TOUCH OF HEAVEN

SPECIAL EDITION

ELICE NANGE

COPYRIGHT

Special Edition Cover by Amanda Walker
Editing by Leanne Rabesa
Diversity/Sensitivity Editing by Renita McKinney
Proofreading by Deborah Peach
Print and E-Book interior design by Elice Nange

eBook ISBN: 9781958937013
Paperback ISBN: 9781958937037
Hardcover ISBN: 9781958937051
Special Edition Paperback ISBN: 9781958937174

First Edition © January 2023 by Elice Nange

DEDICATION

For all the perfectly imperfect individuals who have been bestowed ironic titles.
Embrace it all ~ your imperfections and your weirdness.
The best of us bloom in the shadows!

PLAYLIST

#1 Fan ~ Plies (feat. J.Holiday & Keyshia)
Scars To Your Beautiful ~ Alessia Cara
Shivers ~ Ed Sheeran (feat. Jessi & SUNMI)
Everytime We Touch ~ Cascada
One Last Time ~ Ariana Grande
You Broke Me First ~ Tate McRae
Heaven Is A Place On Earth ~ Belinda Carlisle
Livin' On A Prayer ~ Bon Jovi
The Heart Wants What It Wants ~ Selena Gomez
Haven't Met You Yet ~ Michael Bublé
You Are The Reason ~ Calum Scot & Leona Lewis
Heaven Sent ~ Keyshia Cole
I Put A Spell On You ~ Nina Simone
River Of Tears ~ Alessia Cara
Bust It Baby, Pt. 2 ~ Plies (feat. Ne-Yo)
Unwritten ~ Natasha Bedingfield
Better In Time ~ Leona Lewis
Rise Up ~ Andra Day

FOREWORD

Touch Of Heaven is a dark romance with dark themes. It is a friends-to-lovers, interracial, forbidden love, MMF, ménage/why choose, romantic suspense, dark mafia billionaire romance.
It features a transgender side character.
This story contains harsh language, and some aspects of it will make you uncomfortable.
If dark content triggers you, this isn't the book for you.
It also touches on several sensitive topics, including childhood neglect, dysfunctional family dynamics, sexual assault (alluded to, non-graphic), abusive parents, murder, suicide, explicit sex, pregnancy, vomiting (caused by pregnancy), knife play (consensual), etc.
Reader discretion is advised.

That said, this story contains no cheating and a guaranteed HEA.

For a comprehensive list of content warnings, visit
https://elicenange.com/touchofheaven/

CONTENTS

BLURB

Heaven isn't the dream; it's my wild heart they set ablaze.

DELILAH

Hand-me-downs, runner-up, dubbed the faulty spare by everyone around me I was used to feeling like a burden.

The love of my life knew exactly how that felt too and now I was haunted by their ghost.

Moving on felt impossible so I wished for my heart condition to reunite me with them.

Living in the shadow of my identical twin sister's perfection, I rejected everyone's love around me.

Even my best friend who was hopelessly in love with me.

It wasn't until I didn't have to choose that I realized *I could love on my own terms*.

HARRIS

Expectations, embarrassment, and all the rules I was willing to break got me kicked out of my controlling family at eighteen.

That didn't stop me from spitting on our family name when I rejected law school just to follow Delilah wherever she went.

That landed me in medical school but instead of saving lives, I was saving you from a bad orgasm when I put all my knowledge into making the finest toys.

Imagining Delilah using something I created only fueled stalking her in the middle of the night.

But I wasn't the only one obsessed with her.

Marc was willing to cross lines *to make sure she was ours*.

MARC

Honor, loyalty, fear, and… lies felt like the family motto. Being a Sotelo meant living up to the bad reputation.

My mother was a legend, a mistress, and now I was paying for her absence when my father initiated us into the family business.

Fresh meat I was supposed to be married off, be the father to new heirs, when all I wanted was to be myself.

All I wanted was her.

Even if that meant taking what I wanted. Even if she didn't know she wanted us yet.

Together we felt like heaven, even if we were considered *a special brand of nightmares*.

PROLOGUE

DELILAH

Step-by-step instructions on how to talk your twin sister off the proverbial ledge less than forty-eight hours before her wedding are so not covered in the standard maid of honor handbook. I checked.

Okay, I Googled it, but I got the same result.

I always knew this wedding wasn't going to be smooth sailing, just like everything else that involves that family. It never is.

Whatever.

It's her life. She can live it however she chooses to.

Given how I choose to live my own life, it's not my place to judge hers. At least that's what I tell myself. For the most part, I love this life, the one I've chosen for myself. But it does have its drawbacks.

Going home alone is hard.

Going to bed alone is hard.

Staring at the empty side of my bed is even harder.

But knowing that it is by choice, that no one else has occupied that spot in almost two decades, brings me some semblance of comfort.

It's not my fault that I have impossibly high standards. I'm not the type to conform to societal norms and mores, so finding someone else with similar views to mine is hard enough.

But I digress.

My point is that I did not think I'd ever need such a book in my wildest dreams, not ever, in my lifetime.

Until my identical twin sister showed up at my doorstep, three nights before her wedding, with bloodshot eyes and a pink nose.

Then she said the magic words, *"He doesn't love me, Dee."*

Suddenly, all is right in the world again. My world, I mean.

Not so much hers.

PART I

1

DELILAH

The internet is good for a lot of things.

Communicating with people around the world, for starters. Expanding the reach of Brewer Health, of which I am co-founder and co-CEO, from national to international and subsequently to global. Diversifying your collection of sex toys because you've accepted the fact that you'll forever be alone, and as such, your orgasms are your responsibility.

Okay, so I'm being a little bit dramatic with that last part. The point is the internet is good for a lot of things.

What is the internet not good for? Advice on messed-up weddings and relationships.

Somebody should write a book on that. I'm sure there's a market for it, albeit a niche one, but there has to be. I'd buy the book, even more so now.

I didn't even think I'd ever need such a book in my lifetime.

At this point, I feel like I'm in the Twilight Zone. It's déjà fucking vu all over again. I already lived through this scene seven years ago with my best friend, Harris. And now my sister?

Is there something in the water? Or do people just feel inclined to dump their messy feelings, so I can absorb them, marinate in them, and spit out a palatable version for them that makes it all better?

I'm good at that, aren't I?

Being an emotional sponge for others. Being the dumping ground for all of their emotional baggage. It's why they come to me in the first place. Not only would I not breathe a word to anyone else, but I'm literally on death's door; I'm as emotionally closed off as a person can get. According to some people, getting information out of me is like pulling water out of a rock... whatever that means.

I'm not as cold and unfeeling as people think I am. Not only that, but being a sponge is a lot harder than it looks. And I hate being that for others. I fucking hate it.

But since it's not my style to veer too far off from that — studying, observing, absorbing, and reporting on information is what I do for a living; I'm a geneticist, after all — I always do it because they need me to. They need me to be that person for them. They need me to be that unwavering constant, one who absorbs the worst parts of their personalities and, in turn, makes it all better.

But when it comes to my sister... Well, let's just say it's hard to feel sympathetic to someone who's so deeply entrenched in what I can only describe as insanity. Doing the same thing over and over again, expecting a different outcome. It's not going to come, and I've told her time and time again.

But now's not the time for *I told you so*.

I can't even say anything sarcastic, though. Not when she's sitting in the middle of the living room, head bowed as she bawls her eyes out. She's looking like someone just stabbed her in the heart.

That someone being Curtis. Her fiancé.

Ex-fiancé?

I never know with these two. They've been doing this dance for two decades. He's such a pussy hound, but she always takes him back for some reason. I've waited, hoped, and dreamed of the day when Dahlia would come to her senses and break it off with him for good. Maybe now isn't the time to pray that this dream comes true, but still.

I know it was our parents' dream for her. They hoped it would come to fruition in their lifetime, but sadly they died before that dream became a reality. Once Mom even let it slip that she was counting on me to be the one to finally talk some sense into Dahlia, seeing as we are best friends and share this strong twin bond.

Or rather, this weirdly strong twin connection that, in true Brewer fashion, tends to defy the very laws of logic.

I wish I were making that up.

Growing up, I used to have panic attacks. Intense, debilitating panic attacks. They were horrible. I wouldn't wish that on my worst enemy. Then something happened between us in college, some stupid fight that neither of us remembers. Because neither one of us wanted to walk away from it in the heat of the moment, transference happened, and she ended up with my debilitating panic attacks. I haven't had one since. Scientifically speaking, no one can explain why it happened in the first place, only that it did. No one can explain why her symptoms and the intensity of her panic attacks are almost identical to mine. They can't even pinpoint what triggers them, only that they happen. Dahlia, being who she is, hides them. She's so committed to this perfect façade that she puts forth, because heaven forbid the rest of the world knows she's as normal and human as anyone else.

But I still love her all the same.

My twin sister Dahlia is indeed my best friend. Or Daa, as I like to call her. In turn, she calls me Dee, which is short for Delilah. We called each other Daa and Dee ever since we were one. It didn't make sense to anyone else but us, and thus the nicknames stuck.

Dahlia can be quite headstrong when she digs her heels into something. Once she does, there's little anyone can do about it except to let things run their course. I say almost two decades is long enough, while she thinks there is still hope for Curtis but not so much his parents.

I, on the other hand, wrote them off years ago. After everything went down with my ex-girlfriend Simone — who was their daughter, even though they will deny it and her till kingdom come — I washed my hands of them. My parents, bless their hearts, tried to be cordial with them even though they were on the same wavelength as I am. But they did try, for Dahlia's and Curtis's sakes. He was as much a victim in all of it as Simone was. As I was. As Dahlia was.

It's been eighteen years since then, so how much longer will he play the victim card? Not only that, my loyalties lie with my sister, not him. I'm even less sympathetic to him when she shows up at my doorstep looking like this.

As the maid of honor and the only living person in their wedding party, it's my job to ensure that the bride makes it down the aisle in one piece. Even if I have a very vested interest in this wedding not happening.

Does that make me a bad sister? I'm sure it does.

Do I care? Absolutely not.

If it means that my sister doesn't get even further tangled up with that family, then so be it.

"Why don't you stay the night?" I offer.

Between the dark circles under her eyes and how her brown hair falls on her face, my twin sister looks more worn out than I feel.

She chews on her lower lip as she mulls over the question. "No. I... I better go. I didn't mean to impose."

I reach for her as she rises to her feet, and she looks startled when I not-so-gently push her back down onto the sofa.

"First of all, Mom and Dad left the house to both of us. This house is as much yours as it is mine. Second, you aren't imposing. It's Wednesday night, which means I'm usually either home or at the lab." Or hanging out with Harris and Marc, but I leave that part out.

"O-okay."

God, she really is a wreck. I can't wait to hear every last sordid detail of what he's done this time before deciding whether I will be killing or simply maiming him. Harris's dad lost his middle finger years ago. They can be twinsies.

"I'll get you some water, okay? Then we'll talk."

"Can I have some ginger tea instead?"

Okay.

Strange, but okay.

She hates ginger, so it's strange that she would specifically ask for it.

"Sure. I think I have some in the tea drawer." The same one Harris keeps stocked for me, but again, I won't tell her that. Those two don't like each other, so I can only imagine the conniption fit she'll have if I tell her he bought it. "I'll be right back. There's blankets in the..."

I trail off at that because I've lost her. She's staring into the distance, her eyes seemingly fixated on the large, twenty-two by thirty-two-inch picture above the fireplace. I leave that picture there in place of a flatscreen TV since it holds more meaning for me. It's a picture of the four of us — myself, Simone, Dahlia, and Curtis. The four amigos. We were all kids then and so full of life. Simone was seventeen and the rest of us were fourteen. Dahlia took the picture, too. It was her first time using a tripod and delayed capture. Still, for a budding amateur photographer, it actually came out well.

Maybe if she stares at it long enough, it will re-ignite her passion for photography. And maybe dim her obsession with Curtis in return.

A girl can dream, right?

As I go through the motions, I can't help but wonder what it is Curtis did this time. He's done some pretty shitty things over the years, but I don't think it was ever this bad. This isn't even the first time she's shown up on my doorstep in tears over something he's done.

But this is the first time she's used the magic words, "He doesn't love me, Dee."

'He doesn't love me, Delilah.' Harris's voice pops into my mind from seven years ago. *'I can't believe he fucked a woman, right under my nose too.'*

Talk about déjà vu.

I didn't even have anything to do with it this time, but it still managed to find me.

Fifteen minutes later, I walk back into the room — a glass of water in one hand and a mug of ginger tea in the other — to find her pulling a couple of pills out of an inconspicuous pill bottle and popping those into her mouth. Then comes the sickening crunch.

I hate it when she does that. Whatever happened to good ol' swallowing?

"Don't you need water for that?" I ask incredulously.

She shakes her head. "The tea will wash it down just fine."

I set the steaming mug on the coffee table before her and pick up the pill bottle. Not as innocuous as I thought since it does say Diclegis on the outside. It also lists Charlena Cantor-Dietrich as the prescribing physician.

Charlena is our friend. She also happens to be one of those odd fixtures in Dahlia's and my lives. We met her in medical school, and for some bizarre reason, that friendship stuck. Her family is well-off, so she doesn't have to work but chooses to. And for some equally inexplicable reason, she chose to come work with me doing research. We are both geneticists, after all. We work in labs, analyzing data. We're not the kind of doctors who dole out prescriptions of any sort, much less nausea medication. We could. We both have the credentials to do so. We just choose not to.

Or, at least, *I* choose not to. Charlena makes the occasional exception, it would seem.

With a sinking feeling, I ask, "Why would Charlena write you a prescription for nausea medication?"

Her eyes meet mine, and I watch as she struggles to blink back tears.

Oh.

Oh, dear.

Please don't be pregnant.

"Are you pregnant?" I ask incredulously. Then I hold my breath as I wait for her reply.

It takes a while, but it comes in the form of a slight nod. An acknowledgment of the one thing I've always been afraid of. For her, that is.

Okay.

This changes things.

"I'm sorry," she mumbles.

She's sorry? "What for?"

She gives me a tight smile. "I… you know how I feel about…" A pause, then, "This doesn't change how I feel about them. Having kids, I mean."

Yeah, well. That last part is unfortunate.

Even I know that motherhood is not a good look for Dahlia. She's an excellent doctor, but that doesn't make for a good mother. At least she has enough self-awareness to put two and two together. So yeah, I do know how she feels about them. I can tell she's trying her best to tiptoe around the issue since she knows how *I* feel about them.

"How far along are you?"

She ducks her head and chews on her lower lip. "Thirteen weeks," she mumbles. "It's a boy."

Dahlia might not have envisioned herself as a mother, but motherhood is my dream. I love kids. Dahlia, on the other hand, does not. Personal choice. It's the one thing about her that's been constant since we were kids. She never wanted any. She always saw herself in the role of fun aunt.

If I'm ever fortunate enough for the opportunity to become a mom, I'd love for that to happen. But as it happens, my defective heart is getting in the way of that.

No time to dwell on negative thoughts, so I shake those off.

Sinking into the seat, I scoot over to sit next to her and slide an arm around her waist, pulling her close. For a moment there, she settles in next to me. Leaning into my body. Letting her breathing even out.

"Tell me everything," I finally say. "Everything he did. Leave nothing out."

2

HARRIS

I love Friday mornings.

They're one of my favorite days of the week because I get to have breakfast with one of my two favorite people in the world, my best friend, Delilah Brewer.

We go to different places for breakfast, and usually I get to pick where since she is hilariously bad at it. She likes to describe herself as having a singular palate, something I can confirm after years of friendship. If it weren't for me, she'd never try new foods or even attempt new experiences.

Today though, she asked if we could keep it simple and meet in the café in their building, Brewer Health. I'm not one to split hairs over this, though. She already has enough on her plate, with her sister's wedding happening this weekend.

Her identical twin sister, Dahlia Brewer.

Or as Marc and I like to call her, Hurricane Dahlia.

I got her a wedding present too, since I'm generous like that. I even plan on tastefully covering it up in non-obscene wrapping paper.

But first, I need Delilah's take on it, so I slide the box across the table towards her. "I was thinking about gifting this to Hurricane Dahlia."

She takes a moment to study the box, turning it over in her hands. "Why would you give her something like this?"

That something is a crimson handheld bar wench 'Ring For Sex' bell, complete with constructive instructions etched onto the box. Instructions like *'ring once for "Dearest, I'm ready,"' 'ring twice for "Sweetie I'm waiting,"'*, or my personal favorite, *'ring three times for "GET UP HERE ALREADY!"'*

I shrug. "A peace offering, of sorts."

"Peace offering, huh?" she asks, tilting her head to the side. Golden-brown eyes roam my features, studying them and committing them to memory like she always does. From the look in her eyes, I can tell she isn't judging me or my twisted sense of humor. Instead, she's simply observing me, since that's what she does. She observes and reports for a living. Or in this case, she commits to memory. "You don't do peace offerings, Harris. Why start now?"

Another shrug. "There's a first time for everything."

"Yeah, I suppose so." A small smile flickers on her lips before it vanishes, and she shakes her head. "It's a good gag gift, but now might not be the time for it."

"What better time is there to gift a woman a sex toy? I say now, seeing as I wasn't invited to the bridal shower—"

"No one was."

"It's only right that I give it to her now."

She shakes her head again. "I wouldn't joke about something like that."

"She can't be that big of a prude. I'm sure she'll have a sense of humor about it."

She shakes her head again. "No, she wouldn't. She's…" Trailing off, she blows out a frustrated breath. A beat passes, then, "Can I get the code of silence?"

I hate the code of silence.

I fucking hate the code of silence.

I hate it with a passion.

Because I take too long to answer, she mistakes my hesitation for a refusal. "Forget it then."

"Fine, you can have the fucking code of silence." On instinct, I lean forward and take both her hands in mine. "Now, let's hear it."

For the first time in a very long time, she doesn't shy away from my touch. Or stiffen. Or jerk her hands out of mine. Her body doesn't tense up like it does on occasion. It's taken us years to get to this point, with several setbacks included, but I'm glad we're here.

"Things aren't great between them," she says.

She lets that hang in the silence between us, and when the silence stretches for some time I take that as my cue to add, "You say that like it's something new, Delilah. It isn't even newsworthy at this point. Not when they've been doing this weird-ass dance for two decades."

A look of annoyance flashes on her face, and she goes to pull her hands out of mine. I clamp down on them in response. For the first time in months, I get to hold my best friend's hands out in public, and I'll be damned if I let the moment end so soon.

Delilah and I have been best friends since college. We met in our freshman year — in freshman biology to be exact — and we have been inseparable since then. At least I'd like to think we've been inseparable since then. After all, I'm the one who spent years chasing after her, begging her to be my friend while she kept me at arm's length. She had been in a deep depression at the time, having lost her girlfriend only three years prior, something I still don't think she's quite gotten over. But over time, she's come out of her shell. As far out of her shell as she's comfortable with. She's also let me inside that shell, and what a beautiful shell it is.

I never thought it possible fifteen years ago, but look where we are now. She's come to warm up to me. And after several setbacks, she's come to warm up to this — a hug here, a touch there. Holding hands in public, too, that's a big step for her.

Other than my partner Marc, she's the only other person I'm close to. She's also the other person I'm in love with. So yes, I am a cliché. I am head over heels in love with my best friend.

"Why don't I rephrase that," I say, "this time with a splash of tact somewhere in there?"

She scoffs. "You, tactful? I highly doubt that."

Ignoring her pointed jab, I continue, "Things weren't always great between them. As much as she likes to pretend otherwise, we both know she isn't happy with the state of their relationship. It certainly doesn't help that he's such a pussy hound."

This is where she laughs or says something condescending about herself — I still don't know why she does that, putting herself down to make others look better in comparison — but instead, she goes silent.

That is not a good sign.

"She's pregnant," she eventually says.

She lets that hang in the silence between us.

I let out a deep exhale, after which I say nothing. Absolutely nothing, because there is nothing to say. I feel for her. I really do. It's hard to watch as everyone else achieves the one thing you want but can't bring yourself to reach for.

For Delilah, it is children.

The kicker is Dahlia doesn't even want kids. But Delilah does. She's a natural with them. Kids love her, and rightfully so because she's a joy to be around. A pure soul. A rare breed too. I know that she wants kids someday when the time is right. Except she's thirty-four years old, and the stars haven't aligned for her.

She does have a point there. The Brewer sisters have been quite busy in the last decade or so. Between medical school, residencies, launching Brewer Health, setting up their respective practices, and seeing their careers take off, the Brewer sisters have been consumed with their jobs for the last five years.

But then there is the rare occasion when she lets slip that she doesn't think she'll live long enough to have them, much less raise them. That her heart isn't strong enough to withstand the grueling nature of pregnancy and childbirth. I still think she should have them. The medical field has made many strides in recent years, and I'm sure she will be fine.

Take Yna Sandstone, for example, the other public figure in this town with whom Delilah shares certain aspects of her medical history. She was also born with a congenital heart defect, except she's had her aortic valves replaced three times compared to Delilah's getting both of her aortic valves replaced. They both lived after all that. Yna had her second child not too long ago, so there's hope for Delilah.

Perhaps seeing her sister finally taking the plunge and settling into this ill-advised marriage is the thing that will spur something in her.

Hopefully, spur her in our direction, Marc's and mine.

I mean, what's not to love about her?

Delilah is my best friend, but she's always been much more. The thing is, I was never interested in Delilah as one-half of the famous identical Brewer twins. Granted, I knew of her — who wouldn't? They are practically celebrities in this town, being two of the first IVF babies, and ones that cost a fortune at that — but I didn't make the connection until much later.

Not to mention she's drop-dead gorgeous, always has been.

She has the most beautiful shade of pale porcelain skin I've ever seen, so creamy that it feels like velvet to the touch. Her golden-brown eyes have a mesmerizing allure, which sinks into your soul's depths.

Her body is not the only thing that I love about her. It's her mind too. I knew her long before discovering she was one of the famous Brewer twins. Her professionalism caught my attention when we were partnered on our first lab project in freshman biology. Like many others back then, I was equally captivated and intrigued by her charm and presence. As time passed, I realized that she was intelligent, funny, and loyal — sometimes to a fault. She cares about the well-being and happiness of others, sometimes to her own detriment. That makes her unique and sets her apart from her identical twin sister.

She describes herself as a self-proclaimed wallflower, which is mostly true. Over time, the more I got to know her, the more traits I learned that set her apart from the sister everyone loved to lump her with.

She also owns the other piece of my heart.

Something I believe she knows and struggles with daily, for some stupid-ass reason too. All because I already have a partner. Which is bullshit, if I'm being honest. It's not that I'm oblivious to it. It's more the fact that she's attracted to him too. And the feeling's very much mutual. Except she's the only one who doesn't seem to realize that.

Baby steps.

On the table, Delilah's phone chimes. And since I'm the nosy best friend, I spare a glance at the message that comes through.

Daa: Are we still on for this morning?

What did I say?

Hurricane Dahlia knows about our standing Friday morning breakfast. Of course she would come up with something mundane to infringe on our time.

After some back-and-forth text messages, Delilah sets her phone face down on the table.

"I'll have to leave soon," she says.

I nod. "Okay."

Like I said, she's loyal — sometimes to a fault. I know she'll drop everything to go to her sister.

"I wish she would just leave that fucking family already," she mutters.

That's something else that I never quite understood about this whole situation. Delilah isn't the vengeful type, but she hates that family with a vengeance. That hatred seems to be directed at just the parents though — at Andrea and Matthias McWhorter. She hates those two almost as much as I hate my dad, but I think she's got me beat there.

She won't talk about it. I've asked, but she's brushed me off. Not even the fucking code of silence could entice her to spill the beans.

The whole thing's baffling.

Their families used to be friends, that much I know. Their mothers were even best friends growing up. The McWhorter and the Brewer children used to be in and out of each other's homes. There's even a picture of the four of them as kids hanging in her living room. It's front and center, with all the other pictures of them at various stages in their lives flanking that one picture. Then there's the matter of her sister dating their only son, for crying out loud.

Whatever it was, it had to have cut deep, way deep.

She snaps her fingers before me. "You zoned out again, didn't you?"

Clearing my throat, I sit up straighter. "I was just thinking about the Brewer-McWhorter feud. Are you ever going to tell me about—"

"No."

That's what I thought. "Okay. Just know that I'm here for you, always. If you ever need to talk—"

"We talk plenty. We're talking right now. Besides, I don't need to rehash ancient history when there are more pressing matters to deal with."

"Like Dahlia getting knocked up before her wedding? Don't tell me you didn't see that one coming."

"Not from Dahlia, no. She's a lot of things, but she would never use a baby to keep a man. The hormonal imbalance that comes with pregnancy doesn't bode well for any of her... issues, medical and otherwise. Not to mention, the stretch marks aren't worth it. Also, do you know how hard it is for a woman to get a hysterectomy? I know things like that because she's been wanting one for years."

"It's too bad she can't just order one for herself."

She laughs, and to this day, it remains one of the most beautiful sounds I've ever heard. "With a mindset like that, you would've made for a terrible doctor. Ethics be damned."

"You know me. I'm all about pushing those fucking boundaries."

She rolls her eyes. "I wasn't born yesterday, Harris. You don't practice just to spite your dad."

"That too."

Her face goes serious. "The code of silence still stands, right?"

"Delilah—"

"I'm only telling you this because I trust you to keep your mouth shut. You cannot breathe a word of this to anyone. Not even to Marc."

That'll be especially hard since Marc and I tell each other everything. But for her, I'll do it. "I won't tell him. But you know he'll find out eventually, right?"

"Yeah, with the rest of the world, I suppose. How long will it take before an official press release gets sent out? A week? Before the ink dries on their marriage license?"

Another sigh. "I wish she'd just call off the whole thing already." She flips over her phone to read the last message, then flips it back face down. "I'd rather not have anything more to do with that family. Not if I can help it."

3

DELILAH

Dahlia sounds slightly miffed by the time I get to her place. It's what I expected, but I didn't count on the roadblocks at her house. Is it retaliation for when she came over two nights ago?

"You can't go up there," Laurie, Dahlia's assistant, declares. Her breathing stutters as she follows me up the stairs.

Instead of this pointless gatekeeping, what she needs to do is more cardio. It would help with the strain of going up and down these ridiculous flights of stairs several times a day.

"On whose command?" I ask, not really caring for an answer. "And what part of 'she's expecting me' didn't you understand?"

"But—"

"But nothing." We reach the top of the stairs and I make a beeline for the master bedroom. She doesn't stop me this time as I push open the door and step inside. "Hey, Daa. Sorry I'm late."

Not surprising is the fact that Laurie still hovers behind me.

"It's all right," Dahlia says, waving her off. "Delilah has full access to the house."

"But Mrs. McWhorter said—"

"I don't care what Mrs. McWhorter says. I live here now, and I say my sister is welcome anytime."

A brief silence, then, "Understood."

"That will be all." Dahlia waves her off.

She doesn't answer but leaves, closing the door behind her with a gentle click.

"What was that about?" I ask, shrugging off my coat.

She shrugs. "Andrea."

"Hmmm. Well, she's your mother-in-law now. Legally. Well, sort of," I say as I walk over to drop it onto the upholstered leather high-backed armchair next to Dahlia's dressing table.

"And yours," she adds.

I shake my head. "Nope, can't claim her. I refuse to claim her and resent the implication that I have to."

"That would have been the case if—"

"Don't even go there," I snap.

We both know where she was going with that sentence, just as we know there is no need for her to finish it, especially in this house, where the walls have ears. There is no shortage of listening ears lurking, always ready to report back to their bosses.

She chuckles as if this is all one big joke to her, even though we both know it isn't. It doesn't matter that we've known the McWhorters for most of our lives. That doesn't make this particular quirk of Andrea's any more palatable.

I wish I didn't have to deal with her, but we don't always get what we want. Even when we speak it into existence. Dahlia's insistence — pleas, really — that we are Switzerland in this certainly isn't helping matters any. Taking the high road in all this only gives them ample opportunity to walk all over us. It's what Curtis has been doing to her for years now, blatantly taking advantage of her. It's also no secret that she lets him get away with much of it.

Even after his recent snafu, she still plans on going through with this wedding. That's why I'm here, to help her pack for her honeymoon.

I gather my hair up and off my neck, pulling the locks into a loose top-knot ponytail. Positioning myself in the middle of the room, I silently survey the items Dahlia has laid out and about.

There are several stacks of clothing, some still on their respective hangers. An assortment of heels, flats, and slippers are strewn about the floor. Two open suitcases lie on the bed, with two others off to the side for overflow.

The nickname Hurricane Dahlia was bestowed upon her for a reason.

"I'm afraid to ask, but why do you need all of these?" I ask, planting both hands on my hips.

She pulls her frizzy light brown locks over one shoulder, twirling the ends. "I like variety."

There's no logical explanation as to why variety should include every single article of clothing she owns.

This has always been our thing — Dahlia's and mine. We pack together for our travels, a tradition we began as soon as we were old enough to accompany our parents to medical conferences. It's one we carried on throughout our teenage years, undergraduate, medical school, and adult lives. It's a tradition we intend to continue for the foreseeable future.

Unlike me — who focuses on packing the basics only — Dahlia might as well move to wherever it is they will be honeymooning. She still won't tell me where, but what she pulled out indicates somewhere warm and tropical. After the ceremony, she will need it since theirs is an outdoor wedding in April in the fucking Midwest. All Andrea's idea, no doubt.

As I assess the damage, it doesn't escape my attention that she is studying me in return. She had been working when I first came in, but now she shuts down her laptop and sets it aside. As always, she's looking for something I am confident she won't find.

"Dee, what's going on with you?"

Here we go again. Whatever she is on today, I want no part of it. So I give her a blank look. "Why do you ask?"

She shifts in her position, seated on the edge of the bed, and a more serious expression crosses her face. "So, about Harris—"

"What about him?" It takes everything in me to keep my face expressionless, even though my cheeks are warming up from the inside out. As her gaze stays on me, the warmth spreads through my body like wildfire — untethered, unchecked. Her free-roaming gaze pauses at my neck, her eyes narrowing. "Dee, what did you do?"

Without thinking, I pick up a sundress from the bed and take it off its hanger. "What about this one?"

"Dee!"

My eyes meet hers. "It's nothing you need to concern yourself with."

I know what has her attention. The hickey Harris gave me in exchange for my invoking the code of silence. She can read into it all she wants, and I'm not inclined to explain myself.

She draws in a sharp breath. "I say this with your best interests at heart—"

"*My* best interests?" That's rich, coming from her.

"This thing with Harris has gone on long enough, don't you think? It's time you distanced yourself from him. From both of them, actually. You can't be seen cavorting with the boyfriend of a known member of the Italian mafia. Even if, as you say, he is just their lawyer. It looks bad for Brewer Health and our reputation in the medical community. It also calls into serious question your judgment as a medical professional. And mine, by extension."

"Uh-huh." Planting both hands on my hips, my eyes shoot daggers in her direction. "Are you sure you're not just saying that because it makes your in-laws look bad?"

"Well, there's that too."

"Your precious fiancé's Casanova reputation is doing that on its own." It's a pointed jab, but a necessary one at that.

"Unproven," she counters, even though we both know it is a lie.

"Don't even get me started on your in-laws' holier-than-thou attitudes."

She purses her lips. "That I can't comment on."

If I had my way, Dahlia would have been done with that family eighteen years ago. I know I am. Forgiveness is a concept I have always struggled with, even more so with the McWhorters.

And if I am being candid, Dahlia could do much better than Curtis. He doesn't deserve her. He never did, and sometimes I wonder if she realized this from the get-go. Or if she's decided to look the other way as he blatantly uses her, exploiting her feelings for personal gain. I can point that out until I am blue in the face, but if she can't see that for herself, it just means she is a lost cause.

The man told her to her face that he doesn't love her, in the worst possible way, yet she stays.

"Tell you what. Worry about what goes on in your relationship, and I'll worry about what goes on in my friendships. Deal?"

"No deal. This is serious, Dee."

Okay then. If that's the way she wants to play this, I have no choice but to add, "You don't get to dictate who I can and cannot be friends with or even associate with."

She rears back at this. "That's not even—"

"Stones and glass houses, Daa," I point out. "Now, do you actually need my help? Or are you just going to shit on my friendship all morning?"

4

HARRIS

S ome people just aren't built to handle large social gatherings.
    Me.

I am some people.

Long before this evening started, I was ready for it to be over. Maybe it's because everyone is so intent on exchanging the usual pleasantries, which in true Midwestern fashion means a five-minute exchange runs twenty minutes at least.

I don't get how or why people gravitate towards me. Delilah says it's because I am this charismatic creature. I most certainly am not. I just haven't perfected the resting bitch face like she has.

At least no one has groped my ass yet. That unpleasantness is usually reserved for Marc's family gatherings, where they claim to do so in jest — a grope the ass-fucker contest. Except the sleazeballs only do it when Marc isn't looking.

Talk about cliché.

At least here, the most I have to do is stand here like an unmoving tree stump and get sucked into pointless conversations while simultaneously observing as people I don't particularly care for plant fake kisses on either cheek.

The ones who are scared of being corrupted — or losing a limb, since they all know who my partner is — don't dare approach me, for one. Of course, that doesn't stop them from telling me about their latest exploits, since I am the go-to guy for enhancing their sexual pleasure. It keeps me rich and them happy, so it's a win-win for everyone.

It takes over an hour, but I eventually break away from this group and make my way to the bar.

"Léandre," someone calls out as I am halfway to my destination.

As if this night couldn't get any worse, *he's* here. The man I have the displeasure of sharing DNA with. A man who insists on calling me by a name I haven't answered to in over sixteen years.

So I keep on walking until a heavy arm connects with my shoulder.

Oh dear god, the man actually placed his fucking hand on me.

"Did you not hear me call out your name?" he asks in that condescending tone. "Or are you still pretending to be someone else?"

Shrugging his hand off my shoulder, I turn around to face him. "I have a name," I manage to bite out. "I would have answered had you bothered to call me by my fucking name."

"Language, son." I barely hide the grimace that forms over the moniker. "Whether you like it or not, it is still your name."

A name I had changed the moment I was legally able to. This is a conversation we've already had several times.

"You were named after several important men in history," he continues. "A name that carries great weight. A symbol that whoever bears it would do many great things. Tell me, exactly what it is that you're doing with your life?"

I lift an eyebrow. "Living it on my terms?"

He *tsks*. "By selling sex toys? Léandre, you have a medical license. When are you going to grow the hell up and get a real job?"

The man never did approve of my life choices. But he's not wrong. I do sell sex toys for a living. It's more of a hobby, even though it makes six figures a year. Not that that means anything to the smug son of a bitch. He's more interested in being right, not in conversing with me.

For the record, it has been over two years since we last spoke. Not quite long enough, if you ask me.

"Do you really want to do this here?" I ask, returning his equally condescending tone. "I hear things aren't going so well at your law firm. Is that why you're here? You need the McWhorters as clients that badly?"

"At least it's all legal. I can't say the same for the lowlifes you associate yourself with."

By lowlifes, he's referring to Marc. Or rather, the Sotelo family.

My gaze drops to his right hand. "Shouldn't have stopped at just one," I say, my gaze narrowing on his middle finger. His prosthetic middle finger. "Seeing as you love to run that mouth of yours about the Sotelos, you must be itching to lose another."

"Is that a threat?"

"No, it's a promise." I force a smile. "Marc's here. Should I go get him?"

I would love to see him say that to Marc's face. Just once. He wouldn't because the man is too much of a coward.

It is then that I feel someone else. Another presence, stepping into my bubble. This one is warm, calming, and inviting.

Marc.

He loops his arm around my waist, pulling my body into his. "Victor Toussaint," he addresses my father, his voice deathly calm. "This is an unpleasant surprise."

Victor's eyes narrow in on the gesture, particularly the protective manner in which Marc's arm encircles my body. "That we can both agree on," he says dryly. "It is unpleasant. We have got to stop meeting this way."

"You mean outside of the courtroom? That's funny. I never took you for a bitch."

Victor winces slightly. "Sadly, I can't say the same for you."

Marc's fist curls up against my side. "If you don't mind, H and I have much more pressing matters to attend to."

"I do mind."

"It wasn't a question. Or a request." There's a deathly calm and dangerous bite to Marc's tone that has my cock twitching.

Victor roots himself to the spot like that's supposed to make a difference. "Whatever it is—"

"It concerns matters of the flesh," he adds with a straight face. "You want front-row seats? Funny, I never took you for a voyeur. Then again, I highly doubt you'd want to watch as I fuck your son now, would you?"

You could hear the thud of my dad's jaw hitting the floor.

At least it gets the fucker to leave.

"Thank you," I say, and my relief is genuine. "I wasn't sure if I'd be able to get out of that conversation."

He chuckles and presses his lips against my temple. "You mean the pointless conversations the asshole insists on roping you into?"

I nod. "Victor is very concerned about my wasted potential and the idea that my dead name is wasted on me."

He throws back his head and lets out that infectious laugh of his. It's music to my soul and not a sound I often hear. "What was it this time? Your supposedly lavish lifestyle?"

I turn to face him before saying, "I wish, but it was the sex toys. And the fact that my medical license is wasted on me. You would think he footed the bill for it. Asshole."

Amusement dances in the depths of Marc's stormy gray eyes. "You should have told him sex sells. It's pretty much recession-proof."

"Why bother? It's not a real job in his eyes." I can't help but giggle out loud at the look on his face just before he stormed off. "Thanks for the visual, by the way. That should keep him at bay for another two years. Maybe even longer."

"Anytime." He spins me around and points in Delilah's direction. She appears to be having a heated conversation with Hurricane Dahlia, her twin. "Go check on our girl, would you?"

I can't help but smile at his use of the term *our girl*. That's what she is. Ours. Even if she doesn't know it yet.

She will though, in time.

"Delilah looks fine to me."

She invoked the code of silence, so I can't tell him what that's about.

His fingers press into my shoulders. "We must not be looking at the same thing then," he says dryly. "Keep an eye on her. I have some funny business to put a stop to."

"What funny business?"

"Who do you think?"

Only one name comes to mind.

Clark David Holcomb.

5

DELILAH

The charade continues.

The fanfare, it makes me sick. Absolutely, positively sick.

Not only do I not know eighty percent of the attendees at this rehearsal dinner, but I also don't believe Dahlia knows who they are. I suspect most, if not all, of them are Andrea's guests, since she appears to be chummy and on a first-name basis with most of them. The media is here, as usual, so they'll get their faces splashed across the pages of posh magazines. It's what they came for, clout, the kind that comes with the McWhorter name. If only they knew what it was they were getting themselves into. With those two — Andrea and Matthias McWhorter — there's always a price to be paid, and when push comes to shove, I doubt any of them would be willing to pay up.

Hypocrites. The lot of them.

I'm here for my sister, that's it. Not this charade, although I wish she would wake up and call the damn thing off already. This shit is painful to watch. The rehearsal was as awkward as I imagined it would be. Dahlia couldn't wait to run off right after, and I watched helplessly as she disappeared. Curtis followed after her, crowding her as usual, like the clueless idiot he is. Someone who doesn't understand the concept of space.

You would think that after twenty years together, he should be able to pick up on her not-so-subtle cues. For someone who so freely helps others, she won't ask for help when she so clearly needs it. When overwhelmed, she gets this scaredy-cat look in her eyes, like she'll bolt at the slightest touch. I know she won't; she's far too loyal for that. Instead, it'll just trigger another one of her panic attacks and that's the last thing she wants. It's been months since I've witnessed her having one, so I think she's got this under control.

Still, I'm a good sister so I go after them. In a not-so-stealthy manner, I follow after her and listen in on her conversation with Curtis. I'm just a good sister, and it would have been sacrilegious not to. Their talk went well, I thought, but we're back to this charade.

Now, hours later, it's painful to watch her go through the motions. It's just as sad watching the both of them feign politeness around each other.

That's why I can't help but ask, "Does this mean the wedding's off?"

She doesn't answer, but she stares, dazed, with a vacant look. My hand has a mind of its own as it reaches for her, pausing midway as it remembers that Dahlia doesn't like to be touched. It's a thing with her. It's always been her thing, this aversion to touch.

Thixophobia.

I didn't understand it until Mom and Dad explained it to me. Even with exposure therapy, the only people whose initiated touch she was okay with were me, Curtis, Simone, Mom, and Dad. Now that list is down to two.

It's only gotten worse as we've gotten older, except she's gotten better at hiding it, like she does with her panic attacks. It's ironic because she does touch people. She touches a lot of people. All the time. As an OBGYN, she cannot not touch people. Except its always non-sexual touches, and she's always the one who initiates the touching. It's how she's gotten around it. I've witnessed her visibly cringing when other people touch her, followed by the stuttered breathing.

Once she gets like this it could still happen, even if it's me. So I let my hand hover over her shoulder for about a minute, so her subconscious can pick up on my nearness before our skin touches. She flinches slightly, blinks twice, then draws in a sharp breath. I wait for that to sink in — my hand on her shoulder — so she can face me of her own accord.

Brow arched, I press two fingers into her shoulder. "What's going on in that head of yours?"

She blows out a frustrated breath. "I wish I knew."

In times like these, I wish I did too. Unfortunately, our twin connection doesn't include the powers of telepathy.

I know that I am ready for this charade to be over. I'm slowly but surely suffocating under its weight, and I'm not even the one who's getting married.

It would seem she is too.

"The happiest," she mutters under her breath. "Bride. That's what I am. So happy. So much joy. So much fucking joy and happiness."

"O-okay then." A barely repressed chuckle escapes. If she's back to talking to herself and hyping herself up to go through with this, we might have some serious problems. "You don't have to pretend when you're with me."

She blinks again, then sighs. "I'm sorry. You asked me something. Before the *'what's going on in that head of yours'* question. What was it?"

Staring into her eyes, golden brown like mine but holding some sort of diminished lifelessness in them, crushes my heart. "You know you don't have to do this, right?"

"Do what?"

"Any of this, Daa," I say, hoping she will listen to me for once. "You can walk away. From him. From that family."

Something indecipherable crosses her eyes as she says, "I can't. It's… it's not that simple."

The fuck it isn't.

"If it's penance you were going for, I say twenty years is a fucking long time, don't you think? You put in your time, now cash in your chips and move the fuck on."

God. Dahlia can be insufferable at times. I still don't know why Mom and Dad always used to say she listens to me. Dahlia doesn't listen to anyone. If Mom and Dad were here, she still wouldn't listen to them.

It's times like this that I wish Simone were here. She would know what to do. If anyone could reason with Dahlia and help her see how foolhardy this whole wedding thing is, it would be her. And if Dahlia didn't listen, she would trash the entire place. Maybe the shame of a less-than-perfect venue would shame Andrea into backing off this lavish, over-the-top wedding.

Just thinking about her reignites the dull ache in my chest that I believed I'd long suppressed. The kind that creeps up on you when you least expect it, burrowing its way smack dab in the middle of your chest and settling right in.

It's been eighteen years since I laid eyes on her. Eighteen years since she last kissed me, made love to me, held my defective body in her arms, and promised me forever.

Eighteen years since she went missing, and yet it feels like she never really left us. Her presence, her very essence, looms over us.

She should be here with me. With us. She should be standing or sitting next to me, watching this shitstorm unfold. Knowing her, she would have concocted at least three elaborate schemes to stop this charade.

Instead, she's gone. And now, so are Mom and Dad. Everybody leaves. They always leave me. It must be the defective stigma. At least I still have Dahlia, and soon I'll have my nephew. At least I think I'll have him, if Dahlia decides to keep him.

Maybe I can talk her into an arrangement similar to what Marc has with his sister, Courtney. Like Dahlia, Courtney never wanted children. She's even worse in that regard. Not only is her relationship with Charlie's dad ambiguous at best, but she's also the illegitimate daughter of the infamous Lorenzo Sotelo, one of a handful of mob bosses of the Italian Mafia in the Midwest region. Any relationships she has will always have that cloud hanging over them.

And given that their mother had them in an eerily similar manner to which she had Charlie, it's no wonder she never wanted him. But Marc is big on family, so they have an arrangement where he gets his nephew two days a week, which was more like five days a week in the beginning. It helps, I think. And it works, from what I can tell. Maybe it'll work with Dahlia too.

"Who was that?" she asks, her voice surprisingly soft and... *dreamy?*

I chance a look in her direction and that vacant look is back, but it's... different.

Now *this* I have to see.

"Who was who?" I ask, leaning in but not touching her.

Her arm lifts, her pointer finger angled in the general direction of a group of guests.

An eye-roll comes on and I don't stop it. "You are going to have to be more specific. There are a lot of — *oh my god*!"

"What is it?"

"I can't believe he actually showed."

"Who showed?"

I scoff, angling my chin in the same direction. "Him."

"Why would you be surprised that Marc showed?"

"Because he said he wouldn't?"

"I was under the impression that you wanted them both as your plus-two long before Andrea put them on the guest list." She lets out a mirthless laugh. "I'm pretty sure they both arrived at the same time."

"Who—" My brow scrunches as it dawns on me that we aren't on the same wavelength. "I wasn't talking about Marc." I knew Marc was coming. Andrea specifically requested a representative of the Sotelo family be present and Marc drew the short end of that stick. Or rather, none of his legitimate half-brothers, sisters, cousins, aunts, or uncles wanted to come, so his dad laid the guilt on thick. The man can be sneaky and underhanded like that. So I scoff, and this time I make it a point to point out my intended target. "I meant him. The guy Marc is talking to. Clark David Holcomb."

A beat passes, then, "Holcomb. As in Holcomb Enterprises?"

"The one and only," I say breathlessly.

And, as if he hears us — Dahlia and me — his eyes lift in our direction, specifically landing on Dahlia.

Huh.

This *is* different.

I heard all about this from Harris. The David Holcomb effect. Apparently, there aren't many people who can resist the effects of his seductive prowess. Harris swears by it. Glancing between the two, it's apparent that not even Dahlia is immune to it. There's a pink flush crawling up her neck and cheeks. Her chest heaves in unsteady breaths, and a slight shudder wracks through her. It's all... good things?

She shifts in her seat. "Why is *he* here?"

For how much she claims to love Curtis, I don't think I have seen her react this way around him. Not in a long time. And as much as I would like to see this one play itself out, it's not exactly the time or place for this.

"Andrea and Matthias invited him. From what I hear, they insisted on it."

It is never a good thing where those two — Andrea and Matthias — are concerned. That said, it does beg the question. Why would David be turning up the charm on my sister, at her wedding rehearsal dinner no less? Then again, if he is the catalyst that puts an end to this debacle, then by all means, he can carry right on. Maybe I'm not as immune to it as I thought, especially knowing he's had both Marc and Harris — they had a thing six years ago — and I haven't.

"I can't believe it. One whole year…" I trail off at that as something else slithers around my skin, leaving pin prickles behind. This feeling, it settles in the pit of my stomach. It settles in knots, tighter than the ones Harris is so obsessed with.

Jealousy?

I thought I was done with this shit. Evidently not.

"What?" Dahlia asks, but the question barely registers. A minute passes, then she adds, "Can't believe what?"

"I can't believe they f—" With a slight head shake, I add, "Never mind."

No way I'm telling her that. I'm sure she knows, or at least suspects, they had a thing six years ago. All three of them, Marc, Harris, and David. It happened not too long after the… thing. I was crushed then, but I swallowed up my personal feelings on the subject and tried to be the best friend I always was. The role I had relegated myself to. The position I had insisted on having, not wanting to blur those lines — only to go right ahead and blur them anyways.

Pathetic, huh?

To point it out now means to admit I was jealous. Still am jealous. I mean, I love Dahlia, but this isn't something I want to get into with her, especially not tonight.

I don't think she quite gets the memo.

"Dee—"

"Don't worry about it." There's a bite to my tone, one I don't bother disguising.

So I want both men — Harris and Marc — but Marc turned me down seven years ago. Harris just went on pretending everything was all right between us. Still, he did take it upon himself to regale me with the details of their sexual exploits. Some of it, not all of it. But just enough to keep me salivating for those details. And despite that initial rejection, I have been hanging onto Harris's every word.

"You know you can talk to me, right?" Dahlia says. "About anything."

And say what, exactly? *Hey sis, maybe I am as sick and depraved as people say I am. Defective Delilah lives up to her name again.*

I slowly shake my head. "You don't care about this stuff."

"I do care, Dee. I do. I just—"

"Stop, okay? Just... Please, leave it alone."

There are still a few more hours left of this rehearsal dinner, and I am so sick of it all. The people, all pretending their posh lives are picture perfect. Don't even get me started on the charade. The nauseating fanfare, the pretending to be normal. I think I'm going to throw up.

Maybe not here. Forcing down the rising bile, I mentally note to let it all out tonight. Or maybe tomorrow.

An exasperated breath slowly moves through me as I lean back in my seat. "Have you ever wanted something different?"

"Something like...?"

"I don't know, just different." Shrugging a heavy shoulder, I fold my arms and hands over my chest. "Different, as in something outside the legacy Mom and Dad left behind." I miss them every second of every day, but they are both gone. Dahlia and I are still here, holding on to their legacy. Sometimes it feels like we never had a choice. "Something other than the life that we were born into. Something outside of medicine, or even STEM. Something that's not this," I angle a chin in the general direction of the room. My eyes find Marc, then Harris. A beat passes before I add, "Someone other than Curtis."

I don't miss the slight hitch in her breath as she says, "He's all I've ever known."

"I know, Daa." A bitter laugh erupts from my chest, ending all too soon. "Simone's all I've ever known too."

That's the problem, is it not? For me, it's her. Simone. It's always been her. She's been gone for eighteen years, yet some days I'm still stuck in the mindset of a sixteen-year-old girl. Full of hopes and dreams. Full of promise.

My hand moves over to my right side, fingers trailing over it. The ghastly deformity is reminiscent of just how defective I am. How defective I have always been. Not only is it so fucking hideous, but it also runs along the side of my ribcage, just below my right breast. This one's from the second open heart surgery over a decade ago. It's like someone couldn't figure out how to get at the organ that's barely keeping me alive, so they carved right into the skin as haphazardly as they could.

"Perfect Dahlia, defective Delilah." The names spill out before I can rein them in.

Dahlia places a hand on my shoulder, then gives me one of her obligatory sighs. "We never asked to be who we are, you know? It just sort of happened."

What a crock.

"Nothing about this," I say, gesturing between us, "just sort of happened. But it is what it is." My eyes dart to her still flat stomach, and I can picture her months from now, swollen and cranky and hormonal, all of which is not her style. So taking both of her hands in mine, I continue, "You have a chance to change things, to do something different. Why don't you?"

"Because, Dee. It's not that simple."

The fuck it isn't.

"You don't have to marry him just because you're having his child. As far as reasons go, that one's pretty shitty. And this isn't the fucking Dark Ages."

"But it's not just that. It's... complicated. You of all people should know that."

"Look, I get that you love him, okay? That you'll do anything for him. Heck, I know that you've done things for him, and you'll continue to do things for him. Anytime he asks. Anyhow he asks. I know that. He knows it. You know what else? Simone knew it. And even though he's her brother, we both know she would've been the first to tell you to walk away. Just bite the bullet and walk away from it all."

"Like she did, you mean?"

Her words send a sharp stab through my chest. Drawing in a quick breath, my eyelids flutter, then close. "That was uncalled for."

I know Dahlia can be crass, but it still doesn't take the sting out of her words. Because they are true. Simone is gone. Whether or not she left of her own accord, it doesn't change the fact that she's gone.

The ache in my chest only spreads. My breathing comes in short spurts. I keep my eyes closed while I force myself to steady my breathing.

This trip down memory lane, I hate it. It's hard to believe she just up and left. To this day, I still refuse to think that's what happened, that she really did up and leave. Not after what we meant to each other. Not after the things we shared. Not after the promises we made to each other. Certainly not after—

Everybody leaves. Everybody dies.

Eighteen years and she hasn't come back to us. To me. And to think that in some cruel twist of fate, I was the one who first noticed she was gone. Or missing. Or whatever the hell that was.

"I'm sorry," Dahlia says, and to her credit she sounds contrite. "I shouldn't have said that. I miss her. I loved her too, you know? Not like you loved her, but still. I fucking miss her, every second of every day. And if I'm feeling this way after eighteen years, I can only imagine how you're feeling, and—"

"It's fine, let's not turn this into a back-and-forth thing," I cut her off. I'm not doing this with her, not tonight. Not when she still plans on walking down that fucking aisle and promising forever to the idiot who will never honor it or her. "You've made your position clear, and I get that. You like the way things are. You like your life the way it is. You like the comforts that come with being attached to that family's name. I'm sure you'll love being Mrs. Curtis McWhorter. So stay. Fucking stay with him. Marry him, have his babies, and live your fucking fairytale life.

"But we both know that it won't be a fairytale. More like a fucking nightmare. Or maybe I'm the only one who sees it. Then again, I suppose your standards have dropped so low that you're willing to put up with a man who calls you by another woman's name while he hate-fucks you."

She grimaces. "When did you become such a bitch?"

A slight tinge of regret creeps up, and it gets swept away just as quickly as it appeared.

Bitch?

She hasn't seen anything yet.

"A long time ago," I answer her, placing a hand over my chest. "I guess this is good for something." I let out a bitter laugh as my fingertips rasp over my defective heart. For some reason, she seems intent on working extra hard tonight, the resilient heart muscle. For one thing, she's feeling extra vindictive. "You're not the only one with ironic nicknames. Hurricane Dahlia." Another bitter laugh. "More like Spineless Dahlia."

6

DELILAH

M isery loves company.

Which is ironic because I'm not very good company right now. Quite far from it. What I am, though, is a bitch. God, I am a bitch. I'm worse than Dahlia, and that's saying something.

A hypocrite.

Dahlia's face falls. Without another word, she stands and walks away from me. As I stare at her retreating figure, I cannot find a single part of me that regrets the words that came out of my own mouth. All I can hear is *hypocrite, hypocrite, hypocrite* repeatedly echoing in my mind.

That's what I am, a fucking hypocrite.

Here I am, doling out life advice like some two-bit guru, yet I've been stuck in the same place, emotionally speaking, for eighteen years. Holding on to something that never was. Holding on to someone who's never coming back. Someone who has been legally declared dead for the past eleven years.

A waiter passes by and I snag a champagne flute off his tray. Another comes by with hors d'oeuvres and I wave her off. The last thing I need is to give anyone the impression that I was up for some company or idle chit-chat tonight.

I'm not the only one, it seems.

My gaze falls on his as I idly survey the room with my resting bitch face on display. He stands off in an inconspicuous corner of the room, leaning casually against the wall as he strikes a pose. The picture of indifference — arms crossed, hips hung loosely to the side.

Unlike me, he doesn't have to be here. I'm the bride's identical twin sister, her maid of honor, and the only other living person in the wedding party, so it goes without saying that I have to be here. Technically, he doesn't. Even though Andrea specifically requested that the Sotelos send a representative. His dad laid on the guilt thick, ensuring he was here as a representative of the family, but he could just as easily have sent his sister, Courtney. But he didn't, not this time.

Family. Obligation. He takes those duties very seriously.

Too seriously. I don't, for the most part. It's not exactly a hardship on my part either, not when I only have one living family member.

A cluster of chatty guests obstructs my view of him for a brief moment. Once they walk past and he's back in my line of sight, he watches me with a heated look that has butterflies taking flight in the pit of my stomach, their wings fluttering to life.

I take a sip of my champagne, and my eyes rake over him from head to toe and then back up again as my mind creates a mental tally of his physical assets.

Simply put, he's perfection personified. A god of a man.

I can't help but notice his muscular arms, clothed in his perfectly tailored charcoal-gray suit that matches his eyes. Then there's his basic facial architecture — his jet-black hair, parted on the side and feathered to the back, highlights his perfectly chiseled cheekbones. Features that most men and women would kill for. Luminous dark skin, courtesy of his Italian heritage.

A girl can look, can't she?

It's what I indulge myself in every chance I get.

Our eyes meet. A delicious shiver runs through me and I swallow hard.

Coyly, those stormy gray eyes, the color of thick, prowling clouds in a thunderstorm, partially close. A roguish smile teases the corners of his lips. His gaze glides over my body slowly, sensually, evenly, and without faltering.

I should look away. I really should, but I can't.

Even if everyone left, the whole world would fade away and our eyes would still find each other like a moth to a smoldering flame. His eyes are the kind that draw you in and make you speechless. The type of gray that puts you under a spell so you can't look away and warns you not to look, all in the same moment.

His eyes, they are the things nightmares are made of. I have always been one to flirt with the edge of danger, sometimes jumping right off the cliff, knowing full well I wouldn't survive it. Not that I want to. I am trapped in his stare, this unspoken connection zipping between us. As always, neither of us is fighting it, but we're not readily accepting it either.

He's not the first one to look away like he always does. Tonight, it's like we are at some sort of impasse — playing a game of cat and mouse with our instincts — and I'm not sure which of us will swerve first.

It won't be me; that much is certain.

It has to be him because he is a dangerous man, a fact we are both aware of.

He's also off-limits.

Very, very off-limits.

For starters, he's gay. Very, *very* gay. As in, there's not even a little bit of wiggle room in there. He's been gay forever — since he could talk, at least. Rumor has it those were the first words he spoke from the moment he could string coherent sentences together.

I have it on good authority that his sexual proclivities are very singular. But that's not to say he doesn't occasionally indulge in watching other men fucking women. *Look, don't touch* is his life-long motto. One he's lived by for most of his adult life.

Yeah, I know far too much about his sexual habits. I know all this because he is in a very committed relationship with my best friend, Harris. Has been for the last sixteen years.

So yeah, he's taken. Very much so. And even though their relationship is an open one, I should not be lusting after him.

I should *not* be getting lost in his eyes.

I should *not* be exchanging wistful, longing looks with him.

I definitely should *not* be walking toward him in purposeful strides.

None of this is enough motivation to heed my own warnings or even stop what is about to happen. One foot in front of the other, my feet move of their own accord in his direction, closing the distance between us. Then, pausing a foot before him, I lace my hands behind my back — crossing them in front of my chest would seem preposterous — not once breaking eye contact.

This is a bad idea. I so should not be doing this.

I am so doing this.

"I need your help," I say, not once breaking eye contact.

He lifts a perfectly arched brow. "With?"

Dear lord, how do people do this?

I have done this once before — asked him this question — but that was seven years ago and I was drunk off my ass. Funny, how articulate one can get after two shots of tequila — only to find out later that it was more like ten. I lost count after the fifth one, but I was told by a reputable source that it was ten. Right after the colossal shit storm that followed. Either way, suffice it to say I learned my lesson after that and haven't touched the stuff since then.

I would kill for a single shot right about now.

"D?"

His use of the moniker he has specifically reserved for me sends a tingle straight through me. One of these days, I will ask him what it means. Tonight, I need just enough courage to ask for what I need. Consequences be damned.

Wiping my sweaty palm against my dress, I continue, "I need your help with… the thing I asked you. Back then."

A ghost of a smile teases the corners of his lips. "What thing?"

The all-knowing smirk on his face tells me he knows exactly what I'm referring to, but he will make me say it out loud.

It's what he does, so I shouldn't be too surprised. Get the wallflower all twisted up into tangled knots. And he's enjoying it too. He takes great pleasure in toying with me. He loves to see me squirm.

His gaze stays on mine — scrutinizing, studying, taking me in. I resist the urge to fidget under his intense scrutiny, but I don't shy away from his gaze. I keep my hands laced behind me on purpose. If they weren't secured behind me, they would be itching, fidgeting with the jagged, raised scar that runs along the side of my ribs.

But no, I have more control than that.

I force myself to take a deep breath. This will be fine.

"Seven years ago."

The smirk disappears off his face in a flash. For a moment, there is a shiver that runs through me — and not the good kind, I might add.

He pushes off the wall. Something flashes in his eyes that looks dangerously close to anger... and... is that a hint of lust I see? It disappears just as quickly, gone in a flash.

I lied.

This is *not* fine.

"With me," he growls in a low, threatening whisper that has both my stomach and pussy violently clenching in response, desperately seeking the type of relief only they can give me.

Now I know I've definitely said the wrong thing. He doesn't spare me another glance before he spins on his heel and walks into the room. It stuns me, but only for a moment. Then my legs are whipped into action, following — clamoring after his long, purposeful strides with short, reluctant strides of my own. It's not until we almost arrive at our destination that it fully dawns on me what he meant.

Harris's eyes watch us as we approach. His gaze briefly darts to Marc's before settling on mine. He smiles, and it's a genuine one at that. All the tension in my body seeps away, falling off my shoulders.

It's what he does to me — Harris, I mean.

My best friend.

His easy-going smile accentuates his perfectly chiseled chin and highlights his dimples. Like me, he has brown eyes, the mesmerizing kind that draws you in and don't let go. The type of brown that puts you under a spell so you can't look away. Like Marc's do to me.

But with Harris, I want to be drawn in. Like a helpless moth to yet another flaring flame, his are the kind that truly takes your breath away. They steal away all of your air, leaving you drowning and gasping, but you fall in because you can't help it. You want to be breathless because he breathes life right back into you.

Unlike Marc's, Harris's eyes are the things dreams are made of.

For the first time, I chance a smile at him. I allow myself to relax a little.

As always, he's surrounded by people. People are drawn to him, drawn to the charisma and animal magnetism that he exudes in copious amounts. Actually, he is a man of frightening intelligence and charisma. He has the uncanny ability to charm the pants off virtually everyone he meets.

I'm not the only one who's powerless against it.

Marc, on the other hand, has the exact opposite effect on the group that is gathered. Something about the way he approaches them has whoever is speaking falling silent.

I can't help the frown that comes over my face. Marc's not usually this menacing. He could be friendlier if he wanted to be, and I want to tell them this, but he beats me to it.

Something he says, directed at Harris, has the group dispersing faster than you can say Uncle.

"You didn't have to do that," Harris says.

Marc scowls harder and folds his massive arms across his chest. "It was necessary. We need to talk."

7

DELILAH

O f all the truly terrifying conversations I have ever had, this one ranks in the top ten.

"This can wait," I speak up first, surprised at how easily the lie falls from my lips.

It is comical how we got here in the first place. I am the quintessential good girl — also known as the invisible one. Or the Defective Twin — this title is my favorite, all because I was born with a defective heart, something I had no control over.

Not that I minded. I have always been content to live in Dahlia's shadow, who also happens to be the Perfect Twin.

The problem with labels is that nothing is ever as it seems.

We are each flawed in our own way. The labels bestowed upon us are nothing but a cruel irony.

Letting out an exasperated sigh, Harris runs his fingers through his hair — dirty blond hair that I help him dye once a month — as he takes us in.

Takes me in, more like. Harris does to me what I did to Marc earlier. His gaze glides over my body slowly, sensually, evenly, and without faltering — from head to toe and back up again.

I should look away. I really should, but I don't. Because I do the same to him.

After all, a girl can look, can't she?

Again, it is something I indulge myself in every chance I get. I admit it has been a while, but I'm doing fine. It is probably a little pathetic, but that's what happens when you meet the love of your life at thirteen. No one else has compared since then, but these two come pretty close. Still, I managed to make it this long, so why did I have to go and rock the boat again?

And why did I spew all that psycho-babble at Dahlia earlier?

"Are you all right?" Harris asks. His concern for me, though palpable, is misguided.

I nod at first, then shake my head. Then, for the umpteenth time, I'm wondering why he favors the hair dyes. He doesn't need it, something I've told him countless times. Like mine, his natural hair color is brown and I love it just the same.

Love. Such a foreign concept.

"Talk," Harris deadpans.

Even though the single word is directed at Marc, his eyes stay on me, as they always seem to do each time we are in close proximity to each other. Conversely, Marc shifts on his feet as his eyes stay on us, watching, studying, dissecting, and analyzing this exchange like he always does. It's a thing with him, and I don't have the mental fortitude or patience to analyze that right now.

"Can we skip the staring contest?" he asks, impatience lacing his tone. "We have more pressing matters to discuss without you two ogling each other."

I flinch at his words.

Harris closes the distance between us and places both hands on my shoulders. "What did Marc say to you?"

"Why do you assume I said something to her?

"Because you always do."

"Yeah, well, I didn't," Marc says rather petulantly. "Tell him what you said to me, D."

Ah, it's just like old times. Our conversations — interactions, really — are usually mediated by Harris. Except for that one time, seven years ago, when I unwittingly triggered a shitstorm.

God, I miss tequila.

Swallowing thickly, I repeat my earlier words to Marc. "I need your help."

This time I don't need to further elaborate. They exchange a look, the kind of all-encompassing, all-knowing look that Marc had on earlier.

Which tells me they know.

They fucking know.

I get this uneasy feeling in my stomach that something is off. Blocking out all external distractions, I hone in on the one thing that's out of place — their knowing looks, their exchange. It's... relaxed. Unfazed. It's like they were expecting this.

But why would they? It has been seven years; Harris would have said something by now.

Wouldn't he?

Harris's eyes return to mine. "You need our help," he repeats in a low, rough voice. It's more of an acceptance, an acquiescence that they will grant me my request.

Except what I have in mind isn't going to be like one of their usual arrangements. I'm not interested in making this a long-term thing. Or even a short-term thing.

Pulling in a stuttered breath, I add, "For one night only."

Harris lifts a perfectly arched brow. "One night?" he asks, barely disguised mirth in his tone.

Urgh.

Why does he have to say it like that? Like Marc would. When two people have been in a long-term relationship, their mannerisms mirror each other. And theirs do, to some extent.

"One night," I repeat.

I cannot budge on that.

"Will that be sufficient?" Harris asks.

He knows the answer to his question, so I'm not sure why he bothers asking. My answer will always be the same.

Life is short. It is fleeting.

Some lives are remarkably shorter than others.

Like mine.

I am who I am — the defective twin, a title I will wear proudly. That is who I will always be, and I chalk it up to having learned my lesson at the age of sixteen and in the most brutal way possible.

For this reason, I refuse to risk any more emotional entanglements, no matter how insignificant. Or significant. Spending any more of my precious time overthinking the impossible is a waste of my precious time and life. I'm done dissecting this. Or even fighting it. This pull I feel towards both men. This unspoken connection constantly pinging back and forth between the three of us. So rather than accept it, I would prefer we all fucked it out of our systems.

One night should be enough to do just that.

"It has to be," I mutter, my voice as rough as gravel.

It's what I asked for the last time, and that part hasn't changed. From what Harris has told me, they are good. Like, really, really good. They would be perfect for this, seeing as they do this already. And I trust them — both of them, implicitly.

I trusted them enough to want to do this. Seven years ago I did, and I asked but was turned down. I truly believed I had missed my chance and lost out on the opportunity forever.

Or so I thought.

Until now, that is.

It was never about me being a prude. No, far from it. Lord knows I'm far too kinky for all the sex I'm not having. My collection of adult toys is enough to make RuPaul blush. Still, most days, I'll settle for watching my sister's cheeks pinken at the uninhibited detail of my latest exploits with my trusty toys.

For someone in a long-term relationship, Dahlia is an even bigger prude than I am. And she's supposed to be the one having sex on the regular. Or not on the regular, it would seem, per our conversation last night.

Which is what spurred this discussion in the first place.

Life is far too short and fleeting, so why not do the things you can now? If I were to drop dead tomorrow — a real possibility given the state of my heart — I would rather die without any regrets than spend all eternity resigned to the what-ifs.

"Not for me," Marc says, his tone clipped.

"What?"

"One night won't be enough."

My breathing stutters at his words. I waited, for years, for this opportunity to come again. And it did. Only now, I can feel it slipping away once again, just like back then.

"It needs to be," I can't help but reiterate, directing my response to both of them. "It's all I can do."

I'm grasping at straws. My gaze lifts to meet Marc's. What I see in there cements his answer. Though his eyes are molten, his gaze darkens as he stares at me. Stares me down somewhat. I suspect his answer remains the same as before.

I can't, D. We can't do this.

I roll my shoulders, then they slump in resignation. "I understand," I mutter, my voice low. It's a shame, really. We would've been good together. Even if it was for one night only.

A noncommittal but angry growl comes from Harris's direction. Still, neither speaks up, further cementing that this was a bad idea. Perhaps the worst one I've had in ages. The finality of their silence drives home that point. Now that I've asked, putting it all out there only to be turned down twice, it tells me everything I need to know. Staying in my lane is what I must do for the rest of my life. I hope I haven't driven an irreversible wedge between them a second time. Once was enough.

Fucking tequila.

I take a step back from them, and Harris's hands fall to his sides. "Sorry I asked. Can you... can we just... p-pretend I said nothing?"

With that, I turn to leave but Harris has other ideas. He reaches out and grabs my wrist, pulling me against his lean, muscular body.

"H, no," Marc warns, his tone steely.

His hands move to my waist and he tightens his hold on me.

"Damn it, H. Let her go."

Another noncommittal growl rumbles through his body. Pushing against him does nothing to lessen his grip on me.

"I'm not losing her a second time," Harris says.

"Doesn't matter. We are not all on the same page, so she took it back."

It's happening again. Déjà vu. I've always known I wasn't a good best friend to him, and this is the final nail in the coffin. Best friends don't go about propositioning their—

"She didn't take back jack."

"Harris, I can't be the thing that drives a wedge between you two again," I mutter into his chest. "I'm sorry."

"You have nothing to be sorry for," he tells me, his arm still tight around my waist.

The silence stretches between us. I imagine Marc and Harris are doing the eye thing again, having full-blown conversations without saying a word.

"Fuck," Marc hiss-whispers.

"When?" Harris asks.

It takes my muddled brain a minute to process his question and accept that this is really, truly happening.

"I'm not sure," I say, my voice a breathy whisper. "I haven't thought that far ahead yet."

He knows it's not a no. We've known each other long enough that he understands this isn't a no. It's a *'my mind is too jumbled up, and I haven't thought this through, but I want to do it more than anything'* answer.

"Where?" he asks, and I forget to breathe for a second.

I bite down on my lower lip. "My place."

Harris presses his lips to my hair. It's a gesture he has done many, many times before. This time, I feel it throughout my body as shivers ripples down my spine, right to my toes. Marc comes up behind me and places both hands low on my hips. "You realize what you're getting into?"

I nod against Harris's chest. "One night, that's all I need."

Marc snakes a hand between Harris and me, splaying his massive palm against my stomach before moving in, sandwiching my lithe body between them. His cock is already hard as he moves behind me, swinging his hips and mine from side to side, sensually, slowly.

"Thank you for trusting us with this," Harris whispers against my hair.

I nod against his chest since this is classic Harris. Always supportive. Ever so charming. That is one of many reasons why I'm drawn to him.

To both of them, actually.

Marc's hand remains splayed on my stomach, and he gently kneads into the flesh before pressing in, making his intentions clear. My body involuntarily shivers at the possessive gesture.

One night, and we can all get it out of our systems.

It will be worth it. It has to be, for all of our sakes.

8

HARRIS

I have always been a glutton for punishment. Even better, I dish it out just as good as I get.

Tonight is no exception.

"You didn't have to say that to her," I tell Marc later that evening as we get ready for bed.

Marc doesn't answer me right away. Instead, he shrugs out of his suit jacket as he strolls into the connected master bedroom's walk-in closet.

Closet isn't the right term for it; more like a completely different dressing room.

On principle, I refuse to follow him there, even though we both know he's expecting me to. To get him to take me more seriously, I must stop doing what he's come to expect of me, especially tonight.

Thirty seconds later, he pokes his head back out to find me still standing where he left me — in the middle of the room, arms crossed over my chest.

He raises a brow and leans against the doorway. "Which part?"

"All of it." I force a smile. "We have been waiting for her to come back to us. Took her a while, but she did. You didn't need to scare her off a second time."

"I still stand by my words," he says. "If you think one night will be enough to get her out of your system — our systems — then you've got another think coming."

Oh great, he's still grumpy. The thing is, Marc is just as stubborn as I am, and tonight something has to give.

"You heard what she said," I remind him. "It has to be enough."

He scoffs. "And your friendship?"

"What about it?" I ask incredulously.

"H—" He swipes a hand down his face and sighs heavily. "D is not going to be like the others. She's not a fuck 'em and leave 'em type of woman, regardless of what she says. The sooner you stop deluding yourself about this, the easier this will all go."

"Nothing about this will be easy," I admit with a weary sigh.

Stormy gray orbs stare at me with such hunger, such possession, deepening with desire. "She's not an experiment either," he counters. "Treating her like one will get you nowhere fast."

"We need to start from somewhere."

He reaches into the pockets of his slacks and pulls out his signature pocket knife, the blade glinting in the evening light as he flicks it into place.

"And your bond, is it strong enough to survive this?"

"It's the strongest it's ever been," I say with a shrug.

His jaw sets, then moves from side to side. "You sure about that?"

No, I am not sure about anything when it comes to her. But I can't tell him that now, so I give him another shrug. "We will survive it."

"That's a fucking low bar if I ever heard one." He pushes off the doorway and advances upon me. "It's an insult, you know. A fucking insult to her character and to yours."

"What about yours?"

He comes to a stop before me. Up close, I can see flecks of gold and brown in his eyes. "What makes you think I care about trivial things like that?"

"No, I suppose you don't." I let out a strained laugh. "I don't care what Hurricane Dahlia said to her, only that it ended up being in our favor."

"Is that really what you think it was?" he asks dryly. "We must not have been at the same dinner then."

We are standing close, chests heaving, breaths warming each other's faces. I could stay like this with him forever, and I wouldn't mind it one bit. It's no secret that I have always been drawn to the color of his eyes, the depth of emotion hiding underneath the surface. For now, he needs to cut this shit out. I started this mess, so it stands to reason that it's my job to clean it up, not his.

"Quit overthinking shit, Marc. We took one step forward tonight. We are not taking seven steps backward because you can't settle for one night."

His gaze stays on mine. "You're right. I won't settle, and neither should you."

The sharp edge of Marc's knife glides under the edge of one of my sleeves, from cuff to armpit, then he does the same to the other side. Next he cuts the fabric beside the buttons from hem to throat, taking my shirt off. The sharp tip barely grazes the surface of my skin, yet one wrong move on either of our parts and this would end very differently. He's counting on that too, the sadistic fucker.

Still, it sends my heart racing, shooting bolts of electricity through every nerve ending in my body. Marc has always had a thing for that damn knife. He gets off destroying my clothing and sticking that knife of his in places it doesn't belong. Even after sixteen years, I still haven't figured out what that's about, only that it makes him happy. And whatever makes him happy makes me happy.

Except for this thing with Delilah. I get the sense that we won't agree on this for a very long time. But the one thing we *do* agree on is that we both want her. We will take her however we can get her. It's everything else she comes with, that's the part we aren't on the same page about.

Perhaps Marc is right, and maybe I am being short-sighted about this. I know first-hand that nothing about her is simple or easy. Are any of us?

"This will be a lot more fun if you fight me," he says, eyes intently searching mine.

"Which is precisely why I won't," I say, keeping my tone as neutral as possible. My gaze falls to his lips. His strong, thick lips. "Do your worst, babe. I can take it. Punishment. Pleasure. Do it all. Just know that I am not losing her again."

"And what about me?" he asks, his tone cold and angry. "Will *I* survive it?"

Before I can answer, his lips are on mine, insistent, tongue teasing to gain entry. I can't think straight, much less react. He grabs me by the throat with one large hand, squeezing lightly, not enough to make me black out, but enough to coax my lips apart. I gasp and his tongue darts between my lips.

He kisses me rough and wild, his hold on my throat firm and punishing, along with his mouth. By god, does he taste good. Hints of whiskey and olives on his tongue, on his breath. I can't get enough.

I draw his lower lip between mine, licking at the moist softness. He moans against my mouth, and his hold on my throat tightens.

"Marc…" I barely manage to force out his name.

As if only realizing what he's doing, his hand falls off my throat, and I feel the loss of it instantly. Those hands go to my chest instead and he shoves me back. Hard. Stumbling, I take a step back and he takes one forward until my calf connects with the edge of the bed.

A smirk plays at the corners of his lips as he places both hands on my shoulders, then leans forward to look me in the eye. "Make me the bad guy if that's what it takes."

"We are equals, not—*oomph*!"

He shoves my body down and into a sitting position. "You want her, and I get that. I fucking do." He drops to his knees and shoves my thighs apart before wedging himself in the space between my legs.

"Babe, we are equals," I try again. "She's always been a part of us, and this just—"

"I can't give her what she wants," he interjects, making quick work of my belt and pants, "not without you. But can't you see? I'm desperate, H." He reaches into my boxers and pulls my cock out, already rock-hard and pulsating in his hand. He licks his lips before opening his mouth and swallowing me, his teeth pressing down on the tip.

"That's not what she wants—*fuck*!" With a crazed snarl, I grab fistfuls of his hair with one hand and tug hard. "Bite me again and you'll regret it."

His eyes meet mine and he raises an eyebrow at me. "Less talking," he hums around my cock, then the fucker sinks his teeth in again, harder this time.

Groaning, I lean forward to grab hold of Marc's shoulder. My fingers dig unforgivingly into the skin of his shoulder as I pull him closer while pushing my hips toward him. Inch after inch of my cock disappears into Marc's mouth, gliding effortlessly down his throat, the wet warmth and the pressure sending a delirious shiver over me.

Then, just because I can, I pause all movements. His inner muscles stretch and flex as he swallows thickly, suctioning me deeper and deeper down his throat.

"You can end this anytime," I tell him as a sheen blurs his sight.

Both hands grip my thighs as he holds me in place.

"Marc."

A lone tear escapes the corner of his eye and trickles down his cheek. His hand tightens on my thighs as he draws a ragged breath, releasing it slowly. Then another, and another.

"Babe, stop." I cover his fingers with mine and gently pry his fingers off my thighs. The skin will bruise, that much I am sure of. And so will his throat, since that's what he wants. "I call a truce, okay? Anything goes; just... don't do this."

He hums his agreement as his hands fall away. His throat relaxes, and his breathing slows, almost returning to normal. Out of consideration for what I plan on doing to his throat, I give him sixty seconds to catch his breath — as much of it as he can get with my cock still stuffed down his throat. Once time is up, I drag my cock nearly all the way out, then grab fistfuls of his hair and push back in.

That's all the warning he gets before I resume a not-so-consistent rhythm as I plow into his throat. Harder and harder. His eyes stay on mine, so serene and peaceful, even as hot tears stream down both sides of his cheeks as I fuck his throat.

When I'm bordering on coming, I start to pull out of his mouth. His fingers fly to my thighs again, and he tightens his hold on me instead, applying more pressure on his suctioning. My roar fills the room as I come apart, shooting hot streams of cum down his throat.

He releases my cock with a pop, eyes still on mine. With his thumb, he swipes remnants of cum from around his mouth and sucks off all of it. Then he pulls my pants and boxers off in one smooth go, with his hands this time. A small part of me wishes he would have used his knife for this, but it doesn't make another appearance.

Rising to his feet, he sheds the rest of his clothing in record time before joining me on the bed. Drawing my spent body to his, he nestles my body in his arms before claiming my lips with his in a hard, possessive kiss. I take the time to savor how he tastes. My cum commingled with his taste has my flaccid cock stirring again. Running my hands down over Marc's bare chest, I savor the feel of his ripped muscles.

He releases my mouth with great reluctance, a nibble on my bottom lip before releasing it.

"Turn around," he groans.

I do as he asks and get on all fours, only for him to shove my face down on the bed. His hot breath tickles my ass before he presses a kiss to it. He licks it, then sucks on my skin. Spreading my legs apart, Marc reaches under me to grab my cock, pumping on the entire length a few times before switching to fondle my balls. He massages them in his palm as he plays with the delicate skin using the tip of his tongue.

Wild with greedy hunger, I can't help but squirm against his tongue and hand. He knows what I want, what I need from him. It's frustrating that he's planning on drawing this one out.

"Fuck, Marc. I..."

He groans out his agreement as he kisses and licks his way back up to my puckered hole. His tongue teases my entrance before gliding in slowly, and a shudder barrels through me. He chuckles against my cheeks before proceeding to tongue-fuck my ass. It's not long before he has me writhing and squirming against his face again. Then, and only then, does he introduce his finger. Then a second one. Then a third.

Jesus.

My breath heaves. I'm on cloud nine, barely registering when he reaches between my legs, raising the lower half of my body up to my knees, my hips in the air. Spreading my cheeks apart, he rubs the head of his cock over my puckered hole, smearing pre-cum against the tight muscle of my asshole.

"Lube?" he grunts.

Even though our truce is still in effect, it's the one thing he has always been so considerate about.

I shake my head. "Not tonight. I want... I want to feel you."

No sooner do the words leave my lips than he pushes into me, all in one go, not stopping until his entire cock is stuffed inside of my ass, all the way to the hilt.

"Fuck, that's good," he grunts, and I'm inclined to agree because the pressure is unbelievable.

He withdraws and does it again and again, the pressure mounting to new heights. With each thrust, he moves faster and his groin bumps my ass. I fist the sheets, back arched, as I moan and wriggle and grind harder against him, making it easier for him to get inside me.

"Harder," I demand.

He blows out a hot breath. "Yeah?"

"Fuck yeah, give me all of it. Do your worst."

Marc grabs both hips, fingers digging into my flesh as he repeatedly pounds his cock into my ass, his fingers sure to leave punishing bruises all over my hips. Like I did to his mouth.

But it's not enough.

"Marc, quit playing around and fuck me like you hate me," I demand of him again.

I shouldn't goad him like that. I know I shouldn't, but I just can't help it. It gets him to react how I need him to. He pushes up on one knee and adjusts his angle as he continues driving his cock home. I push back into him as I scream his name, forbidding him to stop. Just like that, we grind together, his thrusts getting rougher and harder as he fucks me bare and lube-less in the ass.

My climax builds like a volcano, ready to erupt. Muscles burning, I desperately long to come while wanting to feel like I am hanging onto the edge forever. Marc roars through his release, hot and powerful streams of cum shooting up my ass. The feeling is glorious, and I hold on to it for a moment longer, savoring and marinating in this feeling only Marc can incite in me.

He collapses on me, spent, and his half-mast cock slips out of me. My face turns towards his and he captures my lips with his, wrapping his fist around my cock simultaneously. He squeezes hard, then pumps faster and faster. Moments later, I come again. His hand stays on my cock as he coaxes me through my climax.

We stay that way for some time, then he leaves to retrieve a warm, wet cloth from the bathroom. He does his thing as he wipes me clean, and I move as he directs, content and boneless.

"Truce over?" he asks, his voice soft and pained.

The question draws a smile out of me. Marc has always hated the *anything goes* truce, but tonight it was necessary. More for him, less for me.

I nod, and he leans in and kisses my forehead before trailing kisses down my cheek and pausing on my mouth. It's soft and slow and over far too soon.

"I love you," I whisper against his lips.

He pulls away and tilts his head, studying my features closely. I don't miss the conflicting emotions — frustration and lust — in his eyes. Eventually both clear, and he smiles. "I love you too, H."

I reach up and touch his face. "I will always love you," I tell him because it's the truth. "I love her too," I add, and his grin falters. "I can't live without either of you."

He draws in a sharp breath. "I know."

God, we are so twisted.

She will fit right in.

9

DELILAH

"When I said lose some weight, I meant lose two or three pounds, not twenty," Andrea chastises Dahlia the following day.

What woman in their right mind does a weight check on a bride on the morning of her wedding? I was there when she ordered Dahlia to lose weight. She should have specified how much. If anything, it's her fault that she wasn't more explicit.

"Andrea," I speak up when Dahlia doesn't say anything in her defense. "The dress fits. What more do you want?"

As always, Andrea ignores me. It's what she does to anyone who dares to contradict her. "You." She points to her assistant, whose name escapes me. "Get her on the pedestal and go get the steamer. Those creases in the bottom need to be smoothed out." As they do as she demands, she looks around, searching for the next victim to bark orders at. "Hey you." She snaps her fingers in the general direction of Dahlia's assistant, Laurie. "Go get the seamstress."

Laurie scrambles off to do as she asks. On the other hand, Dahlia just stands there on the lazy Susan-type pedestal with a vacant look in her eyes.

All in all, she looks like a glorified mannequin in her custom Valérie Messika diamond-studded Swan Princess necklace that hangs around her slender neck like a leash, and her gorgeous wedding dress that is a custom-made, off-the-shoulder, cream-white mermaid-shaped dress showcasing her hourglass figure.

Losing twenty pounds was a bit much, but weight loss in the first trimester is not uncommon. Despite the weight loss, the dress still fits her just fine.

She is drop-dead gorgeous, but she is still a glorified mannequin.

Although I don't think Andrea cares all that much. She rounds the pedestal like a cheetah encircling its trapped prey. If her intention is to get a reaction from Dahlia, I hope she's realized she won't get one. Not because Dahlia can't, but because she won't. She refused to engage Andrea throughout this wedding debacle and pleaded with me to leave it be as well.

It's no secret that I cannot stand the woman, but for my sister's sake I have been on my best behavior this entire time.

That's not to say Andrea didn't find every one of my buttons — the ones she knows about — and push them.

Dahlia and Curtis declined to have a full wedding party, so she retaliated by picking out every single article of clothing on my body, down to my bra and underwear. The strapless A-line chiffon bridesmaid dress she decided on is flattering to my figure, but it is lilac. Complete with a dual trail of embroidered lavender flowers that span the waistline and run the entire length of the dress's thigh-high split.

It is not a coincidence. Even if Dahlia doesn't want to acknowledge it, Andrea did this purposefully. It is just like her to pour salt in an already open wound.

"Took you long enough," Andrea says as soon as Laurie returns with Cora the seamstress in tow. "Did you bring everything I asked for?"

Cora nods, holding up her kit.

It wouldn't kill the woman to use people's names when addressing them, but that's exactly what she hasn't been doing all morning. Including now, when she launches a new set of orders for her.

"The neckline is crooked, and it's too loose around the waist. Take in the neckline there and there." At least she points, without touching her. "The waistline should be cinched. There, there, and there. As tight as you can get it. Sew her into the damn dress if you have to, but be careful not to step on the train while you are at it."

My heart sinks as I take in all the places Andrea wants the dress cinched.

The baby.

Meanwhile Dahlia says nothing, the vacant look in her eyes remaining constant.

Cora, on the other hand, looks conflicted. She shifts from one foot to the other, glancing at Dahlia, silently imploring her to step in and say something.

As I expected, she gets nothing.

Dahlia stands, unflinching, as Andrea's assistant runs the steamer along the bottom of her dress. For the record, there are no creases on the dress itself, just the train. The detachable train, I might add. But that's not enough for Andrea. The woman doesn't care if Dahlia gets burned by some steam, just that she looks the part today — perfect and on display for the world to see.

This whole wedding has been an Andrea McWhorter production through and through. We are all just glorified puppets, starring in what has been dubbed the wedding of the year. Not once has Dahlia voiced her opinion on what she wants or needs. Not a single piece of this has been a part of Dahlia's or even Curtis's vision. And instead of speaking up for herself, it's worse than I thought. Much, much worse.

She's mentally checked out of this whole thing.

Time to bring her back.

I step into Dahlia's line of sight, sparking something in her. With a hint of recognition, her eyes widen slightly as she takes in my dress. It's the first time she's seen it, since Andrea played this card close to the chest.

She reaches out and takes my arm in hers. "Dee..."

"Does she know?" I keep my voice low so only she can hear me. My gaze drops to her still-flat stomach.

She answers with a slight shake of her head. "I'm sorry," she says quietly. "I didn't know..." Her eyes roam up and down my dress. "I-I would have said something."

"You can now, Daa. You can put a stop to all of this right now."

She purses her lips, and that spark I saw just moments prior dims.

"What are you waiting for?" Andrea says dryly, addressing Cora. "That dress won't alter itself, and I don't pay you to stand around."

"No?" I lift a curious brow, keeping my eyes on Dahlia. Another head shake is all I get from her. "Well, I've had enough."

"Honestly, people. Am I speaking in Latin?" Andrea huffs impatiently.

I turn to Cora. "You can go."

Cora's eyes dart back and forth between us. "Umm…"

"Everyone, give us the room."

"No one moves an inch," Andrea interjects, shooting daggers in my direction. "Just who do you think you are, giving orders? My employees are not yours to command."

I pin her with an answering glare of my own. "You really want an audience for this?"

"Her hair and make-up still need to be touched up," Andrea declares in a smug tone. She crosses her arms over her chest before adding, "Yours too. Don't think you're getting out of this."

Like I would willingly subject myself to any more of her underhanded tactics. Best behavior took a nosedive a minute ago.

"She's not a fucking puppet." It's pointless feigning politeness at this point, so I don't bother. Fuck keeping the peace. This charade has gone on long enough. "You've had your fun, and you've made your point. It's time to knock it the fuck off."

Her lips curl up ever so slightly. "Calling a truce already? But we're just getting started."

If she thinks I'm still that scared, broken sixteen-year-old girl she once knew and could push around, she's got another think coming. "The next person that touches me or the bride will be relieved of one or more of their limbs," I warn everyone and no one in particular. "Unless it involves getting her off that fucking display and into a chair. Any takers?"

Cora and Laurie spring to action; Andrea seethes as they help Dahlia down off the pedestal and onto one of the seats. She's like a glutton for punishment. Her gaze stays on them the entire time this happens.

"You just earned yourself another fifteen minutes with the steamer," she declares in a patronizingly smug tone.

"Bring that thing near my person and I'll use it on your face." A small part of me wants her to do just that and challenge the validity of my words.

"Dee, don't."

"You are already getting everything you wanted," I continue, ignoring Dahlia's pleas. "This entire production is all about you. It has been this way right from the start. Not to mention this stifling charade. And where is your wedding coordinator? I haven't seen her all morning. I know she's here, but last I heard, you've had her running pointless errands. What was the point in hiring Felicia only to waste her time and considerable skill set the morning of? Was that your intention all along? Distract the wedding coordinator while you drive the bride up a wall? Haven't you had enough?"

"Delilah, stop," Dahlia repeats, louder this time. "Everyone, out. You too, Andrea."

I thought I had misheard her for a moment, save for the priceless expression on Andrea's face. "You can't possibly mean—"

"I don't care where you bark out your orders, just as long as you take it outside," she repeats, her tone steely.

A backbone, finally.

To say Andrea looks shocked would be the greatest understatement of the century. But she does as Dahlia asks and shuffles out of the room, her staff in tow. She expresses her displeasure at being kicked out of the room by slamming the door so hard it reverberates on its hinges.

"Taking your frustrations out on everyone else isn't fair to them either," Dahlia chides me the moment we are alone. "Especially since they are just following the orders of a raving lunatic."

At least we can both agree on one thing. Andrea's momzilla tactics passed the realm of absurd months ago.

"I'm sorry about the others," I say, trying to keep my tone as neutral as possible. "Truly, I am. But we both know Andrea was asking for it."

"And threatening her with bodily harm will get you nowhere fast. I begged you, didn't I? Not to start anything with her. Especially not today. She pushes people's buttons for the sake of it. It's what she does. She has always been this way, so would it kill you to suck it up for a little longer?"

"I'm trying, okay? Look, I'm even wearing this stupid dress," I say, doing a single three-hundred-and-sixty-degree twirl for emphasis. "Just so you know, I hate it. If I had my way, I would cut this hideous monstrosity off my body. But I haven't because I'm trying for your sake. So cut me a little slack."

Face upturned, Dahlia blows out a frustrated breath. "Clearly, you haven't been trying hard enough, so fucking try harder."

"For how long? The next few hours? The next eighteen years? For the rest of our lives? For how long do you plan to drag out this charade, Daa? This crap should have been over and done with eighteen years ago. Yet here we are, still doing the same song and dance."

I knew the moment the words left my lips it was the wrong thing to say. As it so happens, I just can't help myself.

She rises and closes the distance between us, eyes swimming with barely contained rage. Where the fuck was all this energy just moments prior?

"I heard you last night, loud and clear," she says, her face only inches away from mine. "Not everyone gets to live their lives the way you do. Free to say whatever the fuck you want, with little to no regard for the consequences. Just because I was dubbed the Perfect Twin doesn't mean I want to live the rest of my life that way. And neither do you, despite being dubbed the Defective Spare. But it fucking happened, and these are the cards we've been dealt. I'm trying to make the best of an already shitty situation. For a time, I thought you also understood that. Or at least you pretended to understand, despite your not-so-subtle hints that I cut all ties with his family."

"I still stand by my words," I counter. "And I wasn't being subtle about it either. I said this before, and I'll say it again — you don't have to marry Curtis just because you're having his child. Those two things are mutually exclusive, but if that's why you're going through with this... well, as far as reasons go, that one's pretty shitty. And this isn't the fucking Dark Ages."

"And I told you, it's not that simple. Life simply doesn't work that way. How I feel about this," she gestures at her stomach, "is inconsequential and has no bearing on what needs to happen."

That sets off all sorts of warning bells in my head.

"Are you being serious right now? *'What needs to happen?'* Is someone threatening you? This won't—"

"You're missing the point," she interjects, cutting me off. "We don't always get what we want just because we speak it into existence. Then again, you're just as much of a coward as I am."

"Excuse me?"

"I'm not the only one stuck in the past."

"What's that supposed to mean?"

"Eighteen years ago, I made my choice. And while it was unfortunate that yours was made for you, it still wouldn't have changed the outcome. If the situations were reversed, you would have made the same choice. But here's the thing — Mom and Dad understood that. They supported your right to choose just as much as they supported mine. They didn't agree with my choice after everything went down the way it did, but that didn't stop them from standing by me. From standing by both of us, actually, because that's how they raised us. So tell me, why should I be the one to give up Curtis when you're not willing to let Simone go?"

I take a step back from her. "Who says I—"

She rolls her eyes. "Eighteen years is more than enough time to get over her. So why haven't you? And seriously, don't give me that crap about not having found someone. Not when you have two at your beck and call."

My cheeks go warm, and I take another step back from her. "This isn't about me."

She holds up a hand. "I see the way Harris looks at you, and I see the way you look at Marc. So do me a favor and spare us both the sanctimonious bullshit. You showed up at the house yesterday with a hickey on your neck. Which one of them did that? Harris?"

She's not wrong. Harris did spring that one on me in exchange for my invoking the code of silence. I can't help but get butterflies every time I think of it.

"Stones and glass houses, Dee," she says when I don't answer her. "Like you, I've told you exactly how I feel about them, but you don't listen. That's your prerogative. So fuck them both and get it out of your system. Or don't, that's your choice.

"Likewise, charade or not, this is my life. This is my choice. You don't have to like it, just as I don't have to like yours. So fucking try harder, okay? Just know that for the next few hours, we will go out there and smile and pose like the dutiful daughters we both are."

PART II

10

HARRIS

This whole fucking day has been wrong. It should never have happened in the first place, thus making the turn of events that much sweeter.

First, Hurricane Dahlia fled from her own wedding.

I saw that one coming. Hell, I could have predicted it a mile away. The only ones who didn't see it coming were... Well, everyone else.

Almost everyone else.

Her not-in laws, for example. They seem to be under the misguided impression that Delilah knows where she is. Everyone watched her strip just before she took off, a collective *fuck you* to all of them.

Not to mention, we all watched as Dahlia left. Alone.

"Who are you trying to fool?" Delilah asks for the third time. "You don't sound fine, Daa."

She's on the phone with her sister. They're talking in hushed tones, but I can still sense something's wrong.

As it should be, since no one knows where she is. Especially the McWhorters, who are very eager to find her. They really need to learn how to let things go. Curtis never deserved her in the first place, so good for her to finally see that for herself.

What I didn't appreciate, however, was Andrea's death grip on Delilah's arm. Or the thinly veiled threats issued. What really had my blood boiling was when Matthias alluded to the fact that Curtis still needed a wife, implying that he expects Delilah to step into that role.

Not only that, but he said this in front of the spineless idiot with not a shred of tact in his demeanor, like the Brewer twins are some sort of commodities to be passed back and forth to Curtis.

Had Delilah not been there to stop me, Matthias would have lost a finger. He and my dad could be twins.

On the other hand, Curtis just stood there the entire time with that same cocky look on his face, the same one he had on as Dahlia took off. Like he knows something we all don't, and things will work out in his favor one way or the other.

Just as we could tell Delilah was itching to slap that stupid look right off his face. Or worse. That's our girl. It wouldn't even be the first time she's assaulted someone publicly.

At least we got her out of there before things got too out of hand. It's also how we ended up here, since she decided she wanted to do this tonight.

"I know, but you said that already." Delilah tilts her face upward and pinches the bridge of her nose with two fingers. "That doesn't tell me where you are." She listens for a bit, then says, "I'll sleep better knowing where you are, so humor me, okay?"

She resumes pacing, taking several steps away from me. I register words like 'lake' and 'quiet' as she rounds the corner and disappears into the hallway. It's only a matter of time before her voice fades, then a door opens and closes.

Leaving Marc and me alone in her living room.

I've been here before, countless times. This home, a modest three-bedroom suburban home, was their parents'. It's the house they were born and raised in, and their parents left it to both Delilah and Dahlia upon their passing. By all accounts, it is smaller than the estate Marc and I live in, but it is by far the homiest place I've ever been in.

Given their parents' profession — Derrick and Jordana Brewer were biomedical researchers — one would expect this place to have stark white walls with many accolades and no sign of children. It's quite the opposite. There are accolades of all sorts lining the walls in this house — that happens when two geniuses raise a set of genius twins — but there are just as many pictures of the family, plus the McWhorter children. It is clear that there was, and still is, an abundance of love in this house.

The carpeting looks worn in certain places but is well cared for. The living room and hallway walls still bear handprints and crayon marks from when the twins were children. The wall next to the kitchen still has the markings for height charts for the Brewer and McWhorter kids. Even though their parents made a decent enough living, they were the type to live far below their means. It's how they were able to leave the twins a modest inheritance when they passed away.

I've always questioned why certain areas of the house are locked up tighter than Fort Knox. The house has a keyless entry, and they change the entry code monthly. Most of the basement has always been off-limits to guests, with two rooms requiring a retinal scan and fingerprint for each door to gain entry. I know what's in each of those rooms — one houses a sizable sensory deprivation tank, and the other is a sensory deprivation room.

When Delilah and I first met fifteen years ago, she used to have these debilitating panic attacks, and that's why their parents had both of those installed in the basement. Hers stopped not too long after her second open heart surgery, but the twins still keep both rooms secure. If I had to guess, it has something to do with the bad blood between the Brewer and the McWhorter parents, and as these things go, it sometimes spills over to the children.

Which is rather unfortunate because the children were friends. Or at least friendly. There is a very large, twenty-two by thirty-two-inch picture of the four of them — Delilah, Simone, Dahlia, and Curtis — above the fireplace. It's my understanding that Dahlia took that picture. She might have been a kid then, but she clearly has a good eye for this. I often wondered why she didn't keep it going, but Delilah has been surprisingly very tight-lipped about it.

The not-so-stealthy thud of approaching footsteps alerts me to Marc's presence. Moments later, a warm hand touches my elbow, then he wraps his muscular arm around my shoulders and pulls my body into his.

"It's rude to eavesdrop," he whispers directly in my ear.

I scoff. "Like you weren't doing the same thing."

"True, but I'm not in denial about it."

"What's that supposed to mean?" I ask, leaning into his touch.

He nuzzles down my cheek, sharp bristles from his five o'clock shadow tickling my skin. "D isn't going anywhere, H."

Dignifying that with a response is pointless, so I don't bother.

That's just the thing when it comes to Delilah and romantic relationships, one never knows. It's taken us seven years to get *back* to this point. Last time it didn't go so well. It never went anywhere, period. I'm not sure I'll be able to wait another seven years for an opportunity like this to come around again.

After an eternity Delilah re-enters the room, hangs up, and walks over to us.

"Is she all right?" I ask.

Her eyes meet mine, and I'm taken aback by the emotions cycling through her.

Anguish. Worry. Concern. Pain. Anger.

If it were any other day, I would hate for Delilah to give so much of her emotional energy to someone other than me. But not today. After our discussion at breakfast yesterday morning, I have half a mind to march over to wherever Hurricane Dahlia is and drag her back home.

"She just needs time," Delilah eventually answers. "And space."

"She can have those two things in abundance," Marc adds. "Preferably at home, without making everyone worry."

Delilah's eyes narrow. "You've never had your entire world flipped upside down, have you?"

"You know I have," he forces out.

"Then you know." She heaves a heavy shoulder. "She's gotten as far away from here as possible." A bitter laugh, then, "To Antarctica, of all places."

Marc and I turn to each other, exchanging a look. It's not even on purpose; these things just happen.

"Do you have to do that tonight?" Delilah asks with a laugh.

"Do what?" I tentatively ask.

She shrugs. "I thought tonight was supposed to be about me."

"It is."

"Then why are you two doing," she waves a hand between Marc and me, "that thing you always do. The thing where you know something I don't. If you know where my sister is, fucking spit it out."

A tense silence settles.

Delilah sighs. "Please, I need to know."

"I don't think she went to Antarctica," I tell her.

She curls her arms around her waist, folding into herself. "I know that too. Dahlia wouldn't have answered if she were on an international flight."

Marc's hands fall to his sides, and he steps back from me. "For what it's worth, I don't think she went too far."

"I know that, Marc, but that doesn't answer my question. Do you know where she is?"

Marc takes a few tentative steps toward her. "Would you like me to send someone to find her?"

Her eyes meet his, glimmering with unshed tears. "No, that's the last thing I want. It's the last thing she needs too."

I knew that the question was more of a formality, really. Marc sent a few of his men after Dahlia not long after she fled the wedding ceremony, and they didn't find her. She wasn't answering her phone either.

In times like these, I would call the only person I know who can track her location through her phone's location services. But as it so happens, he has mysteriously disappeared too. A shame, really, since David and I still need to chat about what the fuck that was last night. What did he do to Hurricane Dahlia that pissed her off so badly that she threw his fucking drink in his face?

"I should have gone after her. She shouldn't be alone. Not now, not when she's not in a good space, mentally." She bites down on her lip. "I should be with her, yet here I am, about to—"

Marc finally steps up to her and places both hands on her shoulders. "We don't have to do this tonight."

"I do. I want to do this." She looks away, a rose-colored blush blossoming on her cheeks. "I need to do this."

The relief that floods through me is palpable. I don't think I could walk away from her, from this. Not tonight. Not when we are so close to this, to making her ours.

Marc hooks a finger underneath her chin, forcing her gaze to meet his. "If you're having second thoughts, promise me you'll say something, yeah?"

Her breath hitches as she nods. "I'm not having any."

"This will change things between us, D. Forever," he continues, his eyes searching hers. "Are you prepared for that?"

She worries her bottom lip and nods again.

A beat passes, then he asks, "Where do you want us? Out here?"

She chuckles. "As tempting as that sounds, no. I'm a little out of practice and would rather do this in a bed." Then her eyes go wide open. "Shit. My room, it's a mess. I should go tidy up. I... I don't have anything. Shit, I didn't prepare for this tonight. It's all—"

"What are you going on about?" Marc asks.

"Lube. Condoms. I don't have those. I have your lists. Harris..." She laughs, and the color in her cheeks spreads, "...he told me what you each like, and I planned on getting them. I've just been so busy with the wedding, and—"

"We don't need any of that, Delilah. It's safe," I say without thinking.

Twin pairs of eyes turn to me, each sporting similar looks of confusion.

Shit. Why did I say that?

Granted, I'm the sick fucker obsessed with knowing every little detail about her, including intimate details of her cycle. Still, she doesn't need to know that just yet. And as it clicks for Marc, he lifts a curious brow but doesn't say anything. No, he waits for me to haul myself out of this hole I dug.

Which I'm about to, but she does it for me.

She shrugs and steps away from Marc, his arms hovering in the air for a few seconds before falling to his sides.

"Give me five minutes before following me, deal?"

Without waiting for an answer from either of us, she turns and dashes for her bedroom. I know where it is, so I set a mental timer for us.

"Safe, huh?" Marc grins at me. "You really are twisted."

"Pot calling the kettle black?" I counter. "Besides, it's late, and you have particular tastes. So where do you think we'll find the stuff you like at such short notice?"

"We won't, and that's okay. You're gonna fuck her tonight, and I'm just gonna watch. Up close and personal."

That's just too easy and I don't buy it. "What about you? And what if she asks?"

"One night won't be enough."

"That's not what she asked for."

"Well, I asked again and she nodded. You saw."

"She didn't know what she was agreeing to."

"H, I told you. I'm not playing this game anymore. Our girl awaits us."

Before I can say anything, Delilah calls out, "Guys, I'm ready," with three minutes to spare. Marc's grin only grows wider as he turns and heads in the direction of her voice. For someone who claims to only want to watch tonight, he sure is eager.

When I get to the bedroom, Delilah's sitting at the edge of the bed, legs crossed, arms folded and tucked just underneath her breasts. Even though they are covered, her nipples are hardened to twin peaks.

She's staring at Marc, who is leaning against her antique dresser in a stance almost identical to hers — arms crossed over his chest but with that sinister grin on his face.

"Come here," Marc orders, his finger curling in a come-hither fashion.

He really needs to learn to play nice. I can tell Delilah isn't amused by that, even though she's trying not to show it.

"Marc," I warn as I step inside and close the door behind me.

Delilah looks between the both of us, worrying her lower lip. Then, to no one's surprise, she rises to her feet and stiffly walks over to me instead, looping her arms around my neck. My hands go around her waist, pulling her body flush with mine.

Rising to her tiptoes, she steals one last look at Marc before pressing her warm lips against mine. Her eyelids drift closed, and she gently pulls my bottom lip between hers.

When I don't respond, she releases it with an annoyed groan. "Are you planning on kissing me or just standing there as still as a statute?"

"I'm just wondering what the fuck it is you're doing?" I whisper against her lips.

"Giving him a show," she says. "Also, I don't like to be ordered around. Or goaded. Or whatever else he's planning on doing tonight. It only makes me want to rebel."

Smiling against her lips, I finally claim her lips with mine. She sighs against me and her lips part in invitation. Her slender body melts into mine, the tension easing from her shoulders as she ultimately gives in to the kiss.

The kiss is everything I ever imagined and then some. She tastes like she feels — soft, warm, and supple, like my every dream and nightmare, all rolled into one decadent treat.

On the other hand, Delilah doesn't seem to be in a hurry. Instead, she takes her time exploring my mouth with her tongue, swiping over my bottom lip and teeth, then doing the tango with our tongues.

By the time we break apart for air, her cheeks are flushed, and her lips swollen.

"Where did you learn to kiss like that?" The stupid question falls from my lips before I can rein it in.

She looks away, her eyes meeting Marc's once again. A scarlet-colored blush creeps up her nape, spreading over her arms. "I... umm... you don't want to know."

Now I really do want to know. Especially now that goosebumps feather along her arms, following the trail of the most adorable blush I have ever seen.

She's always been this way. She blushes with her entire body, not just her cheeks or neck. I'm dying to see just how far it goes. If her pretty pussy blushes the same way. The thought instantly has my cock going hard, straining against the zipper of my pants.

Placing both hands on her cheeks, I force her eyes back to mine. "Tell me."

Her eyelids flutter and then close like she can't bear to look me in the eye while she answers. "You don't want to know, Harris. You only think you do, but you don't. Not really."

"Is that what you think?"

She nods.

"I want to know everything about you. I always have, and I always will. Call it an obsession, if you will."

"Including who taught me how to kiss like that?" she asks.

"Especially that," I say.

Tilting her head, she leans into my touch and turns her face in my hands. Her eyelids part and her gaze hones in on Marc's again.

Something dangerously close to a growl bubbles up from my chest. "Why do you keep looking at him when I'm asking you a question?"

"She's answering your question," Marc chimes, and I can picture the smug look on his face. "You just aren't paying close enough attention."

I hear the underlying implications in his words. *You're not the expert on all things Delilah, as much as you'd like to think you are.*

"It's how Marc kisses you," she finally says, still looking at him. "I watched, and I learned. I'd like to do it again if you don't mind?"

Mind?

I could kiss her all night long and never get my fill of those lips. Or of her.

11

DELILAH

It's a little intimidating, having both men in my bedroom.

Truth be told, instead of feeling shy or overwhelmed like I initially expected, I'm suddenly feeling emboldened.

This is my choice, giving myself to both men, even if it's just for one night.

I don't particularly care for Marc's bossy attitude, but he's always been that way. It was worth seeing the pure, unadulterated hunger in his eyes as Harris and I kissed while he watched.

And now I want more.

Still emboldened, I move to the side dresser and pull out a pair of scissors. Then, with both sets of eyes still trained on me, I reveal my body to them, layer after layer.

Let's get one thing clear, there is absolutely nothing sexy about the manner in which I go about this.

Every single article of clothing on my body was picked out by Andrea McWhorter, down to my bra and panties. Since I have no desire to keep any of it, I cut it right off my body. The fabric doesn't stand a chance, not even this chiffon bridesmaid dress that, admittedly, is quite flattering on my figure. It has to go, all of it. It makes me happy to watch the sharp edges of the scissors cut haphazardly through the fabric, scraps falling to the floor.

Both men remain frozen in place, silently staring at me with identical heated looks of pure hunger in their eyes.

"Well, I can't be the only naked one, now can I?"

That spurs them both into action. As they slowly discard their clothing, I take the time to study both men, appreciating the unfamiliar yet comfortable process. My eyes travel back and forth between the two men, settling on Marc first. He has a body built for sin, amongst other things. Everything about him that drew me to him in the first place — tall, dark, and broodingly handsome — is prominently displayed.

Then there is Harris, who has always felt like my soulmate in more ways than one. His gentle, nurturing side appeals to my own broken, defective soul. For years, he has always been my constant calm in the weathering storm that rages deep within me.

In so many ways — physically, mentally, emotionally — these two couldn't be more polar opposites even if they tried.

Harris's blond hair is a direct contrast to Marc's short, jet-black hair. Likewise, his natural olive skin tone is in slight contrast to Marc's tanned skin tone. Marc easily towers over Harris, but Harris holds his own, muscular but not overly so.

That's just their physical attributes. That's all I have the mental capacity to process at the moment. Before I chicken out and call this whole thing off.

"What now?" The question is directed at Harris, but my eyes can't help but be drawn to Marc's. His stormy-gray eyes are trained on me, studying and analyzing my every movement. I hate that I'm such an open book to him — to both of them, and that they each know it.

That earlier feeling of being emboldened? It quickly dissipates into a cowardly retreat as it dawns on me just how out of practice I am.

Marc settles in on the bed, back against the headboard. Spreading his thighs, he taps against the inner muscles of his thighs. Wordlessly, I go to him, settling in between his thighs and just out of reach. I'm sitting sideways too, so I can look at both men simultaneously while I disclose this tidbit.

The deep rumble in Marc's chest tells me he is not amused by this. "On me, D," he says.

I swallow. "I... just give me a minute."

"You having second thoughts?" Harris's voice is slightly panicked as he asks this.

I swallow again. "No. Never. I just... I've never had anything... back there."

Marc chuckles. "You've never tried anal?"

I nod, then shake my head. "There's that, but I've never... done this before. Any of this."

"We know you're a virgin, D," Marc says, chuckling again.

"I am not a virgin."

Harris and Marc exchange another wordless look, the same one I am not a fan of. I don't care that my words give off a *the lady doth protest too much* vibe. It is presumptuous of them to assume I am, though at this rate I might as well be.

"What I meant was... it has been a while since I... you know."

Marc scowls. "How long?" he asks, his voice quiet.

Swallowing around the lump in my throat, I say, "Since Simone."

Silence falls over the room as various emotions cycle through both men's faces. Disbelief, mostly. Hints of anguish and frustration. Just the right amount of worry. Don't forget lust — that one remains a constant.

"Eighteen years?" Marc forces out the words. I nod, embarrassment flooding my cheeks. "What the fuck have you been doing all this time?"

"Marc," Harris warns.

"No, fuck that, H. I'm done playing this stupid game."

Icy-hot panic seizes me as memories from seven years ago come flooding back. Memories from the last time I laid it bare with Marc, who unceremoniously turned me down.

"You... don't want me?" God, I hate how weak I sound. How broken.

I guess I really am defective. So defective that—

"That's not what I meant, D." Marc swipes a hand over his face. "I just... Come here?"

With a huff, I cross my arms over my chest. "No. Quit ordering me around, Marc. You keep doing that like you own me or something. Which you don't. This isn't a game. Not to me, at least. But it is to you. Clearly. A stupid game. Since you think that way, you are welcome to leave."

Marc goes utterly still. He goes so still I think Lady Liberty, the statue, has more life to her than Marc does at this moment.

"Both of you," I add when neither man moves an inch.

"Delilah, no one thinks of this as a game," Harris says.

"So what did Marc mean by that?"

"He was talking about me."

My brow furrows. "About you?"

"No, not me per se. Just about—"

"—about this stupid game you've had us in for the last seven years," Marc interjects, suddenly finding his voice.

My eyes jump between both men. "What stupid game?"

I hate that this has my interest piqued. Both men can see how my body reacts to this, and I hate it even more.

Perhaps having this discussion naked wasn't the best idea after all.

"If I promise to tell you later, will you... leave it alone?" Harris asks.

I laugh. "Not a fucking chance."

"Just for tonight, then?"

My lips press into a fine line as indecision wars within me. On the one hand, if this stupid game involves me, I want to know about it. But, on the other hand, I want this so badly that I'm willing to overlook all of that.

So what does that say about me?

Option one wins out.

Squaring my shoulders, I say, "I want the Cliff Notes."

"One night is not enough," Marc states solemnly, his shoulders still tense.

"Not those Cliff Notes," I scoff, turning to Harris. "If you even think about regurgitating what Marc just said, I'll chop off your left testicle."

Both hands instantly move to cup his balls. The low rumble of Marc's laughter echoes throughout the room.

"I'm nowhere near done with you," I bite out at Marc. "Somebody better start talking."

The bed dips as Harris climbs on and sits directly in front of me. I suppose it's a smidge of consideration, so I can continue to look both men in the eye as we have this discussion. Plus, there's the fact that both of their cocks are at full mast, pre-cum streaking down both tips. It is tempting, and since I can't keep staring like some sort of sex-depraved kitten, I force my eyes to stay above their shoulders.

"Anyone?" I rasp.

"We don't want anyone else," Harris says, the words falling out of his mouth in a hurried whisper. "We just want you."

"For one night?"

Harris nods, and Marc shakes his head.

"Seriously, guys. One night is all I can do. You get carte blanche over my body, so feel free to do what you want. Fuck me in the ass for all I care, just for this one night."

Harris reaches out and takes my hand. "This might all be too much for you. After eighteen years," he chokes on the number, "it's not exactly like riding a bike. We'll get you warmed up plenty, trust me, but we don't have to do anal tonight," Harris says, directing this at Marc even though he's addressing me. "Right, Marc?"

He makes a noncommittal grunt. "We'll just take turns fucking you then."

"Easy," Harris growls.

I give Harris a smile. "It's okay, I can take it," I tell him. "I asked for this, didn't I?"

Marc chuckles. "Oh, the fun we'll have corrupting you."

I don't know why, but that has my defective heart blooming to awareness.

Harris gives my hand a gentle squeeze. "Before we start, I need to know. Why?"

"Why the eighteen-year dry spell?" I finish for him. The question was bound to come sooner or later.

Both men nod, and Marc leans forward with interest.

"Her picture is all over this house. Well, except for in here, but that's only because I use this room for sleeping." They're still staring at me, sporting similar looks of confusion. "I'm talking about Simone, my girlfriend. Ex-girlfriend. She's been missing for eighteen years. Legally dead for the past eleven years."

A beat passes, then Marc says, "I don't see how that translates into an eighteen-year-long dry spell."

I don't like spelling this part out, but not because I'm ashamed of it or of her. It's because I hate seeing the look.

For those who knew her, it's a look they still give me even to this day. For those who didn't know her, it's a look that always follows, without fail, the moment realization dawns.

"Simone was… is…" Trailing off at that, my eyelids flutter and then close. A long, heavy breath moves through me. "Simone is transgender. Anatomically male. Still was, when she went missing."

I keep my eyes closed because I can't bear to see the look in their eyes.

Disgust.

I suppose after so many years have passed, I should be desensitized to it by now, but I'm not. Loving Simone was never a choice; it just happened. But sometimes, people can be close-minded about what is acceptable and not acceptable when it comes to who you are and whom you love. They can be unforgiving towards those who dare to step outside those parameters.

Simone was no exception. Just as she was judged for who she was, I was judged for loving her for who she was. I guess I still am.

It was bad enough that I was born with a congenital heart defect. But for me to have been with Simone? That was even more sacrilegious. It only fueled their already-formed perceptions about me. I was defective inside and out. The phrase 'rotten to the core' was thrown out a lot.

In the years following Simone's disappearance, I was too heartbroken and numb to think about anyone else in a romantic light. It helped that Harris inserted himself into my life three years after she went missing, thus taking on the unofficial role of physical shield between me and any romantic interests. It's also common knowledge that where Harris goes, Marc isn't too far off.

As the years went by, the look continued. Some even approached me simply to satisfy their curiosity, like I was some elusive specimen on display. The questions eventually got to be too much to keep fielding. Subsequently, I refused to be a notch on anyone's bedpost, or the one that satisfied their twisted, morbid curiosity. Suffice it to say they didn't take that well, and I've been called every name under the sun. Some of which I let roll off my shoulders. Others cut deeper. Eventually, I simply stopped trying. Why bother when I have no intentions of conforming to what society deems acceptable?

That's how a few years turned into eighteen.

If I see any hint of that look from these two, I'm done. And if that's what ends up happening tonight with these two, then so be it. I could do another eighteen years in my sleep. Maybe shorter, if this defective heart of mine gives out before then.

To my left, the bed dips as Marc moves closer to me. His hands find my shoulders and I lean into his touch, my body relaxing into his. His fingers dig into my shoulders, expertly kneading the tension in them.

A satisfied moan escapes my lips before I can rein it in.

"You don't find me repulsive?" I ask, keeping my eyes closed.

"Why would we find you repulsive?" Harris asks, his voice quiet and strained.

"Because." I shrug a shoulder. "Others have. It's not... I am defective, okay? I know that. I am broken and defective on the inside and outside. If anything, I'll be the one corrupting you, not the other way around. This is your chance to save what's left of your souls. Now's your chance to run."

Marc responds by pulling my body closer to his, my back flush with his chest, his erection pressing against my lower back.

"D, there's nothing defective or broken about you," he whispers against the side of my neck, his warm breath sending shivers cascading over my skin.

Before me, the bed dips again as Harris moves closer. A warm breath feathers my right nipple. Like the flick of a switch, both nipples harden to stiff points.

"Perfection," Harris whispers, then sucks the right breast into his mouth, swirling his tongue around the peak before taking it between his teeth.

"More," I breathe, rolling my hips against Marc's cock, desperate for some friction. If I'm not mistaken, the action has Marc's cock growing bigger and harder, the sheer size almost worrying.

My eyelids fall open. "Marc—"

"You can take it," he whispers, his voice hoarse. "Not tonight though."

Before I even get the chance to process, much less respond to that, Harris takes the other nipple in his mouth, and my fingers find his hair. Running my fingers through the soft blond strands, I tug and pull as I try to get closer to him, even though Marc's solid arm now holds my body firmly against his. With each pass of Harris's tongue over the tip, my pussy clenches, making me a needy, whimpering puddle in Marc's arms.

This doesn't seem to faze either one of them. Instead, I sense a hand trailing down the side of my hip, then up my ass cheek before hovering around my tight pucker.

"I'm gonna have so much fun claiming this," Marc adds.

I blush furiously, from the tips of my brows all the way to the top of my toes. "Okay," I breathe.

Harris releases my nipple with a pop. "The color, it really does spread everywhere when she blushes," he says in awe. "Utter perfection."

His mouth is on mine again, his lips warm and wet from the attention to my breasts. It's a bit of a strain leaning into him with Marc holding me back. His hold on me only tightens as Harris deepens the kiss.

Marc presses his lips to the side of my neck, pulls in the flesh between his teeth and sucks hard. I moan against Harris's mouth as a shudder runs the entire length of my body. That'll no doubt leave a mark. A hickey. What are we, twelve?

"Mine," Marc rumbles, sending another wave of shudders through me.

Harris pulls back from our kiss, his lips swollen and his cheeks flushed. "Ours, Marc. Ours."

"Eh, that remains to be seen."

With a slight shake of his head, Harris kisses his way down my body. He pays extra attention to the ghastly deformity that runs along the side of my ribcage, just below my right breast. Marc reaches down and pulls apart my thighs, presenting my glistening pussy to him.

Harris situates himself between my legs and draws in a long whiff. Heaving his body up on his shoulders, his eyes meet mine, glassy with desire. "I wonder if you taste as sweet as you smell."

Marc snakes a finger between my thighs and wriggles my clit. He collects my juices and pulls some to the back hole, his finger disappearing slickly in and out of the tight pucker while his thumb easily glides into my pussy. He keeps up a steady and continuous rhythm. God, the pressure builds so quickly that I see stars.

Almost see stars, because he takes me right to the edge, then backs off again.

"Perfection," Harris groans, heavy-lidded eyes watching as my pussy eagerly pulsates and contracts around Marc's thumb. His head dips between my thighs, and he inhales my scent again. His nose trails the entire length of my slit, and a shiver runs through me, from the tips of my toes all the way to the top of my head.

His nose is soon replaced by his lips. He takes his time, feathering kisses along the outside, lingering just long enough to get me squirming against Marc's still-hard cock.

"Please…" I whimper, desperate for a release.

He lifts his head, looking up at me, his eyes so full of lust it makes my pussy clench in anticipation. "How many?"

I blink once. "How many…?"

"Orgasms, D. How many would you like?"

Seriously? Now?

Are they seriously expecting me to answer that?

My lips part to tell them so, but something else pops out. "What's your record?"

They exchange their look, and the corner of Harris's mouth pulls up into an almost smile. "Seven."

Pfft. He sounds so proud when he says that. He certainly looks it too. "Triple it, then add one for every year of my dry spell."

A beat passes as both men consider their options. Shouldn't have asked that, huh?

"Well, your wish is our command," Marc eventually says, his voice hoarse, strained even.

Not so fast though. "On one condition," I add.

Harris runs a hand over his face. "What's that?"

"Make it hurt."

"Jesus, D." Marc's deep voice rumbles through me, his chest vibrating with laughter. "For the love of all, why?"

"I like pain."

A sinister smile crosses Harris's lips. "Nothing about this should hurt."

"Fuck gentle. I like it rough."

Marc's hand clasps around my breasts, squeezing tightly. "Like that?" he asks, his voice ragged.

"Yeah, just like that," I say in a breathy whisper.

He turns to Harris. "H, you heard the lady. Get on with it."

12

HARRIS

Delilah Brewer will be the death of me.

No, she will be the death of Marc and myself combined. Our headstones should read, *'Died from one too many happy endings,'* or some other sappy shit like that.

What she is, though, is a drug. Highly addictive and one I could never get enough of. Her skin, soft and supple, trembles slightly with my touch. Her eyes are glassy with desire, their expression dreamy.

For the record, she took it all like a champ. All thirty-nine orgasms. Not only that, but she cried *harder*, *more*, and *faster* more times than I've ever heard her say in all the time I've known her.

Marc is right. One night is not enough. There's no walking away from her after this.

"D," Marc whispers against her skin. "Which of us would you like to go next?"

I know he has to ask, but could he give her a break so she can catch her breath first? We drew thirty-nine orgasms from her naive, innocent, maybe out-of-practice wallflower body using only our tongues and fingers. She could use a breath-catching break.

Her brow crinkles. "Do I have to?" she murmurs under her breath.

My eyes meet his over her shoulder, only to find he's trying too hard not to smile. Trying but failing. He presses a feathered kiss to the erratic pulse on her nape. "You have to, D. It's too late to draw straws."

She sighs, all breathy and turned on. "Fine, who has the bigger dick?"

Yep, she really will be the death of us.

"Harris," Marc says, at the same time I say, "Me."

"Well, that was unanimous." She giggles. "Okay, then. I choose you, Harris."

At least we don't have to rearrange ourselves again, so that's a plus.

We did move around several times in this bedroom. Somehow, we ended up in a position almost identical to when we first started — Delilah sitting at the edge of the bed, her body slumped back to chest against Marc's body. It's no surprise that I'm kneeling before her, worshiping at her feet.

"She's ready," Marc mumbles against her neck. "Isn't that right, D?"

She makes a noncommittal grunt in response. Rising to my feet, I line my cock up at her entrance, gliding up and down her slick folds. She looks down at the juncture where we will be joined soon, her eyes going wide.

She places a palm on my chest. "Harris?"

Her voice is small. Almost fearful.

I pause for a second to watch her. "Yeah?"

She bites down on her bottom lip, golden-brown eyes lifting to meet mine. "Make it hurt."

Blood rushes to my cock as I ask, "Why the fuck would you want that?"

"I deserve it."

Deserving or not, that's the last thing I want.

Behind her, Marc chuckles warmly as his thumb trails along the scar on her ribcage, just below her right breast. He's always been fascinated by it.

I'm fascinated by it too, and always have been. It shows that she's a fighter. A person doesn't live through two separate open-heart surgeries and come out of it unscathed. All this talk of being broken and defective, that just tells us she doesn't see herself the way we see her.

A force to be reckoned with. Our sweet wallflower.

Ours.

"It's not polite to keep our woman waiting," Marc says.

She's far too distracted as she moans and arches into him, pressing her ass into his cock. His fingers tighten on both her nipples, rolling and pressing them into fine points.

"You got her?" Marc asks, his voice hoarse.

Make it hurt.

"Yeah, I got her."

Lining up, I press my head between her slick folds and push in. As expected, her body starts to tense up as she watches me. Marc grabs her by the chin and turns her face to his instead. I slam all of me inside of her as his mouth fastens on hers, swallowing her sharp gasp. She's so fucking tight; she might as well be a virgin. Bottoming out, I pause as her inner walls spasm around my cock, pulling me in deeper and deeper.

"Perfect," I say with reverence.

I pull out slowly, then push back in, my gaze fixated on them as he relentlessly tongue-fucks her mouth, plunging his tongue in and out and around. Just watching them has me teetering close to the edge, but I can't. Not yet.

Marc breaks off the kiss, and a tiny whimper escapes her throat.

"Marc…" she breathes, leaning towards him.

"Does it hurt?" he asks, his voice thick and hoarse.

Her eyes cloud over and she licks her lips — her tender and thoroughly-kissed plump lips — then swallows hard. "Yes… I mean, no."

"Which is it, D?"

They both turn to face me, their eyes having identically dazed and foggy expressions. She blinks once, then twice. The fog clears, and our eyes meet, a ghost of a smile teasing her lips. Her gaze falls to her hand on my chest, then lower to the juncture where we are joined. I keep a steady stroke in and out of her, and she watches in reverence.

"No, it doesn't hurt," she says eventually. "Shouldn't it?"

Something sinister flashes in Marc's eyes. "This won't do," he growls. "Get the fucking clamps."

Jesus.

I don't know what has gotten into him. He's not usually this menacing. Then again, he's usually not this involved either. We've shared women before, but never in the traditional sense. Once we get started, he would go into hands-off mode. He never touches them, only watches from a safe-ish distance — six feet away, at least — while I do the work and he issues commands. Then, depending on how they did or how generous he feels in the moment, it ends one of two ways. He would either kick them out or make them watch as he fucks me to oblivion.

That's more Marc's style.

Then again, Delilah has always been the exception.

For years I watched as he barely exercised enough self-control to keep his hands to himself while I took all the touching liberties she allowed me. Of course, being best friends with her has its perks. And now that we've finally reached this point, it's like Marc can't bear to let her go. No matter how we've positioned ourselves, one arm remained possessively wrapped around her torso. Even now, his arm stays in place as he rests his chin on her shoulder, her back against his chest, so they have the same view. I could slip out of her right now — not that I want to — and thrust into his puckered hole and he still wouldn't budge.

I thought Marc was joking earlier when he said he would watch up close and personal, but that's precisely all he has done in the last few hours. Even with that, he still managed to draw out over half of her orgasms. Not that it's a competition or anything. Sure, he's used his hands and tongue on her, but he hasn't tasted her directly from the source. Just on his fingers, my fingers, and my tongue.

And yeah, our girl is into that.

Watching, that is.

She enjoys watching us kiss. Watching as we take turns pleasuring her, watching as we pleasure her together. Watching as I fuck her. Always watching, not wanting to miss a single detail — like this night is all she has.

But it's only the first of many.

It's been decided. Well, Marc did. He's decided we're keeping her, and I'm seconding that. She just doesn't know it yet.

"I said get the fucking clamps," Marc growls, his fingers squeezing her nipples in a vise-like grip. She moans, rolling her head back and I swear, she gets even wetter at this. Her vise-like grip doesn't ease up, but thrusting in and out of her does get easier.

Her hands move to my shoulders, and she licks her lips again.

"That's not what I meant," she moans, breath punctuating as I continue to pump myself into her, savoring every thrust.

"She said pain, H. We aim to please, don't we?" There is a reluctant calm in his tone, so I take that and run with it.

"Not like this," I tell him.

He draws a sharp breath. "Give it to her, or I will."

"Marc, no." Her head rolls from side to side, her nails digging into my shoulders. In a twisted way, her obvious discomfort amuses me. "It hurts, but you did a thorough job distracting me. So thank — oh. *Oh, god!*"

That discomfort soon gives way to pleasure, her moans and whimpering cries urging me on as I slam into her relentlessly. She's my drug, and I'm plowing into her like my life depends on it. Meanwhile, Marc watches, thoroughly entranced by the scene, as he rolls his hips against the small of her back, his cock gliding along the crack of her ass cheeks.

Our eyes meet, and she gives me a slight smirk, which makes me wonder if I'm playing with fire and what exactly she meant when she said she would corrupt our souls. The thing is, I wouldn't mind getting a little burnt by her. Or even a lot burnt. I'm definitely on board with being corrupted beyond salvation — by her and by him.

Once she starts making those delicious mewling sounds again, he fastens his mouth on hers, swallowing her screams. Then a series of violent shudders plows through her body as orgasm number forty rides out. I speed up my thrusting, stilling for a moment before releasing a guttural, feral groan as mine takes over.

Thoroughly spent and satiated, her body goes limp between us, and her breathing slowly returns to somewhat normal. Marc follows not long after, and watching his orgasm rip through his body is quite the sight. His face goes angelic, lips slightly parted as he stills, shooting hot streams of cum up her back. It's more than enough. It leaks down her ass cheeks and onto the sheets between us, mixing with my cum dripping out of her tight pussy.

Marc presses a kiss to the side of her neck. "D?"

She groans and her eyelids flutter, too heavy to stay open. "Content. Stay. Leave me."

None of that makes sense, but we both chuckle as we grasp her meaning. Marc scoots back on the bed, taking her boneless body with him while I head for the en suite bathroom to prepare warm towels. Marc's eyes follow my every movement as I clean us up, his arms still draped over her body as he strokes her hair. Delilah stirs as the towel touches the skin of her thighs, and he tightens his hold on her.

"You'll have to let her go at some point," I tease and he gives me the middle finger.

Her queen-sized bed is barely large enough to accommodate all three of our bodies. Still, I would rather spend the night crammed in her bed, just as long as she's in my arms. Marc feels the same way, the possessive fucker. Our bed at home has always felt empty without her, and it will be even worse after tonight.

Once done, I toss the towels in her bathroom hamper before joining them. Marc makes a face when I settle into the empty space beside her, then growls when I move to pull her body to mine.

"Marc, sharing is caring," she whispers sleepily.

His Adam's apple bobs once, then twice, and he finally lets her go, albeit with great reluctance. But he rolls to his side and drapes a heavy arm over her torso, just not as tightly as before. To appease him, she wriggles her backside into him as she snuggles her upper body into mine and her face into my shoulder.

"I know he's your favorite," he pouts, his voice low and gravelly.

"A girl can have more than one favorite," she counters.

I press a kiss on the top of her head, my gaze locked on Marc. I'm not in the least bit surprised by what I see in his eyes. His lips part to add something else, but he thinks better of it and presses them together.

We hold each other this way, in silence, each of us lost in our thoughts. Her breathing slows, and her soft snores fill the room.

"You were right," Marc finally admits.

My heart swells with pride. In sixteen years, I can count on one hand the number of times he's said that to me. Actually said the words, not just implied them.

"I always am," I tease, and the corner of his lip kicks up ever so slightly. "What was I right about this time?" A beat passes, and I finish his thoughts by stating the obvious. "You love her too."

He runs a hand over his face. "How much do you think she'll hate the idea?"

"That's up to her, don't you think?"

He makes a noncommittal grunt. "I'll just tell her it's your fault."

Yeah, that's not Marc's style. He's more of the take-the-blame type of guy since he makes for a more believable villain. So I ask, "Why?"

He scoffs. "Why else? It's your fault we ended up in this mess in the first place."

"She doesn't know that."

"Then you have to tell her, H. Sooner rather than later."

13

DELILAH

This will be the last time I ask a friend for a favor.

Or two friends, for that matter. One best friend and one sort-of friend slash overly protective lawyer, who also happens to be my best friend's partner. His very gay partner, I might add, and last night only confirmed it. And after what I shared with them about my ex-girlfriend, both men should want nothing to do with me lest I corrupt their souls any further. Yet they look like men who want to have their cake and eat it too.

They've conveniently forgotten I don't do romantic relationships. I haven't had one in eighteen years and I'm not about to start now. I was upfront about this from the start too. One night is all I asked for. In hindsight, I should have gotten their written agreement before we did anything.

He's saying many things — Marc, that is — and as he talks, my mouth falls open in disbelief. Blood rushes to my ears as the twin holes confirm what my brain struggles to register. His delectable lips eventually stop moving, and he winks at me. I think an unintelligible noise escapes my lips — a cross between a squeak and a scream. The noise doesn't cease, and neither does my now frozen-in-place face.

"Huh. Congratulations, Marc. You finally broke her," the other one — my best friend — speaks up.

He should be stopping this madness, not egging Marc on. I'm not wearing my happy face right now, so why isn't he putting an end to this?

Marc tilts his head to the side, a smirk playing on the corners of his lips. "I don't think so, H. Look, her eyes just moved. What look did you say that was? Her thoroughly-fucked face?"

Great.

They've gone back to talking about me like I'm not present. This is just fine because it gives me a chance to seriously reconsider my life choices and choice of friends, and also the most effective way to kick them out of my bedroom for good.

Harris, the traitor, laughs. "No, that's her panic mode face. I see what you mean, though. She was making that face for most of last night. Perhaps an encore might be just what she needs. Less panic, more—"

"I'm sorry. Could you repeat that?" I rasp, forcing the words out as heat floods my face at their words. Mostly embarrassment, but with a healthy dosage of lust as last night's events replay in my mind. Not that I need any more reminders of what happened. I'm not wearing any clothes. The only protection I have are the bedsheets, and I doubt they serve their intended purpose.

"Which part?" Marc asks, that damned smirk still on his face. "The encore or the..." He twirls a finger in front of his face.

"No, before that."

He considers it for a moment. "Ah, *that*."

"Yes, *that*." He's going to drag this out like he did two nights ago.

"You need to be specific, D. I said many things."

"That you did, and you also said the words *keeping* and *you*." My middle finger presses into the throbbing pulse at the base of my neck. "As in me."

They exchange another of their wordless looks, gazes lingering on each other for longer than usual. They have their own language, and eye-fucking each other is one of many ways they communicate. Understandable since they've been together for an eternity. Sixteen years, actually, but it might as well be an eternity.

As far as I know, they are happy. Sickeningly happy. Plus they have an open relationship, which is the main reason why I asked them for this favor. Now that it's done, they can return to doing what they've always done. If they want something long-term, well, they already have each other. What the fuck do they want me for?

"Why me?"

Both pairs of eyes turn on me, undisguised lust in their gazes. The look in my eyes mirrors theirs as reignited desire floods my body. It fills my veins, rolls over my skin, and erupts into tingles on my fingertips.

"So, we are all in agreement then." Marc drags his gaze over my body, leaving goosebumps in its wake.

Yeah… they won't be sweet-talking me into this absurd proposition with promises of making all of my wildest fantasies a reality. Not that I would mind. Life is fleeting, and mine is already shorter than most. I'd prefer to go out in a…

No. Focus, Delilah. That's how they got you the last time.

I clear my throat. "Agreement about what?"

"We're keeping you." His words are delivered in a gentle, calm manner. Like it's the most logical thing in the world.

Logical or not, I disagree, so I turn to Harris, communicating my unspoken plea through my eyes. I wager he ought to be the more reasonable party between them.

"I'm with Marc on this," he says.

Traitor. Why are we best friends again?

I hug the sheet closer to my body. "I'm a person, not an object."

The corner of his mouth quirks. "I'm aware."

I swallow, caught in his gaze. "Of which part? My personhood? Or what it entails?"

He considers this for a moment. "I don't see what that has to do with what we've just agreed on."

"You don't own me, Harris. Neither of you do."

He chuckles. "That's not what you were saying last night."

Again with the innuendos.

Who is this stranger and what has he done with my friend? The Harris I know is kind, gentle, and considerate. This version of Harris is none of those things, and the ego on this one is more than I can handle. He's also acting more like Marc. A small part of me likes it, but telling him that will only feed his burgeoning ego, and I'm not sure it can fit in the room with the rest of us.

Marc clears his throat. "If you two would cease making googly eyes at each other, let's discuss our living arrangements."

My face whips to his. "Living arrangements?"

He gestures about the room. "We can't all stay here, so you're moving in with us."

"Unbelievable. Was this the plan all along?"

"Not exactly," Harris quickly answers.

Marc's gaze flickers to his. They exchange another of their wordless looks. I can't even complain about it now since the night is over.

"There was an elaborate plan in place," Harris continues. "It had lots of wooing, but we've done everything out of order."

My eyes stay on Marc. "So everyone you've fucked got this proposition?"

Something flashes in Marc's eyes, a cross between anger and anguish.

"Not exactly," Harris says.

"Then what is… You know what? Never mind." My eyelids flutter, then close, and I pinch the bridge of my nose. "This was a mistake. Last night was a mistake."

"D—"

I suck in a sharp breath between clenched teeth. "I'd like you two to leave now."

An awkward silence settles over the room, the weight of it deafening. No clothing rustles, no zippers work up. No shuffling of footsteps. No doors opening or closing. Just stifling silence.

Until the bed dips next to me and I'm surrounded by Marc's pheromones. He reaches for my hand and tugs it toward him. The sheet falls, exposing the top half of my body.

"D, look at me." His voice is strained but stern.

I have no choice but to obey. My eyelids flutter and open, and our gazes lock. My pulse spikes, and a familiar ache spreads between my thighs.

Damn him.

"Last night wasn't a mistake," he says. "If anything, it was meant to be."

In addition to the raw, undisguised hunger in his eyes — one that no doubt matches my own — there's also kindness in them, which appeals to me more than I care to admit. It draws me in, anchoring me to him, or him to me, the lines seeming to blur at this point.

I let out a shaky breath. "Then why the speech about keeping me? That's not what we agreed on before last night happened."

He chuckles, then leans forward to press a chaste kiss to my lips. "H agreed, I didn't."

"Semantics, Marc. I'm not doing this."

"There isn't a choice to be had here. H here has an innate sense of duty."

"Duty?"

He nods, stroking my hand between his. "He feels obligated since he was your first."

"Obligated? Are you kidding me?" I scoff, some of the lust-induced haze clearing. "I told you I wasn't a virgin, and this isn't the Dark Ages. You can't decide my fate unilaterally based on... whatever this is."

Something indecipherable flashes in Marc's eyes. "Are you making light of what we shared?"

His words flick a switch deep within. My back immediately arches in response, and both nipples go rigid, hot against the room's cool air. It takes every ounce of self-control not to touch, pinch or roll them between my fingers.

"I'm not making light of anything," I force out, my heartbeat kicking up a notch. "Our deal was for one night only."

"Your body says otherwise," he says, his voice going stern and back to business as usual. "The sooner you stop fighting this, the easier it will be on all of us."

How I wish I could turn the clock back twenty-four hours prior, to when I was the invisible, defective twin. That holds more appeal than this absurd conversation about who gets to keep whom.

Behind me, the bed dips as Harris joins us, scooting close, and his warmth envelops my body. I don't dare turn to face him. If the look in his eyes is anything like Marc's, I know I'll be agreeing to all sorts of things before this conversation is over.

My head tilts to the side. "Is this what you meant?" I ask, keeping my eyes on Marc. "The stupid game you mentioned last night?"

Marc blanches. "I—"

"I wasn't asking you," I say, cutting him off. "Seven years, you said. I left it alone last night, and now you spring this on me. What's next? Blood oaths?"

"If it comes to that," Harris says.

"I was being sarcastic."

For someone who makes it a point to touch me every chance he gets, Harris sure is keeping his hands to himself. Not sure how I feel about that.

Before me, Marc shrugs, his infamous boyish charm plastered on his face. "Aren't you forgetting something?"

My brow twists. "What's that?"

"You chose me first." Harris's breath caresses my ear.

My eyes go wide. "When did I—" I squeak, the words dying on my lips as the memory sends a new wave of desire coursing through me, unfurling in my stomach and spreading between my thighs.

The look on Marc's face turns downright wicked and hungry. "So you agree, we *are* keeping you."

Why does he keep twisting my words?

"That is not what that meant and you know it. You asked me to... I didn't think it meant..." No matter what I say, they'll just read into it however they want to. "That was something else. Something said in the heat of the moment."

Marc's laugh is sinister. "Do you need a refresher? You asked—"

I place a hand over his lips. "I know what I said."

Putting a hand over the mouth is dramatic and juvenile, but desperate times call for desperate measures. He doesn't see it that way. His lips part underneath my hand, and his tongue caresses the sensitive skin of my palm. The sensual gesture has my body vibrating with hunger, a new sizzle of desire coursing through me.

"Don't I get a say in any of this?"

"Not really," Marc murmurs before pulling my hand off his mouth. Then, taking both hands in his, he runs both of his thumbs over my knuckles. "See, I've made it my life's mission to grant H whatever his heart desires. He wants you. It's my job to see that he gets you."

"So, a plaything for Harris. That's what I've been reduced to?"

"You're making it sound worse than it actually is," Harris adds, finally deciding to touch me. Using a single digit, he runs feather-light touches along the back of my neck, enough to send shudders of desire down my spine.

"I don't see the upside," I force out through clenched teeth.

"How about this?" Harris's hands cup both of my breasts, his thumbs tracing circles over the rigid peaks.

I stifle the moan that escapes my lips. "You want me to become a kept woman, like you are."

"And?"

"We've known each other for how long? All this time, what about me says I want to spend the remainder of my already shortened lifespan as a kept woman, a mob mistress?"

"This goes both ways," Marc says quietly, his stormy-gray eyes searching my face, studying and analyzing my every reaction. "D, we are yours, just as much as you are ours."

Why doesn't this sound as horrible as it should? He knows it, too, the plethora of emotions his words unleash in me. I hate that I am an open book to him — to both of them — and that we all know it.

Focus, Delilah. Don't get derailed. It's how they'll get you a second time.

"It's not a bad deal," Marc continues. "What we're offering is far sweeter, with all the perks that come with it. No more dry spells. Free lodging. All the kinky sex your heart desires. Forever."

Icy-hot panic seizes me and my body goes utterly still. "Pass."

Marc's brow crinkles. "Why the hell not?"

Simple — I don't do commitment.

Forever holds little to no appeal to me. They would know this if they bothered to pay attention to what I said last night. Or even how I've lived my life all these years. Nothing lasts forever. It's never guaranteed, and stupidly, blindly believing in it will only end in heartache.

Also, it's the last thing she said to me.

Harris's hands leave my breasts and encircle my waist, pulling my back flush against his chest. He presses feathered kisses along my bare shoulder before resting his chin on it, his head leaning against mine. Against my better judgment, my body relaxes against his because this is the Harris I know — gentle and considerate.

"Maybe not forever," he says, picking up on what bothers me about Marc's proposition. "Maybe for as long as we all shall live?"

"That's the same thing, so no."

A beat passes, then, "How much time do you need?"

Even though he directs the question at me, I get the sense he's also expecting a response from Marc. They are exchanging one of those wordless gazes. Marc's eyes cloud over, and my chest tightens at the sight.

"None," I force the word out. "A deal's a deal. One night only."

His clenched jaw lets me know he doesn't like my answer. My heart squeezes painfully, and I don't know what to make of it. Besides, Marc isn't known for diplomacy or tact. Abrasiveness, yes, and I expect that side of him will be rearing its head any time now.

"One month." Marc's tone goes back to calm and business as usual. "Scratch that. You have one week. You can come of your own accord, or I'll make you. You've seen me do it before, with H. That was me being gentle. Considerate. It will be far worse if you force my hand. As you know, I'm not above resorting to sneaky and underhanded tactics either."

He's insane, is all I can think of.

I picture Harris's dramatic eye roll against my cheek. Then he says, "Jesus, Marc. Would you knock it off already?"

Marc drops my hand in my lap and rises to his feet. "Talk some sense into her," is all he says before leaving the room.

14

HARRIS

"**M**arc is not used to being told no," I whisper against her skin. My arms tighten around her stomach, anchoring her as she relaxes her body against mine. I nip at the sensitive nape of her neck before tracing the outline of her ear with my tongue.

"I wish that made me feel better, but it doesn't."

I laugh. "I know. Marc doesn't make empty threats. When he gets like this, it's best to go along with it."

What little tension I've managed to ease out of her body returns. "Harris, I'm not stupid," she says in a low voice. "This isn't about him. It's about you."

And just like that, the moment's gone.

I draw in a deep breath, releasing it slowly. "Delilah…"

"Save it," she says, pushing out of my arms and scooting off the bed. "If you're going to lie to me, you can shove it up your ass."

I bite the inside of my cheek to keep from smiling. Marc is right; I should have been truthful with her from the start. But I also know how she is. Had she known this was how things would end, she wouldn't have come to us in the first place. Convincing her that this is best for all of us will be no easy feat.

She has her back to me as she retrieves her discarded clothing from the floor and gets re-dressed. Or partially dressed, in her bra and tank top, before she begins frantically searching the room. I'm graced with a delectable view of her supple ass cheeks and glistening pussy when she bends over to check under the dressing table. My cock goes hard instantly, and there's nothing I'd like more than to keep her in that position while I fuck her from behind.

She straightens, then runs her fingers through her long, luscious brown hair. Her breasts perk up, both nipples already hard points pushing through her bra, begging to be touched. I'd kill for the chance to touch them, to touch her again, period.

"I was enjoying the view," I say, unable to resist the urge to tease her.

Instead, she turns and pins me with an angry glare. "Where the fuck are my panties?"

"You cut them up last night." I point to the fabric pile in front of the side dresser.

She sighs. "Not those ones. The purple thong. I had it on that chair with the rest of today's clothes."

So that's why Marc was hovering in that area this morning.

I shrug. "Marc has them." There is no sense in lying to her.

"Those were my favorite pair," she mutters.

"He'll replace them and then some. All you have to do is ask."

Her jaw tenses and she clenches fistfuls of hair in her hands. Maybe that wasn't the best answer, but it was the only one I could think of.

She draws in a sharp breath, and golden-brown eyes fixate on mine, sparkling with revived rage. "Start talking, and don't even think about lying to me."

"I won't. Cross my heart." I let out an exasperated sigh. "Where do I start?"

That damned tic in her jaw goes erratic. "From the beginning is always a good place to start. Starting with this stupid game." She goes straight for the jugular, not that I expect anything less from my best friend.

"I ran into my dad at the rehearsal dinner."

"I know, his name was on the fucking guest list," she says, impatience lacing her tone. "What does that have to do with this?"

"He said some things. The same shit he's been saying for years. I've gotten better at handling it now, though that wasn't the case in the past. The last time his shit got to me was seven years ago."

We both fall silent, letting the weight of that revelation sink in.

I am what most people refer to as biracial or racially ambiguous. I mostly take after my German mother in terms of physical appearance. Not that I'd know, I never met the woman. Long story, lots of family drama there. But because I can pass, it's not something I advertise about myself. Besides, blond hair dye works wonders in altering one's appearance, something Delilah often helps me with. It's also the perfect way for me to stay hidden in plain sight. Few people know I'm biracial. Even fewer can connect me to my well-known father, Victor Toussaint.

It's how I've lived the entirety of my adult life — as far away from his roof, legacy, and control as I could. But as it happens, Victor is a creative fucker who always finds different ways to sneak back into my life. He's not above using the family members I actually care about as bargaining chips. But having practiced healthy boundaries for sixteen years — courtesy of Marc — I shut it down fast each time. It's freeing. Exhilarating, even. And just how I like it.

Unfortunately, he sometimes finds ways to sneak back in by ambushing me like he did two nights ago. Most of the time, it's through Delilah.

"What did you do?" she asks.

I swallow over the lump in my throat. "Something stupid. It cost me you, and it nearly cost me Marc. Hence the... thing. You were there for that."

An uncomfortable silence stretches out between us.

"What did he say?" she eventually asks.

"The usual, with some extras thrown into the mix. It started with the kids thing, then it all snowballed from there."

I can't stand to see the look of pity in her eyes, so I redirect my attention to her obnoxiously colorful bedspread. Talking about or even thinking of my family has always been a sore subject.

Not only was I barely accepted by both sides of my family, I was dubbed the black sheep of the Toussaint family. I guess I still am. Coming out as bisexual was the equivalent of tossing the proverbial gas on the fire. My falling in love with Marc ensured my subsequent banishment from the family, amongst other things. I miss them every day — most of them anyway — but what's done is done.

Despite what my dad says or does, I will never be welcomed back home. Not unless I bend to his will. Not unless I submit to all of his demands, something I have no intention of doing. As such, we are at an impasse.

Which is fine by me. I've done just fine all these years. I don't need him, his connections, or the clout that comes with being associated with my family. After kicking me out of the family, he expected me to flop and fail. He'd expected me to come crawling back home with my tail tucked between my legs, and the fact that I didn't do that irked him to no end.

I know it too. I know I turned out better than most, and I also know that I was lucky to find a home with Marc.

And hopefully, with Delilah too.

The sound of the dresser drawer slamming shut draws me out of my thoughts.

"I know what your dad is like," she murmurs. "But that doesn't explain the stupid thing you actually did. Or why Marc called it a game. Why would he use those exact words? We both know Marc doesn't say shit he doesn't mean. If he called it a game, it's because you called it a game."

My heart clenches. "If I promise to tell you later, will you... leave it alone?"

She laughs bitterly. "Not a fucking chance."

"Just for tonight, then?"

"That only works once."

Now it's my turn to laugh. "I'm a screw-up, Delilah. A failure. That's how he will always see me. It's not something I readily advertise. You know this. So when I say it was bad, it was bad. But I am trying to make up for what I did. To you and to Marc. I just... I can't talk about it. Not yet. But I will, I promise."

She blows out a breath. "Is that why your dad still hates me?"

"That's part of it, yes. I don't think that's ever going to change."

"I have so many questions about that," she says as she pulls on a clean pair of underwear. "But as your best friend, I will wait for you to tell me in your own time. As long as you don't give me a reason to pry. That promise only stands as long as you are truthful with me."

"I like you half-dressed," I say, knowing jeans will follow shortly.

She looks back over her shoulder at me. I just quirk my brow at her, an amused smile playing at the corners of my lips. She rolls her eyes before resuming tugging her jeans on.

"Stop changing the subject," she bites, her words punctuated by the exertion of tugging her skin-tight jeans over her hips.

"Worth a shot."

The good thing about knowing someone for so long is that I seldom have to explain my thought process to her. I don't have to explain why or how the things a person learns as a child tend to stay with them through adulthood, no matter how hard they try to shake it.

Because she knows. She understands all of that because, in many ways, our childhoods mirror each other. That's the thing about damaged souls. They are like homing beacons and always find a way to latch on to other damaged souls.

Marc, Delilah, and myself — we are a unique brand of damaged.

I just need to convince her she belongs with us.

"Last night wasn't a mistake. We are yours, just as much as you are ours. It's been that way for a long time. Last night just made things official."

Her mind is a beautiful thing to watch. I watch as the wheels turn in her brain and the moment it finally clicks. Her face falls, then contorts into an odd shape — a cross between disbelief and shock.

"Please," she draws in a sharp breath, releasing it slowly, "tell me you aren't basing this on—"

I nod somberly. There is no sense in lying, not when she has the uncanny ability to see through me. Marc and Delilah both do. It's one of many things that bind me to them.

For a long while, she says nothing. Her golden-brown eyes fixate on me, searching for something deep within. I don't think she'll find it, whatever that is.

Or maybe she will.

God, I hope she does.

Maybe it's because her chest heaves like she's undecided on whether to give in to her physical desire or continue fighting it.

It's not a bad deal, what we are offering her. I can't speak to whether or not it's what's best for her since that's something she needs to decide for herself. But she needs to decide soon, or he will decide for her since that's what he does best. When he does, she won't like how he goes about it.

I still don't understand why she insists on fighting this. Not just now. She has been fighting this for seven years, maybe even longer. Maybe even for as long as I've known her.

It's no secret she is physically attracted to Marc. Whenever she's around him, her mannerisms make it painfully obvious. He never acted on it out of respect for me, even though I knew he wanted to. He's wanted her since the moment he first laid eyes on her. I did too, and time didn't change that.

But Marc is a whole other beast. He's the type of man who takes what he wants when he wants it. Delilah has always been the exception. All this while, he has exercised remarkable restraint where she is concerned. Until I showed interest in her, in wanting more than just friendship, in wanting her as a part of our family.

She runs her hands through her hair. "All I asked for is one night, Harris. I was upfront with you both about that. You gave me your word. Marc didn't, but I already know that's just how he is." She pauses to catch her breath, and I don't dare to say anything else. "That said, I'm fully aware Marc doesn't mince words and doesn't make empty threats. He wouldn't be digging his heels in this hard unless it was something you wanted."

She goes silent then, so I take it as my cue to speak.

"It's what we both want," I answer her truthfully. "But mostly, it's what I want. I never hid how I feel about you—"

"As a friend, right?"

Is she for real? "As more than a friend, Delilah. I—"

"Don't," she interjects with a slight shake of her head. "Please don't. Not now."

Patience, I remind myself.

A long while passes before she finally asks, "I hate to have to ask this, but did you know…?"

Our eyes meet, her gaze searching mine. I see the question in her eyes, so I finish with, "That Marc was going to do this? Yes. I knew." A beat passes, then, "I thought you would ask him to do it. You took us by surprise last night."

"Again, that's not how it…" she trails off, then blows an annoyed breath. "You're unbelievable, Harris. I can't decide if I should be honored or annoyed."

"How about both?" I ask, giving her a small, tentative smile.

She pins me with an angry stare. "Don't even go there. Flattery will get you nowhere fast."

I lift both hands in mock defeat.

Delilah walks over to join me on her bed, only this time she sits at arm's length from me. I hate it — this distance between us. This tension. It's never been like this with us, and I wish things between us would return to normal — whatever our new normal is going to be.

"What can I do to fix this?" Tears burn my eyes, and I know I need to fix this. Soon. I can't afford to lose her. Not now. Not when I've had a taste of her. "I'll do anything."

I don't sense her scooting closer at first, not until her thigh presses against mine. The sudden intimate touch sends a glow that spreads from my chest into my limbs. It feels a lot nicer than it probably should, and my heart hammers against my ribs in anticipation. I'm filled with hope. Maybe this thing we have is salvageable.

Until she says, "Last night was a mistake."

Hope deflates instantly. I hated hearing it the first time. I loathe hearing it even more the second time. I loathe yet more the emotions those words stir up in me. I've really fucked this one up.

"Delilah, I—"

She rests her arm on mine. "Please, let me finish."

I swallow around the lump in my throat, interlacing our fingers. "Okay."

She doesn't pull her hand from mine. "What's done is done. We can't exactly undo what happened last night." She squeezes gently. I hope it's a good sign, but her elongated silence says otherwise. "Obligation. Duty. Commitment. Forever. I hate those words, Harris. I've been trying to get away from those. That's what last night was about. Not this. Not all this talk about keeping and claiming and owning. We both know only you can call off Marc and his guards. So do what you have to, but make it happen. Like he said, you have a week."

"I can't."

"Can't or won't?" Irritation sparks her voice, but there's something else in there. *Despair?*

An overwhelming sense of urgency takes the place of hope. It builds and spreads and smothers. I have every intention of answering her. My lips part but no sound comes out, so I close them back up as my breathing goes ragged. I can't give her what she wants. What she's asking for.

The wheels have already been set in motion, and there's no stopping this. There is no calling Marc off once he sets his mind to something. He's probably hovering outside the door, listening to our conversation, planning his next move.

"Harris, can't or won't?" she repeats.

My lips thin out, quivering.

She doesn't know exactly how far Marc would go to grant me what I want. He's like a dog with a bone in that regard. That obsession of his now includes her. She now has as much power as I do in this relationship, so it's up to her to strategically leverage it.

But there's no stopping this, and there's no leaving Marc. Not now, not ever. The sooner she understands and accepts this, the easier her transition will be.

"I'm sorry," I whisper.

"Then I'm sorry too," she says, her breathing mirroring my own. Using her free hand, she hooks a finger underneath my chin and turns my face to hers. Her eyes glimmer with unshed tears, mirroring my own. "If he makes me do this, I will resent you for it." She pauses to let her words sink in. A lone tear inches down her face and falls on our intertwined hands. "Not him. You."

15

DELILAH

This dumpster fire of a week finally crawls to a slow, torturous end. Not that I expected any different. After Saturday's fiasco, the media vultures descended upon Brewer Health, hoping to catch a glimpse of the runaway bride. More like clamoring for an exclusive interview with Dahlia, even though it's been made abundantly clear that she won't be giving any.

It certainly doesn't help that all anyone cares about isn't why Dahlia ran away from her wedding. No, they care more that she took the time to strip before taking off, that Andrea's heart attack was completely staged, and how heartbroken Curtis supposedly is to have been left at the altar by his childhood sweetheart.

Bullshit.

Cry me a fucking river.

It's too bad they don't see him the same way I do. A rich, spoiled, disrespectful, pompous, entitled asshole who thinks the world should revolve around him.

I could go on, but as it so happens, there is one other whose sense of entitlement rivals his. None other than his own mother.

Andrea's overly dramatic antics in the days leading up to the wedding, the morning of, and even after Dahlia fled were enough to drive any sane person up a wall. I expected the McWhorters to be on the warpath — and they were, for all of forty-eight hours. By Tuesday morning they went into damage control mode. A blessing in disguise at first, until they put out a press release on Wednesday morning announcing Dahlia's pregnancy to the world.

It wasn't a highlight; that much was certain. It got the media vultures to back off for the time being, but that's only a band-aid. Dahlia would hate that they announced this without consulting her first. Especially since I'm not sure if she'll make it through this pregnancy in one piece.

The icing on the fucking cake? I missed my standing Friday morning breakfast with Harris.

Make no mistake, it was on purpose that I stood him up. He came to me. Or rather, to the cafeteria of Brewer Health, same as he did last Friday. I know he did, because he sent me a picture of himself, in the café, alone in an empty booth. He even captioned it *'Lonely.'* Then he sent me a picture of his and my breakfast orders — twin stacks of mouth-watering pancakes, generously drizzled with syrup, sugar, and strawberries — and another of him leaving with two takeout boxes.

I know all this because I opened his messages, then left him on 'read' like the petty bitch I am. Like I have been doing all week long. With his phone calls too. He's called me several times, and I let it go to voicemail. Then, because I am such a glutton for punishment, I listened to all the sappy messages he left me. Yet I couldn't bring myself to call him back. Or even text him back.

It's not like I have been pining for him either. I've had other more pressing matters to deal with.

Like the case of my missing sister.

Who, as it turns out, is not so much missing. More like hiding.

Not that I blame her.

What I did not count on, however, was the dumpster fire waiting for me at the end of what should be a peaceful weekend.

It comes in the form of Harris, waiting for me at my doorstep. Hands tucked into the pockets of his distressed blue jeans, he crowds the doorway with his massive and impressive body. It's his way of letting me know he doesn't plan on leaving until we talk.

I should've known he wouldn't let this morning's snafu go so easily. It's also not the first time he's shown up at my doorstep unannounced. We've been best friends for fifteen years, so it's only fair that he has some latitude at my place. Although it's the first time he hasn't simply let himself inside, even though the front door's been thrown wide open.

His doing, no doubt.

"I have nothing to say to you," are my first words to him.

There's no point in exchanging pointless and forced pleasantries between us. Screw the *hello*s and *how-do-you-do*s — it's not how we usually communicate, and we're not about to start now.

Then, because I know he is never too far off, I glance over Harris's shoulder and into the entryway. Sure enough, Marc is inside, leaning against the door frame and crowding the threshold with his equally impressive and massive body. He looks casual and relaxed, but I don't doubt for a second that he'll stop me if I attempt to walk away from them.

"Marc." I readjust my purse strap over my shoulder. "Fancy seeing you here."

He makes a noncommittal grunt, eyes still trained on me.

I have to walk around Harris and past Marc to get inside my house. Their body positioning makes it clear that I will have to touch one or both of them to achieve this feat. My body will have to brush against both to reach my destination.

Not that I'd mind that. I already did that, and so much more, a week ago.

But that was the deal — one night only.

Once and done.

Or that was *supposed* to be the deal. Until Marc reneged on it the following morning with unreasonable demands about keeping me and equally unrealistic asks about forever. And since Dahlia is in hiding, I've spent the week juggling two jobs. The last time we spoke was Saturday evening, and it's been radio silence ever since. She needs the break and I understand that.

But it also means that I don't see a reprieve anytime soon. Between dealing with the board of directors for Brewer Health and putting out PR fires left and right, I'm already on edge. My nerves are tattered, emotions riding way too close to the surface. These are all things Dahlia usually does; quite frankly, she's much better at it than I am. So if she ends up being gone for who knows how long, then I need to figure out how I will make it through without her.

The last thing I need tonight is to find Marc and Harris on my doorstep together.

Not when my traitorous body remembers every sordid detail of our night together. And she wants more. More of everything that they have to offer.

"I have nothing to say to you either," I say in cold acknowledgment, addressing Marc this time.

His lips twist into a classic Marc-esque smirk.

"We need to talk," Harris says, not moving from his position.

No, we don't.

I fold my arms across my chest. "Look, guys. It's been a long day. Long days, actually. Can we do this some other day?"

He nods as if he understands my dilemma. "You don't have to talk—"

"Excellent. Leave."

"—you can just listen to what we have to say. Well, listen to what I have to say. I'm the only one who's here to talk. Marc's not."

Talking. That never ends well.

"Fine, I'll listen. Tomorrow. Next week. Any day but today."

"That's not an option, D," Marc chimes in.

My gaze levels with his. "All right then. Doesn't change the fact that I don't want you here. Either of you."

Marc starts to say something else, but Harris levels him with a gaze of his own. "We didn't come here to fight," he says, addressing me even though his eyes stay on Marc's. "Right, babe?"

After a brief staring contest, Marc huffs out a frustrated breath, pushes off the wall and stalks inside.

"Please, by all means, come inside. Make yourselves at home," I say, without bothering to hide the sarcasm and forced politeness in my voice.

"Don't worry, we will," Harris says, chancing a wink at me. Then, with a slight shake of his head, he follows Marc inside.

And I'm left outside, staring at their retreating figures and wondering how my life got to this point.

Because as much as it bothers me to admit it, Marc was right.

One night was not enough. So even if I wanted to, I couldn't exactly kick them both out. Too much of a headache. That, and I think my traitorous body still misses them.

Both of them, actually.

I miss them.

But most of all, I miss Harris. This is the longest we've gone without seeing or talking to each other. To his credit, Harris did try to keep the lines of communication open between us. I'm the one who froze him out. Not that he was any good at taking a fucking hint.

Taking the stairs two at a time, I follow them inside, close the door, then slide all the deadbolts and locks into place like I always do. I hear them shuffling about in the living room. To prolong the inevitable dreaded talk, I take my time draping my purse and coat on their designated hooks. It reminds me of my parents' routine. It's also why I can't let go of this house.

This house is our childhood home. In addition to our first building — the one that houses Brewer Health — Dahlia and I co-own several commercial properties throughout the Midwest. This house just so happens to be the only residential real estate property we co-own.

It's filled with all our mementos, with traces of my parents and Simone sprinkled throughout the house. Their memories, too, still linger on, but the space reflects my style now for the most part. Dahlia didn't care what I did here as long as she took creative rein over our commercial properties.

I don't think Marc understands what he's asking of me when he says I should move in with them. It will mean leaving all of this behind. Boxing up their memories, shoving them in the back of a closet, never to see the light of day again. I'm not sure I can handle that.

Then again, I'm not sure I can handle these two either.

Like I always do, I stop to study her picture, the one hanging in the entryway, framed over the entryway bench. It's one of my favorite pictures of her, one I display proudly in our home because this house is one of a few McWhorter-free spaces. Mom and Dad had the foresight to install a keyless entry to the house back then, and Dahlia and I change the codes monthly, even to this day.

Because Harris is my best friend, I give him the code each time — in the spirit of free rein and all. The codes are due to be changed in a week, and suffice it to say he will not be getting the new one.

Time heals all wounds… I call bullshit on that. I miss her every single day. Time hasn't made anything easier. It certainly hasn't lessened the pain of her loss or the debilitating grief I still feel each time I look at her picture. My grief still bleeds out every day, no matter how much time passes.

So this house is a shrine to my parents and to Simone. And this picture is also one of the rare instances when Simone felt truly free. Dahlia took this picture of her — amateur photography is one of her hobbies — and she captured Simone's essence perfectly in this photograph. It's one of the few pictures that survived after her parents went on a rampage, determined to purge every image or likeness of hers from existence.

After losing her back then, I don't have the emotional wherewithal to survive that rabbit hole again. Yet, I can't help but think that this thing with Harris and Marc does just that. As enticing as it is — as they both are — it won't end well for me. At its core, it goes against everything I believe and everything I'm trying to establish for myself.

Yet I want more. Like a glutton, I want it all.

And Marc, he makes it sound so easy. So simple.

But even I know that nothing is ever that easy. Or simple. Everything comes at a cost. A hefty emotional price. And for every touch of heaven, there will always be a taste of hell not too far off.

16

DELILAH

Eventually, I make my way inside to find that Harris and Marc have taken my sarcastic advice and made themselves at home in various parts of the house.

Harris sits cross-legged in the living room — my parents' living room — sipping red wine from a long-stemmed glass and looking very much like he lives here. While Marc is in the kitchen — my parents' kitchen, but it used to be my dad's domain — and it looks like he's making... *dinner*?

Like it's just another Friday. Except it's not. Fridays are their days, so I'm still not sure why they're here.

I huff out a frustrated breath. "Listen, guys. It's not that I'm not happy to see you. I am. But I was planning on a quiet evening, a long soak in the tub, preferably in silence and with pitch-black darkness. I intend to indulge in that and only that tonight. Preferably without all of these penises swimming around."

"You sure you don't want that?" Harris asks.

"Want wh—" I trail off as it dawns on me, just what I said. "Testosterone! I meant to say testosterone, not..."

I meant to say testosterone, I swear. Not sure why the word penises slipped out instead. But they are both here, with their big, warm, hauntingly yet mouthwateringly gorgeous bodies and seductive eyes. I just want to crawl in between them and settle in there. Or on them.

Whatever.

I can't.

I just need to make it through their seductive glances and delectable bodies, preferably without giving in to my desire. I already know firsthand just how addictive these two can be. The intensity of our chemistry was explosive, and I'd be lying if I didn't admit that I was still reeling from the effects of our one night together.

But I can't go back. I'm not looking for forever — not with anyone, for any reason. People leave. They die, and it hurts too much to be the one who's left behind.

Releasing an exasperated smile, I turn to Marc. "What are you doing?"

He shrugs. "Making dinner."

Huh? "You cook?"

"I do a lot of things." He has several contraptions pulled out of several drawers and spread out on the countertop. I haven't seen some of those in months, ever since Dahlia moved out. Others I haven't seen in years, since our parents died. "Why are the contents of your fridge uncharacteristically sparse?"

"Because I don't cook. I just order takeout most nights."

"Yeah, figures," he says with a laugh. "Your eating habits are horrendous."

Scowling, I can't help but add, "If it's a docile housewife you're looking for, you're not going to get that from me."

He goes utterly still, the smile falling off his face. "That's not why…" He trails off at that. His eyes meet mine, and something flashes in them. Pain, I think. It disappears so quickly that it's hard to tell.

My tongue darts out to lick my lips. "Why are you here?"

His gaze lowers, honing in on my mouth. "Fridays are date night. I do all the cooking on date nights, or whenever I feel like it, really. We have two chefs for our nutritional needs and staff for everything else."

My brain is still stuck on the first sentence. "Date nights are your thing. I want to know why you're doing it here, at my house? Don't you have someplace else to do this?"

"They include you too, D. I meant what I said."

I meant what I said too, but there's no reasoning with Marc.

Pinching the bridge of my nose, I turn my attention back to Harris. "There was a bottle of merlot in the fridge with my name on it. Tell me that's not it?"

"It is." He takes a sip, then finishes it off in another long swallow. "What was left of it, anyway."

I try not to stare at him while he does this, but it's impossible not to. I hone in on the bob of his Adam's apple as the liquid moves down his throat.

He sets his glass down, picks up the wine bottle, and sloshes it around. "I guess there's still some left. Pour you a glass?" he offers.

I shake my head before shoving a hand through my hair. "Whatever. I need to get out of these clothes."

After a long day at work, I'm covered in sweat and grime. I'm ready to shed these stuffy clothes and restrictive bra. Free the girls, so to speak. My favorite pair of onesie pajamas beckons.

Harris springs to his feet, almost toppling the bottle in haste. "I'll join you."

"Please don't," I bite back.

Harris takes several quick steps towards me, angry at my response. "I wasn't asking."

"I wasn't either."

He stops before me and places both hands on my shoulders. "You'll change and we'll talk. It'll be just like old times."

I lift a brow. "Seriously?"

He doesn't answer but spins my body around and walks me toward my bedroom. Once inside, I shrug him off and pin him with an angry glare of my own.

"I don't need a fucking audience," I practically scream at him.

He closes the door behind us, leans against it and crosses his arms. "We need to talk."

"We don't *need* to do anything."

"We're not leaving this room until we do."

I fold my arms across my chest and press my lips into a fine line. The silence stretches between us, heavy and tense. As expected, Harris concedes first.

"I miss you, Delilah. I miss my best friend."

"Friends don't treat each other the way we do."

"You're right. They don't. And you know why, don't you?"

"I don't know, Harris. I don't know anything about you, clearly. This is the opposite of what I asked for. You both are just carrying on unilaterally as if we're in some alternate universe where I said yes."

"You know me, so don't give me that right now. We're more than that. We've always been more than that. We've come too far and shared so much of ourselves with each other. And yes, I love you. I fucking love you. I always have, and if that makes me sappy, then so be it. But I'm man enough to admit it. Are you?"

"It's not about that—"

"The hell it isn't."

My spine stiffens as he advances upon me. His lips are on mine before I can comprehend it, much less process what's happening here. It only takes a few insistent pushes of his tongue for my lips to part, welcoming his. And just like that, the stress of the week falls right off. Our kiss quickly turns frenzied, as it usually does with us.

We stumble backward, tumbling onto the bed in a tangled heap of legs and arms. I might have been slightly miffed about not getting a taste of my merlot, but this is better. Much, much better. I could drink it all off of him and still wouldn't get my fill.

When he pulls away from me, I'm breathless.

"I only came here to talk, I swear," he rasps, the look in his eyes feral. I've never seen him like this, and I like it. "You're... you're a fucking drug, Delilah. I tried to resist, I really did, but I — that day, when you bent over, showing me your glistening pussy, waving it in my face like bread before a starving man, I clung to that image. And now, I—"

He doesn't finish his sentence before his mouth is on mine again. This time it's forceful, which is fine because my arms loop around his neck and my tongue attacks his with as much ferocity as he does mine.

His mouth eventually leaves mine, his lips trailing kisses down my neck.

"We shouldn't be doing this," are the words that pop out instead, even as my face tilts to the side to give him more access.

It's not an entirely unfounded thought. But somehow, I don't think it fazes him. His lips cover the sensitive spot between my neck and shoulder, and his teeth sink into the flesh. Not too hard, but just enough to leave me soaking and needy.

"So tell me to stop," he groans, his breath hot against my ear.

My pussy aches in protest as I feel his throbbing cock grow against me. He is a highly addictive drug that I can never get enough of, and I want him inside me again.

"I can't." My eyelids flutter, then close as I impatiently wriggle my hips under him. "You're not the only one who's powerless to this."

Thankfully he gets the hint, spurring him into action. His hands find my body again like no time has passed between us. I'm not sure how we manage it, given our current position, but most of our clothes come partially undone. The necessary ones anyway. Then he thrusts a finger into my pussy and we groan in unison.

His hands, his body, they feel warm and familiar. They feel like home. They also feel different, like something is missing.

Like someone is missing.

"This is a fucking mistake," I moan, grinding into his hand.

He goes still, slowing down the pace of his thrusts. "Don't say that."

Keeping my eyes closed, I resist the urge to bite my lower lip. "It's the truth."

"So tell me to stop." He wriggles his finger, pressing down on my g-spot. A shudder ripples through me.

"I c-can't," I force out through clenched teeth. My eyelids part to find his eyes on me. "I wish I could, but I can't. I... umm..." There's a part of me that wonders if voicing this is a smart move on my part. If it will only make his ego grow bigger. "I need you too much."

A beat passes, then he plunges a second finger into my clenching pussy, and then the third one, before swirling his finger in a come-hither motion. "Same here, but know that this isn't a mistake. Nothing about this is a mistake."

"So why does it feel like one? I just... we need—"

"—Marc, I know. I'll..." He presses his head against my forehead, and I can feel him growing even harder against my stomach. "Let me take care of you first, then we'll fix this, okay?"

"How?" I roll my hips against him, forcing his fingers in deeper. "He's not in here. Not sure if he—"

Harris leans in and presses his lips to mine, swallowing my words. I can't help the sigh that escapes when his tongue finally invades my mouth, flooding my senses. He takes his time, gently stroking and caressing my tongue with his, tasting me like I was the most precious thing to him. He picks up the pace as he finger-fucks me, and I writhe against his body and fingers, desperately chasing my release.

"Come for me, Delilah. Now," he growls into my ear.

I do as he says; my body is powerless to stop the hurricane-sized orgasm that washes over me, threatening to pull me under and drown me in it. He takes his time teasing me through my orgasm until all that is left is me, as a whimpering puddle underneath him.

"Perfect," he whispers.

My eyes open to meet his, disbelief swimming in them. I don't know about perfect. More like scared shitless, yet that doesn't even begin to accurately describe how I feel.

Then he brings his hand to his mouth and licks his fingers clean, one after the other. His tongue swirls seductively and sinuously around each digit, all while he stares into my eyes.

"Oh, god," I say, my voice a breathy whisper. "W-why do you have to do that?"

"I needed to confirm that you still taste as sweet as I remember, which you do."

"How I taste? Do I want to know?"

He laughs. "I need to be inside you," he says at the same time I say, "Harris, I need you inside of me."

"If you two are done screwing around, dinner's ready," Marc's deep voice bellows from the doorway.

17

HARRIS

Delilah pushes me away, and it is with great reluctance that I let her go. Then the moment I release her, she scrambles to the edge of the bed, pulling the sheets over her body.

Fuck. I didn't hear the door open. But more importantly, I miss the heat of her body almost instantly.

What I don't miss, however, is the vivid desire in Marc's eyes. Or the arrogant smile that teases his lips. "Don't stop on my account."

She drags a hand through her hair. "I... y-you saw that? You were watching us?"

Something sparks in his eyes and his lips curl just a millimeter before they level out again. The vein in his neck throbs erratically, and with the way his jaw keeps clenching, I can tell that he's grinding down on his molars pretty damn hard.

"Get dressed," he says, his tone becoming cold and impersonal. He spins and walks back out, letting the door swing on its hinges before slamming on the frame. The sound startles her lithe body, and a small yelp escapes her throat.

Asshole.

He doesn't realize the tent in his pants gave him away.

"This was a mistake," Delilah murmurs, her body swinging back and forth.

Oh boy.

"Delilah—"

"Not now, Harris. I just… give me a minute, please?"

I scoot down the bed and reach for her hand, half-expecting her to pull it away from me. She doesn't. Instead, her eyes lift to meet mine and what I see in them is the one thing I least expect.

Regret.

It's palpable and a sucker punch to the gut.

She cracks a grin that doesn't quite reach her eyes. "Marc needs you."

I can't help but flinch as tears burn my eyes, and I feel like throwing up. Still, I interlace our fingers and squeeze gently. "And you?"

"I'll be fine."

"Will you?"

She nods, then blows out a breath. "I'm okay with being alone. Really. I told you, I can't be the thing that gets between you two again. I'd rather be alone."

"You were never alone, Delilah. You have us. You've always had us."

"That's not what I meant, and you know it. You can't talk me out of this either, so don't try to. Just… go to Marc, okay? He needs you."

———

I 'm a selfish bastard. I know this. But I always made sure my selfish actions didn't hit too close to home. Especially Marc. He has always been my number one ride or die, with Delilah coming in as a close second.

For years, that was fine before we got into bed with Delilah. Now, I can't help that all my selfish crap is again spilling into our relationship and muddying the waters up.

I find Marc in the living room, shoulders set as he stands in front of the fireplace, staring at the picture of the four amigos.

"That wasn't what it looked like." Not going to lie; that is the lamest excuse I can come up with.

I step up to him and place a hand on his shoulder, not missing the slight flinch in his shoulder, as he tenses up before relaxing.

"'That wasn't what it looked like?'" he repeats incredulously, his voice thick and husky.

I nod, even though he can't see me. "I was being a selfish asshole."

He rolls his shoulders, shrugging my hand off. "You were." His voice cracks, and when he turns to face me, there's a vulnerability in his eyes that I haven't seen in a long time.

Mostly hurt, with traces of regret.

It's a look he gave me seven years ago before he agreed to the game. Or the *stupid* game, as he likes to call it.

I reach up to cup his face in my palm, slightly taken aback by the surprised look in his eyes. But given the circumstances, it's one I'm not quite sure what to make of. Just what does he think is going to happen? I'll suddenly stop wanting him because of Delilah?

He lifts a brow. "Your brain is working in overdrive."

"It is, huh?"

He reaches down to palm my erection and squeezes hard. "What's your excuse this time? You stumbled and your hand ended up in her pants? You should have gone all the way and used your dick."

"That's not what it looked like," I groan as I thrust my hips forward, chasing his touch.

"Seriously, H. I wasn't born yesterday. Spell it out for me, since I have no interest in playing another stupid game. One day, or seven years, I don't want to. Count me the fuck out."

My heart clenches. "Out of…"

His hand falls to his side and he takes a step back. "What do you think?"

I shake my head. "I don't know, Marc. I don't want to choose. You don't want to choose either. Or do you?"

He lifts a brow.

That can't be right.

This can't be happening. There is no leaving Marc, something he's made clear all this time.

He scoffs. "That was never the issue, dumbass. D is not an experiment, and you still treat her like one. Look, last Saturday happened. It's what she asked for, and we gave her that. But we also established that we all want different things, so maybe we should all get on the same page first and establish some ground rules before getting our dicks wet, yes?"

"That's what it was supposed to be, I swear."

His face softens. "I know, H. That's how I feel about you, twenty-four-seven. That's how I feel about her too, twenty-four-fucking-seven. But she's not like the others. She's our forever. *Ours.* Which means we all need to be on equal footing. Starting with the secrets you two keep on side-stepping around. We all have secrets, I get that, but for this to work, we can't and shouldn't be bringing all that baggage into it. Can you do that? Can you make it through the night without—"

Closing the distance between us, my fingers curl around the base of his neck as I lean forward to claim his mouth with mine. His lips part with a husky gasp, and I brush my tongue over his. He hesitates, but only for a moment before responding in kind.

The kiss we share is one of our most aggressive and passionate to date. Teeth and tongues, all wrestling for dominance. Marc's fingers dig into my biceps as he walks us backward until my back comes up against the kitchen island.

"You were saying something about keeping our dicks dry tonight," I tease as he trails kisses down my jawline and neck.

"Don't tempt me," he says, nibbling on my skin. "You have no idea how badly I want to bend you over this island and fuck your tight asshole."

"So do it."

"I said don't tempt me." He finally pulls back, and his eyes meet mine, swimming with unanswered questions, but no words leave his mouth.

I love this man. I love his kisses — crave them, more like. His skillful tongue. The raspiness of his slight stubble over my cheeks. And I fucking love how his stormy gray eyes seem to brighten as he looks at me between kisses.

Like he is doing right now.

So it is with great reluctance that I say, "Same page, got it. I won't touch her again, not until we talk."

He gives me one last nod and steps away, resuming his earlier task. As always, the best thing I can do is stay out of his way while he is in his element.

18

HARRIS

By the time Delilah joins us, Marc has accomplished the impossible. He's scrounged up all the elusive silverware in this house and has the table set.

"Where did all of this come from?" Delilah asks, gesturing at the dining table.

We are having a simple Tater Tots hotdish for dinner, but he's served it up like a feast, like he always does. He takes date night very seriously. Always has.

"Where did that come from?" I ask at the same time, angling my chin at her.

She glances at her outfit. "It's called a onesie."

"It's a giraffe," Marc rasps.

"I'm aware." Their eyes meet for a few seconds, then she adds, "It's meant to keep wandering hands off my person." It's also a pointed jab at me, which I deserve.

"If that get-up is supposed to make you any less desirable, it's not working," he tells her.

"No? Shall I go change into something more hideous?"

Marc laughs. "You could wear a burlap sack and it wouldn't make a fucking difference."

She walks up to Marc and places her hand on his shoulder. Unlike he was with me earlier, he's completely relaxed with her now.

"I'm sorry about earlier." Her voice is quiet, and try as hard as she does, she can't keep the regret out of it. "I didn't mean… God, this is embarrassing. Accident is the wrong word to use in this context, but it feels the most appropriate."

Marc sighs and turns to fully face her, but his eyes light up with a faint glimmer of amusement. "It's fine, D. You shouldn't have to apologize for something that comes naturally to you. Besides, I enjoyed the show."

Her brow furrows. "I don't know what the appropriate response to that is."

He cups her face in his. "I heard what you said to him," he says, then presses his lips to hers. "Thank you for saying that."

She leans into his touch and her eyelids drift closed. "You're not mad at me?"

"D, I was never upset with you."

She swallows thickly. "So we're okay?"

He hums. "With you, yes." He leans in and kisses her, slow and long, and she melts into his arms.

Something stirs deep inside of me, a slightly foreign and uncomfortable feeling.

Jealousy?

So this is what Marc feels. I find I don't like it.

"Don't be too hard on him." Her voice is quiet and the words barely register.

That is, until his eyes lift to meet mine. "Defending him already?"

She shakes her head. "That's not what that was… It's not just… You know, I'm going to stop talking before I dig myself into an even deeper hole with you two."

He roars out his laughter. "Smart choice."

Letting out an exasperated sigh, I run my fingers through my hair — dirty blond hair that she helps me dye once a month — as I take them both in. For the time being, I'm content to watch them. How they interact with each other. What our new normal is going to look like with her.

"Thank you for inviting me to be a part of your date night," she eventually says. "I am honored."

"That's another thing we need to discuss," Marc says as he ushers her toward the table.

She stops a few feet shy of it. "I... umm... I'm gonna move that place setting if you don't mind."

Marc frowns. "Why?"

"No one sits in that chair, not for eighteen years. That's Simone's seat."

"It's just a—" I offer, but he cuts me off.

"H, let it go," Marc interjects, doing as she asks and moving the setting.

See, that's where we differ, Marc and I.

He never questioned Delilah's devotion to Simone all these years, just took it all in stride. He's been in this house several times and never questioned why the place is a shrine to her. Or why the house is basically a fortress.

That's because Marc is the one who meets people where they are at. He gives them what they ask for and also what they need. He'll ask questions, but only when it's vital. Plus, he's more than willing to be the fall guy when things go south since he makes for a much more believable villain.

Me? Not so much.

This shit is not normal. It's an unhealthy obsession with the past, one that she needs to let go of already. Simone McWhorter has always been the bane of my existence. I never met her, and she was a lovely person by all accounts, but she's been the one thing standing in the way of what I wanted for fifteen years.

So unlike Marc, I wouldn't be indulging Delilah in this. Now that I almost have her where I want her, I plan to do everything possible to talk her out of this obsession. To talk her into letting it go, convince her that it's just a seat because I'll be damned if I let her legally dead ex-girlfriend get in the way of our forever.

No time like the present.

"Delilah, don't you think it's time to—"

"Let it the fuck go, H," Marc bites as he helps her into her seat, even going as far as to do the gentlemanly thing and push her chair in. That's usually my job, but we have more important things to discuss.

"It's okay," Delilah says. "You said you wanted to talk, and I suppose that's as good a place as any to start."

Marc pins me with a glare before he goes about dishing out our food.

It's hard work resisting the urge to roll my eyes at him.

"You realize that that is just a chair, right?" I say, settling into my seat. "An inanimate object. One that holds no true... You know what, I'll just come right out and say it. It makes no sense for you to continue holding a place at the table for someone who's gone."

She squares her shoulders. "This is non-negotiable, and I don't expect you to understand."

"Try me," I say dryly.

She picks up her fork and moves her food around on her plate. "No. There's a reason you and I don't talk about the Brewer-McWhorter feud. And given your attitude, we never will. Your interest in knowing about her doesn't strike me as genuine, and I refuse to have the *'it's time to move on'* conversation with anyone, much less you."

"We—"

"Speak for yourself," Marc grits.

"*I* am not asking you to replace her."

"You didn't have to. Your actions speak louder than your words." She purses her lips as she mulls this over. "You know what? Your words do too. Calling that an inanimate object dismisses what it symbolizes. I won't have that."

"Delilah—"

"You changed your name and your appearance when you turned eighteen. You dye your hair, something I help with, yet you don't hear me dismissing it as superficial. Do I think that sometimes? Yes. But then, I get why you are doing it, if not how you choose to go about it. That's what I'm being supportive of as your best friend. You're not the only one going about your healing process in questionable ways, so it's not your place to decide the right or wrong way for me to do this."

"I would never ask you to give up such a large part of yourself."

"It kinda sounds like you are," Marc chimes in, taking her side. The traitor.

"That said, I won't entertain any more of this talk about keeping and claiming and owning," she continues. "To you, it's just words. But what that tells me is you expect there to be no room for anyone else besides you two. I can't have that. If that's why you two came here tonight, then leave. And when I say leave, I don't just mean physically."

A tense silence descends upon us. Delilah pokes and stabs at her dinner, barely getting in a few bites. Marc stares at me, his shoulders squared like hers are, the unspoken warning in his eyes.

Fix this.

The thing is, I don't know how to fix this. I'm a selfish bastard. I want my cake and I want to eat it too. So it goes without saying it is hard to articulate the necessary words in my brain, much less speak them into existence.

So Marc does it for me. "You say *is* a lot."

I was not expecting that. Neither was Delilah, it would seem.

She blinks, then turns to face him. "What?"

"You say *is* a lot," he repeats. "When talking about her, you use the word *is*, as in you believe she is still alive. Why is that?"

She sets her fork down and folds her arms across her chest. "Why are you asking me that?"

"Because I'm curious. Maybe not as nosy as H is, just genuinely curious."

She huffs out a breath, and her lips press into a fine line.

"We all want what we want," he continues, "and there's nothing wrong with that. I just want to know why you still think she's alive."

She shifts in her seat. "I just do, and I don't expect you to understand it either."

He chuckles. "I'm the more open-minded one between H and me. I firmly believe our past greatly contributes to who we are today. Besides, I'm not asking you to give her up, am I?"

"No, but you would do anything Harris asks you to, wouldn't you? Including turning me into his sexual plaything."

The smile falls off his face. "Not everything, D. Fuck closure. If you believe Simone is alive, then she's alive. You want her back; not a problem. I'll find her and bring her back to you. Permanently, if that's what you want."

"That simple, huh?" She is skeptical, and I don't blame her. Marc can accomplish many things, but this is a long shot.

"Yeah, it really is that simple," he tells her. "The world is not that big, and my resources are vast. Just say the word."

The expression on her face morphs from a healthy dose of skepticism to pure fear. I can't explain it, but that turns me the fuck on. And I know for a fact that it does for him too.

"I don't believe you," she eventually says.

His brow lifts. "Is that a challenge?"

"What if it is?"

"I don't do challenges, D. I don't do ultimatums either. If you want something, just fucking say the word. Four words: I want her back."

Delilah flinches at his words, and my cock twitches at her response.

Not sure what's wrong with me that her discomfort brings me such pleasure. If anything, I want to wipe that look off her face. I only want to see the look of sweet pleasure when we finally claim her for our own.

But not tonight, it would seem.

She uncrosses her arms and tucks them under her thighs. "Why would you do that?"

"Three words, D. You. Are. Ours. That's not going to change," Marc says slowly, with utmost certainty and a damning finality to his tone. His body language reinforces this too. "You can run from it, hide, or deny it all you want, but you'll always be ours."

I still like the sound of that.

Ours.

She does too. A pink hue floods her cheeks, slowly spreading down her neck. She looks away from him and reaches for her glass of water. A few sips later, she sets it back down, worrying her bottom lip as she picks up her fork.

"What's it going to take?" His gaze flickers to where she has her bottom lip pinned with her teeth. "Do I play nice, or do I play hardball?"

"Does it have to be one or the other?"

"With you, yes, since nothing else seems to be working."

She turns to me, tucking a loose curl of brown hair behind her ear. "You're being very uncharacteristically quiet over there."

I shrug as Marc answers for me. "He's in a time-out."

"A time-out? What for?"

"Wandering hands, foot in the mouth, that sort of thing. So, what's it going to take, D? Play nice or hardball?"

She huffs out a breath as she sets her fork down and shoves her plate to the side. "Let's say a small part of me is willing to entertain this discussion. What are the rules?"

Marc leans forward and sets his elbows on the table. "For starters, you either come live with us, or we come live with you."

Confusion swirls in her eyes. "You? Live here?"

He nods, a glint of amusement in his eyes, as is the odd little curve to his mouth.

"That's absurd," she says as she waves a hand around. "You barely fit in here."

"And it will be an even tighter squeeze when Dahlia moves back in, even more so when the baby comes."

"Exactly. You couldn't stomach living here with just me, much less with Dahlia. And this isn't what you are accustomed to. Normal people seek to upgrade their living conditions. But you live in a fucking estate, so why would you want to downsize your lifestyle?"

He roars out his laughter. "We lived in a shoe box apartment when I was a kid. This was back when Mom was hiding us from Dad. Those are my favorite memories with her, so it will be just like old times. Except, compared to that, this is heaven. And I can stomach just about anything, and so will H. Just know that this dual household thing won't work for either of us, so we might as well nip it in the bud right now."

She frowns. "Tight quarters or a sprawling mansion. Those are my only options?"

"Yes, those are your only options. Also, you need to make up your mind soon, or I'll be forced to decide for you. You know what will happen if it comes to that."

She shakes her head, even though she does. She was there the last time this happened, seven years ago. It happened in this very house, in this living room. Over on that fucking couch.

Those were fun times.

Not.

Marc reaches into his pants pocket, pulls out a notebook and slides it over to her.

"What's this?" She picks it up and turns it over.

"A book," he says with a friendly chuckle.

Her gaze returns to mine. "What is this?"

"Your book of wishes, lists, demands — whatever you want to call it," Marc continues. "Anything your heart desires, write it in there, and I'll make it happen."

"Did you do one of these?" she asks me.

"Of course he did. Just who do you take me for—"

"I was asking Harris," she says, cutting him off. When I don't answer her, she continues. "Look, we're supposed to be having a discussion about... whatever this is, so this time-out thing doesn't really work for me. Perhaps we can pick this up another day when you're more chatty. Or when Marc is a lot less irritable."

She rises to her feet. Marc and I reach for her by instinct, only for her to shrug us off. "Hands off my person, you two."

When neither of us releases her, she blows out a breath. "Guys, I'm tired. It's been a long week. Either we wrap this up quickly or pick this up another day."

We both tighten our hold on her.

"Fine," she sighs and sits back down. "Say I move in with you. Then what?"

Marc interlaces his fingers with hers and leans back in his seat. "Call it a partnership. The three of us, we are equals."

"A partnership?" she repeats dryly. "It's that simple?"

"At its core, yes, it really is that simple. There are other layers and nuances to it. We will have plenty of time to go over it. But that's basically what it is. A partnership. Then there are open, honest conversations. We have those fairly often."

Her nose scrunches. "You mean the kind where everyone knows everything about everyone?"

"Basically, but it's not that literal. The things that affect everyone," he gives me a pointed look, "need to be shared."

"Like?" she prompts.

"What happened seven years ago."

"Oh." She hums, squirming in her seat.

I do too, but I hone in on her discomfort instead. "Maybe not tonight," I interject, not to give her a reprieve but for selfish reasons. Now is not the time to rehash that day. "To answer your question, yes, I have one of those. He gave me one sixteen years ago. It's how the name change happened. That was on my list."

She nods and presses her lips together. After about a minute passes, she says, "I need more time to think this over. Not that this was what I signed up for when I..." she trails off with a shrug. "Forget it. You'll just do whatever you want, won't you? You're planning on giving me the same treatment you gave Harris?"

"Not unless you force my hand, D. So, how much time do you need?"

She smiles. "You're very pushy, you know that?"

He let out a hearty laugh. "No, just persistent."

"More like pushy. You should get that tattooed on your sleeve. Pushy Marc. It can be the first of many since you don't have any."

"Only you would think that."

"So you do, huh." She leans forward in interest. "Where?"

He takes a moment to study her. "What do you think, H?"

"What does Harris have to do with this?"

"Well, I have to be naked for you to see them. Doesn't exactly bode well for your hands-off request."

"And this?" She worries her lower lip as she lifts their interlaced fingers. "Not exactly hands-off, Marc."

He smirks. "I'm not the only one holding on, D. Don't worry, we will stay forever if that's what you want."

Her face tilts upwards and she lets out an exasperated sigh. "Just for tonight then. Since you've both made yourselves at home, I take it you two are staying the night." She rolls her shoulders forward, then backward. "I already know it's pointless relegating you both to the couch or one of the other bedrooms in this house since you'll just find an excuse to wind up in my bed again."

"Oh good, you're catching on," Marc says sarcastically.

She rolls her eyes. "Actually, I would prefer it if you didn't, but I'll save my breath since you two will do whatever you want. As long as you keep your hands to yourself, I don't care where you sleep. The doors are locked and the alarms set, so no one leaves until I disarm them tomorrow. I would like my hands back now if you don't mind."

"Are you going to run again?"

"No, I'm going to bed. Alone."

19

MARC

My life is complete.

Well, almost complete. We made some strides that got us closer to our objective, so for tonight, I will settle for content. And also the realization that I really am one lucky son of a bitch. Until a week ago, this was a sight I never thought I would see in my lifetime.

As I watch H's and D's sleeping figures, I can't help but wonder how I got to be so lucky. Or the fact that luck just might have nothing to do with it. More like an obsession.

As fate would have it, that obsession goes three ways.

Oh, and that hands-off thing she had going on? It lasted all of fifteen minutes. Not surprising that she wasn't the one who caved first, but she went along with it like she usually does where he's concerned. At least he's keeping his lips in check and his dick fully clothed.

Having had my fill of them, I make my way out to her living room. In the years I have known her, it's a shame I haven't spent much time out here. This house, her childhood home, is obviously very near and dear to her. Recreating this at the estate would be tricky but not impossible, and I will need help with it — as much help as a certain someone will give me.

Pulling out my phone, I thumb through my contacts and pull up her name.

> Marc: I need your help.

She calls back immediately. "Do you have any idea what time it is?"

"This could have waited until morning."

"Bullshit. You knew I was awake."

"You didn't have to call me back. A text message would have sufficed."

She sighs. "What do you need?"

Straight to the point. "The usual."

She laughs. "With you, that could be anything. What do you need from me that couldn't have waited until the morning?"

"Court, please."

A silence stretches on the other end. Then, "You're kidding."

I don't answer her. Why bother when all that would result is a lecture? A lecture that, quite frankly, neither one of us has time for. Not when my family is fast asleep.

"Marc, please tell me you're joking." There's a bite to her tone that I don't particularly care for.

"I wouldn't be asking if I was." I pinch the bridge of my nose between two fingers. "I wouldn't be asking, period."

Another silence, then, "Did you threaten her?"

"Not exactly."

She blows out a breath. "With you, it's the same thing. What did she say?"

"What do you think?"

"Let me guess," she says dryly, "she told you to shove it? No, that would be too tame for her. More like she threatened to chop off your left testicle."

I can't help but laugh. "She said if I made her do this, she would resent H for it."

She laughs. "I'm with Delilah on this one."

"I figured you would be. That's why I need your help."

"What do you want me to do? Use my womanly wiles on her?"

"If it comes to that, yes."

"Men." A sigh. "How is it that you've known her for years, yet are still so clueless as to the two things she values above all else?"

I can think of any number of things, but two resonate with me. "Simone and Dahlia."

"Bingo."

"I'm already working on the second one. As for the first, you know that's not how I operate. She has to say the words."

"That's not what I meant, you oaf," she says with a laugh. "Tell me, brother, how far are you willing to go for her?"

I shake my head, even though she can't see me. "Is that a serious question?"

"Have you told her how you feel? The truth, I mean. Not hiding behind Harris."

"She wants him." Which, technically, is the truth.

"Not even you believe that," Courtney counters.

"She wants him more," I clarify.

"Semantics, Marc. And if you're waiting for her to tell you first, then know that you'll be waiting a long time. The woman is patient, I'll give her that. It comes with the territory, I suppose."

"This isn't helping."

"You didn't call me for an easy solution. Or a palatable one. But since you asked so nicely, I'll make it simple. Drop the fucking ultimatums. Let Delilah come to you on her own."

"She belongs with us." Clearly, Courtney doesn't get the sense of urgency going on here.

"I'm not saying you completely give up on her. But know that if she's going to move in with you, it must be because she wants to, not because she has to. You better be prepared to handle all the baggage that she comes with."

"Okay, I can do that. What else?"

"Tell her how you feel, or don't. That's your prerogative. But know that you will get nowhere fast if you keep using threats. Maybe for once in your life, try being someone you've always been, but without the extra machismo that comes with it."

"What's that?" I ask dryly.

"A protector. A knight in shining armor, or whatever else you want to call it."

"Again, not helping."

"You know I love you, but that possessive streak of yours drives me up a wall. It would drive any sane woman up a wall, Delilah included. So for once, try wooing her like a man in love. And maybe while you're at it, be truthful with her about why you want her. It's because of them, isn't it?"

And by *them*, she means our family — the Sotelos.

I blow out a breath. "I don't give a fuck what they think."

"And yet, here we are. At two in the morning, having this absurd conversation. Where are you, by the way?"

My jaw clenches. "At her place."

"Geez, pushy much?"

I envision the dramatic eye-roll that goes along with it. "Your point is?"

"They've been hounding you to start producing some heirs for over a decade. Don't tell me you're finally caving into the pressure."

I scrub my free hand over my face. "Are you going to help me or not?"

"You are, aren't you?" She pauses, and when I don't answer, she adds, "You're lucky she wants them too. Otherwise, I wouldn't even be entertaining this discussion."

20

DELILAH

One month later

Even though my relationship with her brother is ambiguous at best, Courtney Sotelo and I have always gotten along. When she asks me to meet her for lunch at her place, I don't doubt for one second that he has something to do with it.

Except I wouldn't pass up the opportunity to spend time with her, and I could use the excuse to get out of the house — and away from Dahlia. It's only been a month since she moved back in, and already she's been driving me up the wall.

I mean, I love my sister to death, but there's a reason why she has the nickname Hurricane Dahlia. I can honestly say that in the six months she lived with Curtis, the only thing I didn't miss was picking up after her. For someone so organized in her professional life, she takes messiness in her personal life to a different level.

And since neither one of us trusts a cleaning service inside the house unsupervised, it means I'm relegated to clean-up duty since I care more about that.

"We're set up in the backyard today," Courtney says as we walk through the house.

"*We*? I didn't realize we were meeting with someone else today."

"By we, I mean one six-year-old firecracker, so you don't have to look so terrified," she laughs as she slides open the door to the back.

"Feorie is working on live portraits this month. I volunteered you as her test subject since we've run out of potential candidates."

"Potential candidates?" I can't help but laugh. "What is this, some sort of speed dating or compatibility test, but for artists?"

"Something like that." She purses her lips. "You know how he is. The list of people I trust who can also pass the vetting process is quickly diminishing."

By *he*, she means her brother.

Marc can be a bit much sometimes with his overprotective streak. Harris too, and they still haven't given up this notion that I belong to them. Without fail, they've shown up to the house for date night for the last four Fridays — much to Dahlia's chagrin. Mine too, if I'm being honest. Marc cooks up a feast fit for a football team, even if it's just the four of us.

While Marc does his thing, Harris settles in on the couch and drinks two or three glasses of my merlot while Dahlia sits across from him, scowling the entire time. Glaring at the wine, more like, since she's pregnant and can't have any. We all sit at the dining room table, with Simone's seat left alone. That part surprised Dahlia initially, but I think Marc's cooking might be winning her over.

It might be winning me over too.

That is, until they both retired to my bedroom each week like they did that first night. Since I don't trust them — or myself, for that matter — to keep their hands to themselves, I usually wind up in Dahlia's room. It's the one place they can't follow me, and I don't think she cares too much about that. Or that they both insist on staying the night in my bed without me. Or that I always snuggle up to her in her bed even though she's not a touchy-feely person, but we both agree it's better than the alternative.

But enough about those two. I need to know what's going on with Courtney and Howard, her on-again, off-again... whatever they are.

"What about Howard? How come you didn't ask him to—"

"No, never," she answers a little too quickly for my liking, then hooks an arm around my neck and leans in closer. "We're kind of on a break right now."

I lift a curious brow. "Kind of?"

She's said that three times this year, and it's only June.

"He's sort of keeping his distance since Marc threatened to shred his moneymaker if he comes near me again."

My brow furrows. "His moneymaker?"

She twirls a finger around her face, then wriggles all five fingers in the air. "He needs both, or his fans will come after me. Can't have that now, can I?"

Sometimes I genuinely don't get this thing they have. Howard Beals is supposed to be this rockstar and is pretty popular in certain circles. Although his music is nothing I would listen to, and quite frankly, nothing she listens to. I don't understand their attraction, but it's not my place to question it since the heart wants what it wants.

The issue is that Howard happens to be Charlie's father, so their wishy-washy relationship also means he's barely in his son's life.

"You brought me another victim," Feorie says, as she drums her finger together in a classic evil warlord move. "And she's perfect!"

I turn to Courtney. "Victim?"

She shakes her head and mouths a *'Don't ask'* as she leads us to the patio. Feorie has us settle into the velvet-upholstered settee, then issues directions on exactly how she wants us to position ourselves.

This is new to me, but it's just another day for Courtney. She's an art teacher and gives private lessons out of her home. Seeing as Marc vets everyone who comes into her life, Feorie is the only student she currently has. She also charges an exorbitant amount for her lessons. Still, having seen what Feorie can do, I'd say Courtney is worth every penny. The girl has raw, unfettered talent, like Frida Kahlo and Amrita Sher-Gil, and Courtney pushes her to her limits and then some.

I wouldn't expect a six-year-old artist to be at the level where she does live portraits, but here we are. I'm so excited to see how this turns out.

"Will David be joining us today?" she asks Courtney.

"Not today," she says with a laugh. "He's a distraction, remember?"

I know that David Holcomb sponsors Feorie's art lessons, and he occasionally tags along. As the only surviving member of the Holcomb family, the man has more than enough money to last him several lifetimes and then some. It was his idea that Courtney charge as much as she does, so to spite him, she charges triple when he tags along — which he gladly pays because he has more money than he knows what to do with.

I never understood this arrangement, specifically why he sponsors these lessons. Then again, there has always been a lot about David's relationship with Harris and Marc that I never understood. I never asked because it wasn't my place to ask.

"He's also my direct competition," Feorie counters in her sweet childlike voice.

"That he is," Courtney concedes. "Don't tell him I said that. It will only feed his ego."

"But he's good, so I have to be better. This gift is useless if I can't be better than him."

For starters, what six-year-old talks like that? Second, who is feeding her all this?

Courtney happens to be thinking like I am since she asks, "Sweetie, who told you that?"

She shrugs. "Mom."

Courtney sucks in a sharp breath like this isn't news to her. "Feorie, you are six years old. You only need to worry about being the best version of yourself, okay? Your mom and I will have a grown-up chat about this."

Her face falls. "Do you have to?"

"You know I do, and if you get in trouble because of it, I need you to tell me. Or tell David. Or Marc, Harris, or even Delilah here. And you know why?"

"Because Mom is the adult and I am the kid. It is wrong for grown-ups to take their frustrations out on their children," she somberly recites.

I turn to Courtney and mouth a *'What the…?'*

"This is a safe space," she tells me, twirling a finger in the air. "In addition to art, we are also learning about boundaries, what's appropriate and what's not." She turns to Feorie. "Did you get what you need?"

She nods, walks over to her station a few feet away, settles in behind her canvas, and gets to work.

"Thank you for meeting me here," Courtney eventually says once satisfied that Feorie's sufficiently distracted and engrossed in her work.

"What was that about?" I can't help but ask.

"Feorie is a gifted child. As you know, her IQ is in the high one-eighties. Everyone has ideas about how that talent should be nurtured, but her mother sometimes takes things to the extreme."

"How extreme?"

"Let's just say I grew up with a mother like hers, and the adults Marc and I could trust were in short supply because of... Well, you know. Having a safe space to retreat to outside our home would have made a huge difference, so I now try to pay it forward. Hence the safe space. It's not the same thing, but still."

There have always been several layers to Courtney. To the Sotelo family, she's just another pretty face and spoiled illegitimate mafia princess, and she's more than willing to let them think that of her. But at her core, she's a caretaker who's always looking out for the well-being of others. It's also why we get along so well.

Unlike her brother, she lives a frugal lifestyle because money isn't always everything.

I've always liked Courtney Sotelo's house. It's small and quaint, unlike Harris and Marc's mansion. I know she can afford somewhere bigger, but she insists this is all the space she needs. It's just her and baby Charlie, so she has a point. No one needs that much space to be happy. Again, it's one of many reasons why Courtney and I have always gotten along, despite my ambiguous relationship with her brother.

Speaking of her brother—

"To be honest, I've been enlisted to convince you to change your mind," Courtney eventually says, a smile teasing the corners of her lips.

I wish I could say I was surprised. Marc did say that he wasn't above using sneaky and underhanded techniques to get what he wanted.

"And if that didn't work, I was to ply you with food," she continues. "It'll be delivered in about thirty minutes, so keep an ear out for the doorbell. If all else fails, I've been granted carte blanche to use my womanly wiles on you."

I laugh because that sounds like something Harris would say, not Marc. "Tell Harris that if he wants to talk to me, he knows exactly where to find me."

"It wasn't Harris who called me, but I can see why you would think that."

I completely spaced out on the second half of what she said. "Marc did?"

She nods, but that secret smile doesn't dim.

"Let me get this clear. Marc asked you to seduce me as a last resort. Why?"

"Is that a real question, or are you tugging my chain?"

"I genuinely want to know. Also, why would Marc want me other than as a plaything for Harris? And if Harris wants a human pet that badly, he can get that for himself. As long as it's not me."

She laughs. "You two. I swear, sometimes it's like herding cats."

"I don't know what that means."

She drops the look of mirth. "Look, I won't waste our time talking up Marc's good points since we both know he doesn't have any. Okay, maybe a few, but that's not..." She trails off at that and lets out an exasperated sigh. "I know my brother isn't a good man. A decent man, yes, but not a good man. However, if there's one thing he is, it's loyal, and that's where his over-protectiveness comes into play. He will do the wrong thing — questionable things even — for the right reasons. That's just who he is. It's who he has always been.

"Now, I assume you know all of this already. Or at the very least, you were aware of these things. Otherwise you wouldn't have jumped into bed with them. Twice, from what I've heard. But know this: the things about him that scare you could be your greatest asset. With him, you don't have to worry about the myriad of things that scare you about relationships. Marc is a forever type of guy. He will never leave you, and he will never let you leave him. It's just not how he operates. You can take that how you will, and you can do with that what you please. But know this, he is yours. Irrevocably yours."

I take a moment to let her words sink in. "You don't pull any punches, do you?"

"No, I don't. That said, I think you should do it."

"Do what? Indulge them in this crazy fantasy of theirs?"

"Who says it has to be a fantasy? Just do it. Move in with them. Be their woman. Not a kept woman, of course; that's not your style. But just theirs. They will both be yours. Forever."

I can't help but flinch at that. "It's not that simple."

A beat passes, then she asks, "Because of Simone?"

I nod, unable to quell the ache that erupts in my chest. It's uncanny how perceptive Courtney can be. She and I haven't discussed Simone before — it's not something that usually comes up in casual conversation — but somehow, she gets it. She always has, and unlike Harris, she doesn't push it.

She reaches across the settee and covers my hand with hers. "There's plenty of room in your heart for more than one person, you know? I'm not just saying this because Marc is my brother or because Harris is my friend. I'm saying this because I know them both, and at the heart of it all, you know them too. With them, it will be the real deal. So grab it, and hold on to it with both hands. Be vulnerable with them. Be open and honest with them. You've all had years to get to this point, but make no mistake, this will be no walk in the park. Especially where the Sotelo family is concerned. Certain family members can be assholes, so it will still be challenging initially, but it will be worth it.

"Just do me a favor, okay? Make them continue to work for it. One month is not nearly long enough to make them grovel."

21

HARRIS

I watch as my not-employee, occasional-volunteer-slash-helper, former sex partner, and friend shoves a nipple ring into the same box as a butt plug. Then I fantasize, for the umpteenth time today, how he can meet his slow and torturous end. At my hand, of course, since I don't trust anyone else to do it.

The fucker knows it doesn't go there. I know that he knows it doesn't go there. The only reason why he would put those two things together is that he knows it would piss me off.

And it does. It does piss me off.

But I clamp down on the urge to grab everything from his hands and fix it myself.

"Clark David Holcomb," I say his full name with all the patience I can muster, "you remember that those two things don't go in the same fucking box, right?"

He whips around to face me, amber eyes flashing. "Don't you fucking call me that," he bites. "You don't pay me enough to call me by that name."

"I don't pay you, period."

And I don't have to. The guy is worth billions. He's got more money than he knows what to do with in this lifetime. Or even ten lifetimes, and that money still wouldn't run out. So he has many different interests. Hobbies are what he calls them, including this. And I let him because he needs to stay busy. If anything, I understand the need to not sit on your fucking ass all day, doing nothing. That, and there's a name for people who do this.

Idle people.

Idle people with idle minds, idle hands, and idle lips.

Apparently, those things are bad for you, like my dad used to say. Poisonous even, amongst other things. The man would drill that particular bible verse into my head.

Proverbs 16:27. *Idle hands are the devil's workshop; idle lips are his mouthpiece.*

He would recite it like it was his lifeline. Like it should be my lifeline or even the key to the salvation of my fucking soul.

Well, the joke's on him. I have all of the above and don't see any eternal damnation in sight. There is no fire or brimstone either. In fact, it's what led me directly into the life I have now.

I sell sex toys for a living. It's a small, one-man operation, just how I like it. I even make some of the sex toys that I sell. It helps that with a medical school background, I have an intimate understanding of the male and female anatomy. So while he would say this is a waste of my considerable talents, I just shrug and move on. It's not his life to live. It's mine. And I'll be damned if I don't live my life on my own terms.

For today, I only need to refrain from killing my not-employee. "Are you going to tell me what's bothering you? Or will you keep messing up those orders and creating more work for me later?"

"Or I could hire people to do this shit for you?"

"I think you must have forgotten about the part where I. Don't. Pay. You. You don't get to hire people to do your unpaid labor."

He shrugs and goes back to it. "It'll be more efficient," he mumbles under his breath.

Don't kill him, I remind myself.

He does have a point. I could hire people to do this shit for me, but that would defeat the purpose of keeping this a small, one-man operation. Emphasis on small. It's hard enough managing the different vendors and supplies by myself, so I've been considering outsourcing all of that.

What started as a side hobby ten years ago has slowly but steadily grown into a six-figure business. Shocking, I know, for an operation of this size. I charge thousands of dollars for custom pieces, and people with loads of disposable cash to throw around and who value discretion more than anything still find me and buy them. For this reason, I have yet to do any advertising, period. My business comes through word of mouth, mostly from people in the BDSM scene, where Marc and I were heavily involved up until seven years ago. There have been a couple from Marc's neck of the woods in more recent years, but he vets all of those.

I'm sure some companies handle the administrative side of things, including the vetting, for solo entrepreneurs and small one-man business owners like me. I would happily pay someone else to manage all that for me, or I could ask Marc to look into it since he's resourceful.

Then again, he likes to remind me that I don't have to work and that I could enjoy my life as a kept mafia man. Or is it kept mafia mistress? Mister?

Whatever.

The point is, I fucking love my life.

Except for today, with the urge to strangle my not-so-helpful volunteer hitting hard.

David picks up an ankle spreader and turns it over in his hands like some sort of foreign object. "What does this do again?"

I can't help the look of disbelief I cast his way. "For someone who uses this stuff regularly, you still have to ask? Who have you been fucking lately?"

He sighs. "No one, apparently."

Oh.

Well, that seems to be going around.

Marc has been in a weird-ass funk for weeks, so things have been tense between us. It's like constantly walking on eggshells at home.

It's because all he wants is Delilah. Bad. Not sure why, but he's backed off the threat of moving her in himself. And she still won't come to us, which means we've been thrust into a dry spell. I fucking hate those, especially since it's not by choice. And five weeks is far too long for that.

As per usual, I initiate but get unceremoniously turned down. Several times. All because I still haven't fixed what I broke. Like it's that simple. For him, it's not enough that I'm barely keeping the promise I made not to touch her again until we get on the same page. But in true Marc fashion, the hands-off thing also extends to me.

I fucking hate it.

If you have her next, would that make you happy? I ask each time. He doesn't answer me. Instead, he just stalks off and locks himself in his office.

Friday evening is the only time I see him genuinely relaxed and happy, for five glorious hours. Then he goes right back to his surly mood when she takes herself to Hurricane Dahlia's room.

So yeah, I'm wound a little too tight lately.

David shoves the ankle spreader in the same box as the leather whip, with zero padding, then proceeds to tape the box up.

All right, that's it. "Leave that alone."

Amber eyes lift to meet mine. "Why?"

Focus, Harris.

He's pretty. He really is.

Pretty to look at, that is.

He won't be after I get my hands on him. I'm sure he would like that. Besides the most obvious one, there has to be a reason why he stuck around Marc and me for years after we were done with our relationship. Conversely, there must be a reason we kept him around all these years, but I can't find it in me right now.

I let out an exasperated sigh. "Because, David, I'll have to re-do everything you've just done, and I'd rather not make more work for myself. So drop the fucking spreader and walk away. There's a couch over there. Go plant your pretty tush on it."

It takes him sixty seconds, but he does as I ask.

"Why haven't you been fucking anyone lately?" I ask as I go about undoing what he's just done. Better now than later, and better to distract me from my sexual frustrations. "And what does Nalina have to say about this?"

Something flashes in David's eyes, a cross between anger and frustration. "It's kind of her idea."

I lift a brow. "Kind of?"

Something about that doesn't sit right with me. Then again, a lot about his relationship with Nalina never sat right with me.

David has been dealt some pretty shitty cards, and she was his therapist long before his life became a public dumpster fire. I believe he started seeing her when he was fourteen, almost fifteen. There was the emancipation from his father when he was fifteen, and those court proceedings have been sealed. He took off shortly afterward, the official story being that he went on a global backpacking trip. Barely a month after that went through, he lost his father and aunt in the infamous Holcomb murder-suicide. As the only surviving member of the Holcomb family, he had no choice but to return. Of all the places he could have moved to, he chose to move back into the Holcomb Estate, a place that has been dubbed Hell, Hell on Earth, Rochester's Hell, or some variation of it.

It's where we are right now, so I can personally attest to the place not being half as bad as the rumors claim it is. Is it cursed? Probably. But curses only have as much effect on you as you allow them to — I have my father to thank for that nugget of information.

Also, I might be biased, but I also like what David has done with the place, mainly because he doesn't treat it like a typical mansion of its caliber. This gorgeous Neoclassical-style estate sits on the outskirts of Rochester. It might as well have its own zip code, given how massive the property it sits on is. Like the rebel he is, David keeps adding weird shit to it. My workroom, the one we are in right now, is a perfect example of this. I have one at home just like it, but since he's not allowed in there — no one is — he hired the same architect Marc used to recreate it here.

It's sacrilegious, I know, operating a warehouse for sex toys out of this mansion. It's not the only thing he added to it though. There's a secret tech room somewhere in here, plus the murder room in the basement. Those are only the ones that I know about. Don't get me started on how he's cordoned off the various bedrooms in this house. Knowing the type of person his dad was, a slimy bastard who was probably worse than my own dad, this is the ultimate *fuck you* to him. What's the guy going to do about it anyway when he got his sorry ass murdered?

That said, Nalina might be worse. Much worse.

"I have to stay on task," David says, his voice quiet. Pained even.

"What the fuck kind of vague response is that?"

He bends over and buries his face between his legs. "My new assignment, she's special."

"Define special."

His shoulders heave. "She has something I need, and I have something she needs."

"Isn't that how it always is?"

David has always used sex to feed his demons, something I suspect his dad had a hand in, and as his boss, Nalina coordinates his liaisons. As his therapist, she's also familiar with his peculiar tastes. It's how Marc and I got matched with him six years ago. What doesn't sit well with me is that their relationship is also sexual, and I suspect it started long before he turned eighteen. Neither one would acknowledge it, and David asked us to leave it alone, so we do for his sake.

In return, we keep him around even though we've never done so with any of the others. As messed up as it sounds, Marc and I provide some degree of normalcy in David's life, something I suspect he's never had before.

"It's different this time." He unfolds his upper body and settles his elbows on his knees. "She's different."

I can't help but scowl at that. "How different?"

His lips part but no sound comes out, so he presses them together.

"David, spit it the fuck out." I push the box to the side and cross my arms over my chest. "What the fuck is so special about this one that Nalina is withholding sex to keep you on task?

"It's complicated."

"All right, I'm done with this vague shit. Who the fuck is she?"

He scoffs. "I can't tell you that."

That, I already knew. "Did she sign a contract?"

"Not exactly."

"Dude!"

He runs a hand over his face. "She doesn't know... yet."

I swear, it's like pulling water out of a stone sometimes. "What doesn't she know? The fact that there's a contract to be signed? Or that you've been paired?"

"Yes."

"Yes to...?"

"Both."

A long, exasperated breath moves through me. "What're you waiting for then? Dragging shit out isn't your style."

Another shrug. "She's different."

Okay, I'm done with this.

"I've been watching her," he continues. "She's complicated, you know? What she's asking for with our arrangement and who she is don't match. The more I study her, the more layers I uncover. I happen to like them all, you know? I like all these sides to her, it's like peeling back an onion."

I pinch the bridge of my nose between two fingers. "Let me get this straight. Instead of doing the job you were hired to do, you went off script, following her around like some sort of sick puppy?"

He scoffs. "Only you would hone in on that part. It's no different than what you've been doing with Delilah."

"Is that it? You like her?"

"She's a job."

Okay, *now* I'm done with this. "I'll give you my opinion, even though you haven't asked for it. Ready?"

He makes a non-committal grunt but doesn't say anything.

"Sex doesn't always have to be about sex. Just as what's on paper doesn't always match what's in front of you. Client or not, that shouldn't stop you from reaching for more."

His gaze levels mine. "Been there, done that, not really looking to do that again."

His words feel like a slap across the face, but still, I say, "Who says you can't? Is there a rule in the contracts that says you shouldn't?"

"Not exactly, but why bother?"

"Because, David. Isn't that what you've wanted for so long? What you've always been scared to reach for? If this one is as special as you say she is, go for it. That kind of connection doesn't come around very often. Take it from someone who knows."

He holds my gaze for about a minute, then sighs and looks away. Then, leaning back, he swings his legs onto the couch, stretches out his body, and throws a hand over his face. It's not long before the sounds of his snoring fill the room.

If only it were that simple sometimes.

If only I could take my own advice.

22

DELILAH

D ahlia pokes her head into my bedroom. "Dee, can I get your help with something?"

I set aside my novel and scurry off the bed. "Sure, anything you need."

Upon following her to her room, I find that Dahlia is back to her old tricks again. Her room looks like a literal tornado ripped right through it. Hurricane Dahlia has made landfall.

I could Marie Kondo this room in my sleep. It may be the thing to take my mind off them. It still feels like I am being pulled in several directions, and I can't say that my conversation with Courtney helped. But it did put certain things into perspective. This mess will be a good way for me to ground myself.

Gathering my hair up and off my neck, I pull my frizzy light brown locks into a loose top-knot ponytail. I plant both hands on my hips and stand in the middle of the room, surveying the items she has laid out and about.

"Daa, I hate to ask, but why do you need all these?"

She shrugs from her position on the edge of the bed. "I like variety."

This isn't variety. This is madness.

There are several stacks of clothing strewn about, some still on their respective hangers. An assortment of heels, flats, and slippers are scattered about the floor. Two open suitcases lay on the floor, with two others off to the side for overflow. For what should be a three-day trip to the east coast for a medical conference, she sure has a lot spread about. We will both be going on this and I know she doesn't need this much.

It's like that darn honeymoon trip all over again. Talk about déjà vu.

"I only packed one-fourth of this."

She pulls her hair over one shoulder, twirling the ends of it. "Yeah, well, I'm not you."

At least we can both agree on that.

"I've been thinking about moving," I finally say after some time, voicing what has been weighing on my mind.

"Moving out of Rochester? Moving out of this house?"

I'm not sure why she makes it a point to ask, even though we both know what I'm referring to.

So I humor her with the obvious answer. "This house."

"Yeah, right, like that would ever happen," she scoffs.

"I'm ready for a change."

"After thirty-four years? What gives?"

From my position on the floor — seated cross-legged with my back to her — I can still sense her eyes boring holes in the back of my head. Since I know she's actively studying my reaction to her question and scrutiny, I make it a point not to fidget with my scar today.

Until her fingers wrap around my shoulders, then she settles in before me and mimics my stance.

Her eyes meet mine. "Dee, what's going on with you?"

I give her a blank look, the best I can muster up. "Why do you ask?"

"This thing with Marc and Harris, what's going on there?"

"It's nothing."

She lifts a brow. "Nothing," she drawls. "Look, I've kept my mouth shut long enough, but now I need answers."

"It's nothing you need to concern yourself with."

"Well, I live here, and they keep showing up on Fridays like clockwork. I know they're not here for me, as evidenced by your crawling into my bed each time. So why are you hiding from them?"

"Who says I'm hiding?"

"I wasn't born yesterday." She tucks her legs underneath her body. "From what I heard, you left the wedding with them."

Another blank look. "I did, yes. They were my ride."

"Ride or not," she continues, "you all left right after they threatened Matthias and Andrea."

Only one person I know of could have told her that. Charlena Cantor-Dietrich and her big mouth.

"Your point is?"

"Did you fuck them? Is that why they keep on showing up here?"

"If you're going to give me another lecture about having my best interests at heart—"

"This isn't about that," she interjects. "Look, I shouldn't have said what I said back then. It was ignorant and misguided, and I'm sorry. If you must know, my issue isn't with Marc. It's with his family. Just because his family is part of the Italian Mafia, it doesn't make him a bad person. You see something in him, and I trust your judgment. I might not like it, but I do trust it. Always."

That's all it takes for me to spill all to her, from the mess seven years ago to the talk Courtney and I had a few days ago. Not surprisingly, she doubled down on Marc's threats.

"And this was the day after the wedding?" is the first thing she asks, disbelief laced in her tone.

I nod. "Marc and Harris keep insisting that I belong to them or some other nonsense."

Dahlia roars out her laughter. "Marc is obviously not planning on giving you the same treatment Harris got."

"I don't see what that has to do with anything."

"It's been weeks since he said that, and you're still here."

"He could change his mind at any moment."

"I don't know. It looks to me like they're actively wooing you. Or trying to, yet you keep running away from them."

"I never asked to be wooed. All I asked for is one night, something I was clear about from the get-go."

"This hesitation, it wouldn't have to do with Simone, would it?"

"Maybe. I don't know. Technically, we're still engaged. In a way, this feels like cheating."

It seems silly to hold on to that, especially since not many people know about it. Dahlia and my parents knew, but only because she went through the trouble of seeking their blessing before asking me. If they thought we were too young to get married, no one said anything to either of us back then. Given everything that happened afterward, they thought it best that little tidbit remain a secret.

"Yeah, well, you can't put your entire life on hold because of a promise you made when you were sixteen. And you're not the one who broke that promise. She did. She's gone, Dee."

"Don't say that. She's alive, I can feel it," I drum my fingers over my defective heart, "in here. Every day, I feel her. It doesn't make this any easier."

"I don't think she would fault you for moving on. No one is asking you to forget her. At least Marc isn't, and that has to count for something." She takes my hands in hers. "Besides, don't tell me there wasn't a part of you that knew what you were getting yourself into with them. Then again, you didn't need me to tell you all this. In your heart, you already knew."

She's not wrong.

Marc claims to be a miracle worker, and I have yet to write a single item in my book of wishes. He keeps asking, and I keep stalling.

"Do you still have the negatives for the pictures in the living room?"

"Probably, but I keep those in my darkroom. Why?"

"Could you print some for me?"

"Why don't you just take the ones here?"

I shake my head. "This is her home. It wouldn't feel right to take them out of here."

"But copies are okay?"

"That's not what I meant. They won't be copies, just redos of the originals. Please?"

Dahlia takes a moment to study me. "Sometimes I don't understand you. But yes, I will develop your redos of the originals. Will you tell them you made up your mind or make them work for it a little longer?"

I shrug. "Option two?"

"Will they be here tomorrow night?"

"Why, are they growing on you?"

"Not at all," she scoffs. "It's just that Marc does something with the food. Not sure what it is, but it helps with the nausea."

I laugh. "Shall I tell him that?"

"Don't you dare," she answers quickly. "We hate each other. If anyone is going to cave on that first, it won't be me."

23

DELILAH

Marc will be here today, at Brewer Health, for our standing monthly attorney-client meeting, and I am not prepared to face him. Ever since my chat with Courtney, I've been walking around with a nervous edge of anticipation. Call me paranoid, but Marc did threaten, in so many words, that he would pack up my house and move me into their place, whether I was on board with it or not.

I already missed several standing Friday morning breakfasts with my other favorite person. I'm still not talking to him — except when they show up on Fridays. Harris called me this morning, but I didn't answer. I know he picked a place weeks ago like he always does. I had the address but still chose not to go. Then he sent me pictures of himself looking sad and heartbroken as he sat across from an empty chair. And for a second there, I almost caved.

Then I remembered the words, *'We are keeping you'*, and sobered up fast.

This may teach them not to treat me like an object.

According to Dahlia's and my joint calendar — we share one for all matters relating to Brewer Health — he should be here within the hour. Knowing Marc, he'll be here an hour early since he values punctuality above all else, except that darn knife of his. But we all have our quirks, so who am I to judge?

I can't help but scan the area for a dark-haired, resting-Grinch-faced, impeccably dressed Italian-American man with a body made for sin as I make my way through the lobby, up the elevators, and onto the fifth floor, where my lab is located. I also can't help the disappointment that bubbles up when he is nowhere to be found by the time I make it to the entrance to my lab.

Perhaps the universe is trying to tell me something. This is for the best.

After putting away my jacket and purse, I pull out my phone and shoot Dahlia a quick text message.

> Dee: Can you take today's ten AM meeting with Marc by yourself?

Her response comes through almost immediately.

> Daa: Why? Are you three fighting already?

> Dee: No, nothing like that. I'll owe you one if you do this.

> Daa: Fine.

> Daa: FYI, he asked to move the meeting to later today. Didn't say when though. Or why.

Huh. I suppose Harris told him about this morning. Even better. Maybe this is the one thing that gets my message across.

> Daa: I hate it when standing meetings get moved to open-ended appointments. He's lucky I can be flexible today.

> Dee: You could stand to tamp down on the bitchiness just a little bit.

The middle finger emoji is all the response I get.

Thirty minutes later, I'm completely absorbed by work, and all thoughts of Marc and Harris are pushed to the back of my mind. I even go so far as to venture upstairs and up to the seventh floor later that afternoon. But as I do, I don't go out of my way to look for him. I end up engrossed in a series of meetings between Dahlia, myself, our contractor, and our developer. There are a host of others who join us, whose names and titles I don't remember since I have those laid out in the package before me. It goes on and on — this discussion about the technical aspects involved with wrapping up construction of our latest expansion site in Woodbury.

I'm trying to follow along with all of it, but they might as well be speaking in Latin.

"You haven't been answering H's calls." A voice cuts through my thoughts, startling me to alertness.

My heart skips a beat as the voice and his question slowly register in my muddled brain. I turn to see Marc settling into the seat next to me. I didn't realize he had rescheduled this morning's meeting to after this — or Dahlia knew and she didn't let me in on that part, much less add it to the calendar.

I hate it when she does that.

Still, I can't help but throw back, "What are you, his mouthpiece?"

Not the best choice of words on my part, as something hot and wicked flashes in his eyes, even as his face remains utterly stoic.

"Why are you being so hard on him?"

The only thing that betrays any sort of emotion are his eyes. Stormy gray eyes that roam unabashedly all over me. While I'm used to having his eyes on me, he seldom addresses me directly — not without Harris in the room acting as the go-between with our interactions.

Except for the nights we've shared.

Oh, and that other time.

"We're in a meeting," I say, a hot flush creeping up my neck. "Now might not be the time or place to have this conversation."

As soon as the words leave my mouth, I know that it was the wrong answer to give. I'm just not prepared for what follows next. And by next, I mean Marc pushing back his seat and pulling my body onto his lap like I weigh nothing. Then he rearranges our bodies so I sit in his lap with my legs on either side of his thighs. Two massive palms cup my ass cheeks, bringing me flush against him as he settles me in.

I'm too stunned to say anything, much less fight him on this. So I wait for it, the inevitable sound of someone's throat clearing — Dahlia's, no doubt — before they say something snarky. She would have something to say about this like she does every Friday night when I wind up in her bed.

"Meeting ended half an hour ago." The corner of Marc's lip curls ever-so-slightly upward. "You've been staring off into space ever since."

A quick glance around lets me know that he's right. There's no one else in the room with us.

"What if someone comes in?"

He lets out a sinister chuckle. "Being seen together in public is part of the package. That's what happens when you enter into a relationship with me." His voice goes soft as he says this. Dangerously soft. Even more so when he adds, "I refuse to let you become anyone's dirty little secret, D. Not on my watch."

This changes the dynamics of our already established relationship. But given the circumstances, I'm not sure if the appropriate emotion I'm supposed to be having is happiness or relief now that we don't have to hide it anymore.

His cock strains against his cloth-covered lap, flush against my core as the pressure builds between my legs at an alarming rate.

Warm hands encircle my cheeks, bringing my face to his. His eyes go hooded, stormy gray orbs intently studying mine. "He doesn't deserve your anger, D," he continues, eyes narrowing at me. "I think you know that too."

Looking away from him, I swallow around the lump in my throat. "I'm just frustrated, is all."

A beat passes before he responds. "It's okay to be frustrated. This turn of events complicates things, to say the least."

"You can say that again." My words come out with an edge to them, one I don't intend to be accusatory, but it gives off that impression anyway.

He laughs at my obvious annoyance, the nerve of him. "If you need someone to place blame on — a target for your frustrations, so to speak... Well, that's what I'm here for."

"Yeah, right," I scoff.

"I'm serious, D. I'm here," he says slowly, letting his words sink in as his heavy-lidded gaze holds mine. "I'll always be here."

"In what capacity?" My voice is tentative as I ask this. Hopeful, even.

His gaze darkens. "In any way you want or need."

"And what if that's not what I—"

"Bullshit," he cuts me off in a low growl. "You're already soaked and I barely touched you. Me, not Harris." He fists chunks of my hair and tugs hard. "I'm guessing he doesn't know, am I right? He has no fucking clue how much you like it rough."

Blood rushes to my ears, the rapid thumping of my heart drowning out all other sounds except the ones he's making. His breaths are stuttered and ragged, barely concealing the monster lurking underneath.

My attraction for him initially stemmed from the fact that he is the ultimate forbidden fruit, so to speak. He doesn't fuck women, according to Harris. He does get off on watching Harris fuck women, though.

It does make me wonder how this is supposed to work. He's supposed to be gay. At least that's what he lets other people think of him. But I've seen how he looks at me when he thinks I'm not paying attention. I've also seen how he looks at me when he knows I'm paying attention.

Like now.

And even though I've often wondered, Mom and Dad taught us that shouldn't be what defines who we are on the inside and outside. It's no one else's business who we choose to love, nor should we let that influence who we are or how we live our lives — all of which is easier said than done.

"He's in love with you," Marc continues after some time. I lift my eyes to meet his, stunned. "I'm talking about H, obviously."

"That's not—"

"And you're in love with him too."

He raises a brow as though challenging me to dispute the validity of both statements. My lips part, but no sound comes out. So I snap them shut, because I have no comeback. Nothing whatsoever.

With my luck, if I start protesting this now, I'll be confessing all before I know it.

Just like the last time, seven years ago.

"I don't see what the issue is here. As far as I'm concerned, it's a win-win all around. So what is it that you're struggling to reconcile with? Is it the fact that you're also attracted to me? Or are you concerned about H's feelings on the matter?" His eyes continue to roam my face, scrutinizing me. "Or is it the secrets you keep?" A beat passes, then, "Does he know? What really happened between us that day?"

I frantically shake my head. "I never told him. I don't plan on telling him, ever."

He swipes a hand over his face, looking just as conflicted as Harris did not too long ago. "We don't keep secrets from each other. That includes you."

"Just this once. Please?" My voice goes soft. "It's been years. Telling him now would do more harm than good."

His Adam's apple jumps in his throat, his jaw clenching. "For the last time, D, nothing happened. You were drunk, I was a gentleman, and Harris took you home afterward."

"We both know that's a gross oversimplification of those events."

"Right," he drawls. He looks like he's going to say something else but decides against it. Instead, he says, "It wouldn't have made a difference, you know."

"What?"

"The fact that he was your first. Or if I had been your first. The outcome would've been the same. You're ours now. Forever. Surely there's some part of you that was aware of this when you came to us."

"I hate that word. Forever." The edge to my tone is back. This time, it's bitter and conveys precisely how I feel inside.

"I know. That's why I said it."

That smug smile of his is back.

"The only way you two can be together is if I'm involved," he continues. "I'm sure you've realized it by now, the fact that there's no way around it. We are a package deal. You want him, you get me too. I want him, I get you too. Again, as far as I can tell, it's a win-win-win situation all around."

So logical.

Except for the *"we are keeping you"* part, that is.

I can see why Harris fell head over heels in love with him. Like always attracts like, he says. Maybe that's why I was drawn to him when we first met in freshman biology. It's also why I was just as drawn to Marc when I first met him, a year after I met Harris. I never thought it possible to be attracted so intensely to two men so different from each other. Yet, they appeal to me in different ways. My soul has always been drawn to Harris, just as much as my body is drawn to Marc.

Ever since Simone, I never thought I'd have another chance at this.

Once upon a time those two things — body and soul — belonged to her.

Now, each piece belongs to them — both of them.

Harris and Marc both exude a damaged intensity, each unique in their own way, each appealing to me just as intensely.

With Harris, it's the gentle, naive soul in him that's wrought with pain. It's a feeling I'm all too familiar with. I was born into it as well and raised under a shroud of it, yet flourished despite that. Like he has. It's also how we can be so open with each other. There's no sense in hiding your pain from someone intimately familiar.

With Marc, on the other hand, it has always been about his dominating nature. It's in the way he carries himself, exuding a natural aura of command and control that lingers in his wake. On the outside, he projects this persona of being a cold, hard, remote, emotionally unattached man. Like a lion stalking its prey, waiting to pounce when they least expect it. But he doesn't let go once he has you in his grasp.

I'm not even sure I want him to.

God, I'm such a mess.

"I need to get back to work," I finally say, moving off his lap.

He lets out a strained groan but doesn't stop me. With shaky hands, I gather up my files from the desk and walk toward the door on wobbly legs.

It's not until I reach the door that I realize he isn't on my heels. He's still seated in the same spot where I left him. He doesn't appear to have moved an inch either, but the pained expression on his face is new.

"Marc?"

Heavy-lidded eyes meet mine. "Just… give me a minute." He readjusts himself in his seat. "Make that fifteen minutes."

Oh.

Oh. "I… umm…" Is it appropriate to offer him a blow-job? Would he accept one from me? "Would you like to see my office?" Then, at the incredulous look on his face, I quickly add, "It's, umm… in a secure area."

Translation: we will have more privacy.

The heated look in his eyes deflates a little, and I'd be lying if I said it wasn't a hit to my ego. Instead, he swallows, taking a moment to answer. "That's… thank you for the offer, but it won't quench my cravings."

Oh. Okay.

Translation: I still don't fuck women. Good to fucking know.

"It was presumptuous of me to offer. My bad."

I turn to leave, and my fingers encircle the door knob. No sooner do I do this when I feel his massive body behind me. He crowds my body into the door and presses his erection into the small of my back.

Seriously, that thing has to be massive at this point. And painful. So fucking painful. Why won't he let me help him with it?

"Marc…"

He presses my body against the door, and his hand covers mine on the doorknob, holding it in place.

"I have a lot of cravings," he growls into my ear, just as he snakes his other hand through the waistband of my pants, cupping my ass cheeks. "I've got wicked cravings right now." Fingers slip through the crack of my ass to find my puckered hole. "Especially for this one."

Oh. So he's an ass man.

Good to know.

"Harris told you?"

"No, you did, that night. But H told me before then too."

Of course he did; those two share everything.

Including me.

"I want it," he groans, his words rumbling in his chest and throughout my body. "I want to be your first, back here. Can I?"

Silly man. Doesn't he know it already? My ass, my pussy, my mouth — it's all his for the taking.

I belong to him.

I belong to them both.

PART III

24

HARRIS

As tempting as the thought is, I can't take credit for this.

This wasn't my doing, fixing what I broke, but I'm not about to question it either. Truth be told, I can't recall the last time I was this nervous to see her. It's been a week since I last saw or spoke to Delilah, the longest we've gone without talking. Not for lack of trying on my part. She won't take my calls and leaves my texts on read.

Then three words are all it takes.

Delilah: I'll do it.

That's how this came about; I was tasked with bringing her home. To be safe, I wait for her outside the building, Brewer Health, in which her lab is housed.

Located in what is now considered the heart of downtown Rochester, the Brewer Health building is a mid-rise, ten-story building with floor-to-ceiling windows on each level. They purchased the building right out of college using the modest inheritance their parents left them. Our mentor, Dr. Sonya Goodman, talked them into it. It remains one of many smart investments they made in their early twenties, as the building itself is now worth millions. And so are they.

It's a common misconception that Delilah and Dahlia named the building after themselves. It's named after Derrick and Jordana Brewer, their parents, and biomedical researchers who made great strides in pharmacology. Seeing as their lives were cut short, this was the twin's way of expanding upon their parents' legacy.

Delilah, a geneticist, owns and operates Brewer Diagnostics LLC out of this building, and her lab takes up the fifth and sixth floors of the building. Dahlia, an OBGYN, owns and operates Brewer Medical Clinic, with her practice taking up the third and fourth floors. The spaces on the first and second floors are leased to various specialty services, all medical-related — one of which happens to be Nalina's.

It's not something I readily admit, but I respect the sisters and everything they have accomplished for themselves. One would think that given their notoriety, everything they accomplished would have been handed to them on a silver platter. Still, I know that not to be the case. I know firsthand how many obstacles they've had to overcome, some of which came from the Sotelo and McWhorter families.

As loath as I am to admit it, Curtis stepped in to get his parents to back off of the twins. Likewise, Marc did something similar with his family, which also got them to back off. I admit I did have something to do with that since Delilah is my best friend.

Even then, it hasn't been easy for them. And it pissed me off even further to know that the people who should have been cheering them on were the same people putting up roadblocks and impeding their successes. Especially the McWhorters. Fucking hypocrites. Andrea McWhorter and Jordana Brewer were supposedly best friends, so one would think she would be cheering on her best friend's daughters. Instead, she stood by as her husband put up roadblocks for them simply because he could. It's what prompted Marc and Curtis to make a deal to get their respective families to back off of them — I still don't know how it came about that those two could agree on that, only that it worked.

Now look at what the twins have accomplished without all those pesky little issues in their way. Things like permits and zoning laws and every other trivial issue they kept throwing at them.

The whole premise of Brewer Health is to empower women and educate them on their health and sexuality. That's what the twins do exceptionally well.

Accomplishing what they have and seeing how far they've come in this town fills me with great pride. I'm glad Marc isn't making her give up her career, even though he will struggle with his need to control everything. I have my moments, but I'm more of a homebody than she is. Hell, Courtney does a much better job at toeing the line for her safety. Delilah won't comprehend any of that. She hasn't for years, and that's not going to change just because she's now ours, officially. There's no doubt in my mind that she will give her bodyguards a run for their money. Dahlia too, since that protection extends to her.

Still, even Marc realizes she does too much good for the community. It'd be a waste of her considerable talents to give it all up for a life as a kept woman. That's essentially what I am, a kept man. Sixteen years ago, I chose this life and have no regrets.

Delilah never wanted that, and I don't blame her. But I'm the asshole who will drag her into this anyway. Marc wanted to do it, but he's been uncharacteristically moody. I didn't think it could get any worse. Then something happened between them last Friday, and it got to that point. Even worse after dinner that same night, except unlike the previous times when she glared at me, Hurricane Dahlia seemed to be in on it this time. When Delilah's text message came through seventy-two hours later, Marc wasted no time setting this all up.

Except I insisted on doing this part. Marc's idea of collecting someone means he shows up with a host of bodyguards to physically remove them from the premises. It never ends well for anyone involved. There was a time I tried to run away from him and almost succeeded, except I made the mistake of hiding out at Delilah's. It's embarrassing to think about how easily he found me, how humiliating it felt when he had me collected and delivered home. He's made it clear that no one leaves him, which is why he made sure she witnessed the humiliating ordeal. It's what he meant when he said he would give her the same treatment I got.

His patience with our shenanigans is wearing thin after seven years, so I know he won't be as gentle with her as he was with me. If one can call that gentle.

Staying outside means a decreased likelihood of running into her sister. Dahlia Brewer is a pretentious, judgmental bitch, and it's no secret we can't stand each other. I barely tolerate her because she's my best friend's identical sister, even though their personalities are as different as night and day.

As a backup, I brought a failsafe with me. Delilah might be able to resist me, but she won't resist this.

Because I am an asshole, I make it a point to park directly in front of the building and in her designated parking spot. It will start a fight as soon as she sees me, but fighting with her is better than this tension between us. Fighting means we're talking. Radio silence is much worse. It's what couples do when they've given up on each other and mentally checked out of the relationship. Checked out is the last thing I want. It's the last thing I will ever be when it comes to her.

I spot her the moment she walks out of the building. She truly is breathtaking, as always. Her wavy brown hair hangs loosely around her face and cascades down her shoulders, draped over the front of her blouse.

I do a double-take because this isn't her usual attire. Delilah favors muted, understated colors that make her blend in with a crowd. Today, her outfit complements her pale porcelain skin tone perfectly. She stands out, radiant against the rest.

As expected, she's not alone. With her are three of her employees, two men and a woman whose names I've probably heard a thousand times before but never bothered to remember. She laughs at something one of them says, the melodious sound of her laughter carrying over to where I am, twisting up my insides in reignited desire.

Like a man starving, I hang on to it. It's bad enough that she's kept me waiting all this time, and now her employees are infringing on my time with her. So I wait for her to spot me before raising a hand to wave at her.

Our eyes meet and she pauses in her tracks, the result being one of her male employees running into her. Said hand freezes mid-wave, fists curling in anger. If there's one thing I loathe more than her sister, it's another man's hands or body touching hers. She would brush it off with the harsh reminder of her personhood and that we were just best friends, so I had no claim to her.

Well, that changes now. She's mine.

Ours.

The fact that this isn't common knowledge to the men in her life should be rectified.

Her gaze narrows in on my clenched fist. A beat passes before she turns to address her employees, who have now stopped and are staring at me. Especially the woman. Char-something. Charlene? She looks vaguely familiar and shoots daggers in my direction like a jilted lover would. It takes everything to resist hoisting a middle finger in her direction. Not that that'd help anything, but it would be cathartic.

Char-something turns her attention back to the group and a few more words are exchanged. In true Midwest fashion, they take forever to say their goodbyes before exchanging obligatory hugs. My brows furrow in annoyance when one of the guys holds on to Delilah a little longer than is necessary. I push off the car and head in her direction, intent on stopping it, but my failsafe stops me in my tracks.

They break apart, and she waves all three of them off.

25

HARRIS

Delilah remains rooted to the spot for a few minutes, giving me a curious gaze. A ghost of a smile appears at the corners of her mouth. She brushes her hair away from her face, tucking it behind her ears before heading in my direction.

"You're late," I say once she's in earshot, affecting a stern tone.

"I am?"

She stops before me and then shuffles her feet forward so our toes touch while keeping her gaze downcast. It's her way of saying, 'I'm too pissed at you to say hello, but I'm saying it anyway.'

My lips quirk in amusement. "You are. I've been waiting."

"I could see that."

"I don't like waiting."

Her head lifts, and she glares at me with her hands planted on her hips. "Some of us have jobs, you know. Regular nine-to-five jobs. We actually enjoy them."

"Do you now?"

"I do. They are good for building a routine, adding structure to your day, that sort of thing. You should try it sometime."

"Be another cog in the system? No, thank you."

I do work, just not a regular nine-to-five like her and Marc. One of the many perks of being self-employed is that I get to set my own schedule.

She shrugs. "Suit yourself."

"I like being my own boss," I counter.

"So do I, in a manner of speaking. Most days anyway."

"Tough day?"

Another shrug. "The next time Daa mentions wanting another expansion to Brewer Health, remind me not to strangle her."

"Noted."

"Or better yet, let me strangle her and help me hide the body. Oh, and make sure her soul doesn't haunt me for the rest of my life. And in the afterlife as well."

Chuckling, I say, "You've given this a lot of thought."

"Only for the last two years," she mumbles. "It's not just me she's been driving up a wall. Marc too."

Ah.

Dry spell aside, that could explain why Marc has been extra cranky lately. His law firm represents Brewer Health in all professional and, on occasion, personal matters. I thought regular Hurricane Dahlia was insufferable. Pregnant Hurricane Dahlia is worse, and I don't have to work with her.

I lean forward, bringing our faces closer together. "Did you miss me?"

"No," she quickly answers. I don't miss the slight hitch in her breath.

It's nice to know I'm not the only one affected by this. I hold her gaze for a beat before leaning in to claim her lips with mine. She stops me by placing a palm on my chest, directly over my heart. My pulse kicks up a notch as I respond, placing my hand over hers.

Her gaze softens at the gesture. "Don't go getting any ideas," she says, her voice a breathy whisper. "I'm still annoyed with you."

"I know." Still, I can't help that my heart rate goes into overdrive at the declaration, something I know she can sense. It's why she placed her palm where she did, right?

"Why didn't you come inside?"

"And chance running into your sister? Pass."

"She left three hours ago. I suspect it was a date based on how she was dressed, but she's being tight-lipped about it. But you know, don't you? Since you've been keeping tabs on me. And her too, whatever that's about."

"Not me. Marc."

"Same thing, Harris," she counters with an eye roll. "You're parked in my spot."

Ignoring her not-so-subtle attempt to change the subject, I pull her body flush against mine and wrap my arms around her supple body. Her breath hitches, her nipples hardening to twin knobs against my chest.

"I missed you," I whisper against her throat.

"My car should be parked here," she says but doesn't move or push herself out of my arms. "What did you do with my car?"

"Do you want the truth or a lie?"

She lets out an exasperated sigh. "The truth, please. I can't take any more lies today."

"It's at home." I lean back to look into her eyes, cupping her cheek in one hand while keeping the other secure around her waist. "Marc had one of his men pick it up this morning, drive it to his mechanic, then drop it off at home."

"Why?"

"If you must know, he put a tracking device on your car, amongst other things. Mine too."

"Why stop at that? Why not stick us with GPS tags while he's at it?"

"I don't know. Maybe?" I purse my lips. "That's not a bad idea. Let's run that by him tonight—"

"God, you two are unbelievable." Her other palm moves to my chest, pushing hard against me. I do the opposite and tighten my hold on her.

My eyes move down her face and body, as far down as I can see. "Is this a new outfit? Did you get all dressed up for us?"

She squirms against me, but it only makes me hold on tighter. "Let go of me, Harris, or I swear to god I'll scream."

"If you scream, I'll be forced to gag you."

I don't know where that came from. It just popped out. At least it gets her to stop squirming and not make good on the promise to scream. Her body goes limp in my arms, and I bite down on the urge to take it back.

"Please let go," she whimpers.

I don't. "I like it, but it'll be wasted on Marc. He'll rip it to shreds."

Her eyes go wide. "He wouldn't."

The fight leaves her at that like I knew it would.

"I hardly ever wear the same thing twice. Why do you think that is?"

A flicker of fear passes over her face. As does a flash of pain in her eyes. Both disappear just as quickly. When her body slumps against mine, I can't decide if this is better or worse than her physically fighting me. Squirming shows spirit. This just seems resigned.

I don't understand it. She's physically attracted to him, and he reciprocates, a rare feat for him. Not once has he fucked a woman in the time we've been together, but he gets off on watching me fuck women. And men, on occasion. He'll join in if it's another guy, but he'll kick the woman out or make her watch while he fucks me.

That's not to say that there haven't been women who thought they would be the ones to break his streak over the years. It all ended the same way. Marc tossed them aside once they got too clingy. Or needy. Or both.

Delilah has always been the exception. In more ways than one. He wants her bad, and he's placed first dibs on her once we get back home. I know he won't pounce on her the moment we get there. He might wait an hour for her to get acclimated, but that's as far as his self-restraint goes. I won't tell her that, though. I don't want her to think we only want her for sex because it's more than that. It's forever, come what may. Except she hates that word.

Forever.

She's hated that word for as long as I've known her. We either skirt around the subject or keep it out of our vocabulary. If I had to guess, it has something to do with her ex. With time, I can ease her into this. Get her used to the idea of us as one, forever.

"I brought you a present," I eventually say.

She perks up at that, eyes meeting mine. "A present? Where is it? Why didn't you lead with that?"

She loves presents but hates surprises. Go figure.

"I wanted to see the look on your face." I press a kiss on her forehead. It's chaste and not reflective of the naughty things I want to do to her.

"I'm intrigued. Where is it?"

"Back seat."

Releasing their hold on her, my hands drop to my sides. She wastes no time in making a beeline for the car. Their combined squeals of excitement moments later confirm I made the right decision.

"I know this is a bribe, but I don't care," she says, unbuckling the toddler from his car seat and hoisting him on her hip. "This is the best surprise ever."

I chuckle mirthlessly. "I aim to please."

She attacks him with the tickle monster — his favorite game — and the tiny traitor's happy toddler squeals fill the space, somehow diluting the tension between us.

"Does Marc know you have him?" she asks after some time passes.

I sigh and run a hand through my hair. "I don't need anyone's permission to hang out with my nephew."

"Uh, you kinda do." A smile teases the corners of her lips. "You are hilariously bad with children."

She doesn't say this with malicious intent. It's just how she is. It's how we are with each other. Unlike me, Delilah is a natural with kids.

"I can learn," I mutter, meaning every word.

At this point, I have to learn. Tiny humans keep popping up everywhere I go, so I can't pretend they don't exist. Having kids isn't something I envisioned for myself. For years, Marc and I were on the same page on the subject. Then Courtney gave birth to this little booger, Charles. Or Charlie, as we call him. I wasn't surprised when Marc took to Charlie with natural ease.

Me, not so much. I'm content to watch on the sidelines.

I see the way he is with him, in full-on dad mode. It makes me want that for him. I love him that much, so I'm willing to do anything to make him happy.

Except this.

This fills me with dread, which translates to my face, and Delilah doesn't hesitate to point it out.

"You, learn?" She laughs. "That would be the day."

"I'm not completely hopeless."

"Uh-huh. Tell that to your face."

Again, I know she doesn't say this with malicious intent. It's just how she is.

"How hard can it be? They sleep. They eat. They poop. They require some interaction on occasion. I can do that. I can try, at least."

She pauses and golden-brown eyes fixate on mine, searching as the laughter dies in her throat. "You're serious about this?"

"I think he wants kids." I almost add, 'I know you do too,' but clamp down on the words at the last second.

"I could've told you that," she says. "Given how much Marc dotes on this little guy, it's not hard to put two and two together."

"So you noticed?"

"Duh."

It doesn't help that certain family members are pressuring him to finally settle down and have babies. The ones putting on the pressure are the same ones who still treat me as though my presence in his life is fleeting. To them, sixteen years isn't enough to show I'm not a fling or that this isn't a phase he will eventually grow out of.

I find it ironic that he is the one with the Mafia family, yet I'm the bad influence. Go figure.

Even though Marc pretends otherwise, sixteen years of the same song and dance is finally getting to him. It's spilling over into our relationship. So he's taken to issuing death threats, even though those are a dime a dozen in his world. He tolerates many things from them — something we butt heads on constantly — but he made it clear that their disrespect of my place in his life won't be tolerated. There may or may not be a few framed body parts at home to that effect.

Still, this might work out after all. The two people I love will finally get together and have babies. What more can a guy ask for? Other than the possibility I could get booted out of his life forever.

"How's that going to work, given your aversion to kids?" Delilah asks after some time.

I shrug, shaking off the negative thoughts and returning to the positive. "I'm not averse to them. I just—"

"—don't want any for yourself?" she finishes my sentence.

I give her a small smile, one she returns. This is why we are perfect for each other. We know each other so well. We even finish each other's sentences.

"I don't like a lot of people, especially the little ones. They are needy and demanding, and I'm selfish and self-centered. We are bound to clash every time, so I stay away from them. I don't mind this little guy, though."

"Yeah, I can see that," she scoffs. "You left him in the back seat of the car, all by himself, while you waited outside."

"He was doing just fine."

"He was bored. Where are his toys?"

"I don't know. Courtney put him in there. She must have packed up some toys for him or something."

She plants her free arm on her hip and glares at me. "You expect me to believe she just handed her precious son over to you, just like that?"

"Of course not. She only agreed to this after I told her I was coming here."

"That sounds more like the Courtney I know," she muses. "So, where are his toys?"

"He has plenty at home. Did you know that Marc has an entire section of the estate dedicated to this little booger? He only gets him two nights a week at most, yet he has his own quarters. It even has the Marc flair — lavish, obnoxious, and so him. You'll see."

26

HARRIS

We pull up to the estate an hour later. Ida, Charlie's nanny, quickly comes out and collects him. Courtney could have called ahead of time; even if she didn't, Ida knows how I feel about small humans. All the household staff does, and when Charlie is on the premises they go out of their way to minimize my interactions with him.

Marc has something to do with this too, so I have to work on changing that. The man loves his nephew, I can't fault him for that. It's only a matter of time before the conversation about kids comes up. It will be a two-against-one scenario. So if I'm going to be serious about this parenting thing, then I need to show the people around me that I can be nurturing.

And I really hate the idea of it.

On the other hand, Delilah was uncharacteristically quiet throughout the drive, like a lamb being taken to the slaughter. Not even Charlie's incessant babbling is cheering her up, and it usually does.

"Look, there's your car." I try humor and point to her Mazda MX-5 Miata parked in the driveway. I'm hoping for her smile, but it never comes.

She loves that car. She called it her first adult guilty pleasure purchase. It also took her an absurdly long time, months of research, and at least ten dealership visits before deciding on this one. I remember her dragging me to every single one of those dealerships too.

Her hands twist together in her lap, and her breathing quickens. In, out. In, out. The makings of a panic attack. It's been ages since she last had one. It feels like med school all over again.

"Delilah, I—"

"I heard you," she interjects, her tone curt.

This isn't going well. I thought things were fine earlier, but I misread the situation. Have I screwed things up so badly between us? I reach over to place a hand over hers, but she pulls away from my grasp.

"I don't need comforting, Harris. It's fine. I'm fine. Let's just get this over with." Resignation with a hint of anger laces her tone. It's what I deserve — her anger and her rage.

Her gaze lifts to meet mine, golden-brown eyes lighting up in anger. Unfettered rage pierces through the unshed tears in her eyes, mirroring my own. I'm not surprised my eyes are burning. I'm not usually emotional, but she has a way of drawing that out of me.

"I'm sorry, Delilah," I say truthfully, my tone softening. "It's better this way, I promise. You will be officially under Marc's protection."

"*Officially?*" Out of everything I said, she hones in on that. "What you're saying is, I've been *unofficially* under the protection of the Sotelo family and didn't know?"

"Not the Sotelo family's protection, just Marc's."

"That's not any better."

"And really, is it that much of a surprise? I'm not like you, Delilah. I'm not good with people. I can't see through their bullshit like you can. Ergo, I don't have many friends. Marc vets and keeps tabs on what few friends I have to ensure they don't pose a danger to me and, by extension, him."

"If it's Marc's idea, then it's your idea. We both know he'll do whatever it takes to make you happy."

"It's not like that."

"It's not? How long has he been keeping tabs on me? Undergrad? Med school?"

"Undergrad."

She blows out a frustrated breath. "I must have passed muster since I'm still around. Have you just been biding your time, waiting to take me on as the newest side piece in your relationship?"

"W-what?"

"What am I to you, Harris? A plaything? The shiny new toy you get to play with? Do I get discarded the moment you get bored—"

"Don't do that."

"Do what?"

"Dismiss years of this," I gesture between us, "so easily. We both know that what we have is more than just a simple friendship."

"I don't know what to think. I asked my best friend and his partner for a favor. One night, that's it. Next thing I know, I'm being moved into their house as a... what do I call myself now? A live-in fuck buddy?"

"Live-in fuck — no. Absolutely not. You are not calling yourself that."

"Don't like that? How about sex slave?"

In hindsight, I should have known she wouldn't make this any easier. There's so much I want to tell her about how much she means to me. She's my best friend, but she's always been much more. Not to mention she's drop-dead gorgeous, always has been. If I have to spell it all out for her, I will.

Maybe not tonight, or she'll think I'm just buttering her up for something. Which I am, but only because I can't have her find out my true motives, not yet anyway.

"Fuck buddy implies plaything, and you have always been more than that to me."

"No? How about human pet? I've got more where that came from."

"How about girlfriend?"

"I hate labels," she scoffs as she swipes angrily at her tear-stained face.

Fair enough, I knew that about her; however, "What should Marc call you?"

"I don't know about you two, but I like my name. Why does he have to call me anything else?"

"If it makes you happy, we can keep calling each other best friends. Marc will need a label to call you by. He's sentimental like that."

"That can be tomorrow's problem. Let's just get this evening over with. I could use a shower and a good night's sleep. Maybe this will all be a bad dream when I wake up tomorrow."

27

DELILAH

I step out of the car and slam the door harder than is necessary. Harris follows suit and jogs around the car to find me leaning against it, my face turned toward the sky.

"Still keeping tabs on me? Worried I'll run?" I ask, bouncing my head softly against the car frame in rhythm with my words.

"The thought crossed my mind." He places his massive palm between my head and the car. "Keep this up, and you'll give yourself a headache."

"That's the idea." He mirrors my stance, keeping his hand firmly in place. His concern for my well-being, though palpable, is also misguided. "We've been out here a while. If we don't go inside soon, someone will send out a search party for us."

I angle my face to meet his. "There are security cameras aimed at this section of the driveway." A beat passes, then, "You think he's watching?"

"Who, Marc?"

I nod.

"Probably." He exhales a sigh. "He's always watching. He watches you, you know."

I muster up every bit of self-control to repress a smile at his words. I'm aware Marc watches me. He's been watching me for as long as I've been watching him. I didn't think Harris noticed or cared since he never said anything.

A comfortable silence settles between Harris and me. I take a moment to breathe in the subtle scent of his cologne and natural musk. Brown eyes like mine roam over my face, intently studying my features.

"Do I look okay?" I ask after some time. "You're staring."

A slow smile creeps over his face. "Delilah, you look great. You look gorgeous, as always."

"I meant my face. How smeared is my mascara? How much did I ruin my make-up?"

"You're not wearing any make-up," he says. I lift a brow and his creases in confusion. "Is this a trick question? Are you wearing make-up? You're not, are you?"

I laugh at him this time. "It's called a natural look and is meant to be inconspicuous. How is it that you are still so clueless about women after all this time?"

"But you're not like other women. You are you."

"What's that supposed to mean?"

"I didn't... You are... You don't need..." He takes a deep breath, expands his chest, and then exhales slowly. "You don't need all that, Delilah. You have no reason to impress anyone, much less me. I love you just the way you are."

His words reach inside and twist up a tangle of emotions like they do every time he says this to me.

Love.

It's an emotion he dispenses so freely. Mine, on the other hand, is in very short supply. And since I can't afford to get emotional again, I turn away from him to look at the house.

Mansion, more like. A modern Mediterranean-style mansion with an exterior facade of gray stucco, a terra cotta tile roof, and an abundance of arched windows and doors — too much, in my opinion. It's very Marc-esque, and I don't doubt this is the largest one in this gated community. The house is gorgeous but also secluded, with the nearest house being at least a two-minute drive away.

I've been here several times before but was restricted to the mansion's first floor because Marc is notoriously private. The only people allowed past the first floor are himself, Harris, Courtney, Charlie, David, and a select few household staff. The privilege was never extended to friends and family, something I understood given my own tenuous relationship with the McWhorters. After Simone went missing and our parents had a very public falling out, they made it clear that McWhorters were not welcome in our house, including Curtis.

It still feels surreal that I'm moving out of my home, which has been my home for thirty-four years. Now I'm going to live here. Forever, it would seem.

"I have some make-up remover wipes in my purse. We should make our faces presentable, don't you think?"

He doesn't answer immediately, but I know he is watching me closely. I don't need to see the tightness in his jaw to know that he's scowling at me. I can sense all of that because the air around us is unnaturally tense and dry, and it has nothing to do with the weather. Or the fact that nightfall is upon us.

Instead of dwelling on the tension between us, I focus on the beauty nature has to offer and take in the glorious sight before us — the sunset and the colors that streak across the sky in every shade of red, orange, and gold imaginable. It dances and plays against the terracotta tile roof of the house, its hues reflected against the obnoxiously tall glass windows concentrated on the west side of the house.

Harris moves closer, and the heat of his body seeps into mine. "I know what you're doing, and I'm onto you."

His hot breath tickles against the sensitive skin of my neck, sending a flush of desire straight through my body and pooling between my legs.

"Beautiful, isn't it?" I say instead, pointing to where the sun drops in the sky.

"It sure is. Just wait till you experience it from the inside. It's spectacular." He laces our fingers together, skimming his thumb over my knuckles. "Let's go home, Delilah."

28

DELILAH

Harris takes me on an abbreviated tour of the first floor, since it's an area I'm familiar with. The rest, second floor and upwards, takes longer since I wasn't privy to these sections before. Everything on the first floor — except for the kitchen, pantry, and dining rooms — is duplicated on the second floor but is much more comfortable. They obviously spend more time up here, with the first floor being more for entertaining. That is, on the rare occasion that Marc permits it, something that happens twice a year at most.

We go through the usual rooms on the second and third floors. A family room, living room, library, media room, large bedrooms and bathrooms, and a massive gym with an adjoining indoor pool. We even go through Charlie's quarters on the third floor. The little guy isn't there when we stop by, most likely in some other part of the house. Harris was right. It's lavish and obnoxious, and so Marc. No expense was spared here, like the rest of the house.

"This is a little overboard, don't you think?"

He runs his hands through his hair, blowing out an exasperated breath. "You have no idea."

It's easy to pick up on the undertones of frustration in his words. "I love Charlie, obviously, but isn't this too much space for a child who hardly lives here? Is Courtney planning on having more children? Or is he planning on adopting?"

A flicker of anguish flares in his eyes. Something else does too, something that looks dangerously close to pain. Or is it resignation? Elation? Anger? The emotions cycle through, one after the other and at an alarming speed that's hard to keep straight.

"Something like that," he eventually says.

Huh. "And how do you feel about that?"

A blank look falls over his face, shutting me out. "What do you think?"

It's a loaded question, and I don't dare to answer Harris when he's in this state.

As it turns out, I don't have to. He takes my arm and pulls me out of the room like the devil is on his heels. It's not until the door closes behind us that he breathes a sigh of relief.

"You don't spend much time in there, do you?"

"Not really." He keeps his eyes forward as he says, "Between Marc and Ida, Charlie's needs are taken care of when he's here. They go out of their way to keep him away from me."

"Then why the heck did you take me in there? I would've found it on my own, eventually."

"It's something I had to do."

Interesting choice of words. "Is today the first time you've been in there?"

His jaw clenches and it stays that way. He tugs on my arm and propels us forward. As we walk, I slip my fingers into his hand and his fingers curl around mine. He says nothing about the intimate gesture, just squeezes gently on my hand.

"That's Marc's office," he says once we get to the last door that sits just before the next flight of stairs. "It's his domain, so he spends a lot of time there. It's off-limits unless you've been invited in. It's safe to assume that no one is allowed there, not without his permission."

"Not even you?"

"Not even me." He laughs, but it's weak. "I can count on one hand the number of times I've been in that room."

He might find this humorous, but I don't. Judging by the look on his face, I don't think he's thrilled with that arrangement either.

"That seems extreme. Aren't relationships supposed to be about trust? Why all the secrecy?"

He shrugs. "It's just a room. We each have our own spaces that no one's allowed in. Mine is my studio in the basement. You'll get your own space. Just pick out whatever room on whatever floor you want, and he'll make it so. Except for the fourth floor, that's our shared space."

"Shared space?" I manage to croak.

"Saved the best for last," he says.

He tugs me up the stairs and to the fourth-floor landing, then leads us through a set of double doors into what I can only describe as heaven.

"The master oasis," he chuckles, echoing my thoughts.

My mouth falls open as I turn to face him. "You two were thinking of giving up this?"

"If it came to that. Delilah, you are worth it." He loops an arm around my shoulder and presses his lips to my temple. "Take a look around, as it's your space too."

My space, but to be shared with two men. Except for Dahlia and Simone, I've never shared a room with someone else, much less slept in the same bed as them. Not until a few weeks ago, and that was one time. Now I get to do that for the rest of my life. With two men. Forever.

If I say it often enough, it will sink in.

I take a look around this oasis of a master bedroom. So many things to look at all at once, so little time. The room is more reflective of Harris's tastes than Marc's, but the design aspects here mirror what I have at home. Like the antique dresser in my bedroom, a piece that has survived three generations; this one is damn near an exact replica.

Parted black-out velvet shades frame the row of large, arched windows overlooking the backyard. The carpeting is plush. A leather-upholstered armchair sits next to the windows, and I can take a guess at whose that is.

On the opposite wall are individual portraits of the three of us. Mine is the live portrait that Feorie did two weeks ago. Marc's and Harris's look to be done by her too, and she captured our respective essences perfectly.

"This turned out great," I tell Harris as I study mine. "Did Feorie do all of them? Yours and Marc's?"

"She did. Marc commissioned several pieces of all three of us for the first and second floors. He wants Feorie to do those too."

"That's a tall order."

"She's up to the challenge. Marc doesn't care about age, just talent." A beat passes, then, "Some prints were delivered yesterday. Where do you want those?"

Dahlia came through for me. "Second floor, probably. Or third floor. I don't care where, just as long as they go up."

I head for the massive Alaskan king bed next, sinking in. It is the softest bed I've ever sat on. If they sleep in this every night, I can only imagine how terrible my bed must have been for them in the last couple of weeks.

Harris watches me the entire time, undisguised lust in his eyes as I bounce on the bed.

"We all sleep together," he says, his voice hoarse.

Of course, I expected as much. For weeks they crammed their massive bodies into my tiny queen-sized bed, and I can't imagine that was comfortable for them. This is much better.

I clear my throat. "What if I wanted space from you guys?"

A ghost of a smile teases the corner of his lips. "You can have your space on that side of the bed." It's a huge bed, and he points indiscriminately to a random corner. His gaze stays locked on mine, then dips to my lips before he adds, "Good luck keeping your distance from us, from me especially. I'm a snuggler."

"I never would've guessed," I say sarcastically, my voice as hoarse as his. I tap the space next to me. "Come here."

He looks conflicted as he answers, "I can't."

"Why not?"

"You're sitting in our bed, looking sinfully delicious, and giving me sultry eyes. I can't..." He trails off and draws in a long breath before releasing it slowly. "You're a tough woman to resist, and you're testing every ounce of my patience by doing that."

"Doing what?" I'm enjoying the undisguised lust in his eyes as I continue bouncing on the bed.

"That." He gestures. "I can't sit next to you in our bed and not kiss you. Kissing almost always leads to other things."

Yeah, I remember.

We have unfinished business from weeks ago.

"There's nothing wrong with that statement." I lick my lips, honing in on his chest's erratic rise and fall. Even though I can tell he wants to, he doesn't move. His eyes look like he's trying to convey something, but I can't fathom it.

"Give us an hour," a deep voice booms from the doorway.

29

DELILAH

Harris walks over to Marc, who pulls him in for a long, hard kiss. My lips part on a breathy whisper as their mouths meet, tongues wrestling each other for dominance. I lick my lips, my eyes staying on them as I watch them kiss, liquid heat sliding over me, through me. Harris's hand snakes up into Marc's hair, clenching fistfuls of his hair as the kiss deepens.

The sight gets me aroused and excited at the same time. My heart rate kicks up a notch, hammering in my chest as a softness expands there, stealing my breath. It feels like an eternity passes by the time they slowly break apart, looking thoroughly dazed as they come up for air.

They didn't do this either night we were together; I suspect it was more for my benefit. But boy, do I love to watch. I guess I do have a bit of a voyeuristic trait in me. Watching turns me the fuck on.

Harris's gaze slides over to mine. He gives me a small smile before turning back to Marc. "Be gentle with her," he tells him, his voice breathy.

Gentle?

"What is he talking about?" The question is directed at Marc, who then ignores me.

"When am I not?" Marc's hand slides down to cup Harris's ass cheek, giving it a hard squeeze. That earns a high-pitched squeal from him. I want him to do it again, preferably over here, in this bed, and with no clothing between us.

My mind conjures up the image, heat flooding my cheeks again.

"I'm serious. All of this is a lot to take in. Don't scare her off on day one."

Marc's face turns, his eyes meeting mine as he says, "I promise not to do anything to her that she doesn't want." His words sound sincere enough, even though his tone says otherwise.

Harris isn't convinced either. "One hour, then I'm coming back in here."

Marc turns to look back at him. "Make that ninety minutes."

"In your dreams," he scoffs before walking out of the room.

The door closes behind him, and an ominous click resonates throughout the room. There's no doubt in my mind he'll be back in the time frame stipulated. He'll even time it down to the last second.

For a long while, Marc and I say nothing. Not that there's anything to say, really. I can count on one hand the number of times I've had one-on-one interactions with Marc. But lustful, longing looks do not make a conversation. Here I thought we were being discreet about it, hence the immense guilt that plagued me all these years.

Guilt for lusting after my best friend's partner — his very gay partner — at the same time as him.

I make the mistake of meeting Marc's eyes. In addition to the usual — aloofness, lust, and desire — there's also a darkness in his eyes.

The kind that warns you to stay away, yet it simultaneously draws you in.

The kind that urges you to dive in, yet not too deep, unless you have no fear of drowning.

The kind you want to flee from, yet it anchors you in place, daring you to come closer.

Too close. It ends in regret, flooding every pore of your body only after you've been thoroughly singed by it.

But you'll love every second of it, won't you?

Marc makes his way over to the leather-upholstered armchair and settles in, spreading his thighs open and looking every bit as intimidating as he always does.

My eyes track his every movement. The fluidity and grace in his stride.

The unabashed heat in his stare as he lets his heavy-lidded gaze wander all over my body. His gaze feels like fingertips caressing my sensitive skin. I can't help that my pussy clenches in anticipation of what he could do to me. Mold me, break me, put me back together — then do it all over again.

Again and again.

I'd let him, too. I'm that far gone for him. Always have been.

He's always watching. Harris's words come to the forefront of my mind. *He watches you, you know.*

Does Harris know?

Does he know that I watch him too?

Does he know I've been watching Marc just as much as he watches me, maybe for as long?

Just what does this make me? A bad friend? The world's worst best friend? Worse?

"Here we are." His voice cuts through my thoughts.

"Yep. Here we are. Alone at last. Just how you like it." I remained perched in my position at the edge of the bed. The only thing that changes is I cross my ankles.

A crease forms in the center of his forehead. "You make it sound so dirty."

I have to chuckle at his choice of the word *dirty.* "So, how does this work?"

He opens his mouth to respond, but nothing comes out. It has to be a first, even for him. I can always count on him to throw back one smart-ass comment after the other. I would help him out, but I'm not feeling all that generous at the moment. If he wants me on my best behavior today, the least he can do is work for it.

"How do you want me? On my knees, your cock down my throat?" I shouldn't be egging him on like this, but I can't help myself. "You're not a pussy guy, so I guess that hole's out. How about on all fours then, ass up in the air?"

The crease in the center of his forehead deepens.

"You want my ass raw? Maybe not the first time. But if the mood strikes, you have my blessing to fuck my pussy bare. I won't object to that."

A ghost of a smile teases the corners of his lips, and the crease in his forehead smooths out.

"You should do that more often. Smiling, I mean." I just can't help myself. The words keep spilling out of these troublesome lips of mine. "A real smile. Not the sinister kind you wear like a badge of honor. Or like you do whenever you're sizing people up as prey."

He taps on the inside of his massive thighs. "Come here," he says, his voice quiet.

"Why?"

"I'm not accustomed to making requests twice, D. Get the fuck over here."

Confusion muddles my thinking as I stare at him, baffled at how easy it is for him to accept this. "You want me to sit on your lap?"

"No, my shoulders," he says dryly.

"Why do you want me on your shoulders?"

His gaze lifts, capturing mine. "Why do you think?"

Images of my being sensually devoured by him cloud my mind. I shake them off, willing myself to focus on the threat at hand.

"I think you're toying with me again," I say in deliberate reference to the last time we found ourselves in a similar situation.

"I don't *toy*."

"Fine, squirm. You just want to watch me squirm. It's what you do best." At his indifferent look, I add, "You take great pleasure in twisting the naive wallflower up in knots."

"We both know Delilah Brewer is no wallflower." His tone goes hard as he says this. "If I have to come over there, you'd better believe Marc the gentleman is the last thing you'll be getting tonight."

Oh.

My heartbeat kicks up a notch, my breath quickening. "I never asked you to be gentle."

A wicked grin slides across his mouth. "I know."

"So ask again. Nicely." I throw that last part in there, knowing he would never comply. Not in a million years.

Except he goes right ahead and proves me wrong.

"Come here," he says, his eyes softening before he adds, "Please."

30

DELILAH

That's all he needs to say.

Please.

My feet have a mind of their own as they pivot towards him of their own accord. Once I'm within arm's length, he wastes no time tugging me at him. Not just on his lap but straddling his legs, my thighs on either side of his.

"Marc… what are you doing?" I ask, my voice a breathy whisper.

A wicked grin slides across his mouth as two massive palms cup my ass cheeks, bringing me flush against him as he settles me in. His cock strains against his jean-covered lap, flush against my core as the pressure builds between my legs at an alarming rate.

This feels familiar.

Warm hands encircle my cheeks, bringing my face to his. His eyes go hooded, stormy gray orbs intently studying mine. "What does it look like I'm doing?"

I gulp as my heart rate kicks up in anticipation. "I—I'm not sure."

Half-truths, that's what I'm going with. It feels so wrong, being like this without Harris present. And yet it feels so good. Deliriously good.

"Try again."

Slowly, he lowers his gaze to my lips, which part slightly at the expression on his face. "You're going to kiss me…"

He smirks before saying, "Well, you're half correct," while running a thumb over my bottom lip.

It takes a minute for his meaning to sink in. "But Harris said…"

"Harris said…?" He gently nudges me when I don't say anything for some time.

"He said…" I swallow around the lump in my throat. I can't believe he will make me say it out loud.

"We don't have all evening, D. Fucking finish your sentence," he growls, tracing my bottom lip with his thumb.

Asshole. "He said you don't stick your dick in women."

"I don't."

That's what I thought. "But you like to watch, don't you? Is that what gets you off? The other time, you watched while he—"

"You're the exception," he says, cutting me off.

My breath hitches. "What?"

He presses his thumb into my lower lip. "It would seem that you, Delilah Brewer, are the exception."

My tongue darts to lick my lips, brushing over his thumb. "Why?"

"I'm not sure." His voice is strained as he says this. Pained, even.

"You're not sure?" Talk about a mood killer. "What does that mean?"

"It means just that, D. I'm not sure what I want. But here's what I do know." He exhales on a low hiss, eyes meeting mine again. "I have wicked cravings. All the time. I want your ass. I want to be the first to violate your tight little hole. But I want all of your other holes too. I want to stick everything I can get my hands on in all of your holes. Not just my cock. My fingers, my tongue, my knife, even my…"

Good grief. "…we don't have all evening, Marc. Fucking finish your sentence," I say breathlessly, throwing his words back at him.

Something unreadable crosses his eyes, and he blows out a frustrated breath. "I'm an asshole, D. A ruthless asshole. A controlling, overbearing one at that. But I'm your asshole. I'm not going to change who I am. Not today, not ever. But I'll burn down the whole fucking world for you if you ask me to. That includes those assholes, the ones that hurt you so bad that it took you eighteen fucking years to ever trust someone enough to touch this perfect body of yours."

Good grief.

Does he have to be so fucking sentimental? I didn't know he had this side to him.

Liar. Of course you fucking knew.

"You think… Do you think you can handle it? Being with a man like me? A man constantly obsessed with every inch of your perfect body?"

While he talks, he pushes his thumb into my mouth.

"I'm here, aren't I?" I mumble around said thumb.

Then, just for good measure, I wrap my lips around his thumb, pulling it further into my mouth before sucking on it hard. Like a pacifier.

Except I know this action connects directly with one of his many erogenous points. The evidence of it is his cock that continues to swell against my core.

"How are your multitasking skills?" he groans, his voice strained.

Releasing his thumb with a pop, I say, "Quite good. Why?"

"Let's test it out, shall we?"

Okay? "And how do you suggest we do that?"

A sinister chuckle rumbles through him. "Get my cock inside you before I'm done with your lips."

"Which hole?"

"Lady's choice."

It's not enough warning before he tips up my chin to claim my mouth in a hard kiss.

A few seconds of stunned inertia pass before my brain kicks into gear, prompting my fingers to work on his belt. A moan escapes my chest when he shoves his tongue into my mouth, the taste of peppermint flooding my senses. My heart beats at a frenzied pace as his tongue tangles with mine. Fingers fumble some more before his fly jerks open.

I reach inside, thrilled to find he chose to go commando for this. Convenient, and also fewer layers of clothing for me to wrestle with. His mouth gentles on mine as I give his cock a few hard tugs, tongue languidly licking the inside of my mouth.

When he eventually draws back, we are both breathing hard. I don't know what's going through his mind as we stare into each other's eyes, but I'm thinking, *why the fuck didn't we do this sooner? And can we get back to it?*

His lips. They're sweet and warm, like honey. I can't get enough of them.

"Need help?" he breathes, his warm breath commingling with mine.

"I'm good." I give his cock another tug, harder this time, wondering how on earth I will get him inside me when my pants are in the way. Not without physically standing up, and I have zero desire to do so right now.

He makes a noncommittal noise before his lips return for more, deepening the kiss. My body goes soft and liquid on the inside and outside, hands going limp on him, their task quickly forgotten. My core contracts in anticipation, aching with the need for him.

The sound of fabric tearing draws me out of this delirious haze. I break the kiss first and pull away from him. My skin tingles everywhere — from my lips to the tips of my fingers to the rest of my body.

Well, not tingles — pin pricks along my skin from the tip of the pocket knife he's using to rip the fabric of my brand-new blouse apart at the seams.

"That was new," I say softly, watching as what's left of it falls to the floor.

"I'm aware. That's what you get for taking too long." He moves to the waistband of my pants, the blade tracking along the skin of my stomach. "Hold still, or you'll get hurt."

I'm half-tempted to squirm on his lap just because. He has to know holding perfectly still is easier said than done. Especially when I'm visibly trembling with heightened need. But somehow, I succeed, my eyes tracking the blade's tip as it glides along my skin.

"Not the thong," I protest when he brings the blade back up. "This is my favorite."

"I'll like it even better in pieces." The knife falls to the floor. "You'll learn I loathe fabric getting in the way of what I want. Plan on buying two of everything, always." He hooks a finger into the waistband of my thong, knuckles digging into my sensitive skin. "On second thought, make that three." The fabric snaps in his hands like nothing.

"Asshole."

"You like it."

Hands dig into my ass cheeks, lifting me up like I weigh nothing before lowering me onto his cock. I lean over and brace my hands against his shoulders. My fingers dig into the solid muscle of his arms as I sink onto him slowly, every delicious inch of his hard cock disappearing into my pussy. A satisfied moan escapes my chest once he bottoms out inside of me.

"So fucking tight," he moans, eyes glazed over, neck muscles constricting. "Fuck, D. You feel so good," he sighs, heavy-lidded eyes fixated on me. He grunts as he glides out slowly, teasing my slit, before thrusting back in, stealing my breath. He does it again, and again, and again, all the while chanting,

I've been craving this pussy for far too long.

Innocent little whore.

Mine, mine, mine.

Add dirty, possessive talking to the ever-growing list of things that turn me the fuck on. My pussy gets slicker as the words fall from Marc's delectable lips. He keeps up a steady pace, drilling into me with slow, languid strokes that draw out my pleasure, taking me to the edge but not entirely pushing me off it.

"Marc…"

"Hush."

What a dick. At least he knows I don't care for what he's doing. Bringing me so close to the edge over and over, only to be denied.

Not that it changes anything.

We watch each other's eyes as he slowly lifts my hips back up and brings me back down, hips rising to meet mine.

"Do you always talk this much during sex?" I ask. It starts as a whisper but ends with a gasp as he slides out and thrusts into me again.

"It's called multi-tasking." A hand snakes between us, sifting through my curls to find my clit. "You should try it sometime."

"I can't…" I trail off when two fingers press on the small bundle of nerves, alternating between pinching and massaging. One of my hands snakes through his hair before resting on his neck, with my forehead resting on his. "You'll pull out, right?" I breathe, our breaths commingling as we pant and grunt.

"Not a fucking chance in hell."

I should've known. "I'm not…" A whimper leaves my chest. "What if…"

"If that's what you're worried about, so fucking be it, D. I'm coming in you, and you're gonna take every last drop of my cum, like the innocent little wallflower you are."

Again with the innocence crap. "I'm not—"

He cuts me off when he fists my curls, tugging hard. "Shut up and come for me."

That's all it takes. My vision blurs as I fall apart on him. Blood rushes to my ears, inner muscles clenching and unclenching on his cock as a toe-curling scream tears from my throat. He captures my lips in a brutal, possessive kiss, swallowing my screams while maintaining his steady pace, drilling into me with languid strokes that prolong my orgasm. His thrusts grow frenzied before he stills, then hot streams of cum shoot deep inside of me, lips still on mine as he groans through his own climax, seemingly lasting forever.

Satiated, I settle against him, boneless and thoroughly exhausted, my eyelids drifting closed. Even in my post-orgasmic lust-induced haze, I still feel the atmosphere change when Harris steps into the room.

The air around us — it's electrifying, like him.

His touch, too, as his fingers trail along the bare skin of my back. He hooks a finger in the band of my bra and unclasps it.

"She okay?" I think he's addressing Marc, but I don't like that they're talking about me like I'm not there.

I barely muster up the strength to lift my head, turning to face him with a satiated smile. "I'm okay," I assure him.

"You sure?" His voice is neutral, but I detect a concern for my well-being somewhere.

"She said she's fine." Marc's voice rumbles in his chest against the skin of my cheek. His hand cups my cheek, bringing my face back to lie against his chest. "She's still in one piece, H. I didn't break her."

"No, just her clothes."

Awww, they're squabbling over Defective Delilah. Isn't that sweet?

"Guys, I'm right here."

They ignore me, carrying right on. Maybe they didn't hear me. Whichever it is, I am far too content to move, much less disengage myself from Marc's cock. Which, if I'm not mistaken, is starting to twitch inside me.

More words are exchanged between them, but I don't catch any of it. I drift off to sleep because that's as much as my body can handle. The last thing my muddled brain registers is the feel of solid arms draping over my body, heat from either side of me as I'm sandwiched between them.

I could get used to this for the rest of my life.

31

HARRIS

I could get used to this view.

Delilah's sumptuous brown hair spread on the pillows, her slender body spread out on our sheets. This is one of those rare times when she's genuinely resting. Not a nightmare in sight. Not a nervous or impatient tic to be seen. She's not fidgeting with the incision along the right side of her rib cage. Even better, she's not even hiding it. I could watch her all day without regrets when she's like this.

I would've done it, too, if not for the hard, familiar hands that grab me from behind and pull me in for a hard kiss. One I happily and hungrily melt into, reveling in the commingled tastes of peppermint and coffee — an odd combo but one that is so uniquely him.

I could kill for a fresh cup of coffee, or satisfy my caffeine fix by drinking it from him. Option two sounds much more appealing, even though it's not practical.

Our kisses evolve, going from hard to soft, fast to slow, until I'm the one chasing Marc, trying to bring him back. But as always, he redirects our course and skillfully maneuvers us outside the bedroom. The door closing with a soft click is enough to jar me out of the lusty haze he drew me into.

We're both breathing hard when Marc takes a step back. He takes one of my hands in his, lacing our fingers together.

"Spoilsport," I moan in denial.

"You make it far too easy," he says in a low and gravelly voice. "We need to talk."

"Uh-huh. Before or after you finish what you started?"

I go back for seconds, but he places a palm on my chest. "Before," he answers with a rueful chuckle. "Preferably downstairs. D doesn't need to hear this."

When he gets that sinister tone in his voice, I know better than to argue with him. We make our way downstairs and to the first-floor kitchen, as far away from Delilah as is humanly possible in this humongous estate. Suffice it to say, I already do not like the feel of this.

Marc prepares our morning coffee, moving about the kitchen with ease and grace. Usually, I would sit back, relax and enjoy the view, except I am now far too wound up from the suspense of it all to appreciate it.

"I was served with another injunction yesterday," he finally says as he sets a steaming mug before me.

Ah, coffee. All black and scalding hot, just how I like it. Too bad I'm far too irritated to actually enjoy it.

Despite the numerous barstools that line the edge of the massive island, I hoist myself up and onto the surface, crossing my legs underneath my body in a yoga-type meditation stance.

"What did this one say?

There's a tic in his jaw before he says, "Alienation of affection."

Yeah, I do not like the feel of this at all. "My dad again?"

He nods.

I'm not in the least bit surprised. My dad has been serving Marc with those things for as long as we've been together. Sixteen years. You'd think he would have given up by now, but the man is like a dog with a bone. Before Marc, he served papers to anyone I dated or was friends with, going as far back as middle school. He didn't stop even after I left home and legally changed my name.

Nothing kills a friendship faster than being served with a fucking injunction for alienation of affection. And oops, your friend isn't who he says he is, so here's all these conspiracy theories for you to ruminate on.

Back then, I never knew what he was doing to my friends and their parents behind my back. Not until Marc told me about it. I just assumed I was terrible at making friends, and in a twisted way that brought us closer together. Until I turned out not to be the perfect son he wanted, that's when he threw me out.

Now, thanks to him, what few friends I did make ended up distancing themselves from me eventually. But not Delilah. Funnily enough, getting served one of these letters convinced her to change her mind about being my friend. Never mind that I had been chasing her around for about a year at that point. Then I introduced her to Marc not long after that, and the rest is history.

I guess I have him to thank for that, but the bastard doesn't deserve an ounce of my gratitude. I know she gets these letters from him still, on occasion. She is one of the few people in my life who haven't been scared off by him. She isn't even slightly intimidated by him because Delilah doesn't intimidate easily. On the contrary, she does the intimidating.

She scares him too. So much so that he even went so far as to try and get her killed. For which he was relieved of his middle finger for his troubles. Marc did the honors then — while I watched, of course — since one has to take that extreme approach with people like my dad to drive home the point.

Don't mess with Marc's people.

It didn't get him to completely back off her then, but it did get him to slow down some. I don't think he can afford to lose any more digits, but time will tell. On the plus side, the frequency of the alienation of affection injunctions significantly slowed down, though they didn't stop.

In his twisted mind, it's his way of showing concern for my well-being. Never mind that it's too little too late. What little hope there was for reconciliation between us evaporated the day I discovered he was the one who chased off my mom. He used her and threw her out like trash, all because she wouldn't conform to his idea of the perfect wife. He also thought he could do a better job parenting than she would have, so he set out to raise the perfect son as a single father. He wanted that son to be the perfect mirror image of himself, and he didn't want a woman's influence sullying all that up.

That failed spectacularly.

"How many body parts does the man need to have removed before he gets it through his thick skull that I won't leave you? I'll have to die first, and even then my lovesick ghost still won't leave your sorry ass alone."

He chuckles at my ill-timed rant. "You know I love it when you get like this, don't you?"

I pin Marc with a playful glare. "You poke fun, but it's been sixteen years. Why won't he take a fucking hint?"

He shrugs. "Beats me."

"Can't you just kill the man already?"

He lets out his signature sinister chuckle. "Which man? There's so many to choose from."

"Har har, very funny." I shrug. "My dad has instigated enough trouble in our lives, don't you think? Losing a finger didn't teach him a lesson, clearly. Let's take things up a notch this time. An arm or a leg should do the trick. He can bleed to death for all I care."

I'm not even kidding when I say this. As far as the saying *'blood is thicker than water'* goes — which happens to be one of my dad's most used quotes even though he clearly doesn't comprehend its true meaning — I'm better off with arsenic-laced water. At least I'll have a hand in the thing that kills me, not an unexpected knife in the back.

"And people call me the twisted one." He places a palm over his heart in mock surrender. "The man really did a number on you."

"What do you think? Rumor has it he had my mom killed not too long after he chased her off. There's no love lost between us."

It's never been proven, nor has her body ever been found. For all I know, her demise wasn't as grim and she simply wanted out of their marriage. And as soon as he gave her an out, she took it and ran with it, as far away from him as possible. I know I did. Maybe not as far as she did, but I changed my name and distanced myself from him as much as I possibly could.

Who knows? Maybe she's somewhere out there, living a glorious and fulfilled life.

"Most lawyers in this town are a dime a dozen, your dad included. So no, I will not be killing the man. I don't think anyone would bat an eyelash if someone else did. If he goes, another one will simply take his place. No one can touch you if you make yourself indispensable like I have."

I give him a rueful smile. He might be the illegitimate son of the infamous Lorenzo Sotelo, but he's positioned himself to be truly indispensable. Making sure he knows where all the bodies are buried gives him additional leverage over all the key players in this town, including those in his own family. It's one of the reasons why even though most of them aren't thrilled with our relationship — except for his dad, who fucking idolizes him and his sister — they wouldn't dare publicly oppose him since that means opposing Lorenzo by extension.

That, and Marc has got dirt on them, which could land them in jail or worse. That's his thing. Collecting dirt on people. No one does it like he does.

What they do not know, however, is that he's amassed quite a few bodies himself. The psychopathic fucker takes that knife of his quite seriously. He also takes Halsted's model of "see one, do one, teach one" seriously. Funnily enough, his mom taught him everything he knows in that regard. Shocking, I know. Who would have thought the most ruthless contract killer for the Sotelo's Midwest chapter was the soft-spoken Sarah Bardales? Not me, that's for sure.

To pay it forward, Marc took David under his wing six years ago.

It makes their murderous little hearts happy, so who am I to judge?

Besides, they have standards. Not everyone deserves the sweet relief that death brings. Sometimes it's more fun to psychologically torture them. The threat of death is a compelling motivator, especially when it's followed up by the loss of a body part or two... or five. The ones who lived to tell the tale, like my dad, know better than to publicly name him as their attacker. Not unless they want all of their dirty laundry aired out, or to find themselves on the wrong end of the law with all the dirt he's got on them.

Then there's also the fact that Marc is as ruthless in the courtroom as he is outside it.

"I like toying with him," Marc adds. "He's like a caged bird who acts oblivious to his captivity. That false sense of bravado feeds my demonic spirit."

"I love the way your twisted mind works."

I've always known he's a ruthless demon, but he's my ruthless demon. Mine and Delilah's now. I trust that he would never hurt anyone who didn't deserve it.

"That so?" He glances at my not-steaming mug. "Then you're going to need that for what I'm about to say next."

"I highly doubt that."

His brow lifts as though to ask, *you sure?* before continuing. "The injunction your dad served me with wasn't for you."

There's only one other person it could've been for then, and she's currently upstairs, asleep in our bed, oblivious to the world.

It makes no sense.

The man hates her almost as much as he hates Marc, so why would he serve up injunctions on their behalf?

"What the fuck does my dad want with her?"

"Not him. The McWhorters. Andrea and Matthias McWhorter. Your dad's firm represents their interests now. They must have had a falling out with their old law firm. There's a lot of that going around with the clients of that law firm ever since David jumped ship six years ago."

"Back up, why would my dad work for those pieces of shit?"

He shrugs. "Money. Why else?"

"That's as pathetic as it gets. Sheesh. The man really has no morals whatsoever."

I know he's always been obsessed with money, above all else. It has always been his weakness. Money makes weak men turn into monsters real quick.

It's sad, really.

But what else can I expect from the man who tossed his own child out on the streets simply for being himself? A man whose entire identity as a father was so wrapped up in his version of the perfect son that any hint of something different threatened that, and he tossed said son out on his ass.

It's no wonder said son changed his name to get as far away from him as possible.

Said son is me, for the record.

So maybe I didn't get as far away from him as I wanted, but I legally changed my fucking name as soon as I turned eighteen. I liked that name too, but I like the one I have now even better. It's a nod to my mom's heritage. An acknowledgment of the woman who should have raised me. Not the narcissistic monster who did.

The narcissistic monster who couldn't wrap his head around the fact that his perfect child wanted nothing to do with him as an adult and thus did not take it well. And who has, in turn, set out to make my life unpleasant every chance he got. Ergo, those fucking injunctions, plus a slew of other things I don't even want to get into.

"What do they want with her now?"

He snort-laughs. "The McWhorters paid for all the fertility treatments her parents underwent to have her and her sister. What do you think?"

"What do I think? I think they got her sister for twenty years. Since that didn't work out, are they moving on to her now?"

He indulges me in my thought process. "Well, there *are* two of them to choose from. Dahlia has always been the main choice, Delilah the spare."

"The defective spare, you mean." I can't help the retort or the bitterness laced in the words falling from my lips. "Did they conveniently forget that she's a person who literally had no control over how her body was formed? How is being born with a congenital heart defect her fault? Granted, she's had two open-heart surgeries, and she's survived. So where do they get off on calling her defective? Bunch of idiots is what they are."

Marc nods in understanding. "Defective or not, in their minds she's still their spare. You best believe they want their spare back. The injunction proves that, in so many words."

"Jesus. They are people, not commodities."

"Not according to the contract their parents signed."

"What fucking contract? When was this?"

"Thirty-something years ago."

"Well, I guess it's too bad their parents are dead. How can they enforce it when the people who signed it are gone?"

As if I need any more reason to hate those assholes.

"Because they can. You know that something like this won't hold up in court. This isn't the sort of laundry they want to be airing. What they did back then was lauded as a good deed. Andrea doing a good deed for her infertile childhood best friend. Imagine the backlash of it once their true intentions are made public."

"Is it possible that the McWhorters fudged the details of their contract?"

His brow furrows with a contemplative stare. "Possibly. I'd have to see her parents' version of it, though."

"Have you?" I nudge him impatiently. "Seen it, I mean."

He shakes his head. "It wasn't with the rest of the paperwork from their estate. The twins might have it and not know that they do. If it were me, I would hide it amongst something else. Like with my research papers, that is."

"So it could be in their house then?"

"Probably. I'll chat with D and her sister, then I'll file a response, and we can all forget about it."

"Until the next one."

He waves me off. "Don't be such a downer. In the meantime, I have an idea."

Because I love him, I humor him and go along with it. "What has your twisted mind come up with today?"

He rasps his fingers against the surface of the island. "Their issue is with me since I'm the big bad wolf who supposedly corrupted their innocent little wallflower. So why don't we make a public statement?"

"A public statement?" I don't like the sound of this. "You want to go to the press with this? The same press that keeps printing all those conspiracy theories about the Brewer sisters? They've recently changed their tune but still left a sour taste in my mouth."

Marc laughs. "Absolutely not, and no."

Good. "So, a press release then?" I hate the sound of that even more.

"No. I want to make a grand gesture, so think bigger."

My eyes narrow. "You want a coming-out party," I deadpan.

It sounds absurd saying it out loud, but I'll roll with it since he did say to think bigger. With Marc, this is as big as it gets.

"Yes, a coming-out party, like what we did with you when we announced your name change and all."

He nods as he says this, liking his idea.

I didn't like it then, and that was sixteen years ago. Delilah isn't a fan of parties either, and that's recent. I love him, so I'll humor him and keep on rolling with it.

"And where would this party take place... here?"

He eyes me as if I've suddenly gone crazy. "And have people I don't particularly care for traipsing about in our space? No thanks. We met our once-a-year party quota already."

That's what I thought. "Where would this supposed grand gesture take place?"

His lips curl up and into a sinister smile. What I see in the depths of his eyes freezes the blood in my veins.

"Don't say it…" I whisper, air locked in my throat.

"The Sotelo Annual Ball," he says, his gaze stays on mine. "Or whatever they're planning on calling it this year. It'd be fun."

Yeah… fun is not the word I'd use to describe it. Not when it's just another excuse for the wealthy to throw their weight and wealth around.

Lavishly obnoxious is what it is.

It's also an excuse for the wealthy to show off their affluence and for the hopefuls to get in on the action — rubbing elbows with the rich and powerful.

Why can't they just do it as a fundraiser or something? There are plenty of worthy causes out there that could benefit from an event like this. That way something good comes out of all the schmoozing that goes on in one night.

Marc and I go every year. Courtney, and now baby Charlie, join us. We get dressed to the nines too. I loathe every moment, but I do it anyway because I love him. I know he's doing it to make a statement too. He doesn't care what people think of him or our relationship. Not only that, but he'll rub it in their faces every chance he gets. Especially those members of his family who think it's wrong for someone like him to openly live the lifestyle we do.

What better way to do so than at this event? He did it with me sixteen years ago, and it all worked out for the best. He'll be showing up with both of us, draped on either arm this time. It will be the ultimate grand gesture.

A collective *fuck you* to all of them.

32

DELILAH

Waking up alone is the last thing I expect, especially since I fell asleep with two men flanking either side of my body. But that's what happened the following day anyway.

After a quick shower in the impressive en suite bathroom, I make my way to the master closet with a towel draped around my naked body. Since the tour ended in the bedroom, we never came in here yesterday evening.

It is enormous and impressive, around half the size of the master bedroom, with wrap-around wall-to-ceiling closets sectioned off into three separate areas roughly equal in size. There's even a sitting area in the middle of the room. It's easy to tell which area belongs to whom. To the left is Marc's — his suits, all in shades of black and gray, are a dead giveaway. Harris's is to the right — his assortment of clothes and shoes have a lot more color.

What surprises me the most is the middle section, slightly larger than Marc's and Harris's areas and complete with a built-in makeup vanity dressing table. It's clearly designed for a woman. I know they've never lived with a female partner before, and they didn't bring any former partners to this house — except David. With everyone else, they went to hotel rooms or met at one of their swing clubs.

What's more, this looks like it was always meant to be here and always meant to be mine. It's filled with more clothing and shoes than I know I own. Some of my clothes have been hung up. The bulk are hanging from the racks to the side and still being put away. I vaguely remember Harris telling me I wouldn't have to worry about it.

"Sleep well?" a deep voice says from the doorway.

I let out a tiny yelp, jumping in place before turning to face him. I'm still clutching the towel over my body, a gesture that elicits a chuckle from him.

Electricity shoots straight between my legs at the sound, desire pooling between my legs.

"Don't sneak up on me like that," I can't help but scold, placing a hand over my erratically beating heart. I haven't taken my medication yet, so this isn't helping.

Harris leans against the doorway, looking every bit as delicious as he's always looked. His blond hair is tousled, swept off to the side and away from his face. This showcases his natural olive skin, sultry brown eyes, high cheekbones, sculpted jawline and chin, his chiseled features.

Then, as if he's intent on driving my heart rate up even further, all of those decadent features of his are barely concealed. He's wearing sweatpants that fall low on his hips, and the rest of him is on display as he is shirtless and barefoot.

He tilts his head, eyes raking over me. "Didn't mean to scare you."

I clamp down on the laugh that threatens to bubble up to the surface. If only he knew. He doesn't scare me, not in the traditional sense, but he does other things to me. Whenever I'm around him, which seems to be happening a lot more recently, my stupid heart goes erratic for entirely different reasons.

I let my eyes roam all over his body, as much of it as he has exposed, and now that I know just what he's packing under those pants, I want more. More of him. More of this.

Forever sounds pretty good right about now.

"You didn't," I mutter, clutching my chest and willing my suddenly spiking heart rate to settle down, but for entirely different reasons than being scared.

"I just wanted to know if you slept well. You know, after..." He trails off, his eyes casting downwards.

Heat flames my cheeks. "Yeah, I think so. I don't remember much of what happened afterward. I..."

"You passed out," he finishes for me.

"Oh. Is that what happened?"

That's not how I remember it.

He won't look at me. I don't know why, but this feels an awful lot like cheating. Which makes no sense, I suppose. Then again, nothing about this makes sense. We haven't gotten around to discussing the rules, if there are any boundaries for this. Who gets whom when? Is there supposed to be some sort of a schedule here? Just what exactly is it that I'm supposed to be doing while I'm living here?

"Harris—"

"It's fine, Delilah." He lifts his head, and our eyes meet. "I get it; why you passed out. Your heart, it's fragile. If there's anyone who understands that, it's me."

"Okay."

"We're going to have to do something about that. Diet, lifestyle, the works. Build up that stamina of yours. You can't go through life like some sort of clinical robot, you know? Maybe you like living like that, but you don't have to now. Not anymore."

Harris is saying a lot of things again. Logical things.

The things someone would say as they skirt around their true feelings.

I still remember what Marc said last night about this being a win-win scenario. I was hoping Harris would be possessive when it comes to me, but that's not what I'm feeling from him. All I'm getting is more of his protectiveness, and I don't want that from him.

I'm not sure what I want from him anymore, but I know that my body needs him badly. She desperately aches for him, as in, right now.

Especially with his eyes on me, practically eating me alive. Something I very much want him to do right now. And those lips, moving — wait, they stopped moving.

Why did they stop moving?

Now he's looking at me expectantly.

What was he saying? Is he expecting me to answer?

Think, brain. Think. "About last night—"

He runs a hand over his face. "I said it's fine, Delilah."

My heart stutters at his words. That's what he says when he's masking his feelings.

I'm fine.

It's fine.

It's all good.

He masks the hurt in his eyes, but I still hear it in his voice.

"I wanted you," I power on, side-stepping his non-answer answer. "Last night, I wanted you. I still do."

That elicits a sort of reaction from him, a peek of interest that flashes through his eyes.

"Okay," is all he says. Nothing more.

Or we're back to the mixed signals.

So I take that as an encouragement to continue. "We never quite got around to discussing the logistics of all this. I don't... I'm not used to this, okay? You two have experience with this; I don't. Is there some sort of schedule? Do you two get to pass me back and forth with each other at will? Do I get a say in the—*eep!*"

At some point in the middle of my incessant rambling, Harris closed the distance between us. He picks me up like I weigh nothing, startling a second yelp out of me as my legs wrap around his body, ankles hooking around his waist for support. Moments later, my bottom connects with the extended closet shelf's hard but slightly shaky surface.

"Do you know what I thought the first time I saw you all those years ago?"

I shake my head. "What?"

He rips the towel from my hands and off my body, tossing it to the floor. Then he crowds me in, his hands on my naked hips as he digs his fingers into my sensitive flesh.

"Mine," he growls, his eyes pinning me in place.

It takes me a minute to process his words. "Yours, huh?"

He nods. "I suppose I should amend that to *ours.*"

"There's a difference?"

"No, I suppose not." Another laugh bubbles from his chest, but it's strained. "When I say you are ours, I don't just mean your body. I mean your soul. And since we are greedy fuckers, we want it all. All of you. No exceptions. You are ours, Delilah, and in turn, we are yours. No exceptions either. No holding back."

He's giving me everything I've ever wanted, just like that. It's all too much and just perfect all at the same time.

Drawing in a staggering breath, I release it slowly. "I can promise you the first part," I say honestly. "As for the second part, that will follow with time."

What I don't tell him is that time is already here. I can't tell him I already belong to them, body and soul. I would love to, but the no exceptions clause has me tripping. It means I'll have to confess all to them. Including the two things I want. Marc wants one of those two things, and I also know that is the one surefire thing to get Harris running for the hills.

Which I don't want either.

But that can be a problem for another day.

Today's problem can be easily solved. I need him in me, but he's still half-dressed and I'm fully naked. If the look in his eyes is to be believed, trusted even, I'll be getting my wish this morning. This is what I wanted last night but was too exhausted and thoroughly satiated to ask for.

But this, with him right now... I could use some gentle. That's what he is. Gentle. Intense. Passionate.

The kind that absorbs and enmeshes you. The kind that hurts and heals you.

That's what I want right now. It's what I need, and only Harris can give that to me.

33

HARRIS

"I need you, Harris."

It wasn't until she said the words that I realized how badly I needed to hear them from her. She lets out a needy whimper as I move both hands to frame her face, tipping her chin up so my eyes can rake all over her.

My thumb traces her bottom lip. "I would very much like to kiss you now."

As I lean in she says, "I'm too heavy for this shelf."

I pause to consider it, my eyes piercing hers deeply. "I don't care."

She reaches up, sliding her hands around the back of my neck. "You should. Kissing almost always leads to other things."

My jaw clenches as I consider her answer, a repeat of my words from yesterday. "Since you care so fucking much, where do you suggest I do that then? The settee over there? The countertop in the bathroom?" A pause, then, "Our bed?"

"Yes, please," she breathes.

So I pick her up again, and her legs stay wrapped around my waist. "Which one? Use your words."

"Our bed."

My lips claim hers, and before she knows it, her back hits the bed's surface. I am that far gone for her, and she has no idea. I settle myself between her legs. Lining myself up against her core, it's a sweet, blissful relief when I finally press in. There are still too many layers between us. Too many clothes on me, none on her.

That needs to be remedied immediately. Still, I can't help but say, "Just so you know, this is more than sex."

She smiles. "I know."

Leaning in, I trail kisses along the hollow of her neck with my lips and tongue, lapping up the sheen of sweat that forms as she trembles in my arms. The most decadent mewling sounds bubble up from her throat. My lips are on hers, demanding, insistent. She squirms against me, making her intentions known. Shy of saying *fuck me*, that is.

I won't budge though. Instead, I plan on taking my time with her. My journey of exploration continues at a traitorously slow rate.

"Too many clothes," she groans, her voice breathy.

"Let's fix that, shall we?"

Pushing off her, I discard my sweatpants and boxers before reaching over to the side dresser for a condom. Her eyes stay on me as I roll it on, the look in them alternating between adoration and unadulterated lust. There's a hint of something else. Something that has those doleful eyes widening as I give my cock a couple of hard tugs and has her widening her thighs for me. Neither does she blink when I return to her, like I always will, settling between her legs again.

"We don't need those," she says as I line my cock up at her entrance. "Condoms, I mean."

A host of conflicted emotions thunder through me. On the one hand, I crave that feeling of being inside her with nothing between us, but on the other hand, it'll open up the door to other life-changing things, setting us down a path of no return.

"You sure?"

"Positive."

"What about—"

"We didn't use one our first time." She reaches between us to roll the condom back off. "He didn't use one last night either."

"It was safe then; it's not now."

"What's that supposed to mean?"

"Back then, you weren't…"

"…ovulating?" she finishes for me. "So you're tracking my cycle too. Good to fucking know."

"Delilah—"

"What's done is done. I'm not mad about it. Just curious. Besides, I think I like you bare."

"You think—" She cuts me off by hiking her hips up, taking me into the hot, silky clasp of her body in one smooth motion. I can feel her inner muscles stretching and flexing around my cock as she pulls me in deeper and deeper.

"That's enough talking," she breathes.

This woman will be the fucking death of me.

Drawing a staggering breath, I lean over and nip at her erratically beating pulse point, and she shivers uncontrollably under me.

"You will pay for that, Delilah."

The declaration sends a second wave of shakes snaking down her spine and limbs before convening at her core, making her even wetter than before — as if that were even possible. Moisture pools, and I slip out of her slightly. It doesn't help that she has little control over what her body is doing.

This won't do.

Flipping us over, I pull up into a sitting position. My hands grip her hips as I bury myself deeper before sliding down to her bare thighs.

"W-what are you…"

At the look of confusion on her face, I tell her, "I want to watch you come undone."

"Harris…" she mewls out in a whimpering sob, but I cut her off.

"Pain, huh?" With a growl, I grab fistfuls of her air and tug on it hard. "You like this?"

She frantically nods. "More."

"No," I say, slightly loosening my hold on her.

She hisses out a breath. "Harris, please…" My hand tightens in her hair, the other on her thigh. "I need more…"

The sounds she makes while she begs for this are even more of a fucking turn-on.

Win-win-win, like Marc says.

Except…

"I don't want to hurt you," I say in an attempt to soothe her, but I'm far too driven by lust to process the words coming out of my mouth. Truth is, I'm not even trying to be noble about this. I genuinely don't want to hurt her. Or maybe I do, but I still need to make up for all the twisted things I've done to her without her knowledge.

Maybe it's to make up for last night, when Marc fucked me so hard I could barely see straight, and then we both blew our loads all over her exhausted, passed-out body.

Perhaps it's for what I did seven years ago. For that fateful afternoon when I spiked her drink and intentionally shoved her into Marc's arms, thus setting in motion the sequence of events that finally led us to this point. It shouldn't have taken us this fucking long, though. That part was my bad.

Or maybe it's because I finally get to make love to the woman of my dreams, anytime I want, as often as I want.

Her eyes meet mine, glazed over with desire. "You won't hurt me."

A rough laugh escapes my lips since I have hurt her in the past. "You don't know that—" I start to say, but she presses a finger to my lips, shushing me.

"I know you, Harris," she says as she bounces slowly, riding up and down my cock in slight increments. "I know you'll never hurt me, not on purpose. You always give me what I want. You always give me what I need. Right now, I need that. I need this more than anything. I need you. Besides, I can take it, you know? Anything and everything from you."

"Yeah?" I can barely manage to force the word out. The exquisite feeling of her pussy squeezing on me with each little bounce makes it impossible to think, much less string together a coherent response.

"Do your worst, Harris. I can take it."

She really shouldn't say things like that. It unleashes the beast in me. "Ride me."

Never one to do as she's told, she does the opposite. With both hands on my shoulders, she leans into me and kisses me. It starts out sweet and tender but soon turns passionate, almost frantic. At the same time she lifts herself up on my cock, then slowly sinks down, taking every inch as our tongues desperately wrestle for dominance over the other.

"I said ride me, not fucking kill me," I force out between kisses.

A wicked giggle and a not-so-subtly-timed bounce are what I get for my troubles, forcing a groan of desperation from me. "Next time, ask nicely."

Then she does it again before slamming down on me hard. I hiss out a breath and tug harder on her hair. So she does it again, clenching even harder on my cock as she glides back on this time. I've had enough, so I release her hair and grab her hips with both hands, lifting and slamming her down on my cock with barely coordinated movements.

"Fuck! I… oh, more…" she cries out. Her face slumps into my shoulder as her body gives in to those uncontrollable shakes I crave so much. Her pussy squeezes my cock in rolling waves, snapping the last thread of whatever semblance of self-control I've been holding on to this entire time.

Not that there ever was any, not when it comes to her. The thought propels me close to the edge, teetering on the cusp of hurtling straight into oblivion.

"Eyes, Delilah!" I bite out, even though the hint of breathlessness in my voice betrays me.

It's a struggle, but she eventually does as I ask. It's equally challenging keeping my eyes on hers but I do, showing her everything I've got through my eyes.

She does too, and I see it all laid bare. Something dangerously close to love. Forever. Stability.

Home.

I lose it then, shuddering and groaning as we hold on to each other for dear life. My own climax barrels through me like a freight train, pulse after pulse of hot, all-consuming pleasure taking over as I shoot hot streams of cum deep into her womb. It goes on and on, settling in there, taking root in her very depths. Possibly her soul too, the one thing I so desperately want from her.

Our gazes lock, and we continue holding each other tightly. Even as our limbs shake from the exertion of our lovemaking session. Even as our holds slip, every inch of our skin is covered in sweat.

I could hold her like this forever.

"I love you." My voice cracks on the words as I voice the truth of what I feel.

A glossy sheen springs into her eyes. "I know."

It should be easy to say the words back, but I know she can't — not yet anyway. Just as I know she loves me. Her eyes have always told me as much, even if the words don't come easily to her.

Ultimately, it doesn't matter. I love her. My heart belongs to her and Marc, and that's how it will stay forever.

Her eyelids flutter and close, and a lone tear trickles down her face. Then she places a palm over my chest, right over my heart. "Mine."

Like hers, my own fragile, defective, erratically beating heart belongs to her.

Always has, always will.

34

DELILAH

D ate nights are a big deal around here. I underestimated just how seriously Marc takes this. He showed me a preview, and it still didn't dawn on me just how big of a deal this was.

It is a production from start to finish. He plans the menu, taking everyone's dietary needs and preferences into consideration. He hand-picks every ingredient, preps, and cooks it all. Then he has one of his men hand-deliver some to Dahlia, and we all pretend it came from me.

Since Harris loathes anything to do with grocery shopping, Marc usually goes alone. The first time this happened, I couldn't pass up the opportunity to tease Harris about being the worst house-husband in the history of house-husbands. Which is mostly true. He hates housework, not that I blame him since I'm the same way. But on occasion, I'm not above getting my hands dirty.

On week two, I let it slip that I don't mind grocery shopping, so Marc took me up on it immediately and asked if I would like to accompany him on the next excursion. I said yes, of course, because I really do enjoy spending time with him, something I never got to do a lot of before. Call it my own personal curiosity. Our sexual chemistry is off the charts. I just need to know if our compatibility carries outside of our bedroom.

It does, much to my surprise.

Being with him, it's not easy, not by a long shot, but it is effortless.

He's so domestic when he's like this. Strolling down the aisles, his fingers laced with mine.

The picture of domesticity.

We come upon the produce aisle, and his eyes light up with something indecipherable. Only then does he let go of my arm to inspect some tomatoes.

"Don't you have staff to get the groceries?" I tease, arms crossed as I study him. He looks like a kid in a candy store. Except those aren't candy.

"We," he corrects, "and this is relaxing."

He takes his time to inspect a Roma tomato, turning it over several times. You would think he were studying the Holy Grail or something, with how tenderly he's caressing the fruit. Vegetable. Whatever it is.

"Relaxing?"

He nods.

"Your idea of relaxing and mine are polar opposites."

I'm also referring to the fact that we came here in a limo. Not only is this a production, but it's also an extravagant one since Marc sometimes can be a bit much.

On the plus side, he's not a gentle lover and limos are roomier — the perfect combo.

"Some things are best done in person," he says, stormy gray eyes lifting to meet mine. "I used to do this with my mother all the time."

He doesn't talk about her much. Probably because all anyone ever cares about is his connection to his father, Lorenzo Sotelo.

"Your mom, is she...?"

"Dead? Yes."

"How—"

"Murdered when I was a teenager."

Oh.

"Marc, I'm—"

"No pity, please." The desperation, the hurt in his voice cuts deep.

I shift from one foot to the other, and my lips thin out as I watch him. Marc is silent at first, then a soft sigh comes from him. In a few long strides, he closes the distance between us. His hand touches my arm and he tugs me to him.

"Tell me about her," he says as he looks down at me and yes, into me.

"You first," I counter, returning his stare.

It makes no sense that he would bring her up now. A part of me wants to believe he knew what he was getting into when he made this proposition. We all have baggage. Mine is stranger than most, but it is my baggage. The prints of Simone, my parents, and Dahlia have been hung up at home, on the second and third floors, along with those of Marc's mom, Courtney, Charlie, and Harris's mom. They haven't asked about her since, and I haven't felt the need to explain. But Marc keeps checking in with me about my blank book of wishes.

He concedes first, and his gaze softens. "It's not personal, D. I generally don't talk about her much."

"Neither do I."

He nods. "Closure is a fickle thing," he continues. "Since Courtney took her death harder than I did, I have to pretend for her sake."

"I know." My voice hitches with a soft sigh.

I suspected as much, since Courtney doesn't talk about her much either. We've shared bits and pieces over the years — me, about my parents, and Courtney, about her mother — enough to understand that those wounds still cut deep.

It doesn't explain much about their standing in the family, like why they are still considered quasi-pariahs in his family. It's not lost on me, the things he can get away with. I don't know a lot about how mob families work. I do know his having a male partner doesn't sit right with certain family members, especially given who his father is. He has gotten away with it for this long because Lorenzo Sotelo is a bit of a man-whore, so he has many brothers and sisters to carry on his father's legacy.

"She wasn't a good woman. She just had the misfortune of getting entangled with him."

He doesn't emphasize, and he doesn't have to. The Sotelo family is complicated, to say the least. Marc and Courtney are the only children born out of wedlock to be publicly brought into the fold. There were rumblings within his family when this happened, as it was a ballsy move on their father's part that didn't sit right with many others. Then there was Marc's equally ballsy move that Harris still talks about to this day, which meant there was extra scrutiny on them both.

Marc is their attorney. Courtney is an artist, a forger. Publicly, Marc is the only one entangled in the family business. They both show up at family functions, do what is asked of them, and all that. In exchange, they seem to be mostly left alone. I wonder if it is enough for them to keep their clutches off him and Courtney.

"She wasn't innocent in all of it, so I don't hate him for it. Even though she was only a mistress, they really did love each other," he continues, his expression growing somber. "My father has a lot of enemies. He will get what is coming to him someday. I'm doing my best to ensure the ones I love don't get swept up in the aftermath."

"Oh?"

"I'm a control freak, D."

I roll my eyes. "You don't say."

He grins. "I cherish the ones I love and hold them close."

"Too close?" I tease.

"I do that too, yes." He traces a finger through my hair, following a strand and re-tucking it behind my ear. "I won't apologize for it."

"I don't expect you to. But you need to loosen up the reins just a little bit."

"Not a fucking chance."

His eyes meet mine, and a hardness flashes there, one I knew was in him. I have seen glimpses of it before, but he doesn't vanquish it now like he had the other times. For the first time, I see him. The real him, the one that exists beyond the walls he shows to everyone else, to me, to even himself.

"I don't fucking care if you hate me for it," he continues. "I'm not burying you because I got sloppy. Even if it comes to that, you need to know I don't let go of my things, in life or in death."

"That sounds a lot like forever."

"It is." His eyes stay on mine, staring into the depths of my soul. This is the real him, raw and unfettered, and as hungry as I am, maybe even more.

Then something he said earlier slams into me. "You-you love me?"

A glint of amusement flashes in his eyes, as is the odd little curve to his mouth. "That surprises you?"

That surprises me?

Talk about the understatement of the century.

"Well, yeah. I didn't... I never thought—"

He fists my hair and tugs my head back. "Stop thinking then."

Heat pools between my legs, and I gulp. "Why? Why can't I—"

His grip on my hair tightens. "Stop fucking thinking."

"Okay."

His hands drop to my hips. He pulls my body closer to his and firmly cements mine against his. The heat of his body melds with mine.

"No one touches the ones I love." His head lowers, his eyes still holding mine. They grow more intense as he talks. "Not H. Not you. Not Court or Charlie. I won't bother giving them a chance to live to regret it."

The look in his eyes is haunted and tortured, but a fierceness in them takes my breath away. Everything and everyone around us fades away, and there's only us. Here, in the now. Hunger licks my insides, lighting the fire inside me.

My arms snake around his neck, fingers curling over the back of his neck and bringing his lips closer to mine. "Are we done here?"

He grinds against me, and my breath hitches at how hard he is.

"We can be," he says, fingers digging into my ass cheeks.

Like earlier, my legs lock around his waist and we are moving. No sooner are we in the privacy of the limo than the knife makes an appearance. This is my second set of clothes for the day and they don't stand a chance against Marc and his damn knife.

Unlike Harris, I fight back. It only takes one wrong move on either of our parts for this to end differently, which only adds to the thrill.

What can I say? I know how to pick them.

Marc has a thing for knives, Harris for ropes, and Simone's thing was fire. In hindsight, I have always been drawn to danger. Occasionally, I barely toe the line of what is and isn't acceptable. Most of the time, I fucking jump right over the line, straight into the danger zone. The point of no return.

Defective, for sure.

Reaching between us, I make quick work of his belt and fly, shoving his pants and boxers over his hips. The car takes a sharp turn and we both fall off the seat. He breaks my fall as we slip onto the floor with a thud. It's like the universe is actively working against us.

He rolls us over so I'm underneath him.

Or not.

My legs fall open in invitation, and he sheaths our bodies together, shoving inside me hard.

"Fuck, D. You're already soaked and I barely touched you."

I lift a brow. "That surprises you?"

His jaw clenches. "I love you," he says, giving it a moment to sink in before adding, "but I'm going to fuck you like I don't."

He thinks it should scare me, but it doesn't. The fucking, I mean. Not the other thing.

"Do your worst. I can take it."

A part of me knows I shouldn't have said that, but I enjoy goading him since it has its desired effect each time. Marc's eyes glaze over, heavy-lidded with desire, and his mouth descends on mine hard.

There's nothing coordinated about our movements after that. Not when there's too much rawness and realness brimming at the surface. Even better, Marc is not gentle. I don't want gentle, not from him.

I want to be owned. Claimed. Desired. Tortured.

I want it all. Pain and pleasure, all of it.

I asked him to do his worst, which is what he does. It's exactly what he gives me with each hard, punishing stroke. The first climax thunders through me. It rips me apart and I swear I black out from the pleasure of it. The pleasure grows and blossoms on the inside and out, pulsating, throbbing, so powerful it sends me spinning and gasping out staggered breaths.

But Marc isn't done.

He keeps on thrusting.

His thrusts get rough, almost violent, and my hips lift to match each one. My fingers dig into his shoulders, urging him on. But the angle isn't doing it for him anymore so he pulls out. A needy whimper bubbles up from my chest, then it feels like I'm flying for a brief second. My back connects with the leather seat and he's inside me again, pushing up and all the way in.

"This okay?" he breathes, eyes studying mine.

"Since when do you ask?" I ask as I wrap my arms around his neck, fingers racking through his hair as I drag his mouth to mine.

Then he's back at it, pounding into me like his life depends on it. The back of the limo fills with the wet sounds of our bodies slapping against each other and our shared, heavy breathing. A hand slides between our slick bodies and he finds my sensitive nub. I shudder as he presses down on it with a punishing force while rocking his cock against a sensitive spot inside me. A second climax hurtles through me without warning and I lose it, thrashing against him as wave after wave hits me, searing through my body.

He mutters a string of curses but still doesn't let go, even as my pussy clenches around his cock, still throbbing and hard. His fingers dig into the sensitive skin of my hips, hard enough to leave punishing bruises behind as he continues fucking me.

"More," I hiss against his mouth.

He nips my lip. "You can't take it."

"I can take it," I breathe out. "We both know you're just getting started."

For a brief moment he looks conflicted. Why bother asking if he's going to second-guess the delivery?

Then he swears under his breath and pulls us back to the floor. Correction, he crushes my body against the floor, then he's back inside me. Owning my body, commanding it as he demands things of me. Not just my pleasure, but my heart too. At this moment, nothing else matters. Then again, when I'm with him like this, nothing much matters anyway.

"Say it," he demands just before sinking his teeth into the sensitive skin of my neck.

"More," is all I say in response.

What did he expect, a spontaneous declaration from me? That's not my style.

Slickness, bodies slapping against each other, the delicious feeling of the rug scraping against my back. There will be abrasions all over my skin from the rug, and I. Don't. Care. All I want is him. All I feel is him.

"Marc, I need more!"

Groaning, he pulls out and spins me over on my hands and knees before thrusting back into me from behind.

God, the angle!

I feel so impossibly full with him thrusting into me from behind like this. His hand snakes between my legs and presses down on my clit again. I come undone for the — who knows how many times this is — as my climax takes me apart at the seams, barely putting me back together.

With my pussy clenching hard on his cock, he comes too, with a roar, his body stiffening, jerking. He collapses on me, his entire body trembling against mine. Mine too, and it seems to go on forever, but it's a minute or so at most. I take the weight of his body, a welcomed distraction and blissful torture.

He rolls to his side, taking me with him. As I drift into that blissful space of sub-sleep and sub-alertness, I barely register his lips on my shoulder, his arm draped over my midsection, or the hard body curling behind mine, snuggling my body close into his.

All I know is it feels like heaven.

"Did you mean it?" I can't help but ask.

Marc's arm tightens around me. "H is going to kill me," he murmurs against my ear.

Funny, he wasn't concerned about that not too long ago. Or was it an hour ago?

That's how things tend to go when I'm with Marc. It's like years and years of sexual frustration unleashed upon us. Our reasons for staying away from each other are now obsolete. We're combustible when we come together like this.

And he's not wrong. Harris will kill him, and his funeral will be a hassle.

"I'll be sure to tell him I asked for it," I assure him.

He nuzzles his face in my hair. "We both know that means nothing to H."

I would and should laugh at the resignation in his voice, but I can't. All I can manage is a weak smile. "Did you mean what you said earlier?"

"Will you tell me about her?" he counters like it's the same thing.

It sort of is, but I can't tell him that.

Using his free hand, he cradles one of my breasts in his palm, his thumb brushing over my nipple.

A moan, then a startled gasp escapes my lips. "I'd like to hear it again."

"You first."

"Someday, when the time is right."

"Get some sleep," he murmurs against my ear. "I'll be right here with you."

Music to my ears. My eyelids are heavy, and the blissful sleep slowly overtakes me.

We are still moving. A soothing, rocking movement.

Nothing else matters as I drift off into sleep, swept up and under the blanket of exhaustion.

Although I could have sworn I heard him say, "I love you, D," one more time, his voice low and faint. Tired. Resigned. With a hint of elation somewhere in there. All conflicting emotions.

I'm not sure what to make of those.

35

HARRIS

After being cooped up in my workshop all day long, the sight that greets me in the kitchen truly is one to behold.

Marc doing what he usually does on Friday evenings, making dinner. Delilah helping, although I'm not sure how much helping she's really doing. He's more of a lone wolf when it comes to these things. But like everything else in our lives, Delilah is slowly but surely becoming the exception to all that.

Leaning against the doorframe, I take a moment to just watch them. Delilah is notoriously bad in the kitchen. The woman could burn water, and that would be the tamest of her kitchen antics. The way I see it, she's getting in his way more than anything, but he seems to be relishing the distraction.

Also, she has that freshly fucked glow about her, and she's not wearing any of the clothes I picked out for her this morning — which means my plan worked.

Sort of.

Until she lifts a hand to tuck a stray strand of hair behind her ears. That's when I notice them.

I push off the doorframe and stalk over to her. "Delilah."

She turns to me, her cheeks pinking up. "Hey."

I'm on her seconds later, pushing the arms of her sweatshirt out of the way to reveal more of them. "Jesus, Marc. What did you do to her?"

"Nothing," he answers, too quickly for my liking.

The abrasions all over her arms and elbows certainly don't look like nothing.

Her nose and forehead crinkle in confusion. "What is it?"

"Then why the fuck does she look like someone ran her through a cheese grater?" It's possible that I'm screaming and I don't care. Not when she looks like this. I take her shoulders in my hands. "Are you all right? What did Marc do to you?"

The blush creeps deeper, spreading past her cheeks, nape, and collarbone, traveling down her breasts — which are now inconveniently shielded by her sweatshirt.

"I'm fine," she says, her voice soft.

"You don't look fine. What about this says everything's peachy at Casa Sotelo?"

"What business is it of anyone's?" she asks, quirking her eyebrow at me.

Marc and Delilah exchange a look. He grins, then shrugs. It's one of his *I told you* so looks. It's the type of look that he and I used to exchange. I don't like being the odd man out, the one left out of the inside joke.

All this time, is this how she felt about those?

I give Marc a pointed look. "One of you, start talking," I force out, frustration seeping into my tone.

"Anybody ever tell you that you worry too much?" There's humor in her tone, which I don't particularly share.

In fact, it only makes me scowl harder, eliciting a giggle from her. "What happened here?" I ask, tracing a finger along her shoulder blades. Fuck, the bruises and abrasions span her shoulders. I'm willing to bet they go down her back too. I check, and yep, there they are. Also, on her knees. "Fucking rug burn? Marc, what did you do — fuck her on the limo floor?"

I watch her face as I ask this; in turn, she watches him, a dreamy look settling over her features. Her brown eyes sparkle, and she tucks her bottom lip under her teeth as she tries to hold back a smile.

Marc and I have shared partners before, so I should be used to this. All that was to prepare us for this, with her. But still, this is different. I still can't put a finger on this tightening in my chest. I'm not sure jealousy is the appropriate word for it anymore.

"And if I did?" His voice is low, husky.

I shift my eyes to him, to how they equally light up as he takes her in.

Come to think of it, he never did tell me why he was never interested in women. He just wasn't. Until Delilah, that is.

"Did you have to be so rough on her—"

"Harris, stop. I asked for it," she speaks out. "If anything, I goaded him into it. And even if I didn't, he won't hurt me."

I keep my eyes on him, studying his features. Features I am intimately familiar with. "You asked for it?"

"I did."

Sensing my eyes on his, Marc turns to me. "She needed it."

"Why?" I ask, the question directed at her.

"I'm not fragile, Harris." She hooks a finger under my chin and forces my face to hers, her golden-brown eyes darkening with desire. They go dark and lusty. "I like it hard and rough, and pain is an old friend. I won't break that easily. Not physically anyway."

I tuck a strand of hair behind her ear, my hand cupping and resting on her face. "I'll never stop worrying about you."

She moves into me, our bodies flush against each other. "I know."

Her head goes to my chest and she melts against me. For the first time today, just having her in my arms is soothing, like applying a warm balm to my aching soul. My hand goes up, running from the back of her neck to her shoulder blades, before moving further down on her back. I don't miss the slight flinch of her shoulders, but she doesn't tense up like I would expect. Instead, she's practically purring in my arms as her body turns gooey.

"He didn't do anything to me that I didn't ask him for," she murmurs against my chest. "I needed it. He did too."

My eyes dart up to meet Marc's again. He's watching the exchange between us, lips upturned in amusement, at my expense, no doubt. The apparent desire in his eyes gives him away.

"Mom came up," is all he says.

Ah. That explains that.

He gets overly emotional whenever his mother comes up, then he gets feral.

The fucking is pretty brutal, but it's also fantastic. Raw. Animalistic. As someone who has been on the receiving end of it myself several times, the sex is fucking incredible. And if her body language is any indication, she loved every second of it.

Still, this doesn't give me the warm fuzzies. Maybe that makes me weak or even an asshole, but I want to take care of her. Perhaps someone has to look out for her because she's always looking out for others. Maybe it's because I know how Marc can get — hell, I know how I can get, so I'm filled with this overwhelming need to protect her from us. Or maybe it's to protect her from herself.

I nuzzle my face in her hair and take a big whiff.

"Quit sniffing my hair," she protests, pushing off me. "I'm not sure whether to be flattered or offended when you do that."

"How about loved?"

She takes a moment to mull it over. "Unless it involves pain, I'll pass."

This thing with pain, it guts me that I didn't realize this about her. My best friend, but it simply never occurred to me to look. But Marc, the perceptive bastard, gets it.

All things considered, her need for pain and just how far she can push it is relatively tame. It's something Marc picked up on fifteen years ago — the why and the how she needs it. Just as he did with me sixteen years ago.

She and I are so alike.

While I like pain in many ways, it's a different kind of pain. The physical and sadistic kind, mostly. Hers tends to lean more towards the emotional, with a splash of the physical. Marc is just the guy to give us that exactly how we each like it. Because to us, he is that. Our protector.

But what does he need in return? Our protector, what does he like? And no, making us happy simply doesn't cut it. There has to be more to it than that, and it's something that quite frankly, I'm struggling to reconcile. After all these years, I'm still mainly in the dark. There are the obvious — family and money — but he has those.

Then there's the kids thing. I know where I stand on it. I know where Delilah stands on it. But Marc... most days I have no idea where the fuck he stands on the subject. Just as I didn't know where he stood with women until Delilah came into our lives.

Despite the manner in which we've been going about this — treating birth control like it's fucking optional in this house.

And no, Charlie isn't a fucking test subject regarding this.

As I ruminate on the subject and my own hang-ups about it, it dawns on me that it's not Delilah's cross to bear. Or even Marc's. It's my own fucking emotional baggage to deal with, and I really should deal with it. For all of our sakes, I need to and hopefully soon.

A gasp escapes her lips and she takes a step back from me. "Oh my god! We weren't quiet in the limo. Do you think—"

"Now's not the time to worry about that," Marc deadpans.

Her eyes meet mine, panicked.

"His drivers have heard worse," I tell her. "They all sign NDAs. Or is it something worse? I don't know. Marc takes care of those."

Something dangerously close to jealousy flashes in her eyes. "What the fuck?" she growls. "Who else have you fu—"

Not sure what stops the flow of her words, but they do come to an abrupt halt. It dissipates — the jealousy or whatever else I saw in her eyes moments prior. Something else takes its place. Something I can't quite make sense of.

As I hold her gaze, the look coming from her feels like a sucker punch to the gut. Again, I'm not sure if it is a good punch or not. Only that she is looking at me with this sudden new understanding. Vague understanding.

The kind that says *'I would rather be looking at him instead of you'* right now. Or an *'I'm sizing you up, but I'd rather be doing that with him'* look.

Dear god. I *do* do that, don't I? Complete with the head tilt. I've done that to Marc several times. Not intentionally, of course. But still, it happened.

Then, as if on command, her head tilts the other way.

"No one else," Marc says in response to her unfinished question. "Just you two."

Her head bobs in place, once, then twice, eyes remaining trained on mine. Searching, seeing into all of me, like she always does.

"Does that mean…?" she starts to ask, then trails off.

"Don't make me spell it out for you, D," Marc growls.

That shouldn't have gotten a reaction from me, but it did. Whatever emotion she sees there has a glossy sheen springing into her eyes. Reaching for my palm, she places it on her chest, right above her erratically beating heart. Then she puts hers over mine.

"It's not like that," she tells me. "I get it. I really do. But it's not meant to... I'm trying though."

Okay.

She saw right through me.

I loop an arm around her waist and pull her back in. She comes to me without a fight, like she always does. She fits perfectly in my arms, just as she is supposed to. Like how I fit in his arms. Or like how she fits in his arms.

So what the fuck is this? This strange yet uncomfortable feeling I've been wrestling with? I press my lips to the top of her head, eyes trained on Marc. Because as much as I'm saying this to her, I'm saying this to him too.

"I'm trying too. I just... I didn't think it would be this hard." It's perhaps the closest and the most honest I've come to admitting how I feel about this.

Her heart rate speeds up underneath my palm, in sync with mine.

I really, *really* don't like sharing Delilah with anyone else, and that's the gods-honest truth. Just as Marc never liked sharing me with anyone else. Even though he never came right out and said so, I always knew that it bothered him, yet he put up with it for my sake.

Granted, I never liked sharing Marc either, but it's different with Delilah. It always has been. But if I were to share her with anyone else, I'm glad it's with him. The two people who hold my heart.

Sometimes I wonder how he's handling this too. But he's giving me cool, calm, collected, and reasonable Marc. I don't like that version of him. When the animalistic, feral version of him lets loose, Delilah comes home with rug burns all over her back and knees.

"You two done with that?" Marc says with a laugh, but it's dry, sinister. "Dinner's ready."

Fucker.

36

DELILAH

I was never one to follow the rules. It helps when the pressure to be perfect isn't on you but on your sister instead. For thirty-four years, this has worked out in my favor — until now.

This is why I don't do forever. It comes with strings attached. Rules too.

Where Marc is concerned, there are plenty. Rules. Guidelines. Whatever else he calls them to make it palatable for me. It is not unheard of, given who his father is. But while everyone goes along with his rules, I make it a point to fight him at every turn.

Which is why his rules have now gone from absurd to straight-up ridiculous.

"I don't need a bodyguard," I tell Marc for the umpteenth time.

Even though they are seated on opposite ends of the couch, Marc and Harris exchange a look, knowing that I can see it.

It's *the look*. The same one that drives me up a wall.

I now see why Marc offered to give me a scalp massage. He knew I couldn't turn one down, so what better way to ply my body with endorphins while buttering me up with this ridiculous rule.

Harris joins in on it, scoots closer, and lifts my legs, settling them into his lap.

"This won't work," I tell them as they knead both ends of my body.

It might work. These two have magical and dangerous fingers, and I'm familiar with both.

"They are not typical bodyguards," Harris eventually says.

"That's not the point," I say, turning my attention to him. "I still don't understand why you go along with this. Don't tell me you are okay with someone tailing you everywhere you go, butting in on your business twenty-four-seven? Lurking around your workshop?"

He flinches. "That's not what they do. They don't guard us in the house."

"I know that. It doesn't mean I want them anywhere near me outside the house. I have a life outside of these four walls. I have clients, patients, a business to run. How can I explain their presence when most people I interact with expect confidentiality and privacy?"

Marc's fingers move to my shoulders. "That shouldn't be an issue. They're supposed to remain inconspicuous."

"That makes no sense."

He shrugs. "If you can tell who or where they are at any given time, it means they aren't doing their jobs right."

"What's that supposed to mean?"

"They are not to meddle with our everyday lives," Harris says. "You are not supposed to know who your designated bodyguards are."

"Again, that makes no sense. What happens if I figure out who they are? Or if they get sloppy?"

"They get reassigned." Harris purses his lips as he switches to the other foot. "At least that's what Marc said. I've had bodyguards for years and still haven't figured out who they are."

"You say that like it's a good thing when it's not. What if a fake team swoops in and you can't tell the difference? Then what?" It's not an entirely unfounded concern. Marc has a tracking device on my car and I let it slide. That doesn't mean that it can't be hacked.

"D, that would be impossible. I only hire the best of the best."

"Nothing is fool-proof."

Since Marc and I talked four days ago, I've been trying to give him some latitude with his overprotective streak, but that clearly isn't enough for him.

"I told you, I don't leave anything to chance. I know where you both are every second of the day. I also know what teams are assigned to you at any given time. Any unsavory characters would be taken care of, swiftly and quietly."

I swing my feet off Harris's lap, stand, then turn to face both men.

Or rather, I hone in on Marc. "This isn't a discussion. It's asking for forgiveness, not permission."

Marc's eyes go heated, flaring with some unnamed emotion. It's not anger or lust; whatever it is ignites shivers throughout my body, as if the scalp and foot massages were not enough.

Harris, on the other hand, glances between us. "Do I want to know?"

"Probably not," I tell him. "Still, I refuse to go along with this, and so should you."

"Walter," Marc eventually says.

"Who the fuck is Walter?"

"Your bodyguard." He says this as casually as one would comment on the weather.

"Hey, that's not fair," Harris immediately protests. "You said we're not supposed to know their names."

Marc's jaw clenches. "D is different."

"How is she different?"

"She just is."

"Who's mine?"

"Let it go, H."

Marc's phone goes off and he leaves the room to answer it.

I plant both hands on my hips and blow out a breath. "I'm still not doing it," I tell Harris once Marc is out of earshot.

He gives me a kind but patronizing smile. "Maybe."

There are no if's, but's, or maybe's about this.

Marc is a control freak; he said so himself. However, it still blows my mind that Harris thinks of all this as normal. This is not normal, it's absurd.

I frown. "It's a bit much, don't you think?"

He laughs and taps on his lap. "Come here."

"The bossing me around thing doesn't suit you," I tell him, even though I do as he asks.

He settles me on his lap, front to front. He reaches over and tucks a few loose strands of brown hair behind my ear before cradling my cheek. I lean into his touch as my eyes search his, my heartbeats going haywire, pounding so hard against my chest.

He swallows hard and my gut twists. His eyes scan my face, and I'm not sure I want him to voice whatever he's thinking.

But he does so anyway.

"I think you should do it," he says softly.

I think so too, I want to say, but the words lodge themselves in my throat.

So I lean in and press my lips against his in what is supposed to be a chaste kiss. As always, Harris has other ideas. His fingers curl around the base of my neck as he angles my face just how he wants, deepening the kiss. A moan rips from my throat when he shoves his tongue into my mouth. Our kiss quickly turns frenzied, as it usually does with us. Heat skips over my entire body and pools between my legs.

When he pulls away from me first, I'm breathless.

"D." His breath is shaky as he cups my cheeks in both hands.

I draw in a shuddering breath and close my eyes.

He murmurs, so soft again, "D, look at me."

I shake my head, coming out of my lusty daze. "Only Marc calls me that."

"I know. He calls me H." A chuckle. "D and H, that's what he calls us."

"Does he have something against using our full names?"

"Not really, he just means something else when he says that." He presses his lips against my temple. "Darling and Husband."

My eyes fly open at that. "What?"

He's silent for some time, his head tilted to the side. Those expressive brown eyes of his studying every angle of me. "Darling and Husband," he repeats.

"Yours makes sense. Mine doesn't."

He looks like he's going to say something else but decides against it.

"They still haven't gotten any better," he says instead, doubling down on the bruises on my body.

"Harris, this was my idea. I told you already."

"Still—"

"H, can I talk to you?"

37

HARRIS

Marc means business when he takes us to the third floor, ushering us straight into his office. Just as well, this conversation needs to be had. He knows I'm displeased by the stunt he pulled with Delilah last Friday, so he has been laying it on thick ever since. Or simply avoiding me for the most part.

This works out better.

"Harris, you seriously need to let this shit go," he says as he walks over to the bar to pour himself a drink.

We're using full names now. Just fucking great.

I shake my head. "We're not savages, Marc."

His shoulders tense. "You know, that's rich, coming from you."

"Meaning?"

"You don't have a problem with it when you're on the receiving end."

My heart twists in my chest, even as I say, "That's different."

"How so?" He sets his tumbler down, then turns to face me. "Because she's a woman?"

"That's not it." How easily the lie falls from my lips.

"She wants what she wants. We all do. Nitpicking at her sexual preferences and shaming her for it isn't helping anyone. We're supposed to be partners, Harris. Or did you forget?"

Why does he have to go straight to that?

Like I could fucking forget.

"Is that why you did that?" I'm grasping at straws, picking a fight where there isn't one to be had, but I don't care. "And who the fuck is Walter? Is that really her bodyguard's name, or did you make that up?"

"If you must know, she has three. Dahlia too." He folds his hands across his chest and leans against the bar. "Walter is the only one who alternates between their protection details. Any more deflecting questions?"

"Yes. Who's mine?"

"That's a non-starter. He has a job to do, and I can't have you reverting to your old tricks. In case you forgot, you're the reason they have to remain inconspicuous in the first place."

A flash of annoyance washes over me. "How long before you let that one go?"

"When you grow the fuck up and accept that this isn't a fucking game. Despite what you may think, switching out bodyguards every fucking week is a logistical nightmare. The same person would do a much better job of learning your routines and blending right in."

As far as explanations go, that one's pretty good.

"You got any more questions for me?" he asks, his stormy gray eyes searching mine. "Or will you quit dancing around the issue and fucking spit it out, the thing that has your panties all twisted up in a bunch?"

I take a deep breath, willing myself to stay focused as I slowly release it. "I love you, Marc. With everything I have, with everything I am. But I also need her. Alive. Safe. In one piece."

I don't know what I hope for with that, but this isn't it.

"She's not a porcelain doll," he says, his voice quiet.

"I never said she was."

After an eternity, he lets out a short breath and runs a hand over his face. "Delilah is her own person. What she needs is autonomy over her fucking body. She needs to decide for herself what she wants. What she wants to be done to her, when she wants it, how she wants it. Your hovering at every turn isn't helping. It's only feeding her guilt."

"Guilt? What the fuck are you talking about?" I ask incredulously, my chest heaving with punctuated breaths.

"If you keep treating her like some clueless, fragile little thing, then…"

The fucking bastard leaves it at that.

"Then what?" I prompt.

He says nothing at first. His eyes flick through the room before returning to meet mine. The hardness in them sends chills down my spine.

"Then you are no different from the McWhorters."

His words knock the air out of my lungs. I take a step back from him, then several, until my heel collides with the back of the couch and I sink onto it, dazed.

Marc says many things, and there's often truth to his words. But in this case, it is a hard truth I hadn't even seen myself. She's my best friend, someone I know better than I know myself. Yet, I've been blinded to this side of her all this time.

I shake my head and pinch the bridge of my nose. "I already hate it when you're right. What more do you want from me?"

"We need to discuss the other thing," he continues.

"What other thing?"

"This," he waves a hand between us. "The truth, for starters."

"Can't this wait while I fucking stitch my heart back together?"

He shakes his head. "As much as I'd like to ignore it, I can't. It has to be now."

My shoulders heave. "Fine. What is it?"

"Kids," he says softly.

Another gut punch. "What about them?"

He runs a hand over his face. Again. Slowly, this time. "She wants them."

Man, is he laying it on thick today. "Did she tell you that?"

"It's fucking obvious."

"Or you're just projecting, Marc." Fine, I *am* grasping at straws here.

He sees right through it. "I know you're not that dense, H. We don't use condoms with each other. We're not using them with her." A pause, then, "She's not on birth control."

"You don't know that." Again, I'm grasping at straws here.

"I checked her meds and no little white pills in sight." He lets out a dry laugh. "No IUD. No implant either, I would've felt that shit."

There's nothing wrong with being thorough, except I knew all that already.

"Instead of jumping to conclusions, why don't you get her all of that? You're the fix-it guy in this relationship, are you not?" I give him a moment to answer, and when he doesn't, I add, "I guess that's a hard pass for you, since it's what you want. Kids. What are you all up in arms about?"

He takes me in, lips pressed into a thin line, his jaw firm. While I love it when he gives me his full attention, this look doesn't make my heart flutter.

It fills me with dread.

"I do a lot of things for you, H. Not this. I already let it slide once before, never again."

"You promised never to bring it up again." My voice cracks with the words.

"I never promised. You asked, and I didn't answer. Don't bother asking again; the answer will always be no. I will not hurt her for you."

I wouldn't blame him for taking that stance, except that's not what he promised me sixteen years ago.

Even then, I know my saying this next part isn't fair to him either. "This all works out in your favor, so somehow that makes it okay, hurting me for her?"

He pushes off the bar and closes the distance between us in a few long strides. He crouches before me and takes both of my hands in his.

"H, this was your idea," he continues, his voice quiet. "From the get-go, you wanted to have your cake and eat it too. I'm not saying I'm innocent in all this, but let's acknowledge that I followed your lead for years. Which is why I'm going to say this, not to hurt you, but because I should have said it back then. Because I regret not saying anything back then and not saying anything since."

I shake my head in protest and my lips part, but no sound comes out.

"Seven years ago, you shouldn't have drugged her, then pushed her into my arms. You fucking knew better, but you didn't care. With the state of her heart, that shit could have killed her."

"But it didn't," I mutter.

"No, you got lucky, is all. You've had plenty of chances to come clean all these years, and yet you did everything but. You made her feel guilty for coming on to me, something she had zero control over. Then you made her believe it was her fault that we almost broke up. And this stupid game, what exactly did that accomplish? Other than make her think of herself as less than?"

"Don't you fucking put this all on me, not when your solution isn't any better. You're not using her as a fucking broodmare, not on my watch."

An assortment of emotions — annoyance, anger, resignation, resolution — flash in his eyes in rapid succession.

He's not the only one doing this to her. I am too, but putting the blame squarely on him makes me feel better. Better about this. Better about myself.

And yeah, I'm an asshole. I'm an even bigger hypocrite in saying this.

You.

Not we, you.

Word choices. It's all about the word choices, isn't it? And words, they really do cut deeper than the sword.

"That's not your decision to make. But you will fucking respect it, whatever she decides on. And while we are on the subject, get that stick of righteousness out of your ass. You might think you have a lot of time with her, but you don't. One way or the other, she'll die. It's what she wants."

"She wants to die?" I want to say he's projecting again, but even I know better.

"Honestly, H. I know you're not that fucking clueless. Her house is a fucking shrine to her dead parents and missing ex-girlfriend. She spent years distancing herself from the world, pouring herself into her work."

My heart clenches. "That's not true. She has friends."

His jaw clenches again. "You. Me. Court. Hurricane Dahlia." A pregnant pause, then, "Who else?"

I can't even answer that because he's right.

"Say we gave her what she wanted. One night, then we went our separate ways. What did you think was going to happen after?" There's a bite to his tone, one I don't particularly care for. "I can put all the safeguards in place. I can have a dozen bodyguards around her to guarantee her safety, but I can't protect her from herself. I sure as heck can't shield her from her own body."

"Didn't you say you're a miracle worker?"

"Don't be a dick, H. There's only so much that I can do. Quite frankly, I won't claim to understand why she does half the things she does. Why she came to us after dragging it out for so long, why we are doing this to her, or even why she's letting us. We all know what will happen, sooner or later, and by her own admission, she won't survive it."

Even then. "I can't lose her, Marc. I just can't."

"You're not the only one who loves her," is all he says.

A pause, then, "I know."

He lowers his head and turns away. "Instead of this overprotective bullshit, give her what she needs. Give her everything she needs, even if you don't agree with it. Even if you don't think it's what she wants or should have. Believe it or not, regret is not a path you want to go down. I would know."

Fuck. He does know.

That's the trouble with thinking you have all the time in the world.

Life is a fickle bitch.

Time too.

Like choices, time is an illusion. It's an excuse to linger on in our pathetic existence. While some people use time as an excuse to live recklessly, others use it to hold themselves back.

I know what side of the illusion I fall on. I wonder which side Delilah falls on.

But more importantly, I always wondered which side Marc falls on. That's one card he plays pretty close to the vest. Maybe too close.

PART IV

38

DELILAH

A girl can't have a moment of peace around here.

I can't blink without either of them coming to my rescue, if that's even what we're calling it. For the time being, I prefer the term hovering, but I don't exactly dislike the attention. If Marc and Harris insist on waiting on me hand and foot, twenty-four seven, I'm inclined to let them.

A small part of me acknowledges this is their way of coaxing me into going along with this absurd bodyguard idea, even though it has already been implemented. Then there was their chat, or whatever that was, from two weeks ago. I went to sleep alone for the first time in six weeks. That's how long their talk lasted.

Since then, they have been walking on eggshells around each other.

I don't understand it though. Marc and Harris are solid. All couples fight, it's a given. But this one feels different somehow. This feels like the tides have changed, and not in a good way.

Hence the hovering. Or smothering, if you will. It was sweet the first few days, but after two weeks of this, I feel a bit claustrophobic.

Like now.

Like a ghost, Marc appears behind me and wraps his arms around my shoulders, pulling my body flush against his. My body sags into his, even as every rational thought urges me to overpower this overwhelming lust and desire that takes over my body whenever I'm near them.

"I don't have much time," I say, knowing it won't make a difference.

He places his head on my shoulder, and his gaze meets mine in the mirror, stormy gray eyes questioning. "When's the appointment?"

"An hour." It's more time than that, but injecting a sense of urgency into this conversation might speed this up.

He already knows this. I'm supposed to meet Dahlia for her doctor's appointment in a few hours. He knows I promised to be at every one of her appointments. It's a promise I don't plan on breaking anytime soon, especially with how wishy-washy Curtis is being about this whole thing.

Meanwhile, all I want to do is brush my damn hair in peace, but Marc is in here, cornering me in the damned bathroom, of all places.

"You have thirty minutes to spare then." He tightens his hold around me, securing me in a safe cocoon I don't want to leave.

"That's not a lot of time." Placing the brush on the countertop, I reach up to slide my hand through his hair, clasping the back of his head. "I just bought this outfit, so try not to ruin it too much, please?"

"That's not why I'm here." He presses his lips to my shoulder, then his hand comes around my stomach, his palm splaying over my stomach in a possessive gesture. At the same time he observes my reaction in the mirror, his eyes hooded.

My breath hitches and coherent thought flees my brain. "I'm not... if that's what you're asking. Or implying." Still, my legs give out and my body melts into his.

The heated look in his eyes deflates a little, and I'd be lying if I said it wasn't a hit to my ego. "Is that what this is? Do you want me to be?"

He draws a sharp breath, holds it for a beat, and slowly releases it. "Tell me you're not just waiting around to die," he eventually says.

Talk about random.

Marc has been doing a lot of that lately, asking random questions entirely out of the blue. Most of the time they're about Simone.

"I'm not just waiting around to die."

Maybe he will stop asking if I put something in my book of wishes.

A ghost of a smile teases the corners of his lips. "Liar."

I drop my hands and turn around to face him. "Where's Harris?"

Usually his eyes would light up at the mention of Harris's name. Today he frowns, a sadness shining from him. "I'm not sure."

"Liar," it's my turn to tease him. "You know where we both are every second of the day."

His hands fall to my waist and he hoists me up on the countertop. "Not always, D."

"Since when do you leave things up to chance? That's not your style, Marc. Not even within these four walls."

He positions his body between my legs, his hand tunneling under my shirt. He finds my scar, and runs his thumb along its entire length, back and forth, over and over again. He's not the only one who's been doing a lot of that lately.

"What's going on? Is that why you two have been walking on eggshells around me?" When he doesn't answer, I add, "And around each other?"

His eyes roam my face, alternating between my eyes and lips.

"What happened?" I ask again.

His frown morphs, and so does the look on his face, from sadness to despair. "You."

Dread settles in the pit of my stomach. Still, I pull my shoulders back and force a smile. "Me?"

His chest rises and holds. "You," he repeats.

I reach up to cup both of his cheeks in my hands. "Coming between the two of you was never my intention."

"Yeah, well… it can't be helped."

Marc and his damn word choices. "Is it salvageable?"

I don't dare to repeat what we are both thinking. Which is something along the lines of, will this be a repeat of seven years ago? It nearly ended their relationship. With what followed after, I try not to dwell on it so much.

Neither does he, it would seem.

"Did you write something down?" he asks instead.

Leaning forward, I close the distance between us and brush our lips together. "Stop changing the subject," I whisper against his lips. "How bad is it? The truth, please."

A beat passes, then, "We have fundamental differences about your mortality."

I lean away from him as a flash of annoyance washes over me. "What? Why?"

"I don't know, D." One hand takes hold of my wrist, bringing it back down between us. His thumb strokes over my pulse on the inside of my wrist. "If there's one thing you could have right now. Anything you want, what would that be?"

My eyes narrow. "I'll ask again, why?"

"Apparently, I'm a miracle worker. It's what I do. My specialty is in making people's wishes come true."

"Not this time." I shake my head and pull my hand from his. "It's something I can't have."

He reaches for my hand again. "What's that?"

Even knowing I walked right into this, I can't help but say, "Same thing I always wish for."

His eyes heat up. "Then say the word."

"No."

"Why the fuck not?"

"Nothing is ever that simple. Even if you say it is, I'm not that gullible. And I would rather not get my hopes up."

"So?"

"Let it go, Marc. Please? Just tell me one thing. Why are you here? And why did you bring me into your family? As far as I could tell, you and Harris were doing fine."

"Well, sometimes looks can be deceiving."

"That's it then? What are these fundamental differences that you and Harris have about me? And don't you think you should be discussing them with me instead of amongst yourselves?"

His chest rises and holds. "There's no easy way to answer that."

"Try me."

He doesn't say anything but stares at me with an indecipherable look.

"Dahlia doesn't like that I'm living here," I say instead, even though it is half-true. She doesn't mind it, but she's not a fan of the rules Marc has in place.

His brow furrows. "I don't care what your sister thinks. She's not—"

"—welcome here," I finish for him. The frustrating thing is he wasn't subtle about it either, even after learning why I brought her here. Blowing out a breath, I roll my shoulders forward, then backward. "I know it, and she knows it too. Your attitude a few weeks ago made that quite clear."

Two weeks ago I found Dahlia on the floor of her office and in the middle of a panic attack. A bad one, too, and one she was trying to hide. She tried to convince me she was okay and had it under control, then asked me to take her downstairs to her darkroom and leave her there. Like that was going to fly. While it is true that her cold, frigid darkroom is her happy place and what grounds her, I'll be damned if I would've left her alone in that state.

I remember what it was like to live with those episodes and how debilitating they can be. When hers started, she tried to hide it, since maintaining the façade of perfection was more important to her than her own mental health. I was the one who insisted on dragging her to one professional after the other since nothing about them made sense. The fact that mine completely stopped when hers started, that she exhibits damn near identical symptoms to what mine were, that the intensity of hers is almost identical to what mine were, or the how and why that transference happened in the first place.

The sad thing is, I thought her panic attacks were gone. That's how absorbed I've been in my own shit and hating Andrea for the rollercoaster she put us through with this wedding planning business. It's been almost a year since I saw Dahlia have one, but I didn't realize she had gotten better at hiding it. Just as she should have realized I would be the last person to walk away from her.

So I brought her here, only for Marc to unceremoniously kick her out. Just when I thought those two were making strides in setting aside their differences, it gets reset to square one. He still cooks for her every Friday — and we still pretend those meals are coming from me — so there has to be something else causing him to dig in his heels further on the subject.

Hence the bodyguard talk and the added claustrophobic rules.

Unfortunately, I still don't think we've gotten the half of it. This situation reminds me of when Dahlia dealt with something similar up until three months ago, when she still lived with Curtis in the house Andrea bought and staffed for them.

"I live here too, you know? If Harris has no one he wants to invite over, that's his prerogative. But you do, and you don't see me complaining about it."

"D—"

"The double standard here is appalling. You have to know that.

Dahlia is my flesh and blood. I see no reason why she isn't welcome here. Especially since you two invited yourselves over for weeks in a row and spent the night each time. It's her house as much as it is mine. She could have kicked you out then, but she didn't. So why treat her that way, like she is a stranger? If that's the case, then I might as well be alone."

He pauses. "You're not alone, D. You will never be alone."

"You're missing the point, Marc. If this is supposed to be my home, then it stands to reason that I can invite whomever I want to it, right?"

"You could, but why would you want to? You have us. You have me."

"We had this conversation before. My world does not revolve around you two. It includes other people."

"Other people," he deadpans, then he draws another sharp breath. It sounds painful. "You mean *her*."

My heart stills.

I won't bother dignifying that with a response since there's some truth to his words. It's the fucking elephant in the room. And now it is the thing that looms over us. Constantly.

"If that's what you need, tell me," he continues, his voice breaking. "Frankly, I don't know if we could survive it if you..."

If I died.

Yeah, I know.

It's the other thing that neither of us wants to acknowledge, including me.

Especially me.

They've seen the cocktail of medications that I regularly take just to maintain a certain sense of normalcy in my life. There's not much to live for when everyone you love either leaves you or dies. But that's my cross to bear, not theirs.

"Where is he?" I ask again, slowly this time. "I know that you know where he is."

A tortured look crosses his face. "He's downstairs, waiting by your car."

"Why?"

"He's going with you."

"I don't need a fucking babysitter, Marc. It's just my sister and her doctor. At her very private appointment."

"Precautions still need to be put in place. For you, I mean."

"Yes, and I'm sure there will be Walter and however many bodyguards you have inconspicuously assigned to me. Harris doesn't need to babysit me, and I don't want him tagging along. You might as well come too if that's what we're doing."

"Don't tempt me."

"Believe me, I'm not. You already do — you still have that tracker in my car. Or did you take it out?"

"No. It's necessary."

"You're a control freak, Marc." I place both hands on his chest and push him away from me. He barely moves an inch, his eyes staying on mine as he studies me, a hint of amusement in them. "I could always move back out."

The mirth falls off his face and he flinches at that. "You wouldn't."

"Dahlia needs me," I remind him. "Last time I checked, I'm not a prisoner here. So back up."

"Not until you take it back."

"Back the fuck up."

Finally, he takes a step back, looking visibly stricken. "You wouldn't leave, would you?"

"Don't push my buttons." I slide off the countertop and pick up the hairbrush, attacking my hair with renewed vigor. Our gazes clash in the mirror. "I'd like to be left alone now."

"D, I'm sorry." His eyes reflect his genuine apology, as genuine as he can be.

But even I can see that's all it will ever be — an apology that lacks remorse for his actions. And I'm not feeling very forgiving either.

"Go away, Marc. Tell Harris I don't want company."

39

DELILAH

On most days, I love my sister.

Granted, she's a complicated person to love, but so am I. But on days like today, she makes it very difficult to be supportive of her and her life choices. Particularly now, when she insists on placating a man-child to keep the peace.

"There are women who would kill to be in your shoes right now," is the first thing I tell her once we get to her office.

Me saying this isn't a criticism of her life choices, but from her point of view it would come across that way. Not that I'm particularly interested in being nice or rephrasing my words. My earlier conversation with Marc and Harris still has me in a foul mood, but I did my best to keep all of that under wraps at her appointment because of Dahlia's thixophobia. She already had enough to worry about without me unwittingly triggering another one of her panic attacks. But once we got to her office, all bets were off.

She waits until she's settled behind her desk to acknowledge my words, her movements slow and deliberate. "Is there a point to this?"

"You know I'm happy to go with you. You don't even have to ask. I'll always be there for you. But you and I both know that this is something that Curtis should be doing."

She squares her shoulders, leveling her gaze with mine. "Well, he's not here."

"Where is he then? Where's the fucker who got you pregnant?"

"How should I know?" She presses the bridge of her nose between two fingers before adding, "Curtis is squeamish around blood and allergic to any commitment. Is it really that shocking that he isn't here?"

I lift a brow. "What does that have to do with anything? And why are you still making excuses for him?"

None of this is new information, but it also doesn't change the fact that he is half responsible for this child's existence.

Her shoulders slump. "He was invited, Dee. I don't know what else you want me to say. I invited him to this one like I always do. He chose not to come, like he always does."

"He chose not to?" I let out an exasperated sigh before continuing. "He is just as responsible for this child as you are, so why is he making this your responsibility alone? Is it really that difficult for him to attend one prenatal appointment?"

She runs a hand over her face. "I won't make Curtis do anything he doesn't want to. All that does is make me a hypocrite. Or worse, like his parents."

"No, it doesn't. You're making this all too easy for him. In this day and age, how does he get to shrug off his responsibilities and you don't? Unless..." I huff out a small laugh. "This child *is* his, right?"

She pins me with a glare, tears prickling her eyes. "Are you serious? What do you take me for?"

I shrug. "You *are* acting very nonchalant about this, so yes, I have to ask."

There's not even the slightest hint of projection on my part. Not at all.

Neither of us says anything. We just stare at each other in a battle of wills.

She caves in first, as always. "I had a paternity test done," she says softly. "That's why they can't contest it. That's why they quickly swept the wedding mess under the rug."

And now I feel like a massive bitch for even questioning this. Even after the McWhorters publicly announced her pregnancy without her consent, she's still doing her best to be cordial with them.

I still stand by my words — Curtis never deserved her, and he still doesn't. If Simone were here, she would agree with me.

My gaze softens, still holding hers. "This is nuts. I love you, Daa. You know I do. But this is nuts."

"I know you don't like it, but it is what it is." She lets out a bitter laugh. "What would you have me do?"

"Anything but this. You know what those people are like. You have to know the baby will be better off with you."

"I still haven't changed my mind on this," she reminds me, gesturing at her stomach. "I'm not cut out to be a mother. Should I suddenly decide to keep him without thinking it through, I would only be doing him a disservice. Curtis doesn't want him either, given his actions. But they do. It's a shitty alternative, but it will have to do. Besides, they're his grandparents, not strangers."

"They aren't your only option," I blurt out.

Her eyes narrow. "Let me guess, you want him?"

I do want him, but I'm not sure if she will consider that an option until I explain the why to her.

I bite my lower lip. "You've met Courtney, Marc's sister. I mean, she's like you with the kids thing. So she and Marc have an arrangement where he has Charlie a few days a week. It's unconventional, but it works."

There's a lot more to it than that, but this is the abbreviated version.

She doesn't look convinced though. "Marc doesn't want me in your house, Dee. What makes you think he will be fine with this? Is that why you're bringing this up again?"

My lips press into a fine line, a million thoughts running through my mind. Marc has a soft spot for kids. He might turn Dahlia away, but I doubt he could do the same to her child, my nephew.

Or could he? Is he that heartless?

Marc knows what she plans on doing once he is born. She gave Marc her prenuptial agreement for a second opinion. That was a wise decision on her part since some of the terms were appalling.

Like the part where any and all offspring of their union belong to the McWhorter family. They actually put the word *'belong'* in there, like their children are meant to be commodities.

Marc advised against signing it, and thank goodness she listened to him and didn't sign.

This cordial bullshit only makes them feel entitled to any products of her ovaries, even though the wedding didn't happen.

"Let's say we go that route," she continues after some time. "The McWhorters will fight you tooth and nail. It will be a long, dragged-out custody battle, and the only one who suffers will be him. Is that what you want for your nephew? Because I don't. I would rather take the path of least resistance, if you don't mind."

I can't help but scowl. "And this thing with David? That's your idea of least resistance?"

That's the other thing that has me stumped, this thing she supposedly has going on with Clark.

Clark David Holcomb, sole living heir of the Holcomb family. The same one who was ogling her at her rehearsal dinner, a sentiment she returned. Later that evening, he did something to piss her off so she threw his drink in his face. I remember thinking it was cute at the time, so maybe this is the universe's idea of a joke.

Oh, and he goes by David because Clark was his father, and there's a lot of bad blood there.

As it happens, this isn't a joke but an act of desperation on her part. Dahlia actually hired his services through our mutual friend Nalina. Or rather, *Dr. N. Aidan, M.D.,* a well-renowned psychiatrist who specializes in behavioral therapy and cognitive reconditioning. In addition to that, she also dabbles in sex therapy — or rather, therapy through sex — except this is mainly kept hush-hush, since her particular brand of sex therapy isn't exactly popular amongst the masses. There's no denying that her methods, though unconventional and controversial, are effective. A ninety-eight percent success rate does not lie.

That's how it came to be. Dahlia hired David to sleep with her. At least that's what she told me. She even signed a sex contract with him, which he supposedly does with all his clients. One of her stipulations was that he get a full health screening. She sent him to my lab for this and put her name as the referring party on the form.

I'm glad she found someone whose touch she can handle, but she needs professional help, and this thing with David is simply a band-aid. While I have nothing against sex work — I have nothing against anyone's sexual preferences, period — this whole thing is a bad idea, and it will blow up in *all* of our faces.

Dahlia is my sister, but David is Harris's and Marc's friend and protégé, so the aftermath of it will spill over to all of us.

How can she not see that? Or better yet, how can David not see that?

"Leave it alone, would you?" she bites.

It's my turn to laugh bitterly. "David's lab results came back, and they were clean."

"I know. You sent those to me two weeks ago."

Yes, I did that, but I also hoped she would've come to her senses by now. Not to mention that Nalina has had a thing for Dahlia since undergrad. And David happens to be her favorite, from what Marc and Harris say, except nothing about their tone implies this is a good thing.

"So you'll continue with this then, this band-aid." I don't bother keeping the bitterness out of my tone. "That's what you do, isn't it? The easy way out, always."

"You think this is easy?"

"No, I don't. But what you need is professional help, not a fuck buddy."

She visibly flinches at that, confirming what I feared would happen. "This thing David and I have, it's temporary. It's not a relationship. It's not even a friendship. It's strictly physical, and it will end."

"Your words say one thing, but your body says another," I counter.

It's the David Holcomb effect. There aren't many people who can resist the effects of his seductive prowess, Dahlia included. But this time, I think it goes deeper than that.

"It's hormonal," she says, her voice breathy. "It'll pass."

"I don't think so, Daa. It's in your eyes, too."

She bites the inside of her cheek and looks away. "It's just hormones, Dee. Once this kid is out, it'll pass."

I take a moment to study her. "I don't believe you. You don't believe you either." A beat passes, then, "You like him, don't you?"

She doesn't answer me, which isn't an issue because her body gives me an answer anyway. My gaze hones in on the pink flush crawling up her neck and cheeks. She might think she's fooling me, but the only one she's fooling is herself.

"And what happens when it ends?" I ask her. "Will you be okay?"

She shrugs and turns to face me. That's when I see it in her eyes, the uncertainty that plagues her. Unlike me, she has always been very logical and methodical in her thinking, professionally and personally. A sex contract is uncharted territory for her, and so is this pregnancy. I don't think she will come out of either one unscathed.

Before I can say anything else, there's a knock on the door.

"Come in," she says, then picks up a pen and twirls it between two fingers.

I turn around as the door opens, just in time to see Harris standing in the doorway.

A scowl forms. "Harris," I say, not bothering to disguise the distaste in my tone. "I thought I made myself clear earlier. I don't need a fucking babysitter."

"That's not why I'm here," he says, even as a sheepish smile forms.

"Trouble in paradise already?" Dahlia asks, her tone gleeful. "Does this mean I get my sister back?"

Panic washes over Harris's delectable features as his eyes dart back and forth between Dahlia and me. "What is she talking about?"

A hand shoves Harris's delectable and massive body aside to reveal his entourage. Courtney pokes her head out from behind him, Charlie hoisted on her hip.

"I don't think we've officially met," she announces as she walks into the room, headed straight for Dahlia. "I'm Courtney, and this here is Charlie."

She thrusts a hand towards Dahlia, her tone remarkably cheery and intended to infuse warmth into the room.

It doesn't.

I'm thrilled to see them, all of them, even though I know this is a bribe. I don't miss Dahlia's sharp intake of breath, which is why I place my hand on Courtney's arm and lower it. She turns to me with a question in her eyes, and I give her a slight head shake.

After I check in with Dahlia, I'll explain the no-touching thing to Courtney.

"So, ice cream?" I ask.

Charlie's excited squeal seals our fate.

40

MARC

One month later

I must be a glutton for punishment.
Or a masochist. Or both.

It's the only logical conclusion I can arrive at for insisting on pursuing such a mammoth task, even after Delilah dropped that bombshell on us.

Make that two bombshells — her desire to adopt her nephew, as opposed to Dahlia handing him over to Andrea and Matthias McWhorter. Or the ensuing legal battle that will follow should the twins decide to go that route. She asked that I look into what this will entail but keep it from Dahlia for the time being.

Then there's the fact that she's been actively considering moving back out. She says it's because Dahlia needs her, but we all know it's more than that. It's a culmination of many things, and Harris and I aren't helping.

Since I'm the fix-it guy in this relationship, at the very least, I need to give her her own space at home. She didn't ask for it, but she's getting it anyway. It's her home too, and I don't think I could handle it if she moved out.

Hence this.

Liam, my architect, mulls over the blueprints that he put together, but with an expression that tells me this is somehow news to him, what I'm asking of him, including the condensed timeline for completion.

"This is impossible, Marc," he tells me in an exasperated tone. "I'm good at what I do, but I'm not a miracle worker."

What I also don't care for are his excuses.

"It's been five fucking weeks, Liam," I bite out. "You've worked with shorter deadlines, so I don't see the issue here."

The fucker dares to scowl at me. "You want me to build a fully functional lab on a residential property. Not to mention all of the equipment that you want for it. Most of what you're asking for is meant for a commercial lot, not a residential one. Pulling the permits for that alone is a logistical nightmare. At this rate, we might as well bulldoze the entire house and start all over. And even that would be less painful than this."

"He has a point," David chimes in as he types away at his computer.

"Come again?" For a moment there, I had forgotten he was here.

"You don't need a fully functional lab at home," he repeats, his eyes still not meeting mine. "Either do a scaled-down version of it or get Delilah's input on what she actually wants."

"The whole point of this is to surprise her. I'm not going to her with anything less than a sure thing."

It would have been much easier if she had put this in her damn book. Or anything at all, really. It's been almost three months since she moved in, and still nothing. She won't put her name in the darn book, which is fine; that's her prerogative. But she won't tell me about her either, no matter how many times I ask.

"Do you know what it is that she actually does?" David continues. There's a bite to his tone, one I don't particularly care for. "Or are you being lame and going off what Google says?"

"What the fuck is that supposed to mean?"

"She's a geneticist, right?"

"Your point is?"

"Do you know what that actually entails? Have you ever been in her lab? Or her office? I don't mean the general Brewer Health building, but her domain, specifically. You could bring Harris in on this since he's been in there, but it won't be enough. If the goal is to give her something authentic, then you need someone who specializes in designing medical facilities."

For someone who does neither of these things, he sure knows a lot about this. "Since when did you become such an expert in—"

"I'm not, not that there's anything wrong with doing some research into what it is that you actually need from him," he interjects, still typing away. There's the occasional scowling at his screen; otherwise, he carries on the conversation seamlessly. "All I'm saying is that Liam might not be the right guy for the job. No offense."

"Well, that's Liam's job to figure all that out and tell me. Or give me other options, recommendations, not fucking excuses."

"You didn't tell him that. And before you say otherwise, I was there."

Across from us, Liam clears his throat. "Do you two need the room?"

"No," I say.

"Yes," David says.

He chuckles and rises. "I'm going to get a coffee, be back in thirty minutes. I trust that's enough time for you to settle... whatever this is?"

David waits for the door to close, then his gaze lifts to meet mine. "Why the urgency? Is there trouble in Casa Sotelo? Again?"

"Your job is security, not playing twenty questions."

He makes a tsk-tsk noise. "For a nosy bastard, you sure are doing a lot of deflecting lately. What did you do to piss Delilah off this time?"

My brow furrows. "I didn't... Why? Did Hurricane Dahlia say something?"

He scoffs. "She didn't have to. I know an apology gift when I see one. And why do you insist on calling her that?"

I lean back in my seat and fold my arms across my chest. "Don't tell me you've gone soft on her?"

He squares his shoulders. "She's still a job."

"A job," I say dryly. "Is that why you called Delilah two days ago? How did you get her personal cell number, by the way?"

He slams the lid of his computer down. "You want my help or not?"

My jaw clenches. "I want to know what business you have with my girlfriend. And how you got her number. Did you get it legally or illegally?"

"Are you asking me that as my lawyer, as my mentor, or as my friend?"

I pull out my pocket knife and set it on the table. "Pick one, and I'll decide if you get to keep all of your body parts today."

Or I could just wring his stupid neck and be done with this.

His fists clench in response. "Friend," he grits out.

That's worse. Much, much worse.

I know what David is capable of. I also know that because he's filthy rich, he gets it in his head that conventional rules don't apply to him. And because he's a genius hacker with an IQ in the high one-eighties, he can and does, get away with it most of the time.

But this path he's going down? He's done it before. He was sixteen at the time, so it stands to reason that he was careless and sloppy. At twenty-four, he has since gotten much better at it, but that doesn't mean he won't get caught again.

Not to mention, mixing business and pleasure never ends well.

So I ask, "Dahlia is as straight as they come, so does she know? The true meaning of the contracts?"

He blows out a frustrated breath. "So what if I got Delilah's number illegally?"

"That's not what I asked, David. I went over every single clause with a fine-toothed comb. The whole contract reads like a fucking wish list of sex positions."

He chuckles. "Funny, that's what she said, verbatim, right before she signed on the dotted line."

I slam my fist on the table. "Did you tell her what the contract entails, or did you gloss over those details simply because you were trying to get your dick wet?"

The smile slides right off his face. He leans forward and places his forearms on the table. "If you must know, Dahlia was in a bad spot. She's had a lot of those lately. That's what happens when a woman is forced to endure a pregnancy she doesn't fucking want. But you would know that, wouldn't you? Your own sister went through the exact same thing. So yes, it made sense that I would call *her* sister for help, not you or Harris.

"But you don't care about that. Neither of you does. You only want to see Dahlia as the bad guy in all this, and in doing so, you will alienate one of two people Delilah fucking cares about. That," he points to the blueprints Liam left behind, "is a piss-poor attempt at an apology, and she'll see right through it. So quit riding my ass and work on fixing your own shit the right way."

I run a hand over my face. I hate to admit this, but Dahlia is a good influence on him. For once, he's not being so self-centered. He's starting to care about the well-being of someone other than himself. I'm not sure if this is coming from a genuine place or from his obsession with her body. Or how good of an influence he is on her. Or how healthy this is for both of them, especially given what he is doing.

As is the case with his sex contracts, the deal is mutual usage. I've gone over the one that they both signed. It has over sixty items, and I'll swear on my mother's grave that maybe ten came from Dahlia. There are a lot of sneaky and underhanded clauses in it, both between and on the fucking lines. It's worse than her prenup, and it took us days to take that one apart, after which I advised her not to sign it. She listened to me then, so imagine my surprise when she signed this one.

I still stand by my words. Dahlia doesn't know what she signed up for with him, and from the looks of things David still hasn't told her.

So really, it's not his place to judge how I choose to go about things, not when his way is worse and involves a felony or several.

"This thing with her," I ask tentatively, "how far gone are you? How far over the threshold of no return did you cross?"

When this goes south, will I be forced to choose between them?

"I don't get what is so hard for you and Harris to understand," he bites out. "She's a fucking job, like all the others. This thing with her will end, like all the others. Before you go all Yoda on me and start spouting nonsense about reaching for more, just know that Harris already tried that. I'll tell you the same thing I told him. Been there, done that, not really looking to do that again."

He flips his laptop open and powers it on. "Can we get back to work now?"

41

HARRIS

Despite our fundamental differences of opinion about Delilah's mortality, one thing Marc and I can both agree on is that we can barely keep our hands off her.

In addition to the two bombshells she dropped on us, she also admitted that coming between us was never her intention. This was regarding how tense things have been between Marc and me. We agree that it wasn't fair of us to put that on her, even if it *is* about her. Neither of us wants to lose her, so we're on a quest to prove her wrong since we need her a lot more than she needs us. She doesn't come between us but makes us better and stronger.

Although I'm not sure what Marc is on this evening, but whatever it is, Delilah is down to roll with the punches.

He handles her roughly right in front of me, silently daring me to say or do something about it. I don't, because I'm torn between my need to respect her wishes and my refusal to feed into his ego. She certainly has plenty to say about it, and she keeps egging him on, daring him to do his worst. It doesn't matter what he does to her; she asks for more and dares him to make it hurt even more than it already does.

By this point, between managing Delilah's expectations with my equally conflicting feelings about it, Marc's self-control barely hangs by a thread.

So he pulls out his latest toy, an anal plug vibrator combo, and sticks it in her tight pucker. "This will get you all nice and warmed up for me."

At least he had the foresight to lube it up first, but there was nothing gentle about how he shoved it into her ass.

She frowns. "How does this—*eeep*!" He flicks on the remote, and a tremor runs through her. "H-how…"

He bends over and inches closer to her ear, his gaze level with mine. "Go suck his cock, D. And remember, you don't come unless I tell you to."

She walks over to where I'm seated at the edge of our bed, her legs shaky. She drops to her knees before me just as I lean forward, and the warmth of my palm spreads over her cheek. Her whole body trembles even as she leans into my touch. Her eyelids flutter, then close.

This is what she needs. It's what she craves, the fact that we are such polar opposites with her. Where Marc is hard, unrelenting, and cold, I think of myself as soft, gentle, and warm. So it's not surprising to see the conflicting emotions running through her.

Which of our personas appeals to her most? What emotion does she lean into, even if it's just for tonight?

Marc makes the choice for her and flicks it off. Her body sags in relief and she melts into my hands. Using my thumb, I trace her bottom lip. Her tongue snakes out to wet said lip, running over my thumb.

"Delilah, I need to see your eyes," I say, my voice hoarse.

She shakes her head and hums, both hands resting on my thighs. But just when she thinks there's a little reprieve in sight, Marc flicks the switch back on, and a ripple barrels through her and me. We both stop to ride it out.

"Chop chop," Marc barks out.

I slowly glide the back of my hand across her jaw before sliding my fingers around to the back of her neck. Her entire body trembles, and her lips part in a breathy whisper.

"Ignore him," I whisper, leaning forward to brush my lips across hers once, twice, three times before finally claiming them.

She presses her hands to my bare chest, feeling the strength of my heart as she deepens the kiss. Even though she won't say the words, she pours everything she's feeling and experiencing into the kiss without hesitation. I give my all right back, needing to be devoured by her as much as she seems to want to consume me.

Harsh fingers dig into my hair, clenching fistfuls to painfully hard points, then my lips are wrenched apart from Delilah's. We draw in short breaths, our gazes locked. I take in her swollen lips, flushed cheeks, and a defiant look in her eyes.

That last one is meant for Marc, so she aims it right at him.

"How is it that neither one of you understands the concept of punishment?" Marc says between clenched teeth.

"Is that what that was?" she asks, her voice strained. "You should've been clearer then."

His fingers dig into Delilah's hair, applying equally hard pressure as he does to mine. It's not enough to cover up the undisguised lust in his voice. He's just as turned on by watching us kiss as he is by watching me fuck her.

It's also something he has been doing quite a lot lately. Watching. Watching us. Watching me get myself off. Or just straight up demanding that I fuck him how he likes it, which I always do. But no matter how often I ask or even beg, he won't give me what I want. It only makes my ass crave his cock all the more. The more he denies me, the more desperate I get.

"D, I want your mouth wide open and H's cock crammed so far down your throat you can't fucking breathe. Don't make me repeat it."

She licks her lips and her jaw falls open, then she turns to me with an expectant look in her eyes.

"No," is all I say.

Even though the word is directed at Marc, Delilah leans away from me and her jaw snaps shut. The lust in her eyes dissipates a little. "Why the fuck not?"

I lean forward, my hand snaking to the juncture between her thighs. As expected, she's dripping, sopping wet with her desire. Her eyes flare with renewed lust, and she jerks and moans and grinds against my hand, seeking relief.

"I don't want to fuck your face, Delilah," I say as I press two fingers against her pussy. "I want here instead." Then I push my thumb against her tight pucker, along the edge of the vibrating plug, before pressing in slightly. "Here too."

A shudder runs through her. "Oh god, yes."

"I said no," Marc bites out and she jerks on my hand.

Which, of course, I expected from him. In retaliation for her smart mouth, he's been edging her for the last two hours with no reprieve in sight. He's already fucked her face twice, so her throat's sore. Then there are the nipple clamps he cinched so tight they would draw blood when they came off. He's also fucked her pussy with two different vibrators and still refused to let her come.

I'm cruel, but I'm not *that* cruel.

The problem is that, like him, she gets off on it too, on seeing just how far she can push his buttons. She has perfected the art of dishing out Marc's unique brand of bullshit right back at him. Not to mention, she's fucking savage at it. He just might have created a monster.

Also, I need to start taking fucking notes. Stat.

"I wasn't asking," I tell him, and his eyes widen slightly before his lips curve. "Delilah, get down on all fours, will you?"

All lingering traces of defiance flee her body as she does as I ask. The look in Marc's eyes goes downright wicked as my knees sink into the plush carpet. I line my cock up against her entrance and push in, sliding all the way inside her until my hips smack her creamy, supple ass. Her walls clamp down on my cock, squeezing tight and nearly pushing me over the edge.

She looks over her shoulder and her golden-brown eyes meet mine, lusty and hazy with desire. It's a look that is reflected in mine.

"Harris," she says, her voice a breathy whisper.

"Yeah?"

"Fuck me like I'm yours."

"I plan on it," I say with a chuckle. "And you *are* mine."

"Hard and unrelenting," she adds, forcefully this time.

I lean over her, my sweaty and massive chest covering her back, tiny and supple in comparison. My hand grabs her breast, encircling a cinched, engorged nipple, and I whisper into her ear, "Tell me if it's too much."

"Why would it—*oh!*"

Her lips part on a silent scream-whisper as I use two fingers to clamp down on an overly sensitized tit. Her back arches and she presses into me. I do the same with the other one and a tortured groan rips from her lips.

"Oh, fuck me!"

She doesn't have to say it twice. Both hands move to her waist, and I slowly pump myself into her, savoring every thrust.

"H, quit fucking around," Marc says as he watches us with heavy-lidded eyes, his mouth closed and his jaw firm. "She said hard and unrelenting. You need a fucking demonstration?"

Delilah laughs as I pick up the pace, slamming into her. The sound of slapping from our sweaty bodies colliding rapidly fills the room. She moans and cries out *more, harder, faster*, as I'm all-out pounding into her like I'm starving and she's the last reprieve for my dying soul.

Marc crouches before us and takes her cheeks in both hands. "You are perfect for us, you know that?"

Something about the way he phrases that has pin-prickles running down the entire length of my spine. It's not from the vibrating plug in her ass, with which he keeps upping the intensity. That feeling quickly dissipates once she starts making the most decadent mewling sounds. I know she's close and so am I, so I reach between us and stroke her clit, gently at first, then switching to flicking it hard.

He leans over and whispers in her ear, "Come for us, D. Milk his cock," before claiming her lips in a punishing kiss.

Her body starts to tremble as her orgasm takes over. As she convulses around me, her walls clamp down on me, over and over and over, finally tipping me right over the edge. I let out a guttural, feral groan as my climax barrels through me. Marc releases her face and we collapse into a sweaty and slippery pile as our legs and her arms simultaneously give out. We are both spent and satiated by the time the last wave of shivers leaves our bodies.

Only then does Marc flick off the vibrator. He reaches between us and slips it out of her ass, taking extra care not to slip my throbbing cock out of her pulsating core.

"I was enjoying that," she says as he curls his fingers around the device and brings it to his nose, drawing in a generous whiff.

Suffice it to say I won't be looking at butt plugs the same way ever again.

"You want it back?" he asks, flushed and glassy-eyed as his hungry gaze rakes over our bodies.

She hums. "Maybe."

A flick of a knife draws me out of my daze.

I'd been wondering where that had gone. It's the one thing he hasn't used on her yet. Saving the best for last, it would seem.

The look in Marc's eyes is downright feral as he grabs the bottle of lube and begins generously applying it to the handle. Then the blade.

Oh, dear god. He's not—

"You are *not* sticking that blade in my ass," she warns.

He chuckles. "Not today I'm not." He points to the corner of his lip. "You've got a little drool on your face."

"Not ever," she counters. There's nothing on her face, but she still uses her thumb to angrily swipe at the nonexistent liquid on her cheek before sucking down on it.

Another sinister chuckle comes from him as he takes in the defiant lift of her chin. "Ever, huh?"

Is it too much to ask that we have a moment of peace around here?

She releases her thumb with a pop. "I draw the line at blood play."

"We'll see."

"I fucking mean it, Marc."

"It's not negotiable, D. You'll be begging me for it when the time comes. For all of it. My knife. My cock. My kid. It's all going in you, one way or the other."

Everything goes fuzzy at that as a mental fog descends upon me and muddies up my senses. At least I now know I hadn't misheard the first time.

But now? He's fucking doing this now?

So that's what he's been on about all evening?

She pushes my body off hers and sits up. "You... you want me to have your baby?" Her surprise at his admission makes my heart clench.

Blood rushes through my ears. How could she not have known this was his endgame all along? How could she, a fucking genius, not have realized this? She was the one to first pick up on the fact that Marc had changed his mind about the kids thing. And she's always wanted them. And now here we are. Ergo...

"Why me?" Her voice cracks with the words.

Marc's gaze flickers back and forth between us as though he's not entirely sure how to answer her question. It might be the first time I've seen him uncertain about something. Anything, really. But that uncertainty eventually slides off his face, and the feral look from earlier replaces it.

"You want kids, don't you?" he asks, a hint of a smile pulling at the corners of his mouth.

She swallows thickly. "I do."

This part I've always known. Delilah has never lied about it, and she's not about to start now.

The fact remains that just as my thoughts on the matter haven't changed, neither have Delilah's. She wants kids, but I don't. They scare me just as much as she loves them.

Yet when her eyes meet mine, they're glassy with tears.

Now *that* part is a surprising reaction.

And they mirror my own.

"How many would you like?" While he directs the question at her, I know his eyes are on me. It's what he does, always watching, gauging my reaction, and determining his next move.

Why can't we just take a fucking moment to bask in the after-glow of our respective breath-stealing, leg-trembling, toe-curling orgasms? Why does he have to bring this shit up now?

"Why does it matter?" she asks, her eyes on mine.

"It matters, D. You give and give, yet you never ask for anything in return."

I know she still hasn't written anything down in her fucking book of wishes. She's had it for over four months, and the fact that it's still empty has been driving him up a wall. Changing my name was the first thing I wrote down, and I did that the second he gave it to me.

He checks them constantly too. Delilah currently has hers lying on the nightstand. Mine's in my sock drawer — he put it there as a joke a few years ago and I left it.

She tilts her head. "And if I said I wanted thirty-nine?"

"Let's get to work then, yes?" he groans, his voice strained.

Like Marc's, my eyes also flicker across her face, laced with uncertainty as I hang on to her every word. Her answer could be my saving grace or my eternal damnation. The thing is, I don't have to say it. Not to her, anyway, because she sees me. She has always seen me.

She sees behind the walls that I show to everyone else, to her, to Marc, even to myself. She sees it — my hopes, my dreams, my fears.

My greatest fear has always been the fear of being abandoned. Like my father did the moment he realized I wasn't of use to him. I could no longer elevate his status in society because of who I am, and point-blank refused to inflate his idea of the perfect father. And since I no longer served my purpose, he cast me out on my eighteenth birthday, like the unwanted and defective child I am.

That's how Marc found me all those years ago. But those scars never truly heal. We just learn to hide them better, given time.

The worst part is she shares it too. The fear of being abandoned, of not being good enough. Of forever being labeled as defective, along with the endless list of things associated with it. Easily discarded. Easily written off. Easily breakable. The pain, her pain and mine, seeps into the pores of my skin and settles into my veins. This weakness of mine, of hers, it twists my chest. My heart feels so heavy yet pounds so hard I think it might beat right out of my chest.

Reluctantly, she tears her eyes away from mine before turning to Marc. "I would love nothing more than to have your babies," she continues, hand outstretched in my direction. On autopilot I reach for it, lacing our fingers together. "But not like this. I'm not doing this without him."

"You could be pregnant already, for all we know." His voice is solemn as he states the obvious.

He's not wrong. She could be. Protection hasn't exactly been at the top of our list of priorities. It makes sense now why she never was on birth control, not even to regulate her periods. She never had a reason to be for eighteen years.

Until now.

My gaze lifts to meet his, the unspoken plea in my eyes.

Stop this, please.

He lifts a brow but says nothing.

"If I'm pregnant, then I'll take care of it," she adds.

A painful shiver thunders through me, one the size of a category-three hurricane. She must feel it too, as her fingers tighten around mine.

I hate that idea even more. As expected, Marc does too.

He visibly flinches at her words and the knife falls to the floor with a thud. "You wouldn't—"

"This isn't a contest, Marc. We're equals, you said so yourself. Or was that a lie?"

"I don't say shit I don't mean," he bites, his voice shaky.

"Then we do this together, all of us."

He nods and looks away. "So that's it then? You'll sacrifice your dream of motherhood for H?"

"It's not a sacrifice, and making Harris the bad guy in this isn't fair to him," she says. "This is supposed to be a partnership, Marc. Kids are people, not fucking trinkets. If we bring any into the world, it has to be something that we all want. And if he's not on board with this, I'm not doing it either."

He draws in a sharp breath and bites the inside of his cheek. A beat passes and he turns away from us and heads for the door.

"Marc." His name slips past my lips as panic seizes my body.

Delilah shakes her head as he walks out, taking the time to close the door behind him.

"I'm sorry," I say, eyes trained on the closed door. "I know how much—"

"Don't," she bites, her voice shaky as Marc's was just moments prior. "You knew that was going to happen, didn't you? It's why you two fought weeks ago. And why you've been hovering, treating me like some wayward child who needs constant supervision."

She pulls her hand from mine and stands. I sit up and reach for her again, but she takes a step forward and out of my reach.

"Delilah, please—"

"That wasn't an open or honest conversation. It was an ambush." Her face tilts upwards and she lets out an exasperated sigh. "And a test. You two were fucking testing me, wanting to see whose side I would take. Well, guess what? I pick neither."

She disappears into the master dressing room, re-emerging moments later in a robe. Then she walks out of the room without glancing in my direction.

Leaving me sitting on the bedroom floor in my birthday suit, staring at the closed door and wondering where it all went so wrong.

42

DELILAH

When he was a teenager, Marc made a deal with his father.

Part of the deal, amongst many other things, is that he and Courtney must attend any and all family functions. They are also required to represent the Sotelo family at various events at their father's discretion, of which there are many because he is Lorenzo Sotelo. Oh, and that discretion extends to their respective families — for the most part, this is non-negotiable.

As such, Marc ensures that everyone is impeccably dressed at every event, ready to play their respective parts to perfection. It's safe to say that I underestimated just how much of a big deal this is since everyone includes Charlie and Harris. The latter who, as it so happens, detests having to go to these events more than anything. Since Marc has always insisted that Harris is his equal and not some dirty little secret, he sucks it up and goes.

Now that I'm officially a part of the family, I have to go too.

In true Marc fashion, all our outfits are custom-designed and custom-made to each of our specifications. Color-coded too, because heaven forbid we look out of place. As if our collective outfits aren't enough to identify what family we belong to.

Since it's Courtney's turn to pick colors, she goes with red. You know, since we don't stand out enough.

Our stylist, Loretta, and her team come to us, not the other way around. They're all confined to the first floor since Marc won't budge on privacy.

This is only the third round of fittings for the year. We each have over a dozen outfits to try on. After five hours of this slow and painful torture, I am beginning to see Harris's point. If one has to put up with this part, one feels obligated to go to all of the accompanying events, if only to show off these darn outfits.

It would be too soon if I never had to attend one of these things again.

The boys are cheating a little and going with tailored suits. Harris keeps things simple and opts for two-piece suits, while Marc and Charlie go all out with three-piece suits. They look dashing if I do say so myself, but it is still cheating. Between the three of them, how hard can it be to make and alter thirty-six suits as needed? Except for Charlie, that is. He's a growing toddler so anything he gets will need constant alterations. With no expense spared, of course, because Marc is Marc.

On the other hand, Courtney and I have been poked and prodded every which way, and while Courtney is having a blast with it, I have just about had it. Then a replica of my bridesmaid dress made an appearance, the strapless A-line chiffon dress but in carmine, and out came the scissors. While everyone watched, slack-jawed, as I decimated the ten-thousand-dollar masterpiece, Marc's out for blood and the poor soul responsible for that snafu was immediately dismissed. It was immensely satisfying and also sent a clear message — if I dislike something, snip, snip, snip, and heads will roll.

I have nothing against the dresses themselves. They are gorgeous and Courtney loves every single one. Between the two of us, there is a variety of princess cut, empire waist, A-line, and strapless dresses. Between all five of us, our outfits are made of the finest and most extravagant luxury and designer fabrics that money can buy. Vicuña wool, silk, cashmere, Pima cotton, leather, and mohair are those I can name.

Then there's the styling.

Now, I know my boys are already on edge, and we still have unresolved shit to deal with from a few days ago. Had I known that fucking makeup would be the thing to set Harris off, I would have opted out of it and let Courtney play dress-up to her heart's content.

I'm more of a natural look, nude-toned makeup, hair in a ponytail, flats-wearing kind of girl. Courtney, a self-proclaimed tomboy, uses these events to shed that image and goes all out with the styling. Playing dress-up with her mother wasn't something she had a chance to do growing up, hence the tomboy image. I had that in abundance, and while it was never my thing, it was Mom's, Dahlia's, and Simone's thing. Those were good times.

God, I miss her.

By the time the makeup artists are done with Courtney's makeup, she looks every bit like the illegitimate mafia princess she is. A part she's only too happy to play when the occasion calls for it. She attends these things for the sole purpose of upstaging all of the so-called legitimate princesses, stealing their boyfriends and husbands, and leaving a trail of broken hearts in her wake. Her words, not mine. I'm quoting here.

"They need to match," Marc says once they reveal Courtney's look.

He still won't address or even look at me directly, and not for lack of trying on my part. I followed him that night but he locked himself up in his office. So I knocked and begged to be invited in but that didn't make a fucking difference. After an hour of radio silence, I grabbed one of Simone's pictures, curled up on the sofa on the second floor and went to sleep. Woke up the following day in our bed, still clutching her picture. They were both gone as well. Marc left for work and Harris locked himself in his basement workshop. We've been ships in the night since, including sleeping in separate rooms each night.

I fucking hate it. I hate this awkward tension between us. I hate that they put me in a position to have to choose. And I miss her. God, I miss her so much. I miss her so much it hurts to breathe. I miss her so much that it's her face and theirs that I see every night before I drift off into the meaningless void of restless sleep. There are all these jumbled-up messes of emotions in me that I have no clue what to do with.

I want them.

I need her.

I need them too, but I fucking miss her.

And after exerting all of my expendable energy in shredding that dress earlier, all the fight has left me. I offer no resistance as my ass is shoved into the chair, per Marc's directive. And while they all fuss and ooh and ahh and slather various concoctions onto my face, I sit there lifeless, reminded of the time Dahlia went through this.

It doesn't escape me how big of a hypocrite and raging bitch I was to her then, and here I am doing the same, albeit on a much smaller scale. The thing is, I have some fucking say here while she didn't, and still, I let them do whatever it is they want to my face.

Path of least resistance, right?

I focus on Charlie, currently sprawled out on the sofa, asleep and oblivious to the world. How I wish I could have his childlike innocence, even if it is just for a day.

"She looks trashy," Harris mumbles under his breath once they are done with me.

There's a sharp intake of breath from Courtney. "Excuse me?"

He clears his throat and turns to face her. "She looks like a trashy mafia princess," he repeats, louder this time. "No offense."

She huffs. "Offense taken. Haven't you heard of the phrase 'if you have nothing nice to say, say nothing at all?'"

Loretta clears her throat. "Take five, everyone."

Harris barely waits for the room to clear before answering. "Then I guess I'm the uncivilized asshole here, because that," he points to my face, "is fucking hideous. Yours too, if I'm being honest. But to each their own."

Her face falls, and she rears back like he just struck her. "What's the matter with you? Who shoved that sanctimonious stick up your ass?"

"Oh, I'm sorry," he laughs bitterly. "I didn't realize I was supposed to be tiptoeing around your fucking fragile feelings. Maybe you need all the embellishments to feel better about your non-existent self-esteem, but Delilah doesn't. So don't go around projecting your insecurities onto her."

"H, that's enough," Marc growls.

He whips around to face him. "Enough? You're the one who wanted them to match. Is that what you had in mind? She's fucking perfect just the way she is, and you know it. But since Courtney is your sister, you'll just go along with whatever she wants. It's bad enough that she has us looking like the Three Stooges. Does she also need Delilah looking like a trashy mafia princess to prove a point to your family?"

Marc scowls at that and takes several menacing steps toward him. "Take a fucking walk," he barks.

We all flinch.

Harris takes one last look at us, at all of us, his gaze lingering on me. A beat passes and he turns around and heads for the stairs that lead down to the basement.

Leaving me staring at his retreating figure, wondering why I have to watch yet another person I care about walking away from me for the second time in four days.

Is this my fate in life?

"What the fuck was that about?" Courtney hiss-whispers.

Marc scrubs a hand over his face. "He's fine. He just needs a minute."

That's one way to look at it.

I let out a strangled laugh and reach for a pack of makeup removal wipes.

He will need a heck of a lot more than a minute. Not a single soul in this room is oblivious to Harris's dislike of these things. All of the pre-event preparations and the events themselves. He has always wanted out of it. While I was never a part of it before, I heard all about it. Every single sordid detail of it. I thought he was exaggerating before, but it turns out he wasn't. That's why I wasn't surprised that he chose an opportune moment to pick a fight that would end in him dramatically storming out of the room, effectively getting him out of it. Until the next time, that is. I'm surprised he lasted as long as he did. Five hours of this is a new record for him.

I descend into a fit of manic laughter as I wipe the so-called offensive makeup off my face.

"Is she okay?" Courtney asks, her tone laced with concern.

"She's fine," Marc bites.

There was absolutely nothing wrong with my makeup. Or Courtney's, for that matter. I don't believe Marc would have requested that we match had it looked as hideous as Harris claims. I'm staring at hers as I wipe mine off, and I have to say she looks fucking gorgeous. Not that she wasn't beautiful before, but this look is a scaled-down version of what she did in the past. I've seen the pictures too. Hers is a happy medium of what the two of us like, which is a compromise at its best.

"You look great," I tell her. "Don't take what Harris said to heart. He's just in a bad mood."

We all are, I want to add. Not that it comes as a surprise. She has eyes and ears.

"I know." Courtney walks over to where I'm seated and wraps her arms around my waist. She rests her chin on my shoulder, and her breasts press into my back. "You don't look trashy either," she whispers against my neck, and her gaze meets Marc's. "But someone should check on Harris."

Marc presses his lips together, his eyes pained.

"I'll do it," I say, sliding off the chair.

Let's face it — if tonight is any indication of how these things will go, then I will hate them as much as Harris does.

43

HARRIS

This isn't how I wanted the evening to go.

There must be something wrong with me when a day that's supposed to be about fucking fashion ends in me picking stupid fights and insulting my friend for no reason.

I know that the things I said weren't fair to Courtney or Delilah. And taking out my frustration on them isn't fair to them either.

Then again, that's the thing with me. Me and my big fucking mouth. Me and my selfish attitude.

But it had to come out, one way or the other. It's been days, yet none of us wants to address the elephant in the room. I know I don't.

Fucking kids.

I still don't want them. But the image of Delilah's body growing swollen with our baby is such a fucking turn-on it makes me want to put one in her right now. I already see a preview in the form of Hurricane Dahlia and I like it. Maybe more than I care to admit.

But then the kid comes out and they are crying, needy, whiny bunches. They grow up to be moody teenagers. Once they turn eighteen, and after I've managed to screw up their lives incredibly badly, they'll leave, change their fucking name, maybe move to the other side of the country, and won't look back.

Or maybe they don't move quite that far. Perhaps all they manage is to move to the other side of town. Then I'll become that needy, whiny parent who tracks their every move and follows them around like a fucking whiny puppy. I can't even compare that to puppies since that would be an insult to puppies everywhere.

But still, people suck. Maybe kids don't suck as much, but they grow up just the same, becoming people who suck. With billions of people in the world already, do I need to add one or thirty-nine more into the mix?

I don't.

I really don't because some people are just straight-up pieces of shit and they suck. Or they leave. They always fucking leave.

Or they make you leave since that's convenient.

"You'll get pushed out, eventually," my dad's voice echoes. *"Cast out, like the reject that you are. And when that happens, you'll come crawling back home, tail between your legs."*

Given the present state of things, it could actually happen. The gong has been rung, and there's nothing I can do about it besides accept my fate.

God, I hate this. All of it, especially the fanfare. Once we show up, all three of us together, it will be the beginning of the end for us.

The next thing Marc's family will say is, "When do you get rid of the loser boyfriend?"

Frankly, it's not a conversation I'm ready to have, but knowing Marc, it will happen whether I want it to or not.

I poke and prod and blindly stab at the spreader before me, not caring if it's damaged beyond repair or if a masterpiece emerges from it. Some of my best work was done in a fit of rage. I have clients who just eat that shit right up.

So I keep at it until a gentle knock filters through the room.

Took her long enough.

44

DELILAH

I slowly make my way to the basement after Harris, not in the least surprised that the door to his workshop is closed. The only thing different is the Do Not Disturb sign that isn't flipped over.

Fist clenched, I hesitate to knock and my fist hovers over the custom cherry-stained solid oak wood door. It's a part of the house I'm not allowed in, much like Marc's office. The basement workshop is his domain, and though I haven't seen the inside, there is little doubt that this is one of the few spaces in the estate that isn't dominated by Marc's touch.

Harris mentioned before that I would get my own space; all I had to do was ask. I haven't asked because it's not the space I want.

My knuckles connect with the door once, and my hand falls to my side. With my luck, I will be spending an hour knocking and begging to be invited in, only to be met with fucking radio silence. Still, I am curious about what is in there. What is it about this space that Harris will remain cooped up here for hours on end?

For someone who claims not to want a typical nine-to-five job, there have been days when he'd spend sunrise to sunset in there. When that happens, one of us, usually me, must fetch him for dinner. Or bed. It's not healthy, but I'm not one to judge.

Before moving in with them, I was a workaholic who practically lived at my lab. I still am, if I'm being honest, but the thought of coming home to my men gets me out of the lab faster. It has my colleagues stumped too since they don't believe I'm rushing home to Dahlia these days. I'm choosing not to disclose my current living arrangements. They will all find out soon enough.

"Quit your hovering and come inside," Harris calls out.

He still sounds like he did before he stormed off. Irritated, with a splash of annoyance. I lean against the door frame to wait this out for as long as it takes. Maybe he won't be as heartless as Marc was. Perhaps he'll take mercy on me and come out instead.

The door swings open a minute later, squeaking on its hinges. "Marc sent you, didn't he?"

I shrug, but I don't answer him.

Not yet anyway.

"Why aren't you in here? I know you heard me."

"I was waiting on you."

He braces his arm against the door frame, watching me. "Why?"

"I missed you."

One corner of his mouth tugs up. "You're a terrible liar."

"That a fact?" I ask, crossing my arms over my chest.

He nods, his eyes zoning in on my now-pushed-up breasts. "The only time you're truthful is when my cock is buried inside you so deep you can't see straight."

I look past him to a spot on the wall, ignoring the heat flooding my cheeks. "Why do you do that?"

He continues on, ignoring me. "Hmm, gets your lips and your pussy loose." I envision the look in his eyes going predatory as he runs his thumb along his lower lip. "Wanna test it out?"

"Fine." I huff out a breath, push past him, stalk a few steps into the room then turn to face him. "I'm here. I came inside. Happy?"

"Ecstatic," he drawls. The door clicks shut behind him, and he slides all five deadbolts into place. I count them as he secures the room like it were fucking Fort Knox. Again, I'm not one to judge since my parents did the exact same thing at our house. For me.

Still, there's no one here but us, so I ask, "Is that necessary?"

"I need your undivided attention," he says evenly, and my defective heart somersaults in my chest.

"You didn't have it locked before."

He leans against the door and crosses his arms, his eyes steady on mine. "True, but everyone knows this is my space. No one is allowed in here. Ever."

My brow scrunches and it takes a moment for his meaning to sink in. "Ever?"

A twinge of wistfulness flits across his face. "You're the exception, Delilah," he admits eventually, his voice going soft. "You always have been." A beat passes, then, "I was waiting for you to join me."

So that's what that was about earlier.

Does he have to be so sweet all the time? I absolutely refuse to swoon.

I swallow around the lump that forms in my throat. "Courtney sent me," I say instead.

"Your eyes, they were blank earlier. Where did you go?"

"Is that why you were rude to her?"

He nods. "It was worth it."

My eyes narrow. "How so?"

"It brought you back."

"It was uncalled for." Both hands come to rest on my waist. "You owe her an apology. Go on, I'll wait."

Harris pushes away from the door and goes over to his workstation. I shrug since it was a long shot anyway. One way or the other, he will apologize to her. Maybe not tonight, but soon.

While he settles in, I take a moment to look around his workshop, which is different from what I expected.

Harris is obsessed with locks and knots of all shapes, sizes, colors, and mediums. There are far too many items with those two things crammed into every surface of his workshop. It looks messy at face value, but it's all organized chaos, and so him.

Don't even get me started on the amount of BDSM paraphernalia in this room. Most of his clients come from the scene, so it makes sense he would have these in here. Only, it's like he's building a fucking arsenal in here.

I make my way over to his workstation and tentatively approach him. His body tenses slightly, holds for a beat, then his shoulders slump.

"I don't usually have an audience when I'm working," he says, not looking up to meet my eyes.

"I figured as much. What are you working on?"

"A spreader bar. Ten of them, plus a handful of restraints and some chastity belts."

I blow out a breath. "That's ambitious."

Then again, sex toys have always been Harris's thing. He says he only makes and sells them as an act of defiance against his father, but it's more than that. For how nonchalant he is about this, I know better. One does not turn a side business slash hobby into a six-figure business without some degree of business acumen and talent.

Although I do wonder why he rarely uses them on himself or us. Marc and I use them plenty, but Harris barely touches them for pleasure. I asked, but he refused to tell me why. It would appear that Marc knows why but won't share either, which I find odd and in direct contrast with this honesty policy he has us on.

I know they used to be very heavily involved in the BDSM scene, until seven years ago when Harris ran away from home. Marc then sent his goons to collect him from my place unceremoniously, personally supervising the process. It was a spectacle, and I wasn't sure their relationship would survive it. I wasn't sure our friendship would survive it either.

It didn't help that I blamed myself for it at the time. After all, I was the drunk and horny woman who propositioned her best friend's partner in a moment of weakness. Marc shut me down, like any loyal boyfriend would, then Harris took me home not too long after, none the wiser. But when Harris showed up at my doorstep the next day, shit-faced and ranting about how Marc fucked a woman and lied about it, I was floored, then crushed, and I blamed myself for it. Mostly because I knew Marc wouldn't have done that and also because I was the woman Harris was ranting about.

All these years and Marc never told Harris what I did. He could have, but he took full responsibility for my actions because he understood the damage it would have done to my and Harris's friendship. I know he was also looking to get out of the scene back then, but Harris wasn't, so they compromised by taking on partners. Harris later told me that Marc promised never to fuck any women they brought in, only the men. He got off watching Harris fuck the women, which was supposedly enough for him.

At least, it was until a few months ago, when I came to both of them, asking for a favor. I suppose my asking a second time was the final straw that snapped Marc's already thinning resolve. I shouldn't have been surprised by what followed soon afterward. Marc is not one to be denied when he wants something.

And he definitely wanted me.

All this time, he's wanted me. *Me.*

Even though he lied back then, he turned me down for Harris's sake and mine. I know it's mainly for Harris's sake. By his own admission, Marc will do whatever it takes to make him happy. So I was shocked he kept my secret all this time. He kept my secret back then, even though it almost cost him his relationship with Harris. He holds my secret now, even though he has no reason to. It has been bothering him, keeping this a secret from Harris. So I promised him I would come clean about my role in that shitstorm from seven years ago. It's been months and I haven't found the right time to do so.

Now's as good a time as any, when Harris has my undivided attention. Hopefully, it will provide a sufficient distraction and stop him from decimating the masterpiece he's been working on.

He startles when I place a hand on his arm, his movements stilling.

"Harris," I whisper.

He lifts his eyes to meet mine, soft brown like mine, bathing me in the afterglow of his gaze. "Delilah."

"When do these need to be done?"

He releases an exasperated sigh and pushes the bar aside. "I don't do deadlines. They'll get them when they get them."

He stands and tugs my arm, pulling my body into his. His fingers dig into my waist and he hoists me onto the workstation like I weigh nothing.

"A little warning next time?" I tease as he settles himself between my legs, palms still planted on my waist.

A comfortable silence settles between us.

"Where did this obsession with locks and knots come from?" I eventually ask.

A twinge of wistfulness flits across his face for a second time. "My father," he says in a barely audible voice.

I probably shouldn't have asked. Each time Victor Toussaint comes up, it opens up a can of worms that isn't easily shut. He started it for now, and all I did was push us closer to the edge.

"He wasn't always horrible," he continues, his voice tight. "I have some fond memories of my childhood, albeit few and far between. And fleeting."

This part I did not know. Harris doesn't talk much about his childhood. Neither do I, not when so much of it revolves around Simone and Dahlia. Curtis too, and I'd rather not expend my energy thinking about that fucker.

"When Dad spouts his vitriol, it's a struggle reconciling the man he is today with the man I remember him to be. Once upon a time, I looked up to that man. I used to think if I ever were to..." he trails off, scrubbing his hand over his face. "To become a dad, I wanted to be just like him. Now..." His shoulders heave. "I guess I really am naive, huh? I spent all my formative years idealizing him, and it hit hard when he turned out to be not-so-great. It's true what they say, never meet your heroes. Better yet, don't be raised by one."

"Is that why you've been meeting him?" I ask softly.

He bites on the inside of his cheek, his eyes pained.

For months, he's been meeting his dad and thought no one knew. I don't think Marc knows. He's kept at it, knowing Marc would be livid if he found out. I wonder what his supposedly inconspicuous bodyguard has been doing all this while. If they have been sleeping on the job or reporting back to their boss like they are supposed to.

What's even more troubling is that Victor loves to play head games just for kicks, so why Harris would willingly subject himself to that blows my mind. I've had run-ins with the man over the years, and he is everything Harris says he is and then some.

"I am doing it for my cousin," he eventually says.

"Naimo?" She's one of the few family members he still keeps in touch with.

He nods. "She needs help."

I cup his face in my hands. "Can I trust that you know what you are doing?"

His shoulders slump. "Not a clue, but that's what she wants from me."

"Why?" I ask incredulously.

He looks down and a slow breath moves through him. "All good things must come to an end, huh?"

"Again, how's that a good thing?"

"If this gets her away from her parents, I consider it a win. But for her to get there, I think she wants to watch me as I face my demons. Or force my demon to face me, so to speak."

"Come again?"

His gaze lifts, meeting mine. "There's only so many times the man can sit across the table from me without blowing his gasket. Publicly, I should add. He's still clinging to the notion that he is the perfect father. I've spent years trying to reconcile those two parts of him. It's his turn now. Instead of running, I want him to look his bisexual, biracial son in the eye enough times and keep spouting that nonsense. Or maybe it would shatter the illusion of that naive little boy he's still clinging to. You know, that perfect son upon which his identity as the perfect parent was predicated. If he loses his shit in public, even better."

"Or you could not do any of that? Just a thought."

"Nah. You know me, I just love to push people's buttons, and I've got lots of ammunition for him. It helps that I'm a rebel, shacking up with the Sotelo family's illegitimate son. And now you."

"You're not the cunning wolf you'd like everyone to think you are."

He gives me a small smile in response, but it doesn't quite reach his eyes. "Dahlia's right, you know."

I scoff-laugh. "You need to be more specific. My sister says a lot of things and she's usually right."

"I'm responsible for Victor's maiming."

I lift a brow. "Dahlia said that years ago. I didn't question it then, but I will now."

He leans forward and presses his lips to my forehead. "I didn't actually do it myself but I'm responsible for it."

He says that like it should be news to me, like it should scare me, even though these are things I've always known about him. He's sinister and cruel, yet passionate and loyal.

And he does. He does scare me, but not in the traditional sense. He makes me feel things. He makes me want things. Things I shouldn't want. Things I don't deserve.

Yet he makes me want to reach for them. To reach for the impossible, that is.

"You're being intentionally vague, aren't you?"

"No," he says against my forehead.

"You think I don't know what you are like? What Marc's like? I'm sure you had your reasons. Whatever they were, I'm sure Victor deserved it. Besides, it has been fifteen years, so knock it off with the vague shit."

He leans away from me, his eyes searching. "I told Marc to do it."

Not gonna lie, I'm turned on by this. By the knowledge that Marc truly is as ruthless as the rumors claim and that Harris is his kryptonite.

Not sure what that says about me.

Not sure if I care.

"Did he?"

He shrugs. "I watched him mewl, begging for mercy like a pathetic bastard while Marc cut off his middle finger. I even got off on seeing all that blood gushing from the stump."

"Gruesome."

Another pause, then, "We kept his finger."

"Why would you keep the evidence?"

"Why not?"

"What if he comes after you? What if he comes after Marc?"

Most people would be scared of Marc due to his presence and size alone. With him, what you see is what you get. But as I've come to find out, underneath all that is a gentle giant, a loveable, cuddly giant who loves just as fiercely and intensely as he hurts.

Victor's thing is head games, so he's not above hitting Marc where it hurts the most. That would be Harris, his own son.

Harris scoffs, unconcerned. "It has been over a decade. He doesn't have the balls or the guts to do it."

"Or is he just biding his time? What did you do with it? His finger."

Another shrug. "I had it taxidermied and framed in a shadowbox, and Marc has it hanging up in his office."

"Awesome. Can I see?"

"You'll have to be invited in there first."

My shoulders slump. That will never happen. I saw the look on Marc's face right before I came down here. He believes I'm choosing Harris over him.

That couldn't be further from the truth.

45

DELILAH

Harris snakes under my shirt, startling me back to awareness. Then he runs his thumb along the scar on my ribcage, just below my right breast.

He has been doing this a lot lately. They both have. They find every excuse to touch my scar, courtesy of my second open heart surgery. Marc would stare at it for extended moments, tracing it with both his blade and fingers. Harris constantly massages it with this pensive look, the one he has now. They both pay extra attention to it when we make love. Constantly.

I don't know what to make of their obsession. It's not pretty, I know that. It's a ghastly deformity that's permanently etched into my skin, a constant reminder death forever knocks on my door, biding its time to whisk me away. I wouldn't mind, but death still wouldn't claim me. That son of a bitch has been ignoring me for decades.

"He tried to kill you," he eventually says.

I blink once, then twice.

How did he read my mind?

"My dad," he adds.

Oh.

My lips part but no sound comes out.

Harris tightens his hold on me. His chest shudders with hard breaths, and his fingers dig into the sensitive skin of my thighs. "He tried to sabotage your surgery back then, also your recovery. He knew he couldn't touch Marc, not without bringing the wrath of the Sotelo family upon himself, so he went after the innocent wallflower instead. I know he wanted to hurt me in the worst way possible, and you were the easiest target. It was his sinister way of giving me the middle finger, so I took it. Literally. And he—" he draws in a shaky breath, "he wasn't working alone. I heard him say something about doing this town a favor by ridding it of the defective spare."

This is the first time he's told me any of this, but given his dad's attitude toward me, none of this surprises me.

I know about the defective spare thing, and I'm not offended by it. It is what I am. I was deemed defective at birth. Being born with a congenital heart defect would do that. I've had both of my aortic valves replaced — one as an infant, the other in college. Ventricular tachycardia is my body's best friend. I know my heart could give out at any moment without warning.

It's why I decided not to form attachments to people. Not meaningful ones. The ones who leave don't feel anything, yet the ones who are left behind get to feel the brunt of it.

Pain. Grief. Longing. Despair. Heartache. Heartbreak.

I had to live through all that when Simone went missing, then again when my parents died. I barely survived it then; I wouldn't a third time, and I don't want to put anyone through that either. I put up all the walls I could think of, but Harris and Marc found a way to plow through my defenses.

It makes sense now, the things they told me over the years about people and their weaknesses.

Harris, Marc, and I are a unique brand of damaged.

Harris is Marc's kryptonite.

I am Harris's kryptonite.

They are my kryptonite, both of them together.

So much for not forming attachments to people.

"That's how you came to be under Marc's protection." Harris is still talking. "He didn't want Victor getting any ideas about retaliating. I don't think he expected anyone to come to the defective spare's defense, so it was a lesson he needed to learn the hard way."

I give him a small smile. "Someday, your dad's wish will come true. We all die, Harris. Death eventually comes for all of us, some sooner than others."

He brushes a lock of hair away from my face and tucks it behind my ear. "Why not spend the time that you do have being happy? What good does a life of solitude do you?" A beat passes, then, "Don't give up your dream for me."

My heart clenches. "Don't—"

"It's not worth it, Delilah. *I* am not worth it."

My eyelids flutter, then close, and I take a deep, shuddering breath.

I don't know when, how, or why this happened, but I can't live without them. Not now, not ever.

It takes a while for coherent thought to return. "I used to have panic attacks when I was young. Debilitating ones. They happened so frequently that my parents thought it would be the thing that killed me, not my heart. Then one day they suddenly stopped."

He presses his lips to my shoulder. "They stopped in college, I remember that. I don't see what that has to do with you living a life of solitude."

It's hard not to laugh at his impatience. "I didn't know it then, but Dahlia started having them right around the same time mine stopped. She tried to hide it, but I caught her. After watching me go through it for years, she ought to know better. There's no hiding it; when one starts, it can go really bad fast.

"She insists on keeping it a secret. She didn't want the McWhorters to know, so we've been carrying on like mine never left. I already had everything I needed to manage mine, so she inherited all of that. That didn't stop me from dragging her to several specialists to determine what caused it. They tried everything, including triggering mine back up, but that didn't work. One by one, they each arrived at the same conclusion. One word: transference."

He nods, then shakes his head before asking, "How?"

I shrug. "I have no idea. She had to watch me go through open heart surgery without my parents' support, which might have caused it. Psychologically, it makes sense. Scientifically speaking, it's an abnormality. No one can explain why her symptoms are nearly identical to mine. Or even why the intensity of hers is almost identical to what mine used to be. Some idiot tried to claim it was all in her head, and when that triggered one, he said she was faking it. I may or may not have assaulted him." I let out a dry laugh. "Marc was very unhappy with me. You remember that, don't you?"

He laughs. "Whatever happened to that guy? Did Marc blackmail him?"

"Something like that." That doctor has since been disbarred, disgraced, and bankrupted, courtesy of several class-action lawsuits from several patients. "It's been over a decade and she still has them. To us, it's real. As real as my sitting here with you. As real as breathing."

He leans his forehead against mine. "I like real."

"I know you do. The point I'm trying to make is that transference is real. What if I ended up needing open heart surgery again? What if, by living through it, you both end up getting it or worse?"

"We will cross that bridge when the time comes."

My eyelids part, eyes clashing with his brown ones. "You don't understand," I continue, my voice frantic. "It's already happened once before, with you two. It can't happen again. I can't let it happen again."

His brow furrows. "What're you talking about?"

"I almost ruined your relationship. Seven years ago, Marc was telling the truth. He didn't fuck another woman. That was me. Well, it wasn't me. He didn't... I came on to him. I propositioned him. The lipstick you found on his shirt got there because I put it there. It was my perfume you smelled on him. I was drunk, but it doesn't excuse what I did. But then Marc took the blame for it, and I thought everything was fine. Until you showed up the next day, saying all sorts of things. Mostly about leaving him, and I couldn't bear the thought of—"

"Delilah!"

"What?"

My chest heaves. He tightened his grip on me as I was rambling.

"I knew." His lips stretch to a smile.

It takes a minute for his words to register. "You knew?"

"Of course I knew. I know what you smell like, Delilah. I know what you taste like. And after fifteen years, you best believe I'm intimately familiar with all the sounds you make, in and out of bed. So yeah, I fucking knew it was you back then."

"Asshole," I breathe.

The smile spreads. "You got that right. But I'm your asshole, and don't you forget that."

I shake my head. "This makes no sense. If you knew—"

"I was mad at Marc back then, and I was going to leave him, too.

But not because I thought he cheated, Delilah. We always had an open relationship until you. He never cared about other women either, only the men. And I didn't care about the lipstick. Marc has gotten worse things in far more desirable places, so what's a little lipstick between friends?"

He lets out a deprecating laugh but I don't join him. This is all too much to take in.

"Why did you say he fucked another woman?"

"I said that?"

"You were shit-faced, Harris. Same as I was the day before. So yeah, you did say that, amongst other things."

"Oh." He sighs, then goes quiet. It takes him a while before he says, "He turned you down, Delilah. He's always known how I feel about you, yet he turned you down. That's why I was going to leave him."

He sounds sincere, but something about that doesn't sit right with me.

No one leaves Marc. He's said this to me enough times over the years that it's stuck. If he's being serious about this, and if he were to do it — leave Marc, that is — he would have done so seven years ago. Since he didn't, it tells me that little show, the one I got front-row tickets to, was pointless.

"But you never left," I mutter.

"What?"

I swallow thickly. "You never left him," I repeat. "And you watched me beat myself up over it all this time? Why?"

"I didn't watch. I waited. *We* waited, Marc and I."

His words barely register.

"I don't believe you," I say, with a slight shake of my head.

"We waited for you, Delilah. We were waiting for you to come back to us, sober, and ask. But it took you seven fucking years."

"Bullshit. You guys didn't wait for me."

"We did."

Another headshake. "I had to watch you two fuck other people for seven years, men and women alike, so don't give me this bullshit about waiting."

"We thought — or rather, I wanted to give you time to get used to the idea of us as a throuple. I thought that if you saw us with one other person at a time, it would warm you up to the idea of being a family with us. We gave up the scene and settled for domesticity. Sort of. But we were always waiting for you."

"You have a strange way of showing it."

"I know. If it's any consolation, Marc hated the idea but I talked him into it."

"You? But I thought—"

"You are the only woman he has ever wanted, and if he'd had his way back then you would have been here with us. Not any of the others. Except for David Holcomb. Marc really likes David, so we kept him. He used to do this thing with his—"

He gets a smack on the chest for that. "Tales of her boyfriends' sexual conquests are not what a girl wants to hear. Not unless she's joining in."

His eyes gleam and the smile on his face grows wider. "Boyfriend?"

I shrug. "Marc likes labels."

He cups my cheeks in his palms. "I like them too. Girlfriend."

"Don't use it all up in one day."

He chuckles. "I love you, girlfriend."

"I tolerate you too. Boyfriend."

He pulls me in for a kiss, which soon turns languid and sensual, with a splash of sweetness that is new, even for him.

"Does that mean you're in?" he asks after some time. "No more talk about sacrificing—"

"You're missing the point," I say with a sigh, then place a hand on his chest, right over his beating heart. "This isn't a contest, and I'm not some prize to be won. Don't make me choose, Harris."

"You still don't get it, do you?" He puts his hand over mine and presses down. "Feel that? That's all your doing. I've never loved anyone like I love you. Well, I love Marc, but not like I do you. It's different with you. I can't live without you, Delilah. I just... I won't do it, so if I have to reconcile your hopes and dreams with mine then so be it. Because this sucks. All of it."

I blink and my whole body seizes up. "What're you saying?"

He pulls back slightly, his eyes glistening as they roam all over my face. "I love you, Delilah," he says, his voice low and soft. "I have loved you since I sat next to you in freshman biology. And I know that I don't deserve you. I fucking know it, but I can't lose you. Not now, not ever. Don't make me choose either because I'll..." he trails off, his upper body slips, and he plops his face on my shoulder.

Blood rushes through my ears. This is not what I expected. The only thing that could make this worse is—

"What about me?"

46

HARRIS

We both turn in the direction of the shop door, only to realize that wasn't where the sound of Marc's voice originated from. Silly, since there are five deadbolts on the door and I put all of them in place.

Another door clicks shut, startling us both. We both turn in the direction of the sound. The bookcase.

A secret passageway?

"I designed this fucking house," Marc says in response to my unspoken question. "There are secret passageways within passageways throughout. Assume I know where all of them are."

"This isn't what it looks like," I tell him.

He lets out a strangled laugh. "You need a better catchphrase, H. That one's stale."

Delilah pushes my body off hers and I reluctantly let her go. She hops off the bench and makes a beeline for him, but he takes a step back when she reaches to touch him.

She looks utterly distraught as her hands fall to her sides, and she takes an answering step back from him. For some reason, this angers me.

"You can be angry at me all you want, but don't you fucking take it out on her."

"Oh, I'm angry," he admits, his voice cold. He turns to her before saying, "But not at you, D. I don't want to risk hurting you."

She nods and presses her lips together, her eyes pained.

He runs his hands through his hair and turns to me. "Sixteen fucking years, H. That means nothing all of a sudden?"

"Marc—" I start to say, but Delilah beats me to it.

"Shut the fuck up, Harris, let him talk."

Marc leans against the doorway and sets both hands on his waist. "I know I haven't always been the best boyfriend, but I also know I've never given you a reason to regret being mine. Not ever, H. Not even when your dad made my life a living hell. Not even when he went after my practice. My fucking reputation. All that time, I've never given you a reason to doubt what and how I feel about you. I've given you everything you've asked for." He casts a glance in Delilah's direction before his gaze returns to mine. "And even the things you didn't ask for. Even when I knew it would piss you off. Because I need you to know deep down in your bones that you are the most important thing to me. You will always be the most important thing in my world. I could never love anything or anyone the way that I love you. D's a fucking close second, sure, but it has always been you, H. Always. Fucking always."

He pauses to catch his breath.

That's a lot of words, even for him.

Usually, this would be the time I selfishly point out that he misread the situation, but how can you spin this into a positive? There's no way. But that doesn't mean I won't try.

"Marc, I—" Delilah starts to say, but he holds up a hand to her.

"Not now, D. I know you mean well, but not right now." He levels his gaze with mine. "H will use you, you know? It's what he does. Personally, I never cared because he has always been it for me. But not you. This isn't the first time he's pulled a stunt like this, and it won't be the last. What happens when you wake up sixteen years from now, realizing that you gave up your dream of motherhood for a fucking coward? What then?"

A pained sound erupts from her. She turns to me, eyes shimmering with tears. "What is he talking about?"

I ignore her. "Marc, stop it."

"Why? Why don't you tell her what really happened seven years ago? Or do you need a few minutes to spin this one in your favor?"

"Leave it the fuck alone," I warn, my tone steely.

"No?" He turns to her. "My family has their own cocktail mixer. Her name is Lady Poison, but she also goes by Phoenix. H reached out to her and ordered a custom celebratory cocktail just for you. It was a mix of Scopolamine, Rohypnol, and something else. That's what he used on you that day. You had two shots of tequila, not ten, not fifteen, or whatever number H told you. Two shots, but laced with some heavy-duty date-rape drugs. Then he shoved you into my arms because he was too fucking chicken to do his own dirty work."

She turns to me, her bottom lip anchored between her teeth as her face glistens with tears. "Why?"

I flinch.

"Because he loves you," Marc continues. "He loves you, but he's also a selfish fucker. He wants what he wants, D, and he got tired of waiting."

Her legs give out from underneath her and she crumples to the floor. Marc beats her to it, diving to the bottom to break her fall.

Meanwhile, I'm frozen in place and unable to move. I don't say anything. My head is spinning, and the loud rush of blood swimming around my ears drowns out everything else.

He sits up and wraps his arms around her, burying her face in his chest.

"For the record, I never said I didn't want them," he continues, his voice hoarse. "Just because you didn't care for them doesn't mean I did too. I never bothered because being on the same page and finding the right woman had to carry equal weight. And guess what? You found her. The right woman. She's been with us all along. Right fucking here. She's been by our side, dealing with our shit for fifteen fucking years. You know it, I know it. So don't you dare pretend otherwise."

Delilah makes a strangled sound into his chest, then mumbles something only he hears. He tightens his hold on her, presses his lips into her hair, and then mumbles something in response.

His eyes soften when they lift to meet mine. "Lord knows I haven't done anything at all to deserve you, or to deserve this life we have, or even to deserve you both. But it's not this. You wanna ride off into the sunset with D and live happily ever after? Fine, you do that. But where the fuck does that leave me?"

My lips part but no sound comes out.

He rises to his knees, then to his feet, with her limp body still nestled in his arms. They leave the same way he came in, through his secret passageway.

My face turns up and I blow out a frustrated breath. I really screwed this one up.

47

DELILAH

Everyone leaves me. One way or another, they leave.

Marc left as soon as he deposited my numb body in our bed. He placed a picture of Simone in my arms, the same one I have been clutching every night.

I have no idea where Harris is. He could still be in the basement, or he could have snuck out and gone to Hell. He does have a workshop there, courtesy of David.

That's how it starts. A fight here, a threat there.

Before you know it, it's *Bye-bye, Delilah. Hello, heartache.*

I can't take it anymore, the crushing weight of despair that constantly threatens to sink me. This ships-in-the-night thing isn't working for me. But since I can do something about it, I brush off my pity party and search for him in this vast estate.

Fortunately, I don't have to go very far. He is predictable in his actions, so it makes sense he would take refuge in the one place Harris wouldn't step foot in. Charlie's not here either, but that won't make a difference. Today is one of his days here, so Courtney must have taken him home.

Marc sits in the pitch-black darkness, leaning against Charlie's crib and twirling his signature pocket knife in his hands. I join him on the floor, directly opposite him and in his line of sight. I can barely make out the whites of his eyes as they follow my every movement. There's no discernible physical reaction on his part. Except for his blade, which catches rays of moonlight at just the right angle.

"She is my everything," I say softly.

The words hang in the air between us, heavy and smothering.

"Why are you telling me this?" he eventually asks.

I shrug, shoulders heaving against the wall. "You asked."

He laughs. "It can't be that simple, D."

"Why not?"

"I asked several times already, and you wouldn't budge."

"I've never discussed her with Harris."

"He's your best friend, is he not?"

"He is, but I'm not naive. I know just how selfish and self-centered he is. I also know he will never get it, so I never bothered. But you do. She is to me what Harris is to you.

"Simone is the first person I ever truly fell in love with," I say truthfully. "Not Simon, the boy I grew up with, but Simone, the girl and subsequently the woman she blossomed into. But they are one and the same, and I love them both. I always have, and I always will.

"We grew up together, the four amigos. She is three years older than the rest of us, but that didn't make much difference. With our family backgrounds, we knew our friendship didn't make much sense once we were old enough to understand it. Still, we didn't let silly things like age or status get in the way of our friendships.

"Simon was... complicated, to say the least. He was always angry. Constantly picking fights, pulling pranks, and getting into all sorts of mischief. My parents suspected there was more to it than just simple teenage rebellion, but the McWhorters would hear nothing of it. My parents also suspected some abuse at home. Yet Simon refused to acknowledge it and Curtis always backed up his brother's version of events. My parents knew they couldn't make any accusations, publicly or privately, not without absolute proof. Not only would the McWhorters have had any charges against them thrown out, but my parents would also have been discredited for good measure. Their work was far too important, so they weighed the pros and cons and decided it was best to publicly keep their mouths shut for the greater good. But they did what they could, and part of that was the McWhorter kids spent a lot of time at our house. Hence, the chair.

"When Dahlia and I hit puberty and started getting into all things 'girly,'" I put air quotes around the word, "he took an interest in that too. Curtis wouldn't touch it with a ten-foot pole. He thought we all had cooties, so it became our thing. The three amigos. We would go all out with it too. At first, he helped us do our make-up, pick out our clothes, that sort of thing. Then he started trying it out for himself. Subtle things, here and there. Some lip-gloss here, a little bit of eyeshadow there. Then he and Dahlia *really* got into it and that became their thing. I didn't mind it since I was content with just watching them."

Marc is quiet as he absorbs all of this information, the sounds of his heavy breathing fill the air.

"Do you remember what it was like, the first time you met Harris?"

In the pitch-black darkness, I can barely make out the nod of his head. I can also envision the wistful look that comes into his eyes because I'm sure mine mirrors his.

"I still clearly remember the day she came out to us. To myself, Dahlia, Curtis, and my parents. She was sixteen and fucking terrified. Her entire body shook like a lone leaf in the middle of a violent storm. Can you imagine baring yourself like that, body and soul, to a bunch of judgmental thirteen-year-olds? Even though we were her three closest friends, it was a risk she took not knowing if we would accept or shun her. But she still did it. She took the brave step into the unknown, not knowing which way it would go.

"And well... she... she was a breath of fresh air. It was the first time I'd ever seen her truly happy. Truly comfortable in her own skin. This," I tap my fingers over my defective heart, "came to life, and it was at that moment that I fell in love, head over heels in love, for the first time in my life. I fell in love with her, and I never fell out.

"I think we all did, each in our own way. It was like a cloud had been lifted, you know? This shroud of darkness lifted off of us. The same thing happened with my parents too. I don't think I'd ever seen them so happy. They welcomed another daughter into the fold, no questions asked.

"You know what her parents are like now, well, they were much worse back then. From the time she was sixteen to eighteen, our house became the permanent hangout space for all of us. She was Simone under my parents' roof and Simon everywhere else, until she was ready to go public and figure out a way to deal with her parents. That kind of duplicity is a lot for a teenager to handle, so my parents sought additional help for her. Therapy was one avenue.

"The picture of her I carry with me everywhere was from that day. The day she first came out to us. Dahlia took those pictures." A long shuddering breath moves slowly through me. "The pictures here and at home are the last ones still in existence. Because when she did the same thing three years later, on her nineteenth birthday, it didn't go so well. The second time she came out, it was to her parents, with the five of us present for moral support. Suffice it to say it was a fucking disaster. While none of us expected it to go as well as it did the first time, we never imagined it would end as horribly. They blew up, called her names, called us all names, and threatened my parents. I missed the encore later that evening, but Dahlia told me it was worse. There was extensive property damage involved, amongst other things. She went missing not too long afterward, after..."

I pause then, my body racked with angry sobs. Marc says nothing, but I sense his eyes on me. His anger bleeds off of him in strong, intense waves. It's just like her energy from back then.

He continues to watch me. Just as intently I watch him back, taking in his features. The shadows of the night hide the color of his eyes, but I can imagine the stormy gray gleaming with interest just as clearly as if it were daylight.

"It's taken me a long while, but I choose to focus on the good things about her. The positive memories. It was a once-in-a-lifetime type of love. I never thought I'd ever find anything like that with anyone. Don't get me wrong, I'm grateful to the universe for having known her for as long as I did, and for understanding what it is like to love and be loved by her.

"But I resent the heck out of the universe for taking her from me far too soon. I resent her parents for erasing every trace of her existence from this world, all because they would rather have a dead son than an alive daughter. I also resent them for driving her to her wit's end, for shoving her between a rock and a hard place. Heck, I resent her for not standing up to them, for not putting her foot down and saying enough is fucking enough. She taught me how to do that, so why couldn't she do so for herself?

"For years, I resented anyone and anything that reminded me of her. I resented that I knew how it felt to have loved and lost at sixteen. Not even the pain of losing my parents years later hurt as much as the pain of losing her.

"Knowing her, she would've been praying equally as hard for us, all of us, that we find the strength to go on, make peace with our inner demons, break free of our own anchors. And I would have been fine without all of that. I'm... ready to die. I've been prepared to die since I first understood what it entails. Two open heart surgeries only solidified my belief in my own mortality. I'm ready for my defective heart to give out at any moment, even though it's supposed to be 'fixed,' and I've made peace with it. But Simone never wanted that for me, and she would have prayed that I find love, eventually. And I did. I just didn't count on the fact that I'd find it with two different people. People who remind me of her best and worst parts all rolled into one and imperfectly packaged. Or rather, two imperfect men.

"When I first met Harris, it was three years after she went missing. He reminded me of that light I saw in her. The one that drew me in, tethering my soul to hers in the first place. Her essence. Her boundless joy. Her enthusiasm. It wasn't all rainbows and unicorns like Harris describes, it was the most grueling case of déjà vu I had ever experienced. Yet I thought to myself, *I can handle this. It's fine. It's just a coincidence.*

"Then I met you a year later and my heart fucking stopped. That darkness you have, the one raging a constant battle for dominance inside of you, I recognized it instantly. I fucking grew up with it. That's what I missed the most about her, you know? Not all that fluffy shit that people love to reminisce on. So it was gut-wrenching déjà fucking vu all over again, times two. I thought the universe was playing a fucking joke on me. And why wouldn't it? It took her from me, and then it gave me you two like some shitty consolation prize I never asked for in the first fucking place. No offense."

Marc's hearty laugh fills the room. "None taken. Although I have to say, we've been called many things, but a shitty consolation prize was never one of them."

I can't help but smile at that. "Yeah, well, you must have known I was keeping you both at bay even though you inserted yourselves into every aspect of my life. Harris especially. He's not good at the word no, but I suspect you have something to do with that, given his history with Victor.

"The thing is, I know you are not Simone and Harris isn't Simone either, but that doesn't quell the draw I feel toward you both. Especially you. So I fought it. I spent many years fighting it with every fiber of my being. Not so much with Harris, since he was willing to settle for a friendship. But I'm not stupid or naive. I knew he wanted more. He wasn't subtle about it either.

"I didn't know about the drugging, but I'm not surprised by it either. Don't get me wrong, I'm pissed he lied about it, not that he did it. I've had worse done to me before, but I always knew about it. My love for science didn't come from my parents. It came from her. They laid down the groundwork for it, but she held my hand and jumped over the fucking cliff. She wanted to become a researcher like my parents, so guess who her crash test dummy was?

"But you? You're a whole other beast, Marc. You don't strike me as the friends-only type of guy. More like the 'melt her clothes off her body before she can even comprehend what's happening' type of guy. Then Harris told me that you were gay, through and through. That you didn't fuck women, ever. That made things slightly bearable. But you kept looking at me the way you always have, like you are right now, making me doubt everything. Still, I kept my distance. Not because you were with Harris, but because I always knew I couldn't control myself around you.

"That day, seven years ago, was a slip-up. I'd been doing so well before then. I made sure our one-on-one interactions involved Harris as a buffer between us. Then there was fucking tequila, which I could have said no to, and you were there, and... well, you know the rest. Then it almost broke you guys up, and I didn't know how to live with that, knowing that I was the reason why one of the most stable relationships I knew of ended. And also because..." I trail off at that.

"Because what?" he rasps when I don't continue.

I draw in a shuddering breath. This whole night is exhausting, but since we opened Pandora's box, we might as well see it through to the bitter end.

"You know, I tried, okay? For the last seven years, I tried to make amends to both of you. I watched you two fuck other people and kept my mouth shut even as I died a little on the inside. It was what I deserved.

"So no, I didn't keep my fucking distance because you and Harris were together. I kept my distance because of what's in you. That fucking darkness, it sucks you in and never lets go. But the thing is, I love it. It balances out the light. Yin and yang. Two halves of a whole. That's what you and Harris are to me. I can't have one without the other. It's taken me fifteen years to come to terms with that. If there is any chance of happiness for me, I know it won't be with just one of you. Call me selfish, but I want you both. I will always want you both."

His eyes meet mine, his chest heaving in exertion. "You done?"

I shake my head. "I love you, Marc. I won't deny or make excuses for what I said or what Harris said because those are true. All of it. But that's between him and me. But between you and me, there's…" I blow out a breath, steeling myself before continuing. "I love you, Marc. I love you so much it hurts. It hurts all over, from the tips of my hair all the way to the tips of my toenails. It's the kind of hurt that only you can make better. The kind of ache only you can soothe. I've been operating with the assumption that you'll always be there. But now… now, I can't imagine a scenario, or any semblance of a relationship or future where you're not in it. I can't lose you, Marc. I can't lose him either. And I refuse to let her go. I know that's all kinds of fucked up, and maybe I belong in the fucking loony bin for saying all of this, but it's the truth. My truth. I know what it's like to have loved and lost once already, I don't think I could survive it a second time. I… I don't think I could survive losing you."

I let that hang between us for a moment.

Then I take a deep, fortifying breath and slowly release it. "Now I'm done."

Four seconds later, he's on all fours and his face is inches before mine. Our gazes lock and my heart stops again, as he stares into the depths of my soul, unleashing the full might of his darkness on me. It's raw and unfettered, with no holds barred. As hungry as I am, I eat it right up.

"Thank you for trusting me with her."

My heart clenches in my chest at the pure emotion in his voice, and it takes everything in me not to throw myself into his arms.

Instead, I put my palm over his chest. "There is one other thing that you two have in common."

That odd little curve to his mouth makes a reappearance. "What's that?"

"Charlie. Courtney. Harris. Me. You take care of everyone all the time. Who takes care of you?"

"I don't need to be taken care of," he says, his voice husky.

"Everybody needs to be taken care of. You're only human. It's a natural disposition."

"You're taking care of me right now. I'll settle for that."

"*Settle?*"

Something about the word rubs me the wrong way. I can't explain why. It just does.

"I'm gonna fuck you, D. Right now. I'll use your body to work through all of my frustration. I'll shred your pussy, ass, and mouth like they're my own personal confetti. I will use you, destroy you, put you back together, and do it all over again. We'll start in here, then work our way upstairs. Four hours should do it, maybe more. That all right with you?"

Violent shivers run through the entire length of my body as he describes one of my many fantasies, his voice as calm as it would be while discussing the weather. Then he crawls back to his original position, settles in, and stretches out both legs in front of him.

"Come here," he growls, tapping his blade against the inside of his massive thighs.

Keeping our gazes locked, I rise to my feet, shedding layer after layer slowly until I'm left in my birthday suit.

For practical reasons, obviously. While I couldn't care less about my jeans and t-shirt, he doesn't need to ruin a perfectly good set of lingerie. Not when he has easy access to it all. Also, the brands I like are expensive, not that he cares since I now have several black cards with no limits.

I get down on all fours like he did just moments prior. "You don't need to summon me, ever. I'll always come to you. On all fours. On two legs. On two hands. I'll fucking crawl through a fiery pit, on hot coals, or even through hell to get to you, always. Forever."

A ghost of a smile teases the corners of his lips. "Forever?"

I nod. "Forever."

A full-blown smile blossoms. "I'll take forever," he says, his voice low and soft. "You better not renege on that."

"I won't. So, how do you want me?" I say, wriggling my ass in the air. "Where do you want me?"

"On my lap, with my cock inside you." He laughs. "How about we test out those multi-tasking skills of yours, huh? See if they've gotten any better since the last time."

Sold. "Ass or pussy?"

"I've got other plans for your ass."

My breath hitches. "Knife?"

A sinister look comes over his face. "I warned you, D. Non-negotiable. Knife. Cock. K—" A pause. "It's all going in you, one way or the other."

"Do I get to pick?"

"It depends."

"On?"

"Whether or not we have the same thing in mind."

"Will it hurt?"

"Get your fucking ass over here," he growls, impatient. "You know what will happen if I ask again."

48

DELILAH

It is time I got the phrase *'I love my sister'* permanently tattooed on my arm or as a tramp stamp. Either option will have its intended effect on me and my boys and remind me not to indulge her crazy ideas.

Don't get me wrong, I always will. That's what good sisters do. But while I am at it, I will remind her of it every step of the way.

"You realize this is just plain stupidity on your part, right?" I say for the umpteenth time as we make our way to the basement of our building, Brewer Health.

"I told you that you didn't have to be here," Dahlia says as she punches in the code that unlocks the door to her darkroom. "I could just as easily have gotten someone else to help."

"Bullshit. Why don't I go get fucking Curtis to help, since he's the closest thing to... oh wait, we can't. Your boyfriend put him in the fucking hospital."

God, I really am such a bitch.

A vindictive bitch, that is. It's about time someone knocked that asshole down a few pegs. My only regret is I wasn't there to see it.

"You should be in one, too," Dahlia counters as we walk into the adjoining storage room. "You look like someone ran your entire body through a fucking cheese grater. Just like old times, huh?"

It's pointless, but I still pull my sleeves down over my arms. "Mind your business."

"You're all up in mine, so yours is fair game. Did Marc do that?"

"And if he did?"

"Do I need to—"

"No," I say forcefully. "We've had some things to work through."

Her eyes narrow. "Things? Dee, those bruises appear to be weeks in the making. Layers of them. What kind of things?"

"Just things. All you need to know is that I asked for this. I fucking goaded him into it."

She lifts a brow. "You goad your boyfriend into having rough sex with you? What the hell kind of relationship do you three have?"

"The passionate kind, okay? Also, I told him about Simone."

With that, I square my shoulders, make my way to the shelves with the H files, and start rummaging through the box labels. While I don't have to Marie Kondo this room, these should get my mind off things for a while.

It doesn't take long before my frustration at this soon takes over. In this day and age, no one should still have this many paper files. But that happens when you buy another practice and inherit their medical files. The ones we are going through today came from Sonya's old practice.

Sonya — Dr. Sonya Goodman — was one of my parents' peers and colleagues. She'd also been one of our professors in medical school and took on a quasi-mentor role for both Dahlia and me. When Dahlia and I were looking to officially launch Brewer Health, we were also setting up our individual practices. She suggested we buy existing medical practices and combine those under the same parent company, Brewer Health. She'd been looking to retire and offered us her practice at a steal. And since we could afford it, we took her up on her offer. Eventually, her practice morphed into what is now Brewer Medical Clinic. Shortly after, we made another similar purchase and turned that into Brewer Diagnostics LLC. It's partly contributed to us growing as quickly as we did in a short time. Not only that, but we are actively discussing acquiring some practices that lease space in our building.

I thought it strange Sonya retired when she did. She was still so full of life, even though she had been practicing for a long time. She was a legacy in the medical community. In medical school, students were constantly vying for the opportunity to be mentored by her. From our class, she hand-picked me, Dahlia, Harris, Charlena, Erasmo, and Nalina as her protégés, even though we all had different specialties. Her thing was variety, and women's health wasn't the only thing she specialized in. She only kept that as a cover for the other things she did. It also explains how and why our various specialties blended seamlessly with hers.

"Wow," Dahlia says, appearing next to me. "You told Marc about Simone?"

I nod.

"What part?"

"All of it."

She is silent for a while. "That's huge," she eventually says.

I blow out a breath. "Yeah."

"What did he say?"

"He… umm… thanked me."

"He thanked you? What for?"

"For trusting him with her." I tip my face upwards and stare at the popcorn texture in the ceiling. "He says he can find her and bring her home. Permanently, if that's what I want. All I have to do is say the word. Four words. I want her back."

She places a hand on my shoulder. "Is that what you want?"

I turn to face her. "I don't know." A beat passes, then, "Is this what you want?"

Tears spring into her eyes. "I don't know either."

I take the time to study her tired features. The bags under her eyes. Her gaunt cheeks. "You love him."

Her cheeks flush as she says, "I don't love him." Squeaks, more like.

"Oh. My bad then. You are in love with him," I re-state.

She shakes her head and rolls her eyes. "That's not what this is."

God, she can be dense at times. "He hacked into your phone, Daa. And your laptop. And our medical records. Repeatedly. For months."

We both know all this already, but sometimes she needs these things spelled out.

Her response surprises me.

"Well, he exposed the many loopholes in our system," she says, pulling a box off the shelf. "What that tells me is we should fire our current security company for their gross incompetence and hire a new one who will install better firewalls."

She heads for the work table in the middle of the room, leaving me staring at her retreating figure and wondering what the hell has gotten into my strait-laced sister.

"Maybe we should hire him," I say dryly as I follow her with a box of my own.

"*That* is an excellent idea," she calls out over her shoulder. "Why don't you have Marc draw up the contracts, keep it all above-board?"

"Jesus, Daa. Do you even hear yourself?" I set the box down on the table and then turn to her. "The proper response would be to file charges and let the authorities take care of it. Instead, here you are, looking for his mother's records."

She waves a hand at what we've pulled out so far. "If it'll get him to stop breaking so many laws, then so be it."

"And you're sure it's not because you love him?"

"Nope."

Right. "So, let me get this straight. David beat Curtis to a bloody pulp and got himself arrested. Then you went after him, not Curtis."

She crosses her arms and glares at me. "I don't owe Curtis anything. He started the fucking fight."

"I know. I was there. Sort of."

"You're not so innocent in all this, you know. You're the one that beat Nalina up in a fucking police station."

"And you're the one that slapped her in said police station."

"That's because she called Simone a—"

"I know what she said. I was there. Marc and I heard the whole thing."

I don't think Nalina learned her lesson, so I might go back and rough her up some more to get the fucking message across. Besides, me beating people up on occasion is nothing new, and Marc would attest to this since he's the one who usually cleans up those messes — legally, of course. Dahlia, on the other hand... let's just say Nalina will not be getting into her good graces any time soon. Or ever.

Good riddance, if you ask me. The audacity of that bitch. I don't care if people call me defective. It's who I am. However, I draw the line at anyone disrespecting Simone as she did. Not to mention, Nalina has been fucking David since he was fifteen. There's no coming back from that. It's too bad that David refuses to press charges, even though the statute of limitations hasn't yet passed. He doesn't want that information publicized, and given where we are, I can't help but feel for the guy.

Dahlia does too, even though she's obviously *not* in love with him.

"I think we have four more boxes to pull; then we can start going through these." She sighs and rolls her hips. "Remind me why we didn't have these digitized years ago?"

"We have the perfect, temperature-controlled space to store them?" I offer with a shrug.

Another sigh. "Last two runs?"

"For you, anything."

My shoulders slump and I follow after her.

I thought Sonya was yanking our chain when she came to Dahlia and me talking about retiring. Sure, she gave us some sound business advice, but my alarm bells went off when she offered us her practice at a steal. Her only non-negotiable clause was that any and all existing medical records tied to her practice had to be included in the purchase agreement. Marc's firm looked it all over and he confirmed it was all legit and above-board. Thus, Brewer Health inherited all of her medical records and patient files. So it's been pretty standard for us to do so in subsequent deals, and we owe it all to her initial suggestion.

However, no other practice came with as many paper files as hers. Sonya was a Luddite, but that spanned generations. She inherited files from her mother's practice, who also inherited them from her father's practice, and so on. All of those files predate either of our respective practices. Some of those go back decades. Most of these records are for patients who died before either of us were born. For all we know, it could be a fucking treasure trove that we've been sitting on. We don't have time to digitize these records, and no one is allowed down here aside from myself, Dahlia, and David. Sonya died a few years ago, so it's not like we can ask her what the heck it is that's so important about these.

I know that paper files aren't hackable, so here we are, looking for the physical copies of David's mother's records. Marina Holcomb. Dahlia already gave me the gist of it since it was the only way she could get me to indulge her in this crazy idea. That, and she's almost thirty-four weeks pregnant, so she really shouldn't be lifting anything. But she was planning to anyway if I refused. Though organized, the amount of boxes in this room is staggering, and the thought of me finding her dead body crushed under boxes upon boxes of files was enough to get me to agree. She even played the dead nephew card, knowing I couldn't have that on my conscience.

But since we are both here and went through all the trouble of pulling these out, we take the time to read up on it. It takes us six hours to get through every file, but we do. I'm feeling worse than vindictive when we're done. And I'm ready to resurrect Clark Holcomb, chop off his left testicle and feed it to him. Then string up his entrails and feed them to piranhas for fun. Still, that wouldn't be enough for a monster like him.

At least Marina got to kill him, so thank goodness for small miracles.

On the other hand, Dahlia is still stubborn and bull-headed about this.

"You both deserve a win," I tell her. "Haven't you both earned your happy endings? I can't speak for him, but I can speak for you. You love him."

"I can't be with him."

"Why not?"

"It's not that I don't want to, just… he's been through a lot. If I stay with him, I'd be continuing the cycle of the things he's already been through."

"Knowing what you know now," I tell her, "you can't break up with him. It will be cruel."

I am a hypocrite, pushing her to admit how she feels about David and to sort things out with her lover when I can't do the same with mine. I tried getting them both in the same room together. To talk to each other, at the very least. But they keep avoiding each other like the plague.

As always, she sees right through me.

She gives me a sad smile that doesn't quite reach her eyes. "I'm not you."

"What's that supposed to mean?"

"You're one to talk. You were stuck, for years, after Simone went missing. You've got that look about you now. Trouble in paradise?"

"Who says there's—"

"Harris hasn't called or texted you in hours. Why's that?"

I shift in my seat. "Let's just focus on the task at hand, okay? Are we leaving these here? Putting them back? Is this all of it?"

She scoff-laughs. "At least I'm not the only one with denial issues."

I groan and set my cheek against the table. "Everything is upside down and I don't know how to fix it."

She laughs. "Isn't that Marc's job?"

"I think it's my job this time around."

"So distract me. Tell me all about how shitty your life is. Misery does love company, after all."

"With you, it's the reverse."

"You want my help or not?"

I nod slowly. The tabletop's rough texture feels mildly unpleasant against my face.

"Start talking," she says.

My eyes meet hers, and I take a deep breath. "Harris moved out."

Her hearty laughter fills the room. "Yeah, right. And I'm the Queen of fucking England."

"It's true. He moved in with Courtney." Which means Charlie moved in with us.

The laughter dies on her lips. "Oh."

"Yeah."

He moved out the day after our fight. It's been almost two weeks, a new record for him.

"What does Marc have to say about that?"

I wave a hand over my body. "We have daily four-hour sex marathons."

"Ouch."

"Hey, I'm not complaining. At this rate, he just might get what he wants."

"What's that?"

"Kids."

She purses her lips and sets both elbows on the table, fingers steepled together. "There are far too many chunks of this story missing, so start from the beginning."

PART V

49

DELILAH

One month later

What is with these devils and messing with my car?

I suppose that's what I get, for getting myself involved with two devils.

Although the one currently in my way isn't either of the two I've claimed for myself. It's the other one. My sister's devil.

Clark David Holcomb.

Who apparently prefers David, seeing as his father was *the* Clark. A man so self-absorbed and narcissistic that he named his son after himself, not even bothering to add a *senior* or a *roman numeral* somewhere in there to distinguish between the two.

A man who abused his own sister for years, forced her to have his kid, then lied to the world and claimed said child was born via surrogate. And really, who would bat a pretty eyelash at it? The kid looked like his own sister — who was really his fucking mother *and* aunt — so he easily explained it away by claiming their family genetics made it so.

Well, I'm a fucking geneticist and I stand by the fact that there were far too many holes in that story for any medical professional worth their salt not to have tugged at any of the many, many threads on the edge and taken it all apart at the seams. But they didn't do that. Which only gave him ample opportunity, along with a false sense of

invincibility and unaccountability, so that he continued to do so —
abuse of his sister and eventually his son — without cause for recourse
or even remorse.

Truth be told, if she hadn't killed him, I just might have. Or sicced
one of my very own devils on him. I'm generous like that.

So yeah, a part of me is empathetic to David's story. I can only
imagine what life for him was like, growing up in a household like that.
Growing up with a father like that. Being lied to your whole life about
who your mother was, only to find out that she was right there with you
the whole time and you didn't even get a chance to acknowledge her as
your mother. Then you get a small taste of freedom — by getting
emancipated at fifteen — only for both of your parents to die and you
get dragged back into this shitstorm.

So yeah, I feel for the guy.

I really do.

But I digress.

Said devil, he leans against my car, arms folded across his chest,
looking oh so devilishly handsome and so at home. He's dressed in his
signature red on red on red, like it's the only color in his wardrobe. It
suits him, too.

Diabolus. His favorite nickname, apparently.

Which perfectly describes him too.

Why does he have to look so good? It ought to be criminal, how
sinfully good he looks in red. Then again, it really should be criminal
for him to look this delectable, not when I know how miserable Dahlia
currently is.

Then I remember how fucked up it was that he used her. He'd been
after her long before she left Curtis, before she walked away from that
equally fucked-up relationship. And even at her lowest of lows, when
she was raw and vulnerable and emotionally broken, he still sunk those
devilish clutches of his right into her, used her, fucking toyed with her
emotions.

And all for what? Fucking access to files, is what.

Granted, they were his mother's old medical records, but still.

"If I had my way, you'd be sitting in a jail cell right now," I
tell him.

He blows out a heated breath, standing straighter and tucking both
hands into his pockets. "I know." He nods. "And I'd deserve it."

Had he come right out and asked... we probably would've said no. Well, *Dahlia* would've said no. I would've considered it, maybe asked Marc's and Harris's opinion on the matter since they both know the man — intimately and otherwise — then I would've said yes. Because if there's one of us that would've been easier to get through to, it would've been me.

Delilah Brewer.

The fucking wallflower.

The Defective Spare.

I guess that's what made Dahlia all the more appealing — the fact that she was the unattainable twin out of the two of us. That made seducing her all the more appealing, which is fine, but he should have left it at her body only. He didn't have to go and toy with her fucking heart too.

Probably a good thing that he didn't come after me. Harris would've shredded him to bits if he'd tried, if Marc didn't beat him to it first, that is.

"Dahlia might have forgiven you for hacking her devices, and that's her prerogative. I'm not willing to forgive the fact that you broke into our network. Do you have any idea how that makes us look?"

"It's bad, I know. But if you could just—"

"I can still press charges, you know?" I say, cutting him off. Not really in the mood to hear his half-hearted excuses. I bought it once, when he convinced me to take him to her a few weeks back. I bought his fake concerns, hook, line and sinker. Boy, do I feel so stupid.

"I wouldn't blame you if you did."

"Granted, it will be a waste of both of our time, but still. I know you can just as easily buy off everyone involved — judges, cops, prosecutors, investigators — but it'll be fun trying. It'll be fun messing with this," I wave a hand at him, "persona you keep projecting. And maybe by the time I'm done being a pesky little thorn in your side, you'll learn your fucking lesson. Don't mess with the Brewer sisters. This one," I point to myself, "might be a wallflower, but she's also a viper. She's got a mean bite and she holds a grudge."

He doesn't say anything, but the mask slips. It slips and it falls, and in its place is a man who's just as broken and vulnerable as she is.

Good.

"Move." I adjust the strap of my purse over my shoulder. "You're in my way."

He doesn't move, but his hands twitch inside his pockets.

"Fine. You have exactly five seconds to say whatever it is you came here to say, then move the fuck out of my way."

"I have something for you," he says, pulling his right hand out of his pocket.

"We don't have the sort of relationship where exchanging gifts is appropriate."

"I know that. Still, I think you should have this." He holds out his hand to mine, palm up. In it is a small dog-bone shape, but knowing him my money is on it being a USB drive.

"If you got that through unsavory means, then I want nothing to do with it."

His jaw clenches but he keeps his hand out.

"That's probably something illegal, isn't it? Blackmail? Revenge porn?"

His brow scrounges. "Why would—?"

"Dahlia told me you have cameras installed throughout your fucking mansion. Is that what this is? A fucking sex tape? Is that the best you can do? A sex tape from when you were fucking my sister? What makes you think that threatening me with a sex tape of you fucking my sister would be enough to get me to back off? If anything—"

"It's Simone."

That knocks the literal air right out of my lungs. "What?"

"There are video messages, several of them. Some are specifically addressed to you, Dahlia, and your parents. There's one for Curtis, and one for her parents. And yes, you are correct in that I got them using unsavory means. I hacked into Dr. Aidan's system and found those on a ghost drive. I still can't believe that she's been sitting on these for eighteen years, some for maybe not as long, since she inherited her mother's practice, and by extension those files. Still, Nalina knew about them and didn't say anything…"

I go completely numb at his words. I stand there, as still as Lady Liberty, the statute, watching as his lips continue to move, sounds coming out of his mouth, and my brain struggles to comprehend what my ears are hearing.

"She couldn't have," I eventually say.

He stops. "What?"

"She couldn't have," I repeat. "She couldn't have told us that those existed, because she's still bound by doctor-patient confidentiality. Regardless of the relationship you two have, hacking her network is still illegal. Don't you get it? You did to her the exact same thing you did to us. Not only that, but you also broke into the one practice that she has in our building. Do you have any idea how that makes us look? Good god, David! This isn't the type of thing I can just overlook. You just keep making this worse for yourself, and now I have to break the promise I made to Dahlia and—"

"She loved you," he says, cutting me off. "I'm talking about Simone, obviously. She loved you, more than anything. From the way she talked about you, you were the most important person in the world to her. That's why I'm here, risking your wrath to give you this."

"No," I say, taking a step back from him. "You don't get to do that. Not with me. Not after everything you've done. Not after—"

"I screwed up, okay? I admit it. It was wrong of me to do what I did. I don't know if, had this happened another way, if I ever would have gotten a chance to know your sister. And as fucked up as this sounds, I'd do it again. I'd do it all over again, just for a chance to be with her. For a chance to know what it's like. To love. To have loved. To be loved. To have *been* loved. Like that." He pushes his still open hand in my direction. "To be the most important person in the world to someone. To be the center of someone's universe." He takes my hand in his and presses the drive into my palm. "It's all on there, all of the messages that she made. Do with it what you please."

With that, he turns and walks away.

Leaving me staring at his retreating figure, mouth agape, fingers clenched around the drive.

50

HARRIS

"You are not a blanket."

Stormy gray eyes lift to meet mine, but the face accompanying them is a blank mask.

In hindsight, showing up to Marc's office unannounced wasn't the smartest thing I could have done. But that's me, I don't think things through.

For weeks, Courtney has been dishing out generous dosages of brutal honesty, but the moment she uttered the words *safety blanket*, I ran and came straight here.

Barged in, more like.

Because I'm being stared at. Eight sets of eyes all fixated on me, seven faces with varying degrees of surprise and shock. It's not like I am a stranger. They all know who I am, which could explain the looks on their faces.

Because context, damn it!

One of Marc's paralegals, whose name escapes me, hovers at my back. They must be one of the firm's newer hires within the last year. They also aren't familiar with me or my antics because words like *He's in a meeting* and *You can't go in there* were hurled at my back, all things I don't really care to listen to or follow.

The one I really care about is a blank mask, but not completely unaffected by my presence. Physically, he looks sufficiently put together. The only hint of impropriety is that his tie is slightly crooked, which I always do for him since he sucks at it.

"Give us the room," Marc eventually says, his voice flat and emotionless.

The collective sounds of chair legs scraping are dulled by the carpet. Everyone shuffles out of the room. They all step around me in the process, then leave without a backward glance.

I wait until the door closes before saying, "You were never a safety blanket for me, Marc."

He doesn't answer. Instead, he stands and loosens his tie as he makes his way to where I stand. He doesn't touch me either, but he reaches around me and I hear two clicks. The sound resonates throughout the room, sealing my fate.

Not that I blame him. Delilah has tried to get us together in the same room, and I'm the asshole who keeps running away like a coward. Even now, I'm barely suppressing the urge to flee again, so I counteract that by looking everywhere except him.

As the boss, he has one of those fancy corner offices, complete with meeting and private sitting areas. Based on the number of people in the room when I barged in, I must have interrupted something important. Before the guilt sets in, Marc speaks up.

"Did Court tell you that?" he asks, his voice flat and emotionless.

I nod slowly, not sure if he can see me.

Chances are he can. He always watches, it's his thing.

He chuckles; the sound is sinister. "She misses Charlie." At my puzzled expression, he adds, "It's been almost six weeks, H."

I shift my weight from one foot to the other. The silence stretches between us, heavy and tense.

"Have a seat, H."

I shake my head. "I'd rather stand."

Another sinister chuckle. "So you can run again?"

Maybe, I almost blurt out.

"What's the matter?" he asks, his voice getting closer. "Cat got your tongue?"

Then he comes to stand directly in my line of sight. His face is still expressionless, but stormy gray orbs stare at me with a hunger he was never any good at disguising. Not with me, certainly not with Delilah. His hands are moving, so I glance down. Of course.

I swallow thickly. "You gonna use that on me?"

"You gonna fight me?" His voice is hoarse as he asks this.

"Not today," I say, keeping my tone as neutral as possible.

He spins it in his fingers, twirling it. "It's the first present you ever got me."

That knocks the air out of me. "What?"

Our eyes meet, and something flashes through them. Something close to fury. "You got me this. Don't tell me you forgot."

I shake my head, still stunned by the revelation. "I never forgot. I just thought... You have others. Other knives. Better quality ones. I thought you got rid of that one."

"Why would I? It's my favorite one."

"I rarely ever see you with it."

"It's a sixteen-year-old pocket knife, H. It's my fucking good luck charm. I take it with me everywhere I go."

Wow. I need a minute to digest this information. But it's never a minute, not really. After weeks of this strained silence, the dam breaks and out flows verbal diarrhea. At least I have the wherewithal to take a deep breath and slowly release it.

"I won't deny the things I said because those were true. But that's not the whole truth. Lord knows I haven't done anything at all to deserve you. To deserve your love, intense and damaged and pure and unfettered. Marc, I need you to know that I could never love anything or anyone the way I love you. Hurting you was never my intention. You are the most important thing to me. You will always be the most important thing in the world — to that eighteen-year-old boy you saved from himself, and to this thirty-four-year-old man who stands before you today. Asking, no, begging you for another chance to show you just how much you mean to me. How much you've always meant to me."

I get nothing but radio silence from him. But his hand moves to his corded neck and stays there for a beat. He takes me in, his mouth closed and his jaw firm.

"I believe you, H, but it's not enough."

I blink once, then twice.

"And Court is right. You *are* using me as a safety blanket."

I flinch and take a step back. "That's not true."

He shrugs. "You are. It's just that I don't fucking care. You hear me? I. Don't. Care. I'd rather have that than have nothing at all. H, you are it for me. I meant that. I love you. All of you. The good, the bad, and the ugly. That includes your selfish, self-centered, and cowardly ass. That's my favorite thing about you."

I have no comeback to that. He's not wrong. I am all of those things.

"Now, let's talk about Victor Toussaint."

Yeah, I should have known that was coming. "Delilah told you?"

"No, your bodyguard did. The ones you think you've been giving the slip?"

"So you knew?" I ask incredulously. Also, how can I give someone the slip when I have no clue who they are?

"What the fuck does he want?" His voice is strained, maybe a tad murderous.

I can't think of a lie to give him, but I can't tell him the truth either. "It wasn't for me. Some battles need to be... You know what? You are right. I do use you as a safety blanket. But not this time. This one I need to see through myself, like a grown-ass man."

"A grown-ass man?" The words roll around on his tongue, like oatmeal mixed in with sand.

"I don't need you to fight all my battles for me."

His nostrils flare slightly. "I know, I fucking heard you."

"Then you know." A beat passes, then, "How is she?"

He laughs, but it's more pained than amused. "Why don't you call her and find out? Or better yet, come home. She fucking misses you."

"Is that why she looks the way she does?" The words come out harsh and bitter and not at all like I intended, yet I can't stop the onslaught of words that pour out of me. "I'm gone for what, six weeks, and you've already turned her into your personal—"

"That's the fucking problem," he growls. "You really can't fucking stand it that she won't give you her undivided attention twenty-four fucking seven. Well, guess what? It's not about you. It was never about you. Keep this shit up and you will lose her."

"I already lost her to you. You want the same thing she does, so congratulations. You won. I can't compete with that."

"Did you not hear what she said? This isn't a fucking contest. She's not a prize to be won. If anything, we are the consolation prizes she never wanted."

"What the fuck is that supposed to mean?"

"It means," he leans in, his eyes locked on mine, our faces just inches apart, "don't make Delilah choose. Don't put her in a position to have to choose because she will, and it won't be you or me. So fucking take what you can get from her, or leave her the fuck alone. Those are your only choices."

That knocks the wind out of my sails. I take a step back, then several, until my calves connect with the edge of the sofa. My legs give out and I sink into the charcoal gray sofa, my eyes cast downwards.

"You expect her to let go of Simone," he says, "but I don't. Simone will always be a part of her, whether we like it or not. It doesn't matter what we do or say. We will always be third place in her life, right behind Simone and Dahlia. Accept it. Make your peace with it."

A shadow comes over me. His shadow. My eyes lift to meet his, gleaming with unshed tears.

"Our girl is much more resilient than you give her credit for," he continues. "But no more lies, okay? As it turns out, she doesn't care that you drugged her, just that you lied about it. Hurricane Dahlia will have something to say, since those two share everything."

I let out a strangled laugh. "I deserve it, too."

He smiles, but it's sad and doesn't reach his eyes. "Maybe, but that won't stop me from fighting that battle for you. Or maybe I'll stay out of it. You have David to contend with now, so good luck." He sinks to his knees before me and takes both of my hands in his. "You and me, are we okay?"

My lips part but no sound comes out.

His hand comes up and he trails a finger down the side of my face. "H?"

"I... I don't know. Are we?"

"We have to be. You are mine, H. Mine. What will it take for you to understand I don't let go of my things? What will it take for you to realize I won't let you go?"

His words are meant to be threatening, but his voice sounds strangled. Desperate, even.

The words tumble out before I have a chance to rein them in. "You didn't come for me."

Marc's face blanches. "You needed space. I was trying to respect that. I... Court said I had to, so she sent Charlie over. She said you need to come home of your own accord, not because I'm making you. And she's right. That's why—"

"I was waiting for you. You said it yourself, I'm a coward. I need you to make the decision for me. Punishment. Pleasure. Do it all."

He wipes his hand over his face. "I'm sorry I hurt you."

"Don't you ever be fucking sorry for letting yourself go with me," I growl. "Or with Delilah. I've been an ass about it, but I also know it's what makes you, well, you. She needs it, I realize that now. And frankly, I need it too. I need you—"

The wind gets knocked out of me a second time when Marc yanks me to the floor and his lips claim mine in a punishing kiss. Somehow he manages to keep it going when he flips us over, then presses his entire body into mine and I just about die a delirious death.

A long while passes before we break apart; I'm breathless and my mind is in a fog. And so too is he as his gaze roams my face, eyes heavy-lidded and glistening.

"Sixteen fucking years," he breathes as his eyes hone in on my lips, committing them to memory. Those eyes lift to meet mine and I'm taken aback by what I see in them. "That's almost half my life, you know? I will never tire of you, H. I don't know how to walk away from this, and I don't fucking want to."

"Then don't," I growl as my fingers curl around the base of his neck. I pull on him again, but he stops me, bracing both elbows on either side of my face.

"I wanted you from the moment I laid eyes on you; that has never changed. It will never change. I will always want you. I will always be by your side. You are and have always been my forever, H. I will always stand by you, even when you are an asshole. Especially when your dad is being an asshole.

"Here's the one and only fucking chance you're going to get, so think long and hard about this. Don't give me a half-ass answer. If you don't want this anymore, let me know. If you don't want me, let me know that too. If it's D you want, let me know. I'll let you go. It'll kill me, but I'll let you go. So sleep on it, okay? Sleep on it before answering because this is the first and only chance that you're getting."

I don't need to sleep on it. And I'm done thinking about it. I've done nothing but think for six weeks, longer even, and I came to the same conclusion each time.

"You're not like me."

His brow twists in confusion. "What?"

"You've always been so certain of who you are, what you want, what to do. And I'm the fucking leech that hitched a ride on your coattails. A fucking mold that won't budge. Even worse, you kept me. You claimed me, made me yours. Made me your partner, your equal. You even went to fucking war for me, against your family and mine. Even then, I never felt I could measure up to you. I never felt like your equal. But none of that mattered to you, and that's what I've been struggling with all these years."

He's silent, then a soft sigh comes from him. But he says nothing. Because he knows me, and because he knows I still have more to say.

"You see me, Marc. Even with all of my stupid shit, you see me. You see everything. You always have. And you're here, a constant in my life. I'm grateful and appreciative because I know how amazing you are. I know how supportive, loving, and caring you are, and how utterly blessed I am to have you in my life.

"At first, I was overwhelmed by all of it, and there are moments when I can't fucking stand it. But most of the time, I'm just so fucking grateful for it, you know? It doesn't make sense to me sometimes, but then nothing about this, about us, makes fucking sense. But that's just us. And I love you. I fucking love you. Even when I'm being an asshole. Especially when I'm being an asshole. It means I'm your asshole, and I wouldn't have it any other way."

Neither of us says anything; we stare at each other, chests heaving and breaths commingling.

"I'm in, Marc," I eventually say.

His breath hitches. "In…?"

"Kids. Tiny little humans running around, messing shit up."

He laughs. "That's not all they do."

"Oh, I know. That's what you're for. I'll join in and mess shit up. You'll fix it and make it all better. We've been doing that dance for years anyway, so the more the merrier."

He swallows thickly. "If this is about…"

"It's not. This is all me, and I'm in. All in. You, me, Delilah. Always, and forever."

His warm breath fans my face. "Forever, huh?"

"I'd sign on the dotted line, but we both know I'm a man of my word. Now let's go home. Our woman awaits us."

51

HARRIS

"When you said I was getting my own space, you should've warned me about all the work that would go into it," Delilah calls out from the second floor.

As Marc and I ascend the stairs, I pause mid-step and turn to him. "Space?"

He shrugs. "She's looking over plans for her lab."

"Why would you dump all that work on her? She's busy enough as it is."

"I didn't dump anything on anyone," he says, but I don't believe him for one second. Then he adds, "It was David's idea."

Of course it was. "You know he's only looking for a roundabout way to keep Hurricane Dahlia busy, right? He knows Delilah hates that stuff, but Dahlia will eat it right up. It's only a matter of time before she hands it over to her."

"I'm counting on it, too. It's about time—"

"I know you can hear me!" Delilah's voice cuts through. "I honestly don't have time for this. And some of this equipment doesn't belong here. Not with Charlie in the house. What if he..."

He places both hands on my shoulders and shoves me up the stairs. "Go grovel."

"Damn it, Marc. If this is your idea of—" Her words die out when I come into view.

"Hi," is all I can manage.

Hi? What a lame greeting. What am I? Five?

It's what strangers say to each other. We are not strangers.

She crosses her arms, watching me with a guarded expression.

Are we?

"What are you doing here?"

I give her a small smile. "I live here?"

She lifts a challenging brow.

"This is home," I clarify. "Here, with you and with Marc."

She scowls at that. Her eyes dart to the area behind me, and when they return to mine they are hardened with fury. "Dining room. Now."

"Uh... why?"

She spins on her heel and walks away.

Marc places a hand on the small of my back and leans in, enveloping me with his heat. "I wouldn't question it," he whispers in my ear.

Steeling myself, I follow her to the dining room with Marc on my heels. She's sitting at the table, arms crossed with an expressionless face.

"Sit."

My lips part but Marc gives me a slight shake of his head. He pulls out the chair next to her and settles in.

"Is this an interrogation?" I ask them.

"Do you want it to be an interrogation?" Delilah counters.

I have nothing to say to that, so I don't. Instead, I pull out the chair directly across from them and plant my tush in it.

"Nobody leaves Marc," she says evenly. "That's what you told me for years."

I nod. "I said that, yes."

"So why did you leave?"

"I was angry," I say truthfully. "I was afraid, and I was jealous. *Am* jealous."

"Of?"

"You. Him." A pause, then, "Her."

Something undecipherable crosses her face, vanishing all too quickly. "And now?"

I draw in a deep breath, releasing it slowly. "I'm making my peace with it. It'll be a struggle, and I'll screw it up along the way, but... I love you, Delilah. I'll take what I can get from you. Whatever you have to offer. I'd rather have that than nothing at all."

Delilah and Marc exchange a look, then she pushes her seat back and dives under the table.

"What was that about?" I ask him.

He shrugs. "Maybe you should ask her yourself."

"Ask her what—*oh, dear lord*!"

Delilah's hot mouth engulfs the head of my cock, and I have to clench my teeth not to shout. Her nimble fingers have since gotten faster, so quick that my brain barely registers as she unzips my pants and pulls out my cock. It certainly does the moment the head of my cock touches the back of her throat, and I instantly go hard.

"Del—" I mutter as I scoot my chair back, only to watch myself fill her petite mouth. Her nails dig into my thigh, holding me in place. She caresses my shaft with her other hand, her cheeks hollowing out as she sucks on my cock like it's her most favorite thing in the world.

Like I'm her most favorite thing in the world.

Then I feel the corner of her lips tug upwards into a smile.

"Shit, Delilah. I can't—" I start to say, then I feel her teeth grazing the underside of my cock.

Then she clamps down. Hard.

She bites me. She fucking bites my cock and it sets off something in me.

I yank my cock out of Delilah's mouth, which she reluctantly releases, and pull her up to her feet. She stumbles, her eyes half closed, her smile somehow sweet and naughty.

"What the fuck was that for?"

Sweet soon gives way to naughty. "You liked it, didn't you?"

I huff out a breath. "Says who?"

"Says Marc." Her eyelids flutter open, golden-brown eyes staring right into the very depths of my soul. "You like it rough. Well, guess what? So do I. I am not a fucking wallflower."

"That right?"

She nods. "Tell you what? Either take me right now, hard and fast, or Marc will while you watch, and he is not going to be gentle about it."

Something takes over me. I can't explain it, only that I go feral.

This is supposed to be groveling. I'm supposed to be groveling. Instead, she's on her knees before me, hero-worshiping my cock.

Still, it doesn't stop me from spinning her body around and pushing her by the small of her back until her front connects with the edge of the table. Her body folds over, and I waste no time shoving her jeans out of the way and my long, thick, angry length into her glistening pussy.

"Like that?" I grunt, slamming into her once, twice, thrice before losing count. Her walls clamp around my cock in that very Delilah vise-grip. "Fuck!"

"More!" she demands as I continue pounding into her, her body rocking back and forth on the table in a not-so gentle manner. Laying her head down to the side, she huffs and pants as she says, "I-I need m-more!"

Across the table, Marc chuckles. He already has his dick in his hands, stroking himself as his eyes stay on us, a look of longing and lust and desire in his heavy-lidded eyes.

"You heard her," he says with another sinister chuckle. "Give our woman what she wants, or I will."

Not on my fucking watch, I think as I grab the edge of her blouse and pull the flimsy material apart with my bare hands.

I was guessing earlier, but knowing it was an accurate guess doesn't make it any easier to stomach. The fucking bruises are back; this time they span the entire length of her back and shoulders, even creeping up her hairline.

Rug burns, weeks in the making.

I meet Marc's gaze again, the question in my eyes.

"Let it the fuck go," he says with a slight shake of his head as his movements gain momentum. This time his strokes are frenzied and merciless.

"How is it that she still wants more?" I ask, my hips smacking into her ass, balls heavy and tight against the tender skin of her thighs. Who knows, maybe that will bruise too.

"Guys, I'm literally right here!" she snaps. "Quit talking about me like I'm—*oh god*!"

I roll my hips to get at that bundle of nerves nestled deep inside of her, then I drive mercilessly into it. This only makes her even more restless, twisting and squirming against me like she can't get enough.

Which is fine by me since I can't get enough of her either. My sweet, sweet drug.

My mind goes blank, and all that's left is an onslaught of sensations that threaten to overtake my sanity as I revel in the glorious sensation of how tight, how hot, and how wet her pussy is as she grips me so tightly. It's not long before she shatters around me, her whole body jerking in hard, violent shakes as her orgasm takes over. Not that this stops me. On the contrary, it only encourages me to speed up my thrusting, balls deep inside her sweet, delectable body, over and over. Even as her body goes limp on the table, spent and satiated, it isn't enough to tempt me to give up on her.

Instead, I pull her limp body off the table, lower her to the hardwood floor and drive my still-hard cock back home, deep inside her. Then I drive into her tight, dripping pussy so hard I can barely see straight. Her body springs right back to life, her walls gripping me so hard it's like our first time all over again. The first time my cock invaded her virginal, tight pussy.

"Do your worst," she cries out, her eyes glassy, their expression dreamy, just like that night. "Break me, Harris. Fucking shatter me. I can take it."

Leaning over her, I take both her hands and pin them over her head. Staring into her eyes, I continue to drive into her mercilessly as her tits jiggle on her chest. Her soft and supple skin trembles with every hard thrust inside her. She's gasping, mewling, and making all sorts of incoherent sounds, which further fuels my rage.

So yeah, I fuck her like I hate her.

It's what she asked for, isn't it?

Once she starts making mewling sounds, I fuck her even harder. And when she shatters around my cock a second time, I fuck her harder as her screams tear out of her throat. As her juices squirt out of her tight pussy, on my cock, and onto the hardwood floors, I fuck her harder, mercilessly. I don't ease up even as her body goes limp like a rag doll once again.

Not until her eyelids flutter, then open, her gaze locking onto mine. The smile that tugs at the corner of her lips is satiated and happy. A mischievous glint flits through her eyes, and the smile on her face turns downright wicked before she clenches her muscles everywhere —

thighs, arms, pussy, even her fucking ankles — and she grinds herself against me.

My orgasm takes over, it hits me like a freight train, and I come harder than I've ever come before. A guttural, feral groan rips from my throat as I fill her slick, tight pussy, emptying my balls deep inside her tight hole. It goes on and on and on, and just when I think I'm done she does it again, clamping down even harder, and another surge takes over.

She really will be the death of me, and I will die a fucking happy man. Blessed beyond belief, just for the privilege of worshiping her pussy, her lips, her tits, her whole fucking body.

Because she's a fucking warrior, isn't she? She's stronger than both of us, Marc and I combined. And her body, her temple, is a fucking fortress. She's managed to stare death in the fucking eyes twice and lived to tell the story. That's more than I can say for myself, a fucking coward who runs away at the first sign of trouble.

Then there's this body of hers, this glorious, supple body that opens up to me without reservation, and takes everything I have to give her. She takes it all as I shoot hot streams of cum deep inside her tight hole, not once easing up until my body gives way and I collapse over her, satiated, boneless, and *oh so* satisfied.

Content too.

And deliriously happy.

So deliriously happy that for the first time ever, I think to myself, *Boy, do I wish we made a baby tonight.* I realize now that she can take it. Whatever we have to dish out to her.

Including babies.

52

DELILAH

I wasn't planning on doing this.

Really, I wasn't.

Years ago, I promised myself that I would only focus on the good and positive memories I have of her and with her. It's what made living and fucking breathing somewhat bearable. It's what helped me get out of bed in the mornings. It's what helped me put one foot in front of the other.

I'd like to think it's what kept death from coming for me.

This is in direct conflict with that promise, and reneging on that promise would only encourage that fucker, the one who broke my sister.

So no, I'm not doing it. I'm not going to go down that rabbit hole again. I won't get so wrapped up in her that I lose all sense of myself. It's not like she's back. She's gone. She's still gone, and it still hurts. Maybe not as much as it did eighteen years ago, fifteen years ago, or even seven years ago, but it hurts nonetheless.

Besides, I'm happy now. As happy as I'll ever be. I wasn't back then when she left. Losing her broke me, fucking shattered me. Until I found them, or rather, they found me. Harris and Marc, the two halves of my soul. The ones who make me whole again. The twin souls that complete me.

So I tell myself not to, and I remind my defective heart to keep that promise, to not get lost in the whirlwind of all things her.

Except she doesn't listen to me because she wants what she wants. Also, that thumbdrive is still burning a hole in my purse, where I shoved it two days ago. After pacing and pondering and wondering what I should do, I cave and pull it out. Then I go hide in the media room and have a showing, all by myself. It's not like I can tell Harris or Marc what I am doing. They wouldn't understand why I need to do this. It's not like I'm expecting them to understand what I'm hoping to get out of this.

It starts out fine at first. One of those atypical doctor-patient interviews, the kind I'd seen in the movies. They are more like candid interviews, so to speak, where the camera remains focused on the subject — Simone — while the interviewer — Dr. Sonya Goodman — asks a series of questions and lets the subject's responses dictate the flow of the conversation. I feel a little bit like a voyeur, to be honest, infringing upon such an intimate moment.

But that's okay, I guess. Simone is not here to consent to my watching these videos. It takes me all of about four seconds to grapple with the moral and ethical implications of doing this, shove them aside, and dive right in.

The videos start with sixteen-year-old Simone, who is shy and timid and quiet. A stark contrast to the always angry Simon everyone knew, with his explosive temper and self-destructive tendencies. While I knew both sides of her, it is astonishing to see her memorialized on film forever. Inside Simon was this gentle soul waiting to come out into the light. This beautiful, gentle soul begged to be let out.

I had seen glimpses of this gentle soul long before these videos were made. Curtis called it The Simon-Mood-Swings — I know, very original of him. All I saw was this quiet, super-smart soul who blended into the crowd when she wanted to, always observing everyone and taking notes. Back then, this soul took notes on everything — how to understand others, the things that made them happy, but also what made them sad. The things that brought them joy, but also the things that brought them sorrow. Most importantly, this gentle soul took notes on the things that made the lives of others better, or even easier, because that's all anyone can hope for.

That gentle soul, in return, selflessly poured themselves into making the lives of others better. Easier. Safer. She would throw herself over her brother's body, using this body to shield her brother's even weaker form from the wrath of their parents. That gentle soul would bear the brunt of their parents' anger, disappointment, and rage. She did all that so the rest of the amigos could have some semblance of a normal, healthy, organic friendship. And as soon as she got her driver's license, that gentle soul would often drive Curtis to my parents' house just so we wouldn't need to or have to go to the McWhorter house instead. That gentle soul who was a protector through and through — fiercely loyal to the ones she loved and very overprotective towards us.

I didn't realize then just how deeply conflicted that gentle soul was.

As I watch these videos almost two decades later, I can see that gentle soul constantly agonizing over revealing her true self to the people she loved and who loved her in return — my parents, Curtis, Dahlia, and... me.

Any one of them could have rejected her and she wouldn't have cared. But if I had?

I wish I could have told her it didn't matter because I was so far gone for her. For him first, then her. For the two sides of that gentle yet angry and conflicted soul that drew me in equally.

I wish I had known that my rejection of her was one of her greatest fears. I didn't know it then, and I wish I had. Had I known then, I would have told her it didn't matter. I would have told him the same thing too — that angry soul with the explosive temper and self-destructive tendencies — that it didn't matter because I love all of her. And even after all this time, I never stopped loving her.

Hours later, I get to eighteen-year-old Simone. So full of life. So much promise. So much potential. This is the Simone I knew. I was only fifteen then, but my soul knew what she wanted, and it was her. And him. That gentle yet angry and conflicted soul. The same one that needed my defective soul as a calming, healing balm. So I fell hard. And as I watch, I know that this is the Simone I fell for, hard, as in head over heels in love with hard. This is the Simone I trusted with everything in me. This is the Simone around whom my entire being revolved. This is the Simone that I loved with every fiber of my being.

But, most importantly, this is the Simone I gave myself to — body, heart, and soul. And yes, I knew then too, that she loved me back. There was never any doubt in my mind about it. It was apparent back then in the way she took care of everyone, in the way she took care of me. And now, it is right there, forever memorialized on film, for me to see.

The most shocking thing about this?

The dress.

Her dress.

It appears early in the year eighteen series and stays through the end.

It's a simple lilac sun dress. A knee-length lilac wrap dress decorated with embroidered lavender flowers. It brings out the color of her rare and beautiful violet eyes.

Some of these videos had to have been made in the winter, yet she's still wearing it.

The thing is, I got that dress for her.

It was the very first present I had ever gotten for her. For Simone, that is. At the time, my fifteen-year-old self saw it and thought, *'It's such a shame that such a pretty dress has to hang on a mannequin's body. I bet it would look good on Simone,'* so she bought it.

To my fifteen-year-old self, it was just a pretty dress. To Simone, it was more than that. Acceptance is the word she used then, right before she kissed me. I still remember that kiss like it happened yesterday, my fingers trailing my lips as I recall the feel of her lips on mine, licking and sucking and biting, before her tongue invaded my mouth and she gave all of my insides the same treatment. I still remember it because it was the first kiss we shared as Simone and Delilah. It is the kiss against which I measure all other kisses, a kiss forever seared in my memory.

Or it was, until she tainted the memory of the kiss by leaving the dress behind.

I was the one who found it back then, neatly folded and placed on the top of her bed with a note that read *'I'm sorry for everything',* no explanation as to where she'd gone or why. It didn't sound like her, but it was her handwriting. Still, as my heart shattered and my world fell from underneath me, I knew I wanted to keep the dress.

But her parents said no, there was no way I was keeping it.

They thought it was a phase, see? According to them, it was a phase my parents shouldn't have encouraged in the first place. On the day she officially came out to her parents, on her nineteenth birthday, Matthias said, and I'm quoting here, *'No son of mine is going to live like a tranny, not on my watch, and that's the last I will hear of it.'* Not only did they pretend that Simone didn't exist, but they were also actively taking steps towards fixing this supposed 'phase' of hers. They were furious at my parents, livid that they supposedly *'let this go on under their roof, and then lied to them about it',* as if it was somehow their fault. My parents, bless their souls, took it all in stride because that's just who they were. They loved Simone, so they let her know that under their roof she was loved and could be whomever she wanted — Simone or Simon — and there would be no judgment from them. Only love. Only acceptance. They were terrific like that.

But her parents? They were a whole other beast.

They pretended she didn't exist while she was alive because to them it was better to have a dead son than an alive daughter. And after she went missing, they went on a rampage, adamant about wiping all traces of her existence from the world. They even waited seven years after she had gone missing to declare Simon McWhorter legally dead to cover all of their bases.

But what's even worse is, somehow, the McWhorters found out that I was the one who bought that dress for her — the very same one she left behind along with her note — and all hell broke loose. There was a huge falling out between our parents. They sent their goons to break into and collect any items she had in our home. It wasn't enough for them to violate our house the way they did, they also made all of us watch, including Curtis, as they burned it all, including the dress. We watched as all of our memories, mementos, and physical traces of Simone's existence went up in literal smoke.

So yeah, I hate them. My parents barely tolerated them after that. Our mothers, who had been best friends all their lives, never spoke again. As far as I know, they never talked until my parents died a few years later. I could barely stand to look at them after that, not without seeing the glee on their faces as I cried my heart out, all of my hopes and dreams going up in smoke.

What boggles my mind is even after that, Dahlia and Curtis managed to stay together for another eighteen years. I have long since come to accept that this was her prerogative, not mine. Because the heart wants what it wants, right?

And sometimes, the universe has a way of making things right. By some stroke of luck, they missed Dahlia's negatives. All her film. Which Curtis knew they existed, and I was surprised he didn't tell them about. Surprised and grateful because after my parents banned all of them — Andrea, Matthias, and Curtis — from stepping foot inside our home, Dahlia developed some of that film and replaced most of the pictures they stole. Those are hanging in our house and my home with the boys.

But now, watching her like this means much more than I had ever imagined. I see now that I meant so much more to her, maybe even more than she meant to me. That's why there are videos, right?

Then there's her voice. All dreamy and so full of life, hopes and dreams. And love. So much love. It's in her voice, in the way her voice goes all breathy as she talks about me. It's in the way her eyes light up like a kid in a candy store as she talks about the things we shared. It's in the way her voice hitches as she talks about the things we did, both for and to each other. I didn't realize just how candid this would be until I got to those parts, which I watched over and over. Probably not the brightest idea, as I get all hot and bothered again. It takes incredible self-restraint to not snake my hands between my legs and chase my relief.

Oh, who am I kidding? I fail, of course.

So yeah, I'm so fucking glad and grateful that I decided to do this alone. Because the last thing Marc or Harris need to see is me getting myself off while watching videos of my ex-girlfriend talking about the things she did to me back when we were kids. We might be adults now, but still, it's not acceptable.

And to think that my incredibly naive fifteen-year-old self thought that everything would be all right. She believed that even though the decks were stacked against us, with how her parents and grandparents were, we would be okay because we had each other. Simone had me, Curtis had Dahlia, and isn't that what they wanted anyway?

When we get to nineteen-year-old Simone, the dread sets in. These videos were made in the last few weeks before she disappeared. The year nineteen series videos show a shadow cast over that gentle soul. It's all the things she kept from me. Or maybe it's because I didn't want to see it. Perhaps I was naive and oblivious and only saw what I wanted to see.

There is one session in particular that draws my attention. This one is dated two days after her nineteenth birthday, also her second coming out, to her parents this time. It was a disaster, that part I remember. In the video, she talks about what happened later. I barely remember that night. I had another panic attack then, so they took me home and settled me into my sensory deprivation tank. When I got out later that evening, Curtis was the only one home with me. Dahlia later told me Simone insisted my parents had stayed. She and Dahlia went back to try and reason with them.

She recalls a conversation that she and Dahlia overheard. One in which my parents, in their last-ditch attempt to reason with her not-to-be-reasoned-with parents, my dad said something that had them both stumped. He used the words, *'Dahlia is in love with Curtis, and Delilah is in love with Simone, so really, you're getting them both anyways, just like you wanted. If anything, you're getting exactly what you paid for.'* And when they demanded what my dad meant by that, both sets of parents were forced to tell the truth. That, to her, was the ultimate betrayal.

A truth so sinister it's hard to wrap my mind around. Simply put, Dahlia and I were paid for by Simone's grandparents. Andrea took advantage of her best friend's desire to have a child. Back then, it cost a pretty penny to do IVF and all the fertility treatments that went along with it. Someone had to pay for it, and since my parents couldn't afford it on their meager researcher's salary, the McWhorters footed the bill. Specifically, her grandparents footed the bill.

The catch?

Us.

They wanted us. Or rather, they wanted us to marry into their family. She says she never understood why it had to be us. Surely there had to be easier and cheaper ways of securing partners for their children. But it was all about power and control. Money too, as they so succinctly put it.

Dahlia knew about it all this time. It makes sense now, the things she's said over the years. Why she stayed. Hell, why she's having this fucking baby even though she never wanted any. Why she's giving him to them, knowing what they are like. And why everyone, my parents included, never told me any of this, even after she disappeared.

Her last video crushes me. It wasn't just one of her sessions. It was mine. She made it, but it was meant for me.

Me.

So she knew.

She fucking knew.

She knew she was going to leave me, yet she proposed. She promised me forever. She promised we would have a life together, a home, lots of babies, the whole gambit. And since she was my entire world, I said yes. I will never forget the look on her face when I did. She looked like I had just unlocked the gates to fucking Nirvana. She was so fucking happy and then she left. She fucking left me.

She left me because she loves me. And I lost her because of money.

My parents knew. Dahlia knew. Andrea and Matthias knew. Even Sonya knew. Yet no one thought to tell me.

Why?

Because I'm a fucking wallflower? Because I'm defective? Because I'm fragile and need to be protected?

I'm all of those things, yet I broke anyway. Still, no one thought to put me out of my misery.

The thing is, I can't even be mad at them because I understand it. Maybe sixteen-year-old me wouldn't have, but thirty-four-year-old me does. So I sit here, staring at the woman my defective heart still beats for, and I don't know what to do.

I'm not sure how long I stay that way. I'm not even sure how much time has passed. Hours? Days? I have no idea.

I barely register it when someone sits next to me.

Harris.

I know it's him because the air around us changes. It's electrifying, like him. His touch, too, as his fingers trail along the bare skin of my arm, leaving goosebumps in their wake. Then I feel someone else. Another presence, stepping into my bubble. This one is warm, calming, and inviting.

Marc?

This makes no sense. Since when do they feel different?

Whatever. Now's not the time to question it, not when my whole world is flipped upside down.

This warm presence, Marc, wraps his muscular arm around my shoulders, pulling my frail and shaky body into his. It doesn't help; it only gets worse. The shakes. The jitters. Apparently, it has been happening for a while because one of them has something to say about it. Lots to say about it.

Harris? He is the worrier.

Then it goes quiet. I have nothing to say, so I stare at Simone's tortured face that fills the screen. No one says anything. I'm not sure if they have to or need to.

Some time passes, then I'm floating in the air, then moving.

"Can you do it?" one of them asks.

"That's not how this works, H."

Not how what works?

"Why the fuck not? Look at her. Just this once."

Oh good, they are fighting over defective Delilah.

Isn't that sweet?

"She has to say the words."

What words?

There's a sharp intake of air, and my back connects with something soft.

"I'll say them for her."

"What words?" I manage to force out.

Then it all goes quiet.

53

MARC

"I see you brought them all," an acquaintance of the family says. "Your little harem."

I force a grin. "It's not called a harem, you ignorant fool."

This again. Truth be told, I'm not sure what said ignorant fool's name is, only that he's the son of a friend of a cousin of my dad's. He seems to be under the misguided impression this gives him latitude to talk to me however he pleases. Or even that I would entertain having a conversation with him about my lifestyle.

Bringing my glass to my lips, I take a sip of my whiskey.

Don't stab him, I remind myself. Stabbing him will make for a rather messy evening.

Like Harris, I loathe pretentious black-tie events like these. I just do a much better job of keeping my disdain and disinterest hidden. Like many others I am obligated to attend in person, this ball is one of several charitable functions my family either puts on or sponsors each year. Tonight's ball is the biggest of them, with attendance being mandatory for all of Lorenzo Sotelo's offspring.

Dad and I struck a deal back when Courtney and I were inducted into the family. With Mom dead, he had a vested interest in making us a part of his family. I didn't care either way, since I always knew Courtney and I had much more to offer the family, with little to gain in return. Mom knew it too, hence the reason why she kept us out of the family for so long. But I also knew that if I didn't, he or someone else would drag Courtney into the family, knowing I would have no choice but to follow. Mom taught me to always leverage relationships to my advantage. Do unto others, or it will be done to you.

So we struck a deal, Dad and I. I would go to law school — not on his dime, but on mom's dime since she left Courtney and me a healthy inheritance — and build a career cleaning up the family's legal messes. In exchange, we both get to live however the fuck we want. Date whoever we wish to. And if it comes to that, marry whoever the fuck we want. In addition, he can use me however he wants, but Courtney would always be off-limits. That protection would extend to anyone I put under my protection. None of that arranged marriage bullshit for either one of us, not even in the name of forging connections or keeping the peace.

He was far more impressed that his teenage son had the audacity to propose such a deal, and so he agreed to it. His wife, sons, daughters, extended family and friends, and several of his top men were in the room, so a part of him wanted to save face in front of the son of *the* Sarah Bardales. As it turns out, the joke was on him since I had my demands prepared in advance. I got him to sign it — in ink and in blood — right before all my readily available witnesses. So it's official. He can't renege on our deal because it makes him look bad. Neither can they renege on it on his behalf, whether intentional or not, because he now knows what happens if my patience gets stretched relatively thin.

For the most part, we've done rather well over the years. Dad has held up his end of the bargain and stayed out of my personal life. In return, I've always done my duty to the family and gotten them out of sticky situations, legally or permanently. After all, I still have my mother's legacy to live up to. Plus, I go above and beyond, show up to all of these insufferable things, and play the dutiful son because I'm nice. The dutiful bastard son, since that's what I truly am.

In return, I make sure that my family shows up impeccably dressed and ready to play their respective parts to perfection. That includes H, who, as it so happens, loathes these things more than anything.

Truth is, sometimes I wish I didn't care about any of this. The stupid fanfare. The schmoozing. I can think of other more productive ways to spend Friday date night. Although right now, I'll settle for H being my shield. Just as long as I don't have to make insufferable idle talk with idiots like this one.

Who, by the way, is still talking. Somewhere in his long and torturous monologue, I picked up on the words *Delilah* and *contribute* and *family legacy*, so I immediately don't like the turn this conversation is taking.

It's a mostly one-sided tedious conversation, but still.

"Excuse me?" I ask. The question is meant to be rhetorical, but as expected, the implied threat goes over his head.

"You finally added a woman to the mix," he says, giving me a knowing smirk. It is one I don't find as amusing as he does since I have little to no interest in whatever the inside joke is supposed to be. "It's good to know you finally see the light. I mean, sex with Harris had to have gotten stale after sixteen years, right? Family is everything, you know? We must do everything in our power to keep the family legacy going, so to speak. Now you can get to business and start popping out some babies."

How old is this tool again? He will make for an excellent test subject for Harris's new line of torture devices.

"The brunette, that's Delilah, right?" he continues, oblivious to his impending demise. "It is. *The* Delilah Brewer. How did you manage to swing that?"

"Swing what?"

"Last I heard, she's property of the McWhorters."

I take another sip of my whiskey. "Property."

He nods enthusiastically, seemingly proud of himself for pointing that out. "Yeah. It's a whole thing that was set up with their parents." As if I need him to educate me on that. I am familiar with those contracts. Dahlia found their parents' version of the contracts months ago and gave it to me. "Can you imagine making wives for your kids? Who even thinks about shit like that? The McWhorters, that's who. That brings wealth and privilege to another level, am I right?"

"It sure does," I mumble noncommittally.

"Speaking of making wives, there is someone in the family who will make a good pet for me, but I hear she's off limits."

"That right?" He strikes me as a screamer. That would appease H, even if it's only temporary.

"I'm a fucking Sotelo. Nothing and no one is off limits." The nameless bastard scoffs, like the self-entitled asshole he must be. "If I want a piece of ass, it's mine. Plain and simple. Instead I have to jump through fucking hoops just to…" he trails off at that, then leans in close. "You might know of her. The forger."

That has my already piqued senses on high alert. "The forger?"

This asshole had better not mean—

"Yeah, the forger. Artist. Whatever they call her. What's her name again? Starts with a C. Carrie. Connie. Something like that."

"A pet, huh?" I reach into my pocket and take out my knife, my lucky charm.

He snaps his fingers. "Courtney! That's her name. She's Sarah Bardales's kid, from what I gather. Now, Sarah was an impressive woman, and it's a damn shame that she died in the pathetic way she did. How does one even get the drop on an assassin, a fucking lethal one? It just goes to show you, huh? No one is invincible in this business.

"On the other hand, Courtney would make an extra special pet for me. I don't even care that she's damaged goods, those lips are meant to be fused to my cock and I will do everything in my power to make sure that happens. Who knows, maybe she's got some of her mother's fighting spirit. Just the thought makes my cock so fucking hard. I'm not sure what makes her so fucking special that she's off-limits. Her psychotic brother, maybe. But I plan on taking her before the psycho realizes what's happening."

That does it for me. This fucker just signed his death warrant, regardless of whose son he is. I scan the room for my right-hand man. He also happens to be the same guy overseeing the clean-up crew. Our eyes meet and my gaze darts to the nameless idiot in my bubble, blabbering on about things he has no clue about. Thankfully he takes the hint and gets to work, no doubt assembling a discreet crew to take this idiot to David's place.

If there is one thing I won't tolerate, it is disrespect. Everyone knows that. Well, not everyone, since this one felt the need to run his mouth to me.

"So tell me, how much did it set you back, buying Delilah from the McWhorters? And even if that doesn't work, I have a Plan B. I know you've got the in with Lorenzo as one of his many bastard sons. Who do I need to buy or steal the forger from? She should have been mine ages ago, and I'm getting really fucking impatient—"

The knife pressing into his side cuts him off. "Mention my family's name one more time and this goes in your lung."

He made this so easy for me. He really did. Useless tongue aside, he stepped into my personal space first. To anyone else observing this exchange, we are having a friendly chat like a pair of chummy pals.

He tries to wriggle out of my grip, but my arm looped around his shoulder holds him in place.

"Are you insane?" he squeaks.

"In some ways, yes, I am. Certifiably so. I'm sure you've heard the stories."

He gulps. "As a matter of fact, I have. Marc Sotelo, *the* bastard child. Claims to be the expert on all things knifing. But you are all smoke, no fire."

"That a fact?"

"From what I've heard, you are all talk and no action. Not when you have to follow the law. The law of the land, I mean. Not the law of the mafia."

"Would you like to test out that theory?" I press in slightly before leaning in to whisper in his ear. "Piss me off one more time and I will stab you in the lung."

"You'll stab me?"

"In the lung, yes. Then I'll go right ahead and mingle while you lie there, choking. And if I see one drop of your blood on my suit, I will carve up your entrails right here and have them delivered to your father on a silver platter. Who did you say he was again?"

"So it's true. You really are insane."

"Finally, something we can both agree on. I was beginning to find this conversation tedious, less so now since we are all on the same page."

"No, we are not all on the same page, you maniac. What did I ever do to you to deserve—"

"You pissed me off, then you coveted my things."

"I did nothing of the sort."

"Eh, debatable. But by the time anyone comes to a consensus, you will have coughed your life away on these imported bamboo wood floors. A shame, really, since these cost a fortune to maintain in pristine condition. You know what else?"

Again, it's a rhetorical question, but as expected, the implied connotation goes over his head.

"What?"

"No one can touch me. Not even your dad, whose name you refuse to give me. Not that it makes any difference at this point. By the time anyone realizes you are gone, your body parts will be scattered all over the Midwest. And I will live my life like I always do, like the untouchable bastard son I am. So, life or death, it's not up to you. You had a choice — toe the fucking line or die. You choose wrong."

His lips press together as he grits his next words. "I was only—"

"Measure your next words carefully," I say, then press the knife tip in further for good measure, earning a startled yelp from him. "Consider this to be your fair and final warning. I don't give second chances."

My crew chooses that moment to appear. Once he sees who they are, his shoulders sag a little. "Thank goodness you're here," he starts to say, and I cut him off again by applying more pressure to his side. I'm nowhere near done with him, so that had better not be from relief.

"Now, who's the unfortunate bastard that contributed half of your DNA? I'll be sure to offer my condolences right before I spit on your faux grave. Or, since the idiot never taught you not to covet the things that aren't yours, maybe I'll bury him with you, just for kicks. Who is he?"

Nothing.

Okay then.

"My family. Harris. Delilah. Courtney. Sarah. Charlie. Remember their names. That's what signed your fucking death warrant. Now, you are a dead man; that much is decided. You don't get the benefit of a fucking goodbye because nobody has time for that. We can do it here and give everyone a show, or we can do it someplace else and spare your family the horror of watching you take your last breaths. Your choice."

Still nothing.

Not a peep.

I turn to my number one. "Get him there tonight, no fuss. Keep him alive and coherent since I'm nowhere near done with him. And find out who his father is. While you're at it, I want to know who his family and friends are. I want the name of the guy that gives him those hideous haircuts. Even the guy that mows his fucking lawn. I want every crevice of this fucker's life turned upside down. Call Diabolus if you hit any digital roadblocks."

"You'll never get away with this," the miserable bastard whimpers.

"Again, debatable. You won't be around to see it, and that's a damn shame." I release him then, taking a step back. "A word of advice? In your next life, don't make the same mistake again."

The thing is, people know me as Lorenzo Sotelo's bastard son — that's how he brought Courtney and me into the family. Not very many people know us as Sarah Bardales's children. Not that we went out of our way to hide it. I named my law firm after her, so that should be fucking obvious. But no, ignorant idiots like this never put two and two together.

This fucker will learn that right before his tongue gets ripped out of his mouth.

Or maybe H will do it. I don't care either way as long as it happens. He deserves the same respect that I command, and it is my job to ensure he gets that as my partner, come hell or high water.

That, and he's been working on a new line of torture devices — or sex toys, as ordinary people call them — and this is the perfect opportunity to troll for potential victims to test it on. There will always be an idiot or two in or associated with the Sotelo family that needs to be taken care of permanently.

Like this one.

This one's a goner. H can pick out any others he likes and I'll take care of the rest. That sometimes seems to cheer him up.

David, too, on the rare occasion he shows up to these things. I'm counting on him being here tonight, despite the restraining order. He has unfinished business with Hurricane Dahlia, and I hope those two can settle their differences tonight. Well, if they don't, this ought to cheer him up.

With that taken care of, I briefly glance around the room for my family. Then something — or someone — moves in my periphery, and I have to do a double-take.

Hurricane Dahlia.

She's looking less than thrilled to be here, as one would expect.

It just pisses me off that she came here with her tool of an ex-fiancé after everything we've been through in the last few weeks. On top of that, she's thirty-eight weeks pregnant. So what the fuck is she thinking, strapping those death traps — four-inch gladiator heels — on her feet? I have an idea who put those on her, and it seriously makes me question her fucking judgment since she really should know better.

Don't even get me started on what D will do once she sees them. The sisters already beat up Nalina in a fucking police station, and I had to call in a shit-ton of favors to get them off. That was only a month ago. Not quite long enough, if you ask me.

This, though, just might start yet another fight where I'll have to clean up its aftermath. I can't even be mad about it because she would deserve it and so much more.

But the Brewer sisters? I don't know what I'm going to do with these two. Truth is, their emotions bleed into each other. It's a thing with them. H and I, we've barely gotten D to a good place. If we want any hope of being happy with D long term, we should set aside this passive-aggressive bullshit and start actively helping Dahlia.

Not saying it will happen overnight or anytime soon. It could take years. But we have to try.

An hour later, I manage to wrangle them all together by some stroke of luck. My family, I mean. It's almost Charlie's bedtime, and H has had enough people-ing for one evening. Surprisingly, both D and Courtney had a good time, which is all I could hope for. Even with the thing with Dahlia, which both women have been keeping an eye on all evening.

So really, I shouldn't be surprised that we run into her on our way out, stumbling in those deathtraps without her tool of an ex-fiancé in sight.

D rushes to her first, with H and Courtney close on her heels, catching her just before her body hits the floor.

"What have you gotten yourself into this time?" D asks.

She squirms in their hold. "I'm fine," she mumbles. "I don't need your help."

"The fuck you don't," H says as he wraps his arms around her back and pulls her up to her feet. "Hold still."

"You're touching me," she says incredulously. "Why are you touching me? You always keep me at arm's length, like I have the plague or something."

Well, there is that. But there is also her thixophobia to consider. She doesn't do well with people touching her. Everyone present knows about it. Except for Charlie. Although it can't be helped at the moment.

"Can we gag her?" Courtney asks. Her eyes meet mine, and she smirks before adding, "Delilah, quick, give me your panties."

She's lucky I love her, the troublemaker.

"Nobody is gagging anyone," D cuts her off. "What the fuck are those?"

My eyes follow the direction of her gaze, and finally, someone addresses the fucking elephant in the hallway.

"Shoes," Dahlia says, like it's the most obvious response in the world. Which it is, but it's more than that.

"You're thirty-eight weeks pregnant, Daa. You know better than to wear four-inch gladiator heels at this point. That's foot suicide."

She shrugs. "It was Andrea's idea."

It is just as I thought. That woman really has no shame. None whatsoever.

"This is absurd. Let's get you somewhere to sit—"

It's the last thing I hear before a stream of bile rains down on me.

On all of us, actually.

Including baby Charlie.

54

HARRIS

Well, there are worse ways to exit a party.

Of all the ways I imagined this night would end, six people crammed into a tiny bathroom was not one of them. I wish it were as sexy as it sounds. I wish there were any hints of impropriety in the air. At least that would make this evening slightly worth it.

Instead, we all have to bear witness as one judgmental bitch pukes her guts out while two people hold back her obnoxiously styled hair. A fucking bird's nest is what it is. If she were wasted — even slightly — this would be comical and maybe even worth it.

Instead, she's broken.

Someone finally broke the bitch.

David did. He broke her.

I'm unsure whether I should be proud of him or just concerned since he's been the same way. For four weeks, he's been brooding and moping. And screwing up my orders for no reason. I've already threatened to fire his ass more times than I can count. Except I don't pay him, so those threats are empty. Maybe I'll just stuff him and the bitch in the same room together, so they can fuck it out of their systems, yeah?

Delilah's eyes meet mine, narrowing in displeasure.

Okay, fine. I promised I'd start using her actual name.

Dahlia.

Urgh, it is as distasteful as it sounds.

Just as she is. Hence the reason why we are all stuffed in here, like sardines. It's not like it's too much trouble either. We always have an extra set of clothes on hand, specifically for situations like this. Or, in my case, for when Marc is feeling particularly frisky with that knife of his.

Contrary to what her sister thinks, I'm convinced it wasn't an accident. She projectile-vomited on all five of us — myself, Marc, Courtney, Delilah, and even baby Charlie — at once and on purpose.

Hurricane Dahlia's bitch-o-meter is at maximum capacity. So instead of saying thank you, like any normal person would, she's daring Courtney to gag her with Delilah's panties. The same ones she's using as a wet cloth for Dalhia's neck. From the look on Courtney's face, she's actively considering it. Save for the inevitable asphyxiation.

Also, Delilah would be fucking crushed if she died. Marc knows this too since he's the one who volunteers to take those death traps off her feet.

"She's only trying to help since she's been through this before," Marc says as he unlaces her heels. "Do you have to be a bitch even to those helping you?"

"Maybe you could all start by using her fucking name," Delilah counters. "It's Dahlia, not bitch."

I would, except she pukes again when Charlie squeals. I knew she didn't want kids; I didn't realize it was that bad.

"Why did you come with those people?" Delilah asks, holding her hair back. "And why did you let that woman talk you into these death traps? I thought you were smarter than this."

I thought so too, except I'm staring at her ringed-up calves that say otherwise.

"They threatened to file assault charges against all of us if I refused," she says between heaves. "Plus, I'm carrying their grandchild, so it's not like I had a choice."

"You've always had a choice," she counters.

"Oh, grow up, Dee. We're commodities, not people."

Courtney lifts her eyes to Marc and me as she rubs Dahlia's back in circles. She mouths *'what the actual fuck'* at us, and it takes every ounce of willpower I possess to bite down a chuckle. Conversely, Marc is too focused on getting Charlie out of his vomit-stained outfit to pay attention.

On the other hand, Delilah takes it all in stride, keeping her cool while performing her sisterly duties. "Speak for yourself," she coos.

I don't miss the tension in her body or the stiff way she's holding herself. I hate that she has to go through this with her bitch of a sister. Oops, slipped up again. Hurricane Dahlia is in full bitchy mode tonight, and there's nothing either of us can do except ride it out.

I mean, it's not our fault that she broke up with her boyfriend. Boy-toy. Fuck buddy? Whatever she and David were — and I did warn the motherfucker not to get involved with Hurricane Dahlia, but no one ever listens to me anyway — she's the one who put an end to it. So there's no reason for her to drag us all into her miserable pit of hell.

Then again, they do say misery loves company...

Dahlia's eyes lift to meet Marc's. "Ask your mafia lawyer boyfriend if you don't believe me. It's all in the papers I found."

"What papers?" Delilah asks, then turns to face Marc. "What is she talking about?"

My brow furrows in confusion. If Dahlia is talking about what I think she is — the contracts she needed Marc's help with — then Delilah knows about them. She knows as much as she can stomach anyway, which wasn't much. I was there when Marc gave her the cliff notes, and she said she didn't want to know anymore.

As far as I know, she doesn't know of their contents, but she knows about them.

There's no way she's forgotten about it. It came up the first and only time she brought Hurricane Dahlia home, the same day Dahlia requested that Marc take a look at them. Repeated her request, that is, because she had already asked him once and he said no. It was also the day he unceremoniously kicked her out of the house right after agreeing to do it, all in the same breath. Then Delilah and Marc fought about it for weeks after, so it's still a sore subject and nowhere near resolved. Neither of us is particularly eager to rehash it here, especially Marc.

"We'll discuss this at home," he says, his jaw clenched.

It's been months, and Marc still won't budge on this because he's big on privacy. Then again, Delilah has always been the exception, so it's only a matter of time before that rule goes out the window.

Because Delilah makes a valid point. The double standard here is appalling, not to mention the hypocrisy on Marc's part. Courtney, Charlie, and even David can come and go as they please. Bitch or not,

Hurricane Dahlia is family. Whether we like it or not, Dahlia and Delilah are close, so there's no reason she wouldn't be welcome in our home.

"The papers I found in Dad's things, the ones I needed his help with, remember?" Dahlia continues like she's the center of attention. Which she is, except no one wants that going to her head. "He never told you? I thought you guys tell each other everything."

On second thought... Marc has a point too.

Also, where does Dahlia get all this energy to keep spouting such vitriol? Hasn't she heard of such a thing as a brain-to-mouth filter? It's so simple, even Charlie sometimes gets it, and he's only two.

Not to mention, I don't particularly care for the look that passes between Marc and Delilah.

"For the sake of this conversation," Delilah continues, with a bite to her tone that she doesn't bother disguising, "let's just say he told me. What's this business about us being commodities?"

Now *this* I have to hear, even though I already know the story.

Most of it, anyway.

"The McWhorters paid for everything," Dahlia says. "Fertility treatments for both Mom and Dad, several rounds of IVF, prenatal costs, everything. Mom had two late miscarriages and a stillbirth before you and I were born, and they paid for all that. They owed them, and what do you think they wanted as payment?"

"Let me guess — us?"

Huh.

That would explain David's comment from months ago, about the McWhorters taking Delilah from us being the thing that wakes us up. As if that could ever happen. I know he said this to get under my skin, but I now know there was some truth to his words.

Although I still stand by my response. Delilah is officially under Marc's protection, so I'd like to see them try. Dahlia is too; she just doesn't know it yet. So is David, but at least he knows it.

"We never had a choice, Dee. Or even a say in any of it. We belong to them. Well, I do. You lucked out in that department."

Delilah's jaw clenches. "Lucked out?"

Even I have to cringe at the unfortunate choice of words.

"I... I'm sorry. I didn't mean it like that."

"What did you mean by it?"

Dahlia turns her face to the side, leaning against the porcelain bowl. Courtney almost dips her hands into the bowl to stop the bird's nest from falling in. I have half a mind to ask her to leave it just to see how loud the bitch can screech.

Oops, slipped up again.

"We were paired off, all four of us. They didn't care who ended up with whom, or how or when it happened, just as long as it did. With Simone gone, you're off the hook. Sort of. Until Matthias... he said I had to marry Curtis, that we'd been dating for long enough, and it was time. And also, if I didn't marry him, he'd make you do it."

Again, I'd like to see them try.

"What makes you think I want anything to do with that family? Especially after what happened with Simone?"

"You wouldn't have had a choice. None of us did. Remember the huge fight that happened on Simone's nineteenth birthday when she came out to them?" She waits for Delilah to nod before continuing. "You had another panic attack in the middle of it, and the three of us took you home. Mom and Dad stayed to try and talk some sense into them. Later that evening, Simone and I went back, and you stayed behind with Curtis. We walked in on them having a screaming match. Then Mom said that since you were in love with Simone, they were getting us both anyways, and their little tantrum was pointless.

"I'd never seen Simone so angry. I knew what she was capable of, but it was the angriest I'd ever seen her. You know what happened next. Simone trashed their entire first floor that night while they just stood and watched. Millions worth of property damage. That's why after Simone... went missing, they made you watch as they burned her things. Including the dress. They also tried to get Mom and Dad to sign an amended contract. It was already implied, but they wanted it in writing. Assurances that they were getting their money's worth out of us. But Mom and Dad wouldn't sign. They had that falling out shortly after, then they had the house locked up tighter than Fort Knox."

Delilah doesn't say anything at that. None of us do. The room is deathly silent save for Charlie's babbling, but even he seems to be getting the hint that something is amiss.

That's not the only thing that's amiss though.

It occurs to me then — to Marc too, as we exchange the look that Delilah detests — that none of this surprises her. Her dad's papers told us all this, and she told him she didn't want to know. But since she does now… is this what she was watching a few days ago?

We found her in the media room — Marc and me — with violent tremors running through her entire body as she stared blankly at the screen, with a stilled image of Simone's face. After we got her settled in bed, I wanted to see it for myself, but Marc refused. More accurately, he warned me not to be a nosy fucker, then locked up the USB drive in his office.

I don't think it made a difference since the damage was done. Delilah stayed in bed for days, clutching Simone's picture. Her eyes were empty, and her face was expressionless. It reminded me of the blank look she sported like a suit of armor when we first met fifteen years ago.

I get the sense Marc knows what this is about, but he won't tell me. He stressed that it is Delilah's story, and she has her reasons for not telling me.

I do though.

It has everything to do with the Brewer-McWhorter feud, the same one she refuses to discuss with me.

It's because I'm a selfish fucker. For the longest time, I wanted Delilah to move on from Simone. But ever since Marc put things into perspective, I've been trying to do better. To be better. To come to terms with it. Seeing the woman I love in that state doesn't make it any easier.

She barely got out of bed for this ball, and it's not because Courtney used her womanly wiles on her. She's not even here for Marc or this stupid family obligation. Dahlia is the reason she's here, because she somehow got wind of the fact that she was going to be here with her tool of an ex-fiancé. Courtney's doing, no doubt.

"I thought everything was fine," Dahlia says after some time. "I thought they would leave you alone as long as I stayed with Curtis. Then Matthias said…"

She trails off at that, and my fists curl into balls at my sides. Somehow I know what she's going to say next, and it makes my blood boil.

"What did that fucker say?" Delilah prompts when the silence stretches.

"I don't want children, Dee. I never did, but you do. So he said…

he said he would pull an Ian Doyle on you, locking you up while pregnant so you couldn't abort. Several times, as long as they got a grandson out of it. He also said he'd fix it so that no one would miss you if you went missing, like Simone."

Delilah's gaze darts to Marc's and lingers for a few seconds, before returning to her sister. I don't have to guess what's on her mind, not when it's written all over her face.

Also, why haven't we killed this fucker yet? Just because he's rich doesn't make him above the consequences.

"I'd been actively looking into getting a hysterectomy, so this isn't a coincidence." Dahlia laughs bitterly and points to her stomach. "They knew I was stalling, so they found a way to tamper with my birth control. I thought about getting an abortion too, but then I figured if one of us was going to be a broodmare, it had to be me. You won't survive it. Your heart's not strong enough."

"Well, joke's on them because I will have children, just not with Curtis," Delilah says his name with a sneer. "I am done being anyone's spare, defective or otherwise. Or a commodity. When I decide to have children, it will be because I want to, not because I have to."

"Just because you speak it into existence doesn't mean it'll happen. Now that I'm done with Curtis, you know they'll come for you, right? Not even the mighty Sotelo name will be enough to protect you from —*aww*!"

For a moment there, I thought Dahlia was having another puke session. Only this time, Delilah has her sister's hair clenched in her fists. Evidently, this catches Marc's attention too. Pride surges through my body, seeping through every pore. It's about time someone stood up to the judgmental bitch.

Oops, slipped again.

Delilah's gaze darts back and forth between Marc and me. "And when I *do* decide to have children, they will be fathered by these gentlemen right here. Both of them."

Instead of the dreaded panic, my heart swells with pride to hear Delilah say those words.

Then she leans in and whispers something into Dahlia's ear. What she's saying to her has Courtney giggling like a fucking teenager. Then a, "Can I watch?"

Watch what?

What the fuck are they whispering about? Granted, I'm fucking obsessed with all things Delilah so this is one thing I'm not dropping.

"Depends," is all Delilah says before releasing her grip on the bird's nest and turning to Marc. "Go get David."

"He's not here," Marc says. "He's got that restraining order against Curtis, remember?"

Delilah's eyes narrow. "Go get the fucker who broke my sister, or so help me god, I'll lock both your cocks up in chastity cages and ship the keys off to fucking Antarctica."

I wouldn't mind that, just as long as she gets to suffer along with us. That's just me. Not Marc though. He'll die if he doesn't get to fuck one or both of us at least once a day. Then we'll have to put 'Forced Abstinence' on his tombstone. That'd be a sight.

I won't get the chance though, since Marc gives her a curt nod, then leaves, Charlie in tow.

"Shouldn't it be Curtis who has one against David?" Dahlia asks.

Is she really that naive?

Marc can spin a lot of things to his advantage. That's what makes him a darn good lawyer. Everyone knows of Curtis's reputation as a pussy hound. It wasn't that hard to spin the sequence of events the other way around, depicting him as an obsessed man who provoked his ex-fiancée's new boyfriend.

Then there's Nalina, who doesn't want word of her version of sex therapy getting out. There's also the fact that she's been fucking David since he was fifteen. And that this whole mess happened in her office. She knows that statutory rape charges won't look good on her. David doesn't want that getting out either, since it'll bring up stuff about his mother and that whole media shitstorm from nine years ago. Marc reluctantly agreed to file a restraining order against her on behalf of Dahlia and Delilah in exchange for that not getting out.

"That's just how it happened," Courtney says. "This is my brother we're talking about. There's one in the works for you two against Nalina. She's not contesting it, either; something about not wanting her dirty laundry aired." She purses her lips. "So it's true then, that she—"

"David doesn't want it being made public," Dahlia says, cutting her off.

I'm surprised she knows about that. I'm equally stunned she's considering how he feels about it instead of going all gung-ho white savior on Nalina's ass. She must really love him.

But first, I have to know what all the giggling was about.

"What did you say to her?" I ask Delilah. "After all that whispering and fucking giggling, I have to know."

"We'll discuss this at home," she says. "Along with everything else you two idiots have been keeping from me."

Fair enough. We'll stay an hour, at most, then head home. And if she's up for it, Marc and I will edge her until she's confessing all, desperate for a release.

Courtney rises, and her eyes meet mine. A slight shake of her head and a whispered, "You don't want to know," do little to tamp my curiosity.

Until David walks into the room and all else is forgotten.

I don't know what Dahlia did to him, or what David did to her. Still, the scene that unfolds is enough to make me take back every shitty thing I've ever said or thought about Dahlia. I've only ever seen him look at one other person this way. She's six years old, his daughter, and the center of his universe.

Now he's found another one, another center of his universe. His partner. His soulmate.

It's a good look for him.

Love.

It almost makes him seem… human.

55

DELILAH

"I need your help," David's voice echoes through the phone.

Leaning back in my seat, I let out an exasperated sigh. "The last time you said those words…"

"It's nothing terrible, I promise."

Famous last words.

Famous fucking last words.

"All right, I'm listening. You have exactly five seconds to say whatever it is you have to say, then I'm hanging up."

"Geez, you don't mess around, do you?"

"Four seconds, David."

"Okay, fine. Dahlia doesn't have anything for the baby yet, and since she's only recently decided to keep him, or at least fight for him, the least we can do is have somewhere for the little guy to sleep and all of the other things parents get for their kids. It's been a week since she decided and she's overwhelmed by all that needs to be done before the baby comes. I was hoping to get your help with the whole nesting thing."

I really don't want to like him, okay? I just want to keep him at arms length, and barely tolerate him, for my sister's sake. After all, that's what she did with Harris and Marc for years.

But then, why does the fucker have to go and do things like this?

"Delilah?"

He's crazy, isn't he?

He really is crazy — crazily in love with her.

And romantic too. So fucking romantic.

Fuck him.

"I still hate you," are the next words that come out of my mouth.

Not because I do — or maybe I do — but because he's managed to convince her to do the one thing I have been trying to convince her of for months.

A deep sigh echoes through the phone. "I deserve it, but this isn't about me."

"Yeah, I know that."

"I would buy everything for her, but you told me that Dahlia doesn't want me spending my money on her. That's why I think she would appreciate it more if it were done in a sentimental manner, don't you think? Also, she regrets the things she said to you, and the things she did. She's also hurting, not that it justifies what happened. I know she wants to make it up to you, Delilah. She wants her best friend back, even if she's too stubborn to admit it."

I really, *really* don't want to like him.

"I'll make a few calls and get back to you on that, okay?"

"Thank you, Delilah. You are god-sent."

Right. "And David?"

"Yeah?"

"This took longer than five fucking seconds."

Then I hang up.

My next call is to Courtney, obviously. She's the only person I know who has gone through this nesting thing fairly recently, and if there's anyone who's going to be a wealth of information it'll be her. And after she scolds me for calling her in the middle of the day — like there is another better time of day to do so — she lets me know that she still has Charlie's baby things, the things he's outgrown. She also has thousands of dollars' worth of brand-new baby things that Howard — Charlie's father — got for him, things never got used. These things are taking up space in her garage and she needs the room for extra storage for her art supplies. If I could take it all she would be forever grateful to me.

So I guess she now owes me one, since I agreed to take it all. Dahlia has nothing, after all.

My next step is actually getting the stuff out of her place. For that, I call Marc. Normally, I would call Harris for this sort of thing, but he's only just warmed up to the idea of having children with us, and I don't want to scare him off so early in the process. Babies do come with a lot of stuff, after all, and it took him years to even step foot into Charlie's quarters at home. So he's off the hook for this.

Also, calling Marc is easy since this one is more up his alley. He's all for the idea at first, until I tell him who it is for. Then he goes silent, so silent that I think he hung up on me. Except I can still hear the sounds of his breathing, the ragged breaths he draws in and out, several times, as he decides whether to reward me for doing a good thing for my sister, or punish me for doing a good thing for Hurricane Dahlia. I'll take either option, to be honest, and I tell him just that. When he doesn't say anything, I tell him that I could call Harris instead. To which he says he'll be here at five PM and then he hangs up on me.

The grump.

It's a good thing that I love him.

Speaking of, he insists on coming all the way up to Brewer Health to pick me up. I'm still not sure just how practical this is. His office is located at least thirty minutes away from mine, and that's on a good day with minimal traffic. Rush hour traffic at that time of day is a nightmare, so I know it is no easy feat for him to pick me up. Not when I know this will take even longer, since we will be heading over to Courtney's house first. This only means he'll have more work to do when we get home. Or he'll join us in bed first, until Harris and I fall asleep, then spend the rest of the night working.

But it's what he wants, and I don't refuse him. Just like I promised him that night, I won't refuse him ever again, as long as it is within reason. Now that I understand his need to do this, to watch over everyone, to protect everyone, even though he does go overboard with it sometimes, I'm taking Harris's and Courtney's advice and letting it happen. Besides, it's what makes him happy, so who am I to judge? Denying him will only make him grumpy, and a grumpy Marc means an even grumpier Harris, since their moods tend to feed off of each other, and really, nobody has time to deal with two grumpy men. Least of all me.

So I indulge him.

This, of course, is sure to raise a few eyebrows. If Harris were to walk in here, no one would bat an eyelash. After fifteen years of us being friends, he is a regular fixture in my life. But everyone here knows who Marc is. Not just because Harris talks about him all the time, but because he already draws a lot of unwanted public attention to himself due to being the illegitimate son of mob boss Lorenzo Sotelo Sr. His reputation as a ruthless lawyer also precedes him.

So it goes without saying that Marc showing up at my lab at the end of the work day — instead of on the seventh floor where we hold all business-related meetings for Brewer Health — is sure to raise a few eyebrows. For some reason, I find that I don't particularly care about this right now. It's public knowledge that I went with them to the ball. People can make of that whatever they like. People can judge however they choose.

And as I suspect, that judgment comes a little close to home.

"So… your ride is here," Charlena says, hovering at the doorway to my office.

Charlena happens to be one of those odd fixtures in Dahlia's and my lives. We met her in medical school, and that friendship stuck. She also comes from new money, and her family is well-off. As such, she doesn't have to work, but she chooses to, and for some reason she choses to come work with me.

"My ride?" I ask, lifting my face to meet hers.

"He's out there." She shifts on one foot to the other as she says this. "He knows he's not cleared to be back here due to protocol."

For a moment there I thought she was talking about Harris, since he has been a regular fixture in my life for years. Also, since when does Harris's presence make her nervous? She's known him since medical school. They even completed their residency at the same hospital. We all did.

"That makes no sense," I say, pushing the hair away from my face. "Harris can come in here anytime he wants…" I trail off at that, remembering my conversation from earlier. "Marc?"

She nods. "What's up with that, anyway? Is Harris sick or something?"

"No, he's fine."

I go about my usual end of day activities. Charlena doesn't budge from her position at the doorway, her head tilted to the side, those observant eyes of hers studying every angle of me.

"What?" I ask her.

She gives me an undecipherable look. "You're not..."

"I'm not what?"

She sighs. "You and Harris, I get it. You two are best friends, but you've always had strong sexual chemistry, so I get it if you finally gave in to your basic desires and took it to the next level. But you and Marc? That's just so... wrong."

Yep. Judgment.

A beat passes, then she asks, "What does Harris think about this?"

I shove my laptop into my bag and zip it closed before turning to her. "About what?"

"About you fucking his boyfriend? His very gay boyfriend, I might add."

"What makes you think Marc's gay?"

I mean, I *did* think that too at first, but still.

"Oh please, everybody knows Marc is gay, through and through." She waves me off. "I'll bet you twenty-five cents that if you look up the definition of 'gay' in the Merriam-Webster dictionary, you'll find the name *Marc Sotelo* listed under examples."

Huh. I almost forgot that Charlena used to be a part of the BDSM scene along with them. She might have been one of their partners too, when Marc and Harris had an open relationship. You'd think she would have moved on by now, seeing as it's been seven years. Or eight years, if you factor in their gap year. Or maybe it's longer than that.

"You do realize that it's none of your business, right?"

I know it's not fair of me to say that. Charlena is as much my friend as she is Dahlia's. And she does care. But she's also nosy. Too nosy, in fact.

"So it's true what the rumors say."

"What rumors?"

"That you showed up the ball with Marc and Harris, as a throuple."

"That wasn't a rumor, and it's none of your business." I adjust my purse strap on my shoulder. "But if you must know, I am happy."

"As long as you know what you're doing. Be careful though."

"You sound a lot like Dahlia. I know what I'm doing, okay? I'm a grown woman—"

A commotion outside the lab draws both of our attention. We make it to the open area just in time to see Marc as he comes barreling into the area, followed by one of the receptionists. She's voicing her protests about this being a sterile environment and how he doesn't have the necessary clearance to be in this area, and he's ignoring her, like he does to people who hold little to no interest for him. His singular focus is on me, his determined steps making it clear who and what he is after as he breaks all of the policies and procedures that I put in place for this very reason.

I barely have enough time to wave her off before he pulls my body into his and fastens his mouth on mine. His hands move to my ass and he grabs handfuls of each cheek. I react on instinct, legs lifting off the ground and scaling his solid body. When he determines that I've gotten high enough his fingers dig into my ass and a deliriously sweet shiver runs through my body, arms looping around his neck and my ankles hooking around his waist.

Not once does he break our kiss. Instead, he pushes my lithe body against the wall, angles my mouth just how he wants it and deepens our kiss.

What can I say? Chemistry.

I'm not ready for it when it inevitably comes — the moment when Marc's lips break away from mine as he comes up for air. My chest heaves in a bid to draw more air into my lungs, more him into my body. Just... more. So I try to do just that, but his hands hold my face in place.

"I missed you this morning," he murmurs against my lips, before folding me into his body.

"Who are you and what have you done to Marc?" I ask as his lips skim over my shoulder and I moan against him.

There's an infused sweetness to his words, one I'm still not used to hearing from him. You'd think he'd last seen me a year ago, or even a week ago, instead of just last night. Unfortunately, he was gone by the time Harris and I woke up this morning. Which is too bad, because he missed out on some—

Someone clears their throat.

Charlena.

I'd forgotten she was still here, and also everyone else in the room with us, watching this exchange.

Oops.

"I guess that answers that," Charlena says.

I'm not even going to bother hiding this.

"She thinks you're gay," I whisper into Marc's ear.

At which he laughs. A gut-wrenching, full-body laugh, one that vibrates throughout his body, and in turn vibrates throughout mine. It goes on and on, this laugh of his, the sound a beautiful memory that's seared into my memory for all eternity.

He really ought to do this more often. Laugh like this.

"That's a good one," is all he says, then walks us out of my lab and out of the building,

I guess that answers the question then, for anyone who had doubts about what we are. Like the Charlenas of the world.

It's not until he's opening up the back of his limo to let me inside that I remember I drove myself in to work this morning.

"What about my car?" I ask him.

It's not a completely unfounded concern. He did have my car towed earlier in our relationship, to do whatever he did with it. Besides, only Marc would take a fucking limo grocery shopping. It's not like he has a whole fleet of cars at his disposal.

"Wayne will take it home."

I pause. "Who is Wayne again?"

"Your new bodyguard." He says this as casually as one would comment on the weather.

"I didn't know I had a new bodyguard," I say, climbing into the car. "What happened to Walter?"

"He got sloppy and you saw him," he says, then shuts the door behind me.

Oh yeah, that did happen too. It wasn't Walter's fault though. I was determined to find out who had been assigned to my protection detail. My supposed-to-be-inconspicuous protection detail. So Harris and I might have played a little prank, just to draw him out. And also to draw out his bodyguard as well. We never imagined it would actually get them fired.

Or did it?

I wait for Marc to walk around and climb into the adjacent seat. "Did Harris get a new one too?"

He laughs and raps twice on the separator. "What do you think?"

What do I think?

I think he's an obsessive, overbearing, overprotective, controlling grump. It still blows my mind that Harris thinks of all this as normal. It still blows my mind that I've come to think of it as normal. The Marcway. Even though this isn't normal. This is so not normal.

"It's a bit much, don't you think?"

"Maybe. Perhaps you two will think twice before pulling a stunt like that again."

Leaning back against the leather seat, I cross my arms over my chest and stare daggers at him. "Whatever happened to issuing a written warning?"

"That's not how it works." He chuckles and taps on his lap. "Come here."

Now it makes sense, why we are in a fucking limo.

I wait for us to pull out onto the road before saying, "I like these clothes."

He pulls out his pocket knife and flicks it open. "I don't care, D. I skipped lunch."

"But it took Harris twenty minutes to pick out these clothes today."

I already know my protest falls on deaf ears. His affinity for knives is becoming a problem. This would be the fifth outfit he's ripped to shreds this week alone. It's not like I'll deny him. It's like I turn into another person when I'm with him. A sex-crazed fiend. And after the kiss we shared in my office, my panties are soaked. Which he knows, and he always finishes what he starts.

Marc shakes his head, slowly, the look in his eyes going predatory. "This face will stay between those legs for the next forty-five minutes. Now, we can do this the easy way, or we can do this the hard way. Lady's choice."

"Why don't I take these off first?" I begin the arduous process of unbuttoning my blouse, keeping my eyes trained on his ever-growing erection. The thought of him sliding inside me has me salivating, and maybe if I take that long to get these clothes off he'll give me just that. My fingers shake as I'm undoing the teeny-tiny buttons of my blouse. Harris did pick this one out for me. He's the one who talked me into wearing it this morning. It's like he knew something I didn't.

Damn it, Harris knew this was going to happen.

Marc turns and lays the knife next to him, carefully.

"D, I need you." A pause, then his head lifts and his eyes meet mine, stormy-gray and darkening with lust. "Please."

The lone magic word has me scrambling over to him in record time. After another long, drawn-out kiss like before, he sprawls my body out on the leather seat and pulls my skirt and underwear to my ankles.

"Marc, I—"

"The only words I want to hear from you," he says as he slides his hands up to my knees and pushes my thighs apart, "are *'oh'* and *'my'* and *'god'*, okay? Moans and screams too, but that's it."

The amended code of silence.

I fucking hate the amended code of silence. The old one worked just fine, and I start to tell Marc that when he buries his face between my legs, like he promised, and slowly drags that delectable tongue of his over my folds and clit.

"Fuck!" I cry out, back arching as I buck against his face.

"That works too," he breathes against my pussy. His deep voice rumbles against my skin, sending gentle vibrations straight to my clit, which in turns rumbles throughout my core, sending a delicious shiver down my spine.

Then he fastens those bossy lips of his around my clit and sucks on it, hard, and I lose all coherent thought. I lose count of the number of orgasms he draws out of my body in the forty-two minute drive to his sister's house. He is merciless and relentless in his assault of my clit and my pussy, and all I have to do is lie there and take it. Which I do, because with all of my squirming and bucking, I almost slip off the leather seat. He takes matters into his own hands, slinging my legs up and over his shoulders, then sliding his hands up to grip my hips, holding me in place. At some point his fingers join the party. Even that darn knife of his joins the party too because he promised me it would. He did say it was all going in me — his knife, his cock, his kid — and Marc is a man of his word.

If what I'm getting tonight is one out of three then so be it. There will be plenty of time for the rest.

We pull into Courtney's driveway and only then does he finally let up, fingers and tongue and whatever else he was using on me. Even that darn knife of his. He then takes his time in sliding my skirt and panties back into place.

"What about you?" I manage to ask.

He brings his fingers, glistening with my juices, to his lips and sucks on them. Slowly, his eyes intent on mine, he releases them with a pop. "We still have the drive home, don't we? All sixty minutes of it."

At least he didn't cut my clothes off my body this time.

I have no doubt I'll pay for that later.

56

HARRIS

I t is a beautiful day.

The sun's shining, and the birds are chirping. It should be an all-around happy day. We should be on a fucking date. We should be admiring the beauty nature has to offer, and we are. Sort of.

I mean, look at where we are. We are in our backyard, our gorgeous landscaped grounds. But it's what we are all staring at that has me stumped.

Marc has us on either side of him, hands linked, standing over our headstone. Our giant headstone with all our names etched on it. Because nothing says forever like a physical reminder of our mortality.

Harris Brinkmann - Delilah Brewer - Marc Sotelo
HB - DB - MS
Together for all eternity, in life and in death.

I should cut him some slack though. Romantic gestures are so far out of his comfort zone, and I know he is trying. At least he didn't put the word that shall not be used on there. Forever. Delilah fucking hates that word, and now we know why.

It's because of her.

"I don't do grand gestures," Marc says, his voice tight. "What I *do* do though, is say what I mean and mean the shit I say."

See? Not at all romantic. I just have something in my eyes. Delilah too, as she kneels before the headstone, running her fingers over the markings.

"How long have you had this?" she breathes.

Shoulders tight, he shrugs. "Not long."

"These markings are not recent." Her eyes lift to meet his, gleaming with unshed tears. My heart skips a beat as I take in the love and vulnerability displayed on her face.

Neither of us is immune to her charms. He lowers himself to the ground, kneeling before her. "Ever since that day... when you first propositioned me."

Confusion clouds her features, then the fog lifts slowly. "You've had this for seven years?" she asks in a high-pitched tone.

I am as stunned as she is. We don't have a lot of secrets, so not only am I floored that he had our collective headstone done seven years ago, but he kept it from me all this while.

"When was this?" I can't help but ask.

He swipes a hand over his face. "When you first ran away from me."

I blink once, then twice.

That's what I love about him — he's always thinking five steps ahead, figuring out what we need, and giving it to us ten-fold. He's our steady center, our tether, anchoring us to something more than our respective selves. I know he says the same thing about us too.

That's the thing about damaged souls. They are like homing beacons. They always find a way to latch on to other damaged souls. Marc, Delilah, and myself — we are a unique brand of damaged. It might have taken us fifteen years, but we've finally convinced her that she belongs with us.

"Oh, Marc..." She wraps her arms around his waist and buries her face in his chest.

"There is no me without you," he continues. "Both of you. You mean the world to me. More than the world to me. I'll move heaven and earth for you. I'll maim whoever dares to come between us. I'll even kill for you. In fact, I *have* killed for you, and I'd do it again in a heartbeat. What I dread, though, is a future without you both. I don't think I could survive living a life without either one of you in it."

Seeing him like this guts me. I walk the few steps over to him, lower my body to crouch next to him, and slide my arms around his waist. He leans over and places his face in the crook of my neck, smelling me. It's something he's always done; I'm just surprised it took me so long to notice this about him. He claims my scent drives him crazy.

We stay that way for some time — a messy tangle of arms, necks, and faces.

"I love you," he eventually whispers against the skin of my neck. "You too, D. I love you."

He's been saying that a lot lately. I love you. I want you. I need you. I crave you. All three-word sentences. He chants them like a prayer every chance he gets. Because that's what we are to him. We are his doom and his salvation, all wrapped in one.

"I love you too, Marc," I say, my heart swelling with emotion. "You too, Delilah. More than anything."

Delilah releases a noncommittal moan between us.

"What's that, D?"

Her face lifts off his chest. "I said ditto, you sappy fools," she says, her voice a drowsy murmur.

The tension eases up some. We need more of this. More joy. More laughter. More togetherness. More love. More—

"Marry us," he tells her.

Wow, he just jumps right to it with no warning.

For the record, we had a plan. An elaborate plan, one that involved dinner and a movie. And fucking too, since we can't keep our hands off each other. But Marc just loves to go off script, not that I mind.

But she does mind, it would seem.

"Is that a question or a statement?" she asks.

"It can be whatever you want it to be, D."

He retrieves a small velvet box from his pocket and hands it to her. She opens it and erupts in a fit of giggles.

"Damn it, Marc! Did you put laughing gas inside the box?" I ask him, feigning annoyance.

He lifts both hands in mock surrender, but I don't buy it for one second. He's been known to pull even worse stunts in the past.

She holds out a small piece of paper. "What you're saying is," she says between laughs, "you'll fuck me right here unless I give you an answer?"

Marc solemnly nods. "Pretty much."

"Sound familiar?" I add.

She scowls. "You can't use my words against me in a marriage proposal."

"I never claimed to be original," he says. "So, you in or what?"

She appears to mull this over. "On one condition."

His eyes light up. "Name it. Or better yet, put it in your book."

She shakes her head, and he groans. "This isn't a put-it-in-the-book type of thing. It's just basic human courtesy."

He groans louder. "D, you're killing me."

Strangely, her book is still empty. We have an idea of what she wants, but we're not sure what she's holding out for.

A small smile teases the corners of her lips. "Just hear me out."

"What's in it for me?" Ever the lawyer, he goes straight to negotiations.

As always, she dishes it right back. "You get to put whatever you want in my ass."

He purses his lips. "For the next twenty-four hours?"

She scoffs. "No, within the hour."

He rises to his feet. "No deal."

I can't believe it. Marc has always been an ass man, so for him to turn that down tells me he's officially lost his mind.

She agrees.

"Fine. Your loss." She stands too. "I was going to say yes, but you lost your chance."

My jaw goes slack and I turn to him. "Dude!"

This is why we don't go off-script. You can't get anything past our woman. She'll figure it out and then use it against you. Or in this case, against Marc. Because using this as a bargaining tactic means she wants something, and he won't like whatever that something is.

He runs a hand through his hair. "You win, D. What do you need?"

"You missed your window. What does it say about me if I give in so easily every time?"

"You never give in; you make us work for it each time."

She pushes up onto her tiptoes and cups his cheeks. "And that's why you love me." She leans in, presses her lips to his, and then pulls away before he can tighten his hold on her. "Since I'm nice anyway, the offer still stands for the next fifteen minutes. The sticking it offer, not the proposal. Race you though. Loser gets my ass."

After dropping that on us, she takes off like the devil is on her heels. Marc and I exchange a look, shrugging before taking off after her. Marc could win this sprint in a heartbeat, but the fucker slows down and lets me pass him because he wants her ass.

She beats us to our bedroom by a long shot. When I make it there, she's on the bed in her birthday suit, spread out like a delectable treat. It takes me less than sixty seconds to discard my clothing, join her on the bed, settle her into my lap and slide home.

Marc, the slowpoke, strolls in then.

"I think she's ready for this," I tell him. "She'll need some help, though."

He gets to work picking out what we need while I rock inside her, tight and slow, stretching her out while getting her used to the sensations. Her eyes are glazed over by the time he joins us.

"Perfection," he moans, leaning over to capture my mouth in a kiss.

As he does this, Marc cups my balls with one hand, doing the same to her ass cheeks before running a lubed finger down her puckered hole.

She inhales a shaky breath. "Will it always be like this?"

It's easy to forget this wasn't a regular occurrence for her until six months ago. We've done this before, many times, yet she still asks the question every time, so I give her the same answer each time.

"With us, always," I say softly, trailing a finger along her cheek.

She practically purrs and melts into my hands. The feel of her clenching around my cock feels heavenly. My hand snakes between us to find her clit and I press on it gently at first, eliciting a whimper from her.

"Distraction?" I ask her.

Her eyes go hooded. "Always." She leans in to cover my mouth with hers.

All the while, I sense Marc's eyes on us, seemingly mesmerized by the scene. It's a reenactment of our first night together, and he needs to get on it. My hands move to her cheeks, opening her wide for him. He brings a finger to her puckered hole and presses in. Her body tenses slightly before going boneless in my arms again. He adds another finger, and she squirms against me, her mouth insistent on mine.

It's not long before his fingers are replaced by his cock, as he eases in slowly. She breaks the kiss and rests her head perfectly still on my shoulder. Not tensing, though, so that's good. I feel him through her, sliding past me until he's fully seated.

"D?" I hear Marc say from behind her.

"I'm okay." Her voice is muffled on my shoulder. "I'm just... savoring the moment."

Neither Marc nor I respond because we too are savoring the moment. It never gets old. It's more than a physical act to each one of us. It's forever. A word she's slowly coming to terms with, something she seems to have accepted now. Because like it or not, she's stuck with us for the rest of her life. And us with her, come what may.

"Ummm... guys? You gonna move?"

Marc chuckles as he withdraws slowly, then thrusts back in. I follow suit, working in counterpoint with him. It's not long before we adopt a rhythm of our own, Delilah clenching around Marc and me in unison as we work her and ourselves to new heights, drawing out her pleasure and ours.

She comes first, loud and long as we continue to move within her. Then, in a surprising turn of events, Marc comes next, groaning and grunting through his climax as his stamina and resolve shatter around him. I have half a mind to tease him about it, but I don't because I know how addictive she is and how divine it is to be with her like this.

It's a feeling like no other. Heavenly. It's like touching heaven, daring to reach for the things you know you don't deserve, but they are yours anyway. Yours to own. Yours to keep.

Mine.

Ours.

"I love you," she whispers against my neck. "I love you both so much."

My resolve breaks and the surge of emotion overtakes me in a heartbeat. I spill into Delilah, balls emptying out in a rush that seems to last forever.

Marc leans over her shoulder and kisses me softly, gently.

"I love you," he breathes. "I love you both so much."

They are both very corny today, and my heart squeezes in response like it always does.

"I love you," I tell him. "I love you both so much."

What can I say — originality has left the building.

Not that I mind. I don't mind it one bit.

BONUS CONTENT

DELILAH

Six Months Later

"What do you think that's about?" David asks.

Harris and I flank David on either side, each of us vying for the baby, but he won't relinquish him. He's in full overprotective dad mode, this one. Although as he cradles Harold, rocking his sleepy figure from side to side, his eyes remain fixated on my sister, who is having a chat with Marc. A scolding, more like, but Dahlia can hold her own.

It is somewhat comforting to know that I wasn't entirely wrong about him the first time. He really is whipped. Completely, utterly in love with her.

"With Marc, it could be anything," Harris says.

"Call it what it is, an olive branch," I chime in.

Then Marc's fingers curl around Dahlia's elbow and she goes completely still. A feral growl erupts from David's chest, causing Harold to wince.

"She's fine," I assure him.

"What the fuck is wrong with him?" David growls. "He knows she doesn't like to be touched. The fucker probably did that on purpose."

Harris snickers; I do too.

What can I say? Whipped.

"No, he didn't," Harris points out. "Look."

We all watch as Marc's hand falls to his side and he watches Dahlia. A few beats pass, and when she opens her eyes, he… apologizes?

We are all at a safe-ish distance from them, and I don't read lips either, but it looked like he just said *'I'm sorry'* or something along those lines.

Progress, right?

"I take it congratulations are in order," David suddenly says.

My stomach flips painfully.

"What?" Harris chokes.

He tears his eyes away from Dahlia, reluctantly, I might add, and his gaze meets Harris's. "The rings. All three of you are wearing matching rings. Did you get engaged or something?"

"You can say that," Harris says. "I suppose the correct term would be a domestic partnership. Or brother husbands."

"Brother husbands?" David asks incredulously.

Harris snickers at his own joke. "It's a thing."

"But Marc isn't your brother," David counters.

"It's not literal." He holds out both arms. "Give me the baby."

"No." David turns his back on him. "Make your own."

"We're working on it, but I need the practice."

"Practice?"

His eyes meet mine, then his gaze lowers, lingering on my stomach, before slowly rising, lingering again on my chest, then my cheekbones, and finally meeting my eyes.

His lips part and I shake my head, mouthing a *'Don't'* to him.

I'm not hiding it, but I'm not exactly celebrating it either. Not yet, anyway. I'm late, that's as far as I know. Everything else will come after, and that's when I'll know for sure. There's no need to get my hopes up now with a test. Not when it will say the same thing it's been saying for months.

Maybe it will be positive this time.

It's what I've always wanted. It's what the guys want too. While Marc will be thrilled, I'm not sure about Harris. If I'm pregnant, there's a ninety percent chance that the baby will be his.

"I still think it's bullshit that you can't legally marry more than one person in Minnesota. Delilah refuses to pick one of us, so—"

"When did this become about me?" I interject.

"Isn't it always? We told you we don't care which of us you commit to, just as long as you do."

"Fine." I huff. "Then you won't care if I married Marc *and* took his last name."

"I... there's no need to go quite that far."

"So I should marry you and take *your* last name?"

"What about Marc?"

"My point exactly."

"Can't it be either-or? Marry one, take the other's last name?"

"I happen to like my last name."

"But you just said—"

"I know what I said. You know, maybe you should try taking my last name. Just a thought."

David snickers, having turned his gaze back to Dahlia. "You already bicker like an old married couple. Why bother with all the fanfare?"

Harris wrinkles his nose. "I dislike fanfare. And drama. And people and their fragile feelings to cater to. I still want a commitment ceremony though."

"You hate parties," I point out.

"Big parties. I'm thinking of a small ceremony with just friends and family. Something that makes this official."

"David and Dahlia don't plan on getting married. It doesn't make them any less committed than they already are."

"Why are you bringing me into this?" David complains.

"Because you're right here, hogging the baby," Harris says. "But since you asked, when do you plan on making an honest woman out of her?"

David and I both snort at the same time.

"An honest woman?" David laughs. "What is this, the Dark Ages? Dahlia will chop off my left testicle if I mention marriage. And this one here," he angles a chin in my direction, "won't hesitate to hold me down while she carves them right out."

I nod. "That's right, I will."

No point in refuting. I am handy with a scalpel. He did break my sister once, so it's his job to make sure that it never happens again, or the repercussions will be severe.

"You could at least pretend not to be enjoying this," he says about the sinister smirk that crosses my face. "And I happen to like my balls right where they are."

"Chicken," Harris teases.

"I can live with that, as long as I get to keep her and this little guy." He presses a kiss to Harold's forehead. "Besides, if anyone's going to be proposing, it'll be Dahlia proposing to me and not the other way around."

"Good luck with that." I tap on his shoulder patronizingly.

"I won't need luck. I'll just charm her pants right off."

"Dude, you already do that," Harris points out.

"I'll just turn it up a thousand more notches then."

They continue talking, and we all continue to not-so-subtly watch Marc and Dahlia like the creeps we all are. Because those two are like oil and water; the whole point of this fucking gathering was for them to make peace with each other. Harris came around fairly quickly, especially when he discovered Dahlia's other issues. And also why it was that she stayed with Curtis all this time. It really was to protect me.

Once David convinced Dahlia to keep the baby, it sealed the deal for him. Watching him like this, I'd say David has really come into his own. He loves Dahlia, and since Harold is hers, he loves him too. It is that simple for him.

He makes it so hard for me to hate him.

Marc, on the other hand, is taking a long time to come around. Too long, if you ask me.

Then Dahlia hands a bottle of breastmilk to Marc, and David growls again.

"Dude, would you fucking chill?" Harris laughs. "Marc is an asshole, but he's not that big of an asshole. Taking food away from a baby is one of the worst cardinal sins in his book."

That seems to appease David some. But when Marc smiles at Dahlia, I'm sure he has steam coming out of both ears.

"Is he trying to charm my girl?" he says.

Harris doubles over in laughter. "Oh man, you really are whipped."

David pouts. "He is! He's really doing it, turning the famous Sotelo charm on her. Don't pretend you don't know it. It's how that fucker got his hooks into you two. Besides, I'm the only one who—"

"That's it. Hand over my nephew and go to her," I order.

Playing the aunt card always works in my favor, but I only use it for special occasions like this one. It works too, since David doesn't protest. He just hands Harold to me and stalks to where she is. Marc approaches us with a serene smile; the usual tightness in his jaw is gone. He's also holding a bottle of Dahlia's breast milk like it ranks in the world's top ten most precious things.

Progress, like I thought.

Also, I need something from him.

————

"You haven't stopped smiling, so it went well," I tell Marc as we all walk out of Charlie's nursery where Harold is settled for his nap.

It's been twenty minutes and the serene look on his face hasn't faded. I'm hoping this is a good sign because I need something from him. Not a book thing, but it comes pretty darn close.

"We agreed to be cordial," he tells us as we head for our bedroom.

David and Dahlia are still on the second floor, since they need a moment to themselves. We do too. Or I do, and I can't ask Marc what I need in front of them.

"Cordial, huh?" I test out the word; it feels clinical. "Did Daa say that, or did you?"

"She did. I just went along with it."

"Yeah right. You didn't just go along with it. You turned on the Sotelo charm, and David was very bothered by it. Did you do that on purpose?"

Not that I care, this works perfectly in my favor.

Harris frowns like he just remembers something. "What did he mean by that?"

Oh boy.

I turn to Marc for help and he lifts both hands in mock surrender, the smile on his face morphing into a smirk. So I turn back to Harris and give him a sweet smile.

"What did *who* mean by *what*?"

"David."

I steel myself. "He said a lot of things, Harris. You need to be more specific."

He huffs. "He said, *'I guess congratulations are in order'*, and I know he wasn't referring to the rings."

"It's just a figure of speech," I tell him. "Don't go reading into things."

"Figure of speech my ass. If there's something you're not telling us—"

"Like the fact that D's pregnant?" Marc chooses that moment to chime in, oh so helpfully.

"Who says I'm pregnant?"

I answer my own question by wrapping my arms around my stomach. It's a reflex, I swear.

Harris's gaze drops to my stomach, and a look I can only describe as pure elation comes over his face. It will only make this sting like a bitch when the test comes back negative.

"I am not pregnant," I take a step back from him and whip my face to Marc's. "Take it back, Marc."

He shrugs. "Well, there's only one way to find out."

I take another step back. "I am not peeing on a stick while you two clowns watch."

"We can close our eyes if that makes you feel better," Harris adds.

"I don't think so," I say before I sprint towards our bedroom, knowing they will be close behind. Maybe I'll barricade myself in our bathroom before they make it.

It's just my shitty luck that it doesn't happen.

EPILOGUE

SIMONE

Eighteen Years Ago

TRANSCRIPT

Simone: *shuffles and re-shuffles in seat* This is still weird.

    Sonya (off-camera): Again, it's not for you. It's for them. And this was your idea.

    Simone: Dr. Goodman, you—

    Sonya: We saved the best for last. Curtis's and Dahlia's videos are a go, and Delilah will resent you for not leaving her one.

    Simone: I don't think therapists are supposed to use that word. Resent.

    Sonya: *laughs* We do now.

    Simone: *smiles* You're a shitty therapist, you know that?

    Sonya: And you're a shitty patient. Stay on topic.

    Simone: *smiles*

Hey Dee,
    Yeah, I know. Only Dahlia gets the privilege of calling you that. But, given the circumstances, it's fitting, is it not?

Anyway, if you are watching this, it means I am no longer with you. If I were, I'd be kissing you, not making sappy videos. And I'm sorry, okay? I tried.

deep breath All right, that's enough fluffy shit. We both know I suck at it, and you don't like it, so we'll skip it. For the record, I don't like doing these. I don't mind them, but I don't like them. It's weird, right? I've done hundreds of these already. Maybe thousands, I don't know. I wasn't counting. *leans over* How many of these have we done so far?

Sonya (off-camera): To date?
   Simone: **nods**
Sonya: Including this one, one thousand one hundred and fifteen. Why?
Simone: **smiles** Just curious.
(silence)
Sonya: We don't have all day, Simone.

Hearty laugh That's Dr. Goodman, by the way. You were wondering where it is I disappear to every Thursday afternoon. It's for this. Your parents set this up three years ago. And Dr. Goodman, she's been helping me with this, with all of this. Including all that fluffy shit that you don't like. *weak laugh* Anyway, she's incredible and really good with numbers. Kinda like you. Maybe someday you'll meet her, perhaps when she gives you this. Or all of them. All one thousand one hundred and fifteen videos. And while I didn't mind doing most of them, I truly hate this one the most.

So please don't hate me, okay? *sigh* Even if you do, I love you.
I love you, Delilah.
I will always love you. No matter what happens between us, I will always love you.
And I meant what I said, okay? I want to marry you. I do. It's the only thing I've ever wanted. To be with you. To have babies with you. To grow old with you. To die with you. You, and only you.
But I can't. I can't give you all that because... because... because it doesn't make sense. All of this. It really doesn't. It doesn't make sense

how I feel about you. How deeply ingrained you are in here **puts hand over chest and presses in** *since the day I met you. Since the day you were born. Even now, as I'm doing this. But the thing is, I never fought it. I never questioned it. I never questioned us. Why we work. Why we are. How we are.*

Why we're friends. Why we've been in each other's lives for so long. Remember what Dahlia said years ago? This was after boarding school. She said it should be statistically impossible for kids like us to be friends, much less be together. But it happened anyway, and we've all been carrying on like everything's all fine and dandy. But it's not.

Then there are our parents. Why are they even friends? They have nothing in common. Our moms especially. I mean, Jordana is awesome. She's Supermom. And your dad, he's my hero. Then there's my parents, a pair of stuck-up, pompous, entitled— **deep breath** *You know what they're like, so I'm not wasting your video talking about them. Still, how is it that we never questioned it, Delilah? Dahlia did, but we all thought she was being too judgy. And after what we learned, I wonder why they're still friends. Maybe when they were our age, but as grown-ups?*

And now this?

You know, I was angry when I first found out what my parents did and what they did to your parents. How we're all just pawns in their games. Puppets for them to control. It's what they do. Power and control, that's all they care about. It's all they've ever cared about.

But this is different.

Now I'm questioning everything. Do you love me for me? Do I love you for you? Or is it because we were always put together, by design, because my grandparents bought you for me? Do your parents love me? Or am I the trouble child they were contractually obligated to be nice to? Even with all this, you know? All this. Why did they do this? Why did they get Dr. Goodman to help me? They knew my parents would be mad, yet they put everything together. Is it to stick it to them? Or is it because they really care about me?

silence

sigh

They love me. I know they love me. Jordana and Derrick. They do. They could've lied when I asked, but they didn't. I made them their own video, so they know this. When they get it, they will know. How much they mean to me.

I'm not mad at them. Without them, without this, I never would've met the love of my life. That's you, Delilah, in case you're wondering. Which you shouldn't. Even if I'm doubting this, you shouldn't. It will give me something to hold on to. You give me something to hold on to. Because I don't want to do this. I don't want to, Dee. I don't. I really don't. But I feel like I have to. If I don't, this will always hang over our heads. What my grandparents did. What my parents did. What your parents did. It's illegal. I think. If not, it should be. So I'll just… yeah.

I should leave it at that. I shouldn't waste your video on angry shit. You get enough of that from me already. Here's fluffy shit instead.
blows a kiss at the camera

I love you. I will always love you. Always.

I will always be yours, forever.

THANK YOU!

Thank you for reading TOUCH OF HEAVEN, and I hope you enjoyed Delilah, Harris, and Marc's story.
This book is a labor of love, and I'd appreciate it if you left a review on as many platforms as possible.

Want more on this trio?
Visit my website for Bonus Content and Deleted Scenes:
https://elicenange.com/bonuscontent/

If you want to stay up to date on news about new releases and sneak peaks of new books, sign up for my newsletter:
https://elicenange.com/newsletter/

SIX FEET UNDER

Everything has a price; even love and legacy.

OSCAR

Following in my father's corrupt footsteps was only going to make him
happy and I had every intention of making him miserable.
I was a bastard of my parents' love affair, deemed to be treated like one
until I could prove my worth.
I had everything: money, power, prestige, but none of it mattered until I
found someone to create a legacy with.
Once bitten and twice shy, I didn't look for love but it sure did find me.
When Courtney Sotelo stomped her way into my life I never expected
to fall for someone with a reputation worse than mine.
CC was hiding in plain sight, the heiress everyone forgot about until I
uncovered her.
Courtney dominated me; while CC lived for me. *Together we fill the
voids no one else did.*

CHARLENA

Turned into a martyr, hiding in plain sight seemed like a pretty good
solution when I blended into the life of my parent's killer perfectly.
I was the product of nothing more than a life of unfortunate events that
forced me to survive.
I had everything and nothing at the same time.
Love was still the one thing I couldn't hold onto even after Courtney
made it her mission to destroy my family's name. Love became
benefits, acquaintances, fleeting faces that did nothing more than cure
the lonely nights.
Oscar demanded to be loved when he forced me to see the privilege in
his life instead of his still-beating heart.
Courtney was still stuck in killing everything that didn't suit her.
Courtney found me; Oscar kept me. *Together we fill the voids no one
else does.*

COURTNEY

Killing was all I knew. I was a weapon aimed at the people I loved all my life and there was no stopping my fixation for violence and passion bloodlust.

I was the illegitimate daughter of one of the deadliest Mafia families and destined to be nothing less.

Everything I had left was my son, the only person who would be better off without me.

Feelings were nothing more than ammunition when every bit of chaos seemed to shimmer down.

The two people I should have killed became the two truths I couldn't ignore anymore.

Even love has a price but this time it wasn't engraved in my bullets.

CC made me realize there's more than death; Oscar forced me to live.

Together we filled the voids no one else could.

Start Reading:
https://elicenange.com/sixfeetunder/

ACKNOWLEDGMENTS

It takes a village. Truly.

1. My family, Mr. Nange and ~~Baby~~ Toddler Nange. Thank you for all your love and support as I delve into this publishing journey.
2. Amanda Walker, my PA. You have an uncanny knack for taking my jumbled-up ideas and giving me pretty things. And for indulging my random self at odd times. For giving me this gorgeous book cover (and re-doing the damn thing several times) — which inspired me to quadruple this book's word count. For doing all of the graphics for this book. For connecting me with so many, many book people. For... need I go on?
3. My critique partner, Anonymous – thank you for indulging me and all of my crazy, haphazard ideas. I do have a lot of those, don't I? Then again, you have a knack for keeping me on track with all of these, so thank you — from the bottom of my heart.
4. My beta reader, Deb Peach. Thank you for taking on this trio's story at such short notice. All of your suggestions on how to make the story stronger have been invaluable, so thank you!
5. Leanne Rabesa, my editor. For being so flexible, even as I kept changing dates on you. For reading and rereading this mammoth of a story (both versions of it), and for taking it apart at the seams, over and over again. And for that encyclopedia brain of yours! May this be the beginning of a very, very long partnership.

6. My inspirations. Since all three of you have still chosen to remain anonymous, I'm acknowledging you anyway. Anonymously.
7. Last but not least – to you, lovely reader, who is reading this. Thank you for coming on this journey with me. Hope you stick around. There's more where this came from!

BOOKS BY ELICE NANGE

Sin and Sinuosity series

Taste Of Hell

Touch Of Heaven

Six Feet Under

In Plain Sight ~ *February 2024*

Novellas

Twist Our Hearts ~ *Spring 2024*

Six Feet Dark ~ *Spring 2024*

Promise Me Forever ~ *December 2023*

ABOUT THE AUTHOR

Elice Nange is a Contemporary and Dark Romance author. She writes from the heart, and her stories often address sensitive subjects like racism, sexual orientation, discrimination, etc.

Outside of writing, she enjoys spending time with her family and copious amounts of reading. She is also obsessed with Maya Angelou, ice cream, and the color purple ~ not necessarily in that order.

www.elicenange.com

facebook.com/elicenange

x.com/elicenange

instagram.com/elicenange

goodreads.com/Elice_Nange

bookbub.com/authors/elice-nange

tiktok.com/@elicenange

AFTERWORD

Musings of a delicatesoul88

It still feels so surreal that this is the second installment of this. In keeping with Book 1, let's call this The Making of **Touch Of Heaven** too, and of what I hope to be many, many of these. Same as in Book 1, this is the part where I get to say all sorts of mumbled-up, unedited, and un-prettified things. Think of the emotions running rampant through Simone's mind as she was making those video diaries, y'know, since she *had* to do them, it's only fair that I get to share the load, right?

Also, since you've made it this far (again) and are still reading past this sentence, I'm assuming you are just as interested in reading this as I am writing this — so let's dive in!

But first, let's get those disclaimers out of the way again, shall we?

I write from the heart. While I am not a therapist, generational trauma has always interested me, particularly in how it molds and influences our lives. We all have trauma that we need to unpack, and whether we like it or not, it affects our lives in one way or another.

That said, since I am using this in a fictional context, it goes without saying that I do my research on this. However, I don't claim to be the subject matter expert on anything. This is being applied in a fictional context, but if you can see yourself in any of these characters, then I hope I have done my job to some extent. If not, it was meant for entertainment anyway.

Expect most (if not all) of my characters to be diverse or be in interracial and/or intercultural relationships. My stories are character-driven and often contain and/or address sensitive subjects like racism, sexual orientation, religion, discrimination, etc. Trigger warnings will be provided where appropriate.

Along that wavelength, because these stories are character-driven, heterosexual characters in this series will be the exception, not the norm.

Y'know, this is verbatim what I put in the first book. I'll tweak it some for book 3, but I still intend to put this in all of my books. Until you come to know me and what I'm about. Let's say… 10 books later. This is also stated in my author bio. I am, and always will be, unapologetically authentic about it, so if you do decide to follow me along on this writing journey, welcome aboard.

Now that we've gotten that out of the way, let's get down to my actual ramblings since that's what we are here for.

The Brewer twins (Dahlia and Delilah) have lived in my head for over a decade, just begging for their stories to be told. So I caved, and I'm giving them what they asked for. Somehow they ended up being my debut heroines. That's just how it happened, I didn't plan it.

Neither did I plan for their pairings. Well, Dahlia's… I sort of did. She was always meant to end up with David. Whether or not she married Curtis when this happened was up in the air (read Book 1's musings to see how the cookie crumbled with this one).

But Delilah? Boy, was she a challenge. When I first envisioned who Delilah ended up with, Simone was always her first love, and Marc was always her (*last?*) love? Harris was never in the picture. He was somewhere in the vicinity — as Marc's ex or something — but he did not have a major role. But after he became a full-fledged character there was no saying no to him. Or any of them, really. But mostly him.

Can you imagine Marc without Harris? Or Delilah without Harris? I can't — now, that is — but he joined the party a few years ago and was insistent on being a part of it. He says so himself — he is a selfish asshole who wants what he wants when he wants it. Marc enables it too, encourages it actually. And Delilah just goes along with it because she has her own issues that she needs to work through.

When I say issues, I mean we haven't even begun to scratch the surface of it. Are the twins more alike than they are different? I'll do the very unhelpful thing and go with…. It's up to your imagination. There is an abundance of little nuggets to choose from anyway, so have at it! What I will say though, is here's a classic example of nature-nurture and how it molds us. Jordana and Derrick Brewer were amazing parents, y'know? At the risk of spoiling this for the future, they truly are the exact opposite of Andrea and Matthias McWhorter. I know we didn't get to explore this enough in this story (my bad!) since we needed to focus on the romance. It's a dark romance, but it is still a romance. And we had enough dark and messed up shit to unpack without throwing that into the mix as well. So just in case you are wondering — how the heck did these kids get paired off in the first place? Well, I am wondering the same thing too.

Just kidding.

Of course I know. These characters are loud and opinionated. And sometimes they decide they want more stories told, and I have no other choice but to write them — after all, I just wield the pen. Let's not forget, there is Victor Toussaint (Harris's dad), and also Lorenzo Sotelo and Sarah Bardales (Marc's parents) to contend with. Generational trauma, I tell ya! I just can't seem to help myself. Then again, all three of them are each flawed in their own way and that's the beauty of it all. They really are a special brand of damaged.

I'm writing a short prequel that explains their origins, so to speak. This will be free to download on my website when the time comes. I'm also working on another novella that falls between Books 3 & 4 (titled **Promise Me Forever**, *IYKYK*), and goes over the premise of the Brewer-McWhorter feuds (coming December of 2023). There will be one on their parents (titled **Twist Our Hearts**) coming Summer of 2024.

We haven't seen the last of them (yet). While this trio's story is technically concluded, the ***Sin and Sinuosity*** storyline isn't. And, at the risk of re-stating the obvious — Simone will be back. Obviously. I didn't put her in Books 1 & 2 for the hell of it. She closes out both books for a reason. I'm actually working on her story at the moment and it is a blast!

Alright, that's enough rambling from me. I'm also running out of fluffy words to say, so… see you in the next book, **Six Feet Under**.

In the meantime, stay overly ambitious.

Elice Nange

Printed in Great Britain
by Amazon

61598662R00234